Enjoy!

TOO MANY RIVERS TO CROSS

Art Anthony

Art D. Anthony

Publisher Name: Art Anthony
Publisher Address: 104 SouthPointe Ave. Tuttle, OK 73089
Publisher Phone: 405-326-8077
Legal Name: Art Darol Anthony, Sr

ISBN: 978-0-9988078-4-3 (sc)
ISBN: 978-0-9988078-6-7 (hc)
ISBN: 978-0-9988078-5-0 (e)

Library of Congress Control Number: 2019901409

Cover Art was drawn by Sherry Copeland.
Map of Texas and Mexican Troop movement credit to McGraw-Hill Education.

Rev. date: 12/13/2019

Cast of Characters

Impresarios for the Mexican government Moses and Stephen F Austin. Moses had negotiated the deal with the Mexican government to be in charge of distributing land to settlers coming to Texas, Mexico. Moses the father died before the settlers came and Stephen took over after that time. Austin settled over 350 families, all from the United States. There were several other impresarios in Texas but none as successful Austin.

The Pioneers

1. The Logging Family;
   A.D., 30 years old father, Maggie Mae, 29 years old mother, Art 9-year-old, oldest son, Weldon 7-year-old son. Their only daughter, Patricia, was born in 1831. Mr. Logging is a blacksmith and also farms 200 acres. They were friends of the Stroud's. Duke was the Logging family cow dog.

2. The Stroud Family;
   Frank Sr.,37 years old father, Mary, 34 years old mother, Frank Junior 14-year-old son, Pat J. 12-year-old son, Mr. Stroud was a carpenter and farmed 300 acres. They were friends of the Loggings.

3. Rodney, 25 years old and Cindy Smith, 22 years old;
   They had 3 children Tommy, Cindy, and Rodney all under 6 years of age. They met the Logging and Stroud Families on the road to Nacogdoches. Eventually they settled in Perry Point.

4. Jessie the 45 years old ferry man;

    Man who was held after crossing the Sulphur River. This was done by the Logging and Stroud families to ensure they weren't robbed afterwards by his gang.

5. Dave Collins 45 years old;

    A farmer in Nacogdoches that befriended A.D.'s group while they had to spend over a month in that town.

6. Mr. Mills;

    General store owner at Bryans Mill. He helped the Logging and Stroud families stop some thieves that wanted to steal their wagons and stock.

7. Mister and Mrs. Tims both 45 years old;

    They had a son, Bob, 14 years old who joined A.D. on his livestock drive through East Texas to Perry Point. Bob and his family eventually all moved to Perry Point.

8. The McCoy family;

    Gene the 45 year old father, Betsy the 41year old mother, and two daughters, Jane 14 Jean12 and one boy Gene Jr 10. They were owners of the general store in Perry Point since 1822. They tried to help settlers at Anahuac.

9. Doctor Lily;

    A 30 year old Doctor who began medical practice at Perry Point in 1830.

10. The Adams family;

    Ed the 38 year old father, Betty 36 year old the mother, Watha the 13 year old daughter and sons Gage 15, and Dan, 14 years old. They had a farm 10 miles from Liberty.

11. May family;

    Bea 34-year-old mother, Matthew 14, and Mark 13 year old sons. The father had abandoned them and they were starving. They moved from Liberty to Anahuac to work for A.D., and finally Homesteaded for themselves.

12. Dave Morris;

A married 45 year old Local carpenter for the area of Anahuac. His children Were all raised and on their own.

13. Taylor White 50 years old, John Williams 45 years old, Sol Barrow 40 years old, Dick Allen 43 years old, Ed Henderson 39 years old;

Large ranchers in the Anahuac- Liberty area where A.D. worked for them. They drove and sold their cattle in Louisiana, because they could get more money for their livestock. The smaller ranchers would occasionally go along to sell their own cattle.

14. Sergeant Pedro Gonzales 25 years old, Corporal Juan Hernandez 20 years old and Ernesto Diaz 20 years old;

Ex-Mexican soldiers that had been stationed at Anahuac. When the Mexican soldiers left the Fort, they received large grants of land to settle in the area. They had become friends of the Logging's.

15. Shaw family

Mr. Shaw the 50-year-old father, Ion 14 year old daughter and Onnie 12 year old son. A desperate pioneer family that moved to Anahuac. They worked for A.D. and finally homesteaded for themselves.

16. Yoakums;

A large family of outlaws that robbed and killed on the Atascosito trail that ran from Liberty to the Sabine River. (Louisiana border with Texas)

17. 31-year-old Pastor Buck Bills and his family;

They came to Anahuac in 1837 to start a Protestant Church.

18. Clinton Harris and Andrew Briscoe both 31 years old;

Local area businessman that were arrested by Captain Tenorio for not paying taxes on imported items.

19. Thomas Chambers 40 years old;
> The only lawyer certified by the Mexican Government to practice in Texas caused major land disputes in the Anahuac, Liberty area. He lived in the Anahuac area after Texas gained independence.

20. James Morgan 35 years old
> Lawyer, land speculator, merchant. Defied Mexican tax collectors. Founded town of New Washington (Morgan Point). Mexican Army burned the Texas Army supplies in his wharehouses 2 days before San Jacinto. A Texas Col. In charge of the Galveston Bay area.

Mexican
Fort Anahuac Built in 1830-1832

1. General Meir Teran 39 years old;
> Military Governor of Mexico, Texas 1830-1834. He was a friend of Stephen F. Austin. He committed suicide while in office.

2. Col. Davis Bradburn 42 years old;
> Born in Kentucky and joined the Mexican Army. He rose to the rank of Colonel. He was assigned by General Teran to build a Fort at Perry Point, which began in 1830. Also, he was told to rename the town Anahuac and make it the County seat at that time.

3. Colonel Piedras 46 years old;
> Commander at Nacogdoches who came with a small force to help Bradburn. He briefly took command of fort Anahuac.

4. Lieutenant Juan Cortina 23 years old;
> Took command of Ft. Anahuac when Col. Piedras left. Lieutenant Cortina held this command for only 2 days. The troops then revolted pledging to Santa Anna.

5. Lt. Col. Subaran 38 years old;
    Banished to the frontier, because he was a Santa Anna supporter. He came to the Fort at Anahuac and eventually took command of the Fort. Shortly after that he and all the troops abandoned the Fort, sailing back to the Matamoros.

6. Capt. Tenorio 26 years old;
    Reoccupied Fort Anahuac in1835 with a small detachment of Mexican troops. Forced to abandon the Fort by local pioneers after only seven months occupation.

7. Madera;
    State Official issued land titles to many pioneers in the Anahuac-Liberty area.

8. Tom Thompson;
    A 45 year old Englishman turned a Mexican national. Was in command of a Mexican schooner seizing several Texas and US ships plus cargoes that had not paid their taxes to Mexico.

9. Father Michael Muldoon 56 years old;
    The spiritual leader of Mexico -Texas. Spent most of his time in the Austin colony. He was good friends with Stephen F Austin and even wrote articles supporting the rebellious Texans. He enjoyed life.

10. John Austin 32-year-old:
    Not related to Stephen F. Austin. Commander at the battle of Velasco in 1832. Made Brigadier General of the Texas Militia. Also signed the Turtle Bayou Resolution. He was a businessman. He and two of his children died of cholera in 1834. His land grant is now part of Houston, Texas.

The Alamo 1835

1. General Martin de Cos 36 years old;
    (brother in law to Santa Anna) With over 900 Mexican troops, occupied the Alamo in 1835. In December he was defeated by

400 Texas rebels. His army was unarmed by the rebels and sent back to Mexico, where they rejoined, Santa Anna coming back to retake the Alamo in 1836.

2. Col.Domingo Ugartechea 42years old;
    Brought 400 plus Mexican soldiers to help general Cos defending the Alamo against the Texans in December of 1835.

3. Ben Milam 47 years old;
    Led 400 Texas Troops that defeated Mexican General Cos' 900 men at the Alamo in December,1835. Milam was killed during this battle and Col. Ned Burleson negotiated the Mexican surrender to the Texans. Burleson also led part of the Texas Army at the San Jacinto battle.

The Alamo 1836

1. Lt. Colonel James C. Neill 48 years old;
    Took command of the Alamo in January 1836. He left the Alamo February 20th 1836 to try and recruit men to defend the Fort during the coming battle. He never returned to the Alamo but did fight in the battle of San Jacinto.

2. Colonel Jim Bowie 40 years old;
    A famous frontiersman, sent by the Provisional Government to take the cannons and other military equipment out of the Alamo. Colonel James Neill convinced him that the Alamo should not be abandoned. Bowie got sick during the Mexican Alamo siege and was killed when the Fort fell.

3. Colonel William B. Travis 27 years old;
    Came to the Alamo in February 1836 and was committed to defending the Alamo until the death. He was a lawyer and had been in Texas for five years and was involved in driving the Mexicans out of fort Anahuac in1832 and 1835. He scarcely had 190 men to defend the Alamo. Travis was the commanding officer

during the battle and was constantly trying to get more men and supplies to help them defend the Alamo. He, like all the other Texas fighters was killed during this battle.

4. Davy Crockett 47 years old;
    Famous Frontiersman Brought 20 of his Tenn. sharpshooters to help the Texans defend the Alamo. He and all his men were either killed or executed during this battle.

5. Lieutenant Dickinson 24 years old;
    In charge of the 14 canons at the Alamo. He brought his wife and child into the Alamo and they were set free by Santa Anna after the battle. Lieutenant Dickinson was either killed or executed during this battle.

6. Texas defender Brigido Guerrera 20 years old;
    Had deserted from general Cos Mexican Army in 1835. When the Texans defeated the Mexicans in December. He joined the Texas Army at the Alamo in 1836. When Brigido realized the Texans would lose at the Alamo in 1836, he locked himself in a cell and convinced the Mexican soldiers that he had been captured and put in a cell by the Texans. He was the only fighting man spared.

Texas convention, November 1835

1. Henry Smith 48 years old;
    Elected Provincial President of Texas. The Provincial Government sent Sam Houston to Gonzales, and the Alamo where he decided these places could not be defended. During this time Houston was able to get a treaty with the East Texas Indians, promising they would not join the Mexicans fighting the Texans. Smith was controversially impeached in January of 36.

2. Colonel James. Fannin;
    Attended West Point and had a Texas Army of 400 men. These men were the best trained soldiers, the Texans had at the time. He was

executed along with the rest of his Army, who had surrendered. This was done on orders from Santa Anna, Palm Sunday close to Goliad

Texas convention, March 1836

1. Sam Houston 42 years old lawyer;
    Appointed Major General over all of the Texas Army's. This was the first action of this convention.

2. David Burnett 47 year old lawyer;
    Elected Provincial President of this convention. He did not like, Houston or Thomas Rusk.

3. Lorenzo De Zavala 47 year old;
    Elected Vice President. He had formerly been Mexico's ambassador to France but resigned because he did not like what Santa Anna was doing to the country.

4. Thomas Rusk 32 years old;
    Elected secretary of war and he was a friend of Houston's. He was a large, strong man, and he used his strength, many times, on long-winded delegates at this convention.

5. Robert Potter;
    Was named secretary of the Navy and was an ally of David Burnett. This split in the cabinet was the cause of a lot of trouble during Burnett's Provisional Presidency. The Texas Navy did a good job during the revolution. Little credit is given for their accomplishments!

6. George Childress;
    A lawyer, actually wrote the declaration of independence for Texas. He had only been in Texas six weeks.

6000 Mexican Army That entered Texas, February1836

1. Antonio Lopez de Santa Anna 40-year-old soldier and politician;
   The dictator of Mexico, leading his Army against the rebelling Texans. He brought many luxuries for himself, which included a wagonload of opium. Six months before he had ruthlessly put down another revolution by another state and had executed all of the enemy that surrendered.

2. Colonel Jaun Almonte 33 years old who was educated in the United States;
   One of Santa Anna's aides and could write and speak English fluently. He had traveled Texas extensively. He frequently wrote letters to Sam Houston, telling him he could never beat the much larger Mexican Army and he should give up.

3. Ramon Caro;
   Santa Anna's' Secretary. Many times, Santa Anna would lie about what had happened and Cato would put in the truth in his correspondence.

4. General Juan Urrea 39 years old;
   With 1000 men was sent to Matamoros and to March along the Texas Gulf coast to secure that area for Mexico. Santa Anna also knew that Fannin had a large force of Texans at Goliad, and he told General Urrea he must defeat that force, which he did.

5. General Vincente Filisola 47 years old;
   An Italian second in command of Santa Anna's' Mexican army.

6. General Antonio Gaona 43 years old;
   After the fall of the Alamo, Santa Anna sent him with an army of 750 men toward East Texas.

7. General Joaquin Sesma 57 years old;

After the fall of the Alamo, Santa Anna sent him with an army of 750 men, in direct pursuit of Houston, and his Army. Santa Anna, followed General Sesma with his large army of 3500 men.

8. Melchora Barrera;
    17 year old San Antonio beauty that Santa Anna faked married with while he was bored with the siege of the Alamo.

9. Captain Barragan 27years old;
    Took over command of the dragoons after Colonel Almonte failed to kill Provincial President, Burnet and his party at Morgan Point

10. Colonel Pedro Delgado
    In charge of the large Mexican cannon named the Golden Standard

11. Colonel Mariano Garcia 36 years old;
    Commanding the rearguard of General Cos reinforcements for Santa Anna at San Jacinto. Those rearguard troops never made it to the battle of San Jacinto.

Texas Army of 900, 1836

1. Major General Sam Houston 42 years old;
    Was possibly the only man that could hold this undisciplined unruly group of men together. He devised a plan to defeat the Mexican Army and capture, Santa Anna. Houston never deviated from this plan, and thus Texas became a free country. Houston was the first elected president of the country of Texas.

2. Colonel John Austin Wharton 30 years old;
    Adjutant general, at first, he was a supporter of Houston and towards the end of the campaign was not.

3. Colonel Sidney Sherman 31 year old;
    Commander of the second Regiment. Came from Kentucky, he was an industrialist and innovator in his field. When the Texas

revolution broke out, he sold his factory and used the funds to outfit and finance a company of 52 volunteers for the Texas Army. His volunteers were the most reckless, drunken and lawless men in the Army.

4. Colonel Ned Burleson 38 years old;

   Had a lot of military service in Texas and in the United States. He was a patient effective officer, a veteran of both fighting and controlling an Army, very popular with the men and a famous Indian fighter. He was commander of the first Regiment of the Texas Army. Always a firm backer of Sam Houston.

5. Major Moseley Baker 34 years old;

   Would not take his company to Groce's plantation with the rest of Houston's army, which was insubordination. Did rejoin the Texas Army for the San Jacinto battle. Originally a friend of Sam Houston's, but when Houston did not fight at the Colorado River, Baker was no longer his friend. His company spent the two weeks guarding the Brazos River crossing.

6. Major, Wiley Martin 60 years old;

   Also, would not take his company to Groces' plantation with the rest of the Texas Army, which made him insubordinate. Did rejoin the Texas Army for the San Jacinto battle. Originally a friend of Sam Houston's. But when Houston did not fight at the Colorado River Martin was no longer his friend. His company spent the two weeks guarding the Brazos River crossing.

7. Scout and Spy service;

   Was headed by Captain Karnes, along with 27 other men. Two of the most famous of these men was Deaf Smith and his black friend, Hendrick Arnold. This part of Houston's army did outstanding work.

8. Private Mirabeau B. Lamar 37 years old;

   A poet and newspaper editor from Georgia, joined the Texas Army 10 days before San Jacinto. He had joined under the urging of the Provincial President, Burnet to undermine Houston. The day before the San Jacinto battle, he was promoted to Colonel in charge of the Calvary. Because of his heroic actions, the day before. He was Texas' second elected president.

9. Lieutenant Colonel Henry Millard and Captain John Allen 40 and 26 years old;

    Two regular companies of U.S. Infantry that had been allowed to desert for a short time, taking a fighting vacation with the Texas rebels. These were the most disciplined troops in the Texas Army.

10. Lieutenant Colonel James C Neill 48 years old;

    Put in charge of the two cannons received from the citizens of Cincinnati called the twin sisters. The canons were smuggled to Texas boxed and marked hardware.

11. Captain Juan Seguin 29 years old;

    The leader of the Texas Spanish, in the Army and covered the rear of Houston's army in the retreat. His Dad, Erasmo, was one of the richest men in Texas, and gave a lot of material and money support to the Army.

12. Major Lorenzo de Zavala Jr;

    The son of the Provincial Vice President. He joined the Texans as an aide to General Houston 10 days before San Jacinto. He was the best dressed soldier in the whole Texas Army

13. Chief Kalita;

    Chief of the East Texas Cherokee Indians, who were friends of Sam Houston. He promised the Indians Texas would issue titles to the lands they presently occupied.

14. Chief Bowl;

    Chief of the East Texas Cherokee Coushatta Indians and friend of Sam Houston.

15. Sgt. Sylvester, Privates Sion Bostick, Alfred Miles, Charles Thompson, Joe Vermillion, Joel Robison;

    These are the men that captured Santa Anna after San Jacinto. He rode into the Prison camp with Robison who was the only one in the group who spoke Spanish.

16. Ms. Elizabeth Powell 45year old widow;

    An innkeeper that was forced to entertain Santa Anna and his officers for one night while they were pursuing the Texans. She had her son give Houston valuable information on the whereabouts of Santa Anna.

17. Lieutenant William Kraft 27 years old;

    Artillery officer for the three cannons at Fort Anahuac during the time Mexican soldiers were held prisoners at that location. This was done because the Texans feared that Mexico would attack them from the Bay.

18. Navy Captain Joseph Walters 49 years old;

    Sent by General Rusk to take charge of the captured Mexican man-of-war. It was captured when Mexico tried to free the prisoners at Fort Anahuac. The ship was renamed. Stephen F Austin and was assigned to patrol Galveston Bay. The new Texas sailors did not get along with the Texas soldiers at Fort Anahuac.

Lawyers practicing in South Texas 1829 – 1837

William Travis, Sam Houston, David Burnet, brothers Patrick Jack, William Jack, Jack Jack,, Robert Williamson, Thomas Chambers and George Childress.

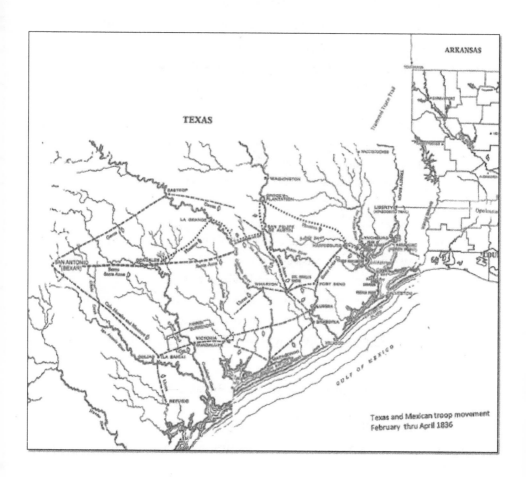

Texas and Mexican troop movement
February thru April 1836

1

CHAPTER

In 1828, the Logging and Stroud families had been living in Fulton, Arkansas, for twelve years. The Logging family consisted of A.D. (Pa) and his wife, Maggie, both in their early 30s, and their two sons, Art, who was nine years old, and Weldon, who was seven. The Stroud family consisted of Frank and his wife, Mary, who were in their mid 30's and their sons, Frank Junior, who was fourteen years old, and Pat, who was twelve. The Logging family had been trying to farm two hundred acres. A.D. also had a blacksmith shop in Fulton. Business the last two years had been terrible because of the drought, and they had not been able to raise enough crops to feed their cattle and hogs. Farmers couldn't even afford to hire him to shoe their horses and mules, much less repair their wagons.

Their neighbors, the Strouds, were trying to run cattle and hogs on three hundred acres, but the drought had practically wiped them out.

The two families had become good friends and usually played dominoes on Wednesday and Saturday nights. Lately, the discussion between the families had been "Where could we go to make a living?" Most of the talk was that Texas was a great place for this type of opportunity. Land grants for a large tract were being given for $60. They had made up their mind they were going to see a man called Stephen F. Austin in Nacogdoches or San Felipe, Texas, wherever they could meet him. The Stroud brothers were really happy because each boy could also get land for homesteading.

Each time they met to play dominoes they spent at least an hour planning how to make the trip.

The Loggings and the Stroud's had been lucky to sell their farms for fifty cents an acre to a nearby farmer.

A.D. told the group, "I would need one wagon for all the household goods, one wagon for my blacksmith and farming material and another wagon for livestock feed. Together we have about eighty-two head of livestock. I have sixteen mules, four horses, twenty cows, fifteen calves and one bull."

"I have four horses, four mules, ten cows and eight calves," Frank said, "I think my family could get along with one wagon for our household goods, and I would let Pat drive the feed wagon." Everyone would have to walk at least two hours a day so it wouldn't be too hard on the animals.

A D. had written to Mr. Austin telling him of their plans to arrive in Nacogdoches about the first part of October, in hopes of getting cheap land. Mr. Austin had sent the Loggings a return letter stating he would try to be in Nacogdoches from the first until the tenth of October and thought the families could get some land.

The two families were talking to everyone travelling down or up the Trammell Trace trail. Trammell Trace was used by most immigrants going to Texas from Missouri or Arkansas. This trail was very important because it was hard traveling with wagons and horses in an area where there was not at least a path to follow. A. D. and Frank were warned that there were a lot of people ready to rob, steal or even kill you if you let your guard down. Each family had two double barrel pistols, two double-barreled shotguns, four Hall percussion breech loading rifles with paper cartridge along with plenty of powder and lead. No one in their party was to go anywhere without a gun at their side. Standard practice would be to post guards each night even if they thought it was safe. Each man or boy would always carry a sheathed knife.

None of these pioneers were overweight because they had to physically work hard each day. A.D. was Six ft. tall and had a friendly face and eyes. Frank was five ft. ten in. tall and had a strong appearance. Both men weighed around one hundred seventy pounds. Both their wives were five ft. two in. tall and weighed one hundred ten pounds. Maggie was a brunette and Mary was a blonde. Both had friendly dispositions. The children were slender because they worked and played hard.

2
CHAPTER

It was September 5,1828 the small corn harvest had been completed and they had sold the corn they couldn't take with them. Their wagons were organized and packed for the journey. That evening they crossed the Red River with four wagons and the livestock. A.D. would guard the wagons and stock that night along with their trusted dog, Duke, who had been a member of the Logging family since he was a puppy.

Art and Weldon had got Duke and his brother when they were three months old from a farmer that was leaving the territory. Duke's brother had died when he was about six months old from a rattlesnake bite. Duke had turned into a great companion for the boys and a pretty good cow dog. The young boys were very upset about losing Duke's brother but it really taught them to be careful around snakes.

The next day, the rest of the group who had gone home to sleep in their Fulton homes, crossed the Red River, walking, and the wagons were underway by seven o'clock.

It was about two hundred miles to Nacogdoches. The group traveled twelve miles that day. The Logging boys were pretty impatient because they were to spend two hours each day with their mother working on their schoolwork. The first day two men riding horses passed them. One was from Fulton, and Pa knew him. They slowed down and talked to him as he drove the wagon.

A.D. asked one man, "Where are you going?"

The man answered, "We are going to Dangerfield to see if we can find work." "There is no work to be found in Fulton."

The other man asked, "Aren't you a blacksmith? My horse has a shoe problem, and I was wondering if you would take a look and see if you can fix it." Pa stopped the wagons and looked at both of the men's horses.

He said, "Both of your horses need a little work and one even needs a new shoe." The two men and Pa went back to his blacksmith wagon and he quickly replaced a shoe on one horse and re-nailed the shoes on the other one.

The man said, "We can't pay you now, but when we see you again we owe you two bucks; thanks a lot." The men then rode on.

Later they met two wagons coming from Texas up the Trace. Both wagons had kids, and Art and Weldon talked to them about five minutes. The boys were happy as the other kids were friendly and they thought it was a big deal to be able to talk to kids they had never seen before.

"Be careful, there are people on the Trace who will steal anything they can," both families of the wagons that were coming northeast warned the Loggings.

That evening Duke was a real tired dog because he had trailed the herd all day. After some discussion they decided he should only be working half days so maybe he wouldn't be so tired. The second day everyone was up by 6:00 a.m. and on the road by 7:00. Breakfast was bacon and eggs from the family hens and milk from the family milk cow which were traveling the Trace with the family. Again everyone took their turn walking for two hours. They also stopped every two hours and rested the mules and horses for fifteen minutes. The Logging boys continued their school lessons, still complaining, but not as much as the first day. The group saw four different pairs of riders who didn't seem to want to stop and merely said hello as they passed. Duke only worked a half day and rode in the wagon the other half day. He seemed to be doing a lot better because he was not nearly as tired at the end of the day. they continued to let him work only half days from then on.

The third day, they met three wagons going North East back to Missouri. They all camped together on the border of Texas and Arkansas. The children played together until nightfall and went to bed exhausted. The parents stayed up and talked about Texas and Missouri.

Mr. Stroud asked, "What about the ferry at Sulphur River?"

The other wagoners told him, "We took the ferry and it cost fifty cents a wagon. That is the way to cross but you can't cross your cattle on the ferry. You'll have to cross them five miles west of the ferry crossing."

Later that night Pa asked Frank, "How are we going to do this cattle crossing?"

Frank answered, "The only way I know is to get the wagons across, and then you and my oldest son take Duke and drive the cattle to the crossing. Your wife, your younger son, my wife, my younger son and I will drive the four wagons to a site five miles south from the ferry on the Trace. Then we'll all meet at that location the next day."

A.D. told Frank, "That will be okay if we can pick up the trail back to the trace. I don't see how we can do it any other way." The plan was explained to the families and they all agreed.

Each family packed plenty of food for this trip, plus they hoped to be able to shoot game all the way to their new homestead.

Two days later they arrived at the Sulphur River without any unusual circumstances. The group arrived about five o'clock in the afternoon.

The ferry man said, "I can cross you now and I think I can cross the cattle also."

A.D. said, "Frank, I'm not sure taking thirty-one head of cattle and twenty-three calves on a flatboat is a good idea. What do you think?"

"Well," said Frank, "It sure would be a problem if they decided to take a swim. I think we should question the ferry man about the possibility of that happening."

A.D said, "If those cows go into the river it will take us at least a day to round them up, if we don't actually lose them."

The ferry operator insisted, "I have crossed cattle, hogs and horses a lot of times. I have a corral which can be quickly assembled and put on the flatboat."

A.D. said, "I think maybe we should try it. This will quicken our trip and won't leave us split up. How about we help put up this corral?" Everyone agreed and pitched in to help. It took until 6:30 to cross the four wagons. They had to assemble the corral and strengthen it on the flatboat. The ferry operator had built the corral so the animals couldn't see through or over the side of the corral boards. They then loaded fifteen cows on the flatboat and into the corral. There was little wind and the river was not running fast so it took fifteen minutes to cross the Sulphur. After unloading on the south side, the ferry had to return and pick up the other sixteen head of cattle and twenty-three calves. By this time, it was getting dark.

The ferryboat operator told the group, "I don't want to cross the river this late."

"Whoa," Pa said as he pulled his pistol, "We cross now! I am not about to leave the rest of the cattle on the other side of the river tonight, and you will not get your money until they are safe on this side!" The last of the livestock was unloaded by 8:30 p.m.

"Well, Frank," A.D. asked, "do you think maybe the ferryboat operator and the rustler or robbers have a thing going?"

"I do believe that is a good possibility," he answered. They both were on guard duty that night. They had to be ready and on guard just in case they were right.

Sure enough, about 1:00 a.m., both men saw four riders coming to where the cattle and horses were located. All the mules and most of the horses were hobbled. Frank and A.D. were standing beside the only two horses they had saddled. Frank Jr. and Pat Stroud were hidden on each side of the cattle. The would-be rustlers rode up with their guns drawn. A.D. shouted, "Halt!" They all started shooting at him but he was behind a large pine tree. A.D. shot one of the men. Frank and his boys shot two more. The last man tried to run away but Pat and Frank Jr. knocked him off his horse. Altogether, one of the men was killed, two were wounded in the arm and the other robber was just shaken up.

A.D., Frank and his boys rounded up the four and took them up to the wagon. Frank ask the three living rustlers, "What are your names? And what is the name of the dead man?" He wrote their names down along with a statement that these men had tried to steal the cattle, horses and mules from him and the Loggings family. He then had the three men sign and date the paper, admitting their guilt. To atone for the rustler's action, they were giving up their horses, tack and guns. This was also put on the statement they had signed.

The settlers made the three rustlers walk behind the feed wagon until noon. The plan was to send them back toward the Sulphur River along with their dead buddy. Before leaving, the rustlers began threatening the settlers and their families. The settlers decided they would not let them go.

A.D. said, "Frank, how about you go to the Bryans Mill settlement and see if there is any law there that could come to our wagons to take care of these men?"

"Sure thing," he replied.

There was no law but he brought back the owner of the general store and post office. The settlers told the mill owner, Mr. Perkins, what had happened and also showed him the signed confessions.

A.D. also told Mr. Perkins, "We took the rustler's guns, horses and tack."

Mr. Perkins replied, "You should've just hung 'em. Then you wouldn't have to worry about what to do with them." It was 3:30 in the afternoon when the rustlers began their seven mile walk back to the Sulphur River.

The homesteaders continued on another four miles before making camp. Pat and Frank Jr. were the night guards that night and they encountered no problems.

The next day the group got back to their regular routine of everyone walking two hours every day and the Logging boys studying two hours. Of course, the boys were already tired of the routine of studying every day. The group was going to camp one mile south of Old Unionville that night. They needed some supplies. A.D. and Frank were going to get the supplies after they made camp. The boys had to gather the wood, hobble most of the mules and the four extra horses, plus put the cows in a pasture which was about fifty yards from the camp.

The two men left camp trailing three mules with supply saddles on them.

Mr. Logging said, "I hope we can get about three hundred pounds of feed for the livestock because it is still about one hundred ten miles to Nacogdoches."

They asked the man in the general store, "What is the trail like to Nacogdoches? And how many rivers do we have to cross?"

The general store owner and a local farmer said, "There are two river crossings, and you'll have to make several stream crossings but we haven't had much rain so you shouldn't have a problem with either one that is if it doesn't rain! You'll have some problems with Caddo Indians as well as whites trying to steal anything you have. Keep your guard up or you'll lose everything. Do you have enough guns, powder and lead?"

"We certainly do," answered the men, "Thanks for your help and advice. We'll be careful." A.D. and Frank began their trip back to the wagons.

Frank said, "You know we are both going to have to be on nightly guard duty because these people are really bad and pretty good at stealing. That means a lot less sleep for us for the next eleven days."

The group headed toward Dangerfield. The second day at noon they passed three miles from Dangerfield. Late that afternoon they came to a big river and another flatboat with the usual loafers around the ferryman's house. They crossed the wagons and mules by 6:30.

The ferryman said, "Leave the cows until in the morning."

At that time A.D., Frank and Duke began heading the cattle and the remaining mules into the river and in twenty minutes all were across the river.

The ferry owner came across and said, "You owe me three dollars for crossing the wagons."

Frank paid him, put a gun in his belly and said, "You're spending the night with us and if your buddies come after us you'll be the first to be shot."

The ferryman said, "You can't do that!"

Frank replied, "Who's going to stop us?" "I've got a wife and kids and they will be worried when I don't come home." said the ferryman.

They answered, "Yes, they will be. Now boys tie him up to that big oak tree in the middle of the camp."

The camp had a quiet night except for Jessie, the ferryboat owner, talking. A.D. finally gagged him so the camp could have some peace and quiet. The next morning three of Jessie's buddies showed up with a lot of threats and bad talk about what they were going to do, but A.D., Frank, Frank Jr. and Pat had guns on them.

Jessie's friends said, "Let our friend go and we won't hurt you."

Frank said, "Either you leave now or we'll kill you along with Jessie. We're going to take Jessie with us today and suggest you run the ferry for him while he's gone." Jessie's buddies knew they couldn't stop the wagons so they left.

This all started when Art heard one of the loafers making plans with another man hanging around the ferry to rob the pioneers. The men didn't see the Logging boy. When Art secretly told his dad, Mr. Logging and Mr. Stroud made their plan to stop the robbers.

The wagons left the River at 7:30 a.m. with Jessie walking behind. About 11:30 they met a farmer that Jessie knew, and they told the farmer Jessie was guiding them to the place they were going. The farmer bought the story and they moved on. When the pioneers' wagons stopped that evening, they let the ferryman go back to his home. It would take him two days to get home unless his men were coming after him. The wagons would be forty plus miles away before they could come after the pioneers. With good horses they could return in a day. By that time the small wagon train could've moved another twenty-two miles, putting them only fifty miles from Nacogdoches.

The group stopped that evening where there was a family with a broken wheel on their wagon. After camp had been prepared for the night, A.D. went to meet the unfortunate pioneer family named Smith. They had three kids under five. The wagon was pulled by two mules that looked as if they were as hungry and starved as the humans they were pulling.

A.D insisted the Smiths come over to their camp and join them for supper and meet the rest of the pioneers. They finally relented and returned with A.D. The Smith family all ate like they hadn't eaten anything for several days and were very grateful.

A.D. sent Art over to feed the two mules and Ace, their hungry dog.

Art returned and told his dad, "I need to take some more feed those animals are starving."

His dad said, "No, you can't because that would make them sick if you feed too much too soon. We'll feed them again about midnight. You did a good job."

A.D. told Mr. Smith, "I could help you repair your wagon wheel tomorrow. I am a blacksmith and believe I could fix it in about two hours. We need to rest our stock tomorrow anyhow."

"Where are y'all headed?" asked Frank.

"We're going to Nacogdoches to get a Mexican land grant from Mr. Austin," replied Mr. Smith.

"Say, we are too!" said Frank.

The settlers had been lucky because they were able to shoot five deer and two turkeys without going over one hundred yards from their wagons. This had given them plenty of fresh meat so far on this trip.

Frank asked A.D. "Do you think we need to worry about Jessie that ferryman?"

"Probably not, as long as we are still posting guards during the day and night," A.D. replied.

Frank Jr. said, "I guess Pat and I will have to do a lot of guarding. Mr. Logging said he could fix this broken wagon wheel and would not do any guard duty tonight." The other pioneer men said, "You know we can't fix the wagon wheel but we can do guard duty."

A.D. said, "Art has slipped over to the Smith's mules and dog to feed them."

When he returned Art's Pa said, "Make sure you feed them again in the morning and afternoon."

Art replied, "I won't forget."

Frank, Frank, Jr. and Pat did guard duty four hours each during the night and early morning. They were the only ones who did not get a great eight hour rest that night. The Smiths joined them for breakfast and again were very appreciative.

After a hearty breakfast of biscuits and gravy, canned jam and fresh milk, A.D. said, "Well, let's get started on that wheel!"

With A.D. and Mr. Smith mainly working to fix the wagon, it was finally finished about eleven o'clock. A.D. told Mr. Smith, "When we get to Nacogdoches you'll need to get another wheel; this one won't last over one hundred miles." A.D., Frank Jr., Pat and Mr. Smith greased the axles on all five wagons.

At supper that night the Smiths asked, "Is it okay if we tag along to Nacogdoches with y'all?"

"Of course," Frank said. "We were thinking that would be best for all of us anyway."

"I don't know what we would have done without y'all coming along. God was looking after us," said Mrs. Smith. A.D., Mr. Smith and Frank had looked at the Smith's two mules and put new shoes on them.

At 7:30 a.m. on September 30, all five wagons and their livestock moved out. They traveled twelve miles that day. The next day they made another twelve miles but were running out of feed for the mules and cattle.

They were still twenty-six miles from Nacogdoches, and there was no place to get any feed along the way. The Smith family and animals had grown stronger since they had been with the pioneers from Arkansas. The group gave all the mules and horses about one half rations. They were down to about fifty ears of corn. Weldon went out and gave each cow one ear of corn. They would not get any more until they got to Nacogdoches. The remaining thirteen ears would be fed to the mules and horses the next night. A.D. had Art shelling the corn off the remaining ears.

A.D. and Frank said, "We will be pulling guard duty tonight."

"No," said Mr. Smith, "I'm going to do it all night and you two can alternate helping me."

"Okay, but we want Frank Jr. and Pat to guard the cows," they replied. "Everyone warned there are a lot of gangs close to these towns."

Sure enough around two o'clock in the morning, five rustlers came slowly into the camp. A.D., Frank and Mr. Smith were hidden and had their rifles trained on them. When they started to holler to wake up the supposedly sleeping wagons three shots rang out and three rustlers fell off their horses. The two remaining robbers didn't even know where to shoot. The wagoners then pulled their pistols and shot the other two rustlers off their horses. The rustlers had sent two more men to stampede the cows, mules and horses but the mules and horses were hobbled. The rustlers did manage to scatter the cows. But the Stroud boys shot and wounded the two rustlers. They were not only wounded but captured.

It took the pioneers about two hours to round up the cows and calves. Everything was in good shape the pioneers only got off ten shots total and three rustlers were dead and four wounded.

Frank said, "We can put the three dead men along with the four wounded in the wagon we used to hold the livestock feed, but one of them has to drive it." After trying to treat the four wounded rustlers, everyone had breakfast and the wagons were under way.

A.D. confiscated all the rustlers' horses, guns, knives and money.

The wounded rustlers were all hollering threats saying, "Y'all will pay for this as soon as you get to Nacogdoches!"

A.D. said, "Either shut up or you will walk back and stop telling us what's going to happen to us, when you came to our camp and started the trouble." Frank rode behind the feed wagon which contained the robbers, and Pat rode in front as A.D. scouted the road ahead. The wagons made thirteen miles that day. The rustler's wagon continued to be escorted by Frank and Pat. They were going to take the prisoners and turn the men over to the authorities. They didn't even know who the authorities were but they continued on to Nacogdoches through the night.

3

CHAPTER

The wagons with the prisoners arrived at 6:00 a.m. and waited until they could talk to Mr. Austin who opened his office at 8:00. While waiting the prisoners were complaining about being hungry and how unfair it was. Pat had gone to the feed store and fed the horses and mules pulling the wagons. A lady came by and Frank bought a dozen tamales from her. He and Pat ate four and gave the others to the prisoners.

Mr. Austin finally arrived and opened his office. They then got water for the prisoners.

Frank told Mr. Austin, "I want to get some land. A.D. Logging wrote you a letter which you answered telling us to come on down." They began to talk about the land that was available.

Frank told him, "We wanted land in the Perry Point area."

At that time Frank's son Pat came in and told his dad, "There's two men out there giving me the devil for guarding their buddies." When Frank went outside they calmed right down. Mr. Austin came outside with pistols drawn.

Frank told Mr. Austin what had happened and he said, "They have to be turned over to the local court." Mr. Austin walked everyone down a block to the stockade looking building and contacted the Mexican authorities.

They repeated their stories and the Mexican authorities said, "These men will be tried in a week. Your group will have to testify at the trials."

The jailer took each wounded rustler and chained them to a ten-foot-tall wooden post. There were twenty of these around the stake contained jail. Six more prisoners were waiting to be tried.

The jailer said, "You need to bury the ones you killed. Take them out north of town; there's a graveyard where you can bury them."

Frank told the jailer, "We could have buried them before but thought maybe their own families might want to see them and bury them."

The jailer said, "Just go on and bury them."

Frank and Pat went out and dug one grave six-foot-wide four-foot-deep six feet long and put the three dead men in the one grave, covering the dirt back over their bodies. Then Frank and Pat went back to search for a place for the other wagons when they arrived later that afternoon.

Mr. Austin had established a place for the immigrants coming into the Mexican territory to claim land but he didn't have a place for thirty cows, a bull and fifteen calves plus the mules and horses.

Frank had told Mr. Austin, "If you are going to be in town Monday, our group would like to meet with you at 9:00 a.m."

Mr. Austin replied, "Sure; that will be fine."

Frank proceeded to look for a place to put all the stock. Finally two miles south of Nacogdoches he found a twenty-five-acre fenced field with a stream running through. Frank located the farmer and owner of the field, Dave Collins.

The farmer said, "You can rent it for a month for $20."

Frank told him, "I think that is pretty high. I'll have to talk to my partner tonight." That was agreeable with the farmer. Frank also noticed that some light grazing could be done and that there were two large stacks of hay on the pasture.

The farmer said, "I have some corn and oats you could also buy."

"I'll get back to you as soon as I have a chance to talk to A.D." said Frank. He and Pat then went to get something to eat and wait for the other wagons to come in to town.

The other four wagons of the group finally arrived at six o'clock. Duke and Ace, the Smith's dog, had barely been able to drive the cattle because they were trying to graze since they were hungry.

Ace had become a fair cow dog working with Duke. Art had saddled up a horse to help drive the cattle. When Frank told A.D. about the pasture they immediately drove the herd to it. A.D. paid the farmer $20 and asked, "How about buying some oats and corn?"

Farmer Dave said, "Everything is one dollar a bushel." He paid the farmer another twenty dollars and the farmer said, "I'll give you an extra bushel of corn and oats to feed right away."

A.D. replied, "We'll take it." He began to scatter the bushel of ear corn for the cattle making sure even the non-dominate cows got their share.

A.D. told Dave, "We'll get the other feed tomorrow." Frank and A.D. discussed bringing the feed wagon out and loading it with the feed they had already bought.

Frank told Dave, "We decided to bring out the feed wagon, and also we'll be bringing twenty mules and ten horses to put on the pasture."

Dave replied, "With that many animals you'll be lucky to keep them on that little pasture for two weeks."

A.D. said, "We'll cross that bridge when we get to it."

A.D. and Frank went back to the others in their group and ate a supper of steak and cornbread. After supper the three families met.

Frank reported, "Mr. Austin said he would be waiting for us at nine o'clock Monday morning, and that he sees no problem getting us land around the Perry Point area."

Art and Frank drove the horses, mules and the empty feed wagon out to the rented pasture and loaded the corn and oats they had bought from Dave onto the wagon.

A.D. told Frank, "Go on back to camp. I will be out here along with Duke guarding our stock for the night."

"See you in the morning," Frank called as he rode away.

While A.D. was watching the stock, Dave came out and said, "No one is going to bother your stock out here." A.D. asked, "Are you going to replace them if someone does steal them?"

Dave did not reply to that but did ask, "Is your livestock marked for easy identification?"

A.D. said, "Yes, mine are all branded with my diamond double A brand." A.D. and Dave talked for about an hour. He relayed their experience on the trail from Fulton, Arkansas, and to Nacogdoches and the reason they had come to Texas seeking their fortune.

Dave said, "I came here with Mr. Austin and now have 4,428 acres, mainly farming and raising pigs. If you need some bacon, ham or sausage I could give you a good deal or maybe we could trade a calf for a hog?"

A.D. asked "where is your family? They died of cholera two years ago" Dave replied. Neither one said another word about it!

Dave continued, "I can also give you some hints on getting to Perry Point. Think I'll get some sleep now." Duke was already asleep under the feed wagon. A.D. stayed in the wagon until 1:00 a.m. and did finally get some sleep. He then went out by two large pine trees to protect the livestock. At 6:00 a.m. Dave brought out some coffee and eggs. A.D. ate heartily and appreciatively. About forty-five minutes later, he headed back to the wagon camp.

Everyone was just waking up and getting breakfast at the wagon camp. It was Sunday, and they all were going to church.

A.D. told his wife, "I am really tired and in bad need of sleep. I might just sleep all day. Duke, Ace and I can stay and guard all the wagons and the belongings." He proceeded to go to bed knowing that he had Duke and Ace to strike the alarm if necessary.

All the rest of the group went to church and returned at 11:30 a.m.

A.D. merely turned over and said, "Let me sleep until 6:00."

Everyone napped and rested that afternoon. Supper was at 5:00 and they all enjoyed a meal of roast deer. At supper Frank, A.D. and Mr. Smith had a meeting agreeing they would meet Mr. Austin the next morning at 9:00.

A.D. said, "I'll be out with the livestock tonight." He rode his horse the two miles to Dave's field.

At the pasture, A.D. began feeding the cattle making sure the dominant cows didn't eat all the food. After that he had to do the same with the eighteen mules and horses. Dave had come out of the house after A.D. had finished feeding all the stock.

He said, "If you are going to Perry Point, you can take flat boats from a place about thirty miles from here on the Trinity River. That trip would only take four days in place of sixteen and would only cost $20. They can take two wagons on each boat if you want to reserve a spot by Tuesday, we can send a message to them tomorrow." A.D. asked, "What about all my livestock?"

"They can't take them so you'll still have to drive them all the way to Perry Point," Dave replied.

A.D. told Dave, "I'll have to talk it over with the rest of the group, and I'll let you know what they decide tomorrow."

Dave went into the house and A.D. thought he had gone in for the night.

However, he came back out of his cabin with checkers saying, "I hope you play checkers. I don't get much of a chance to play or even have time anymore."

A.D. said, "I enjoy checkers and can play a few games till I get tired but I've got to get a good night's sleep. Tomorrow's a big day. We are meeting Mr. Austin in the morning."

Duke had already made himself comfortable under the feed wagon. Dave had brought out two chairs and a candle and they played checkers until about ten o'clock. During that time, A.D. tried to make a deal for a thousand pounds of oats and corn feed for the livestock.

A.D. told Dave, "I am also a blacksmith."

Dave said, "Well, I have some work for you. I need three horses shod and a wagon that needs a wheel replaced so I can either use or sell this other wagon."

"I'll try to do it tomorrow afternoon!" A.D. exclaimed.

He actually went to sleep in the feed wagon hoping Duke would sound the alarm if any rustlers came close. The night was quiet and A.D. woke up at 6:30 a.m. He fed Duke and left him to guard all the livestock.

The Loggings, Stroud's and Smiths met with Mr. Austin at 9 a.m. and they discussed how they could qualify for free land. Mr. Austin told them, "You all can qualify for a league of land each, and, Mr. Stroud, your sons can also qualify for two leagues of land. A league is 4,428 acres."

A.D. explained, "I am also a blacksmith and want to set up a business in Perry Point." Mr. Austin then gave A.D. a piece of land with a one-acre front and ten acres behind in Perry Point for his blacksmith shop. It was right next to the general store already in business there.

Then Austin told them, "The Mexican authorities do not want Anglos to get property within twenty-five miles of the Bay or the Riverhead of the Trinity. I'm going to give you these papers and you're going to need someone to survey where you set up."

"Now, you must understand that you'll have to be careful with the Mexican authorities," he continued, "however, I don't think you'll have any trouble with the property in Perry Point because you will be in business there. You could even be of some help to the Mexican soldiers if they were to happen to come to Perry Point. Also," he asked, "you understand you need to be on the property for three years making improvements on it and that you're going to need somebody to survey the property that won't tell the Mexican authorities." They all agreed they understood everything he told them and each signed the papers and paid Mr. Austin $60 for taxes on their new homestead.

Mr. Austin went on to say, "Each Anglo receiving a homestead in Mexico, Texas, must become a member of the Catholic Church. When you become a member make sure the priest fills out the paperwork for your entire family stating everyone is a member of the Catholic Church. Now I would recommend that you go over to the Catholic Church while you're still in Nacogdoches to become members because there is no Catholic priest or church within one hundred fifty miles of your homestead."

He also stated, "I know the grass is great for stock in the Perry Point area, and you can grow crops almost year-round." He said, "Good luck, and if I can ever be of help to you please contact me."

Austin then turned to A.D. and said, "I have three horses that need to be shod. Can you do it this morning? I would appreciate it and here's three dollars for your work." Mr. Austin then showed him the horses in the corral and in two hours A.D. had finished the job.

As he was working in Austin's corral a man came over and said, "I have several horses and mules that need shod. Would you be able to shoe them?"

"Sure", replied A.D. He worked until five o'clock and made $24 that afternoon. It was after 7:00 when he and his boys went home for supper. He then rode out two miles to feed the livestock.

Dave came out to the feed wagon with the checkers and the two men played until nine o'clock that night. While they were playing checkers Dave told A.D., "There are three more neighboring farmers that have about ten head that need to be shod tomorrow and I was hoping you would help them."

A.D. told David, "I worked all day today shoeing horses and mules and made $24. That's more money than I made in a week the last two year in Arkansas."

"Well," Dave said, "You ought to stay in this area. We don't have a blacksmith, and I'll bet you could make a real good living here."

Dave was thinking, "Maybe I could have a friend locally!"

The next day A.D. put shoes on twenty-one horses and mules. He also repaired four wagon wheels.

The following day A.D. asked Dave, "Are there any cabins or housing my family could stay in for a while? Your family could stay here", Dave answered, "Austin would know better where the other families could find shelter temporarily."

A.D. told Dave, "I'll start at eight o'clock in the morning repairing those wagons."

With Duke guarding the livestock for the night A.D. went to sleep in his feed wagon. Duke barked twice that night. Both times he got up and he and Duke inspected the livestock. They could not find what had alarmed the cow dog. A.D. praised Duke for his alertness and gave him a piece of jerky.

A.D. was up at 6:30 and went to the family wagon for the breakfast. He visited with the family until 8:00 a.m. The three families had a meeting about when they would be leaving for Perry Point.

A.D. addressed everyone. "I'm able to make some real money here and I would like to stay for a while. I know you other folks are anxious to go on to Perry Point, so if you want to leave, go ahead, and we'll meet you there later."

Mr. Smith said "We'll wait here, because in case you don't know it, we are flat broke, and if not for y'all's generosity we would all be dead. We have to stay with you until you stop feeding us."

Mrs. Stroud said, "If we stay, we need to move into a house and get out of these wagons."

A.D. said, "Ok, that means we are staying. Now we need to talk to Mr. Austin and see if he knows about any housing."

They went to consult Mr. Austin and he said, "In the village there is a big house, and the family is gone. You could probably stay there if you don't break anything." Everyone went over and looked at the house. There were four bedrooms and a couple more rooms.

Austin said, "Move in today and leave it just like it is now, and you owe me $10. But you can only stay for a month."

A.D. paid him the $10, saying, "The Smiths and the Stroud's can stay here and my family will stay on Dave's farm."

Mr. Austin told A.D., "There is a ten-wagon train camp north of Nacogdoches that needs a blacksmith to help fix four wagon wheels and at least ten horses need shoeing."

A.D. replied, "I can't do it today but I'll be there in a couple of days." A.D., Maggie and the two boys went to Dave's home.

He came out and said, "Everyone get down and come in the house and make yourselves at home. You can have the two bedrooms in the back. There is plenty of food in the cellar and pantry. We will be gone all day tomorrow repairing wagon wheels so have the boys feed your stock out of my feed in my barn. Have Duke watch the stock and we'll see you all at five o'clock for supper. I hope it's a good day."

They drove off in A.D.'s blacksmith wagon and arrived at the farm in an hour. They worked on two wagon wheels and fixed the wagon tongues on two others. A.D. and Dave ate a lunch of beans and cornbread and drove on to the next farm. By one o'clock they had fixed a wagon wheel and axle plus shoed one horse. He charged that neighbor three dollars. They arrived at the last farm for the day, fixed two wagon wheels and were home by 6:30 not the 5:30 David had promised.

Dave said, "You made $18 today. You would be rich if you stayed here."

Maggie had prepared a great meal and kept it warm until they got home.

She told A.D., "Mr. Stroud, his two boys and Mr. Smith have taken temporary jobs working for six days on a farm two miles west of Nacogdoches. They are building a corral and will receive $25 when they are finished."

Maggie and the boys, Mrs. Stroud and Mrs. Smith and her three young children had gone to the Catholic Church each day trying to get admitted to the church. In order to receive the land from Mexico you had to be Catholic or convert to that religion. All of the group went to church the next Sunday to be received into the Catholic Church. The priest gave each family two sets of papers that confirmed all the pioneer families were members of the Catholic Church. A.D. wanted to give Mr. Austin one copy for the grants given. A.D.'s two boys really didn't understand what was going on, having to go to church, every day schooling two hours and working around the house. Art and Weldon wanted to go fishing, but only had four or five hours a day to fish. The boys caught enough fish for their entire group plus they had given some to the catholic priest to eat on Friday.

The group worked through the week, and they took off on Sunday. Monday morning, A.D. went over to see Mr. Austin and gave him a copy of the paper that confirmed each member of all the pioneer families was a member of the Catholic Church.

He told Mr. Austin, "We will probably be leaving next Sunday."

Mr. Austin said, "You know you're going to be in flat country with more rain, heat and fewer trees than any place you lived so far but you'll have the best fishing you have ever seen." He continued, "You and your friends should not blatantly oppose the Mexican authorities." A.D. assured him, "I don't try to make people upset but we won't let anybody run over us either."

A.D. wanted to say more but thought better of it. He told Mr. Austin, "Thanks for all your help and do come see me and my family any time."

When he arrived back at Dave's there were six horses that needed shoeing and two wagons that had to be fixed. A.D. worked in the barn because it was raining a slow steady rain which amounted to two inches by the end of it. The temperature had averaged about 70 degrees all the month of October and about 80 degrees the previous month of September. This was only the second rain the group had experienced since they left Fulton, Arkansas, thirty days ago. Everyone knew if they had too much rain their heavily loaded wagons would take twice as long as normal to arrive at Perry Point. Too much rain was a worry and fear for everyone. Of course, there was no use worrying about that because no one could do anything about it anyway. Come Friday another two-inch rain fell. A.D. had decided his family should hit the trail to Perry Point on Sunday. He kept up his daily work through Friday and made over $120. He also had enough feed for his cows, horses and mules for at least thirty days.

4

CHAPTER

Saturday, the group loaded their food, and then they all rested, ready for the trip to their final destination. Dave had shown them the safest trails. The plan was to first try to pick up the flat boats on the Trinity River thirty miles South of Nacogdoches. If they couldn't, it would be a hard seventeen-day trip to Perry Point. If they could go on the flatboat it would only take three days on the Trinity River.

Dave told A.D., "I am going to send a local farmer to help y'all until you get to the River. He can show you the trail from the river to Perry Point. He can also help your group make a deal with the flatboat people. Sometimes they drive a hard bargain."

Sunday morning the group, along with Andy, the local farmer, set off for the river. By 7:00 p.m., they had traveled thirteen miles. After they fed and hobbled most of the mules and horses and set up the guards, everyone was asleep by 9:00. They were up by 5:00 and on their way by 6:00. The group was pushing hard to get to the flat boats.

They stopped four miles from where the boats usually docked. A.D. and Andy, the neighbor, rode on ahead to see if the flat boats were there. Luckily there were three flat boats there preparing to depart the next morning. They were anxious to take A.D.'s group down the Trinity.

A.D. and Andy struck a deal with the flat boaters: "You will be paid $60 to take all the wagons and stock all the way to Perry point."

The flat boaters replied, "That will be no problem." The largest flat boat was going to take all the stock. A.D. and Andy didn't think it could be done and told the flat boaters just that. They did get all five wagons on the two flat boats and then tried to load the stock on the larger flat boat. They quickly learned only some horses and mules would be able to be loaded on the third boat.

A.D. and Frank had already discussed this being a possibility and planned what they would do if that happened. They had decided A.D., Duke, Art and Frank Junior would drive the stock down to Perry Point. Art who was nine would drive the stock feed wagon.

An argument ensued with flat boaters. "We are only going to pay $40 because we are only using two boats instead of three," A.D. and Frank reasoned.

"No way! A deal is a deal," the flat boaters exclaimed.

Sober-faced, A.D. quietly demanded, "Unload the wagons and they'll go with the stock. Then we won't use any of your boats." After about thirty minutes, and A.D. unloading one of the wagons, the flat boaters finally relented and returned $10 to him.

The flat boaters and the stock took off at the same time. Five horses, thirty-six cows and calves, one bull and ten mules left on their seventeen-day trip overland.

The first day of this leg of the journey, A.D.'s crew traveled six miles and stopped. After supper, A.D. and Art went to sleep while Frank Jr. and Duke kept guard. At midnight Frank Jr. woke A.D. up for guard duty. No problems occurred that night.

They got underway at six o'clock the next morning and made fourteen miles that day. They were still in the Piney Woods area. The trail they were following went without incident for the next seven days. The last day they found a grassy three-acre spot with a stream running through it. They decided to stop and rest for a day. A.D. put Art on guard duty while he and Frank Jr. slept through the day.

A.D., Frank Jr. and Art worried about their families that were on the flat boats which should already be in Perry Point. The flatboat trip had encountered only one incident. Five men came up to the camp pointing their guns at the wagon settlers only, because the flatboat men had their own camp about fifty yards from the settlers. The loud-mouthed leader's name was Charlie. He told the settlers they were going to take all of their stock and belongings. They began to do just that.

Pat was relieving himself in the cover of the surrounding trees when he heard what was happening. He ran to the boatmen's camp for help.

The six men came up quickly and quietly with their guns drawn and ready. They surrounded the outlaws, telling them to drop their guns. Immediately all of them turned to shoot the boatmen. Three of the rustlers were shot and one boatman was wounded. Frank Sr. and Mr. Smith grabbed their double-barreled pistols, and everyone ran for cover of the surrounding trees. A few more shots were fired and the rustler leader shouted out.

"If you want a truce we will leave and not shoot anymore because we have to take care of our wounded."

The boaters replied, "No! You will give up your horses and guns." Just then Mr. Smith shot Charlie. With a shout, the outlaws all threw their guns down put up their hands and surrendered.

The boatmen tied up the uninjured men to a tree away from everyone and told Pat to shoot them if they tried to escape. Then everyone began tending to the wounded. First, they took care of the one boatman who had been shot in the ear. It was bleeding pretty badly. Ms. Stroud sewed it back on as well as she could, hoping he wouldn't lose the ear. Two of the rustlers died within one hour of their attack. The other two rustlers were treated for leg wounds, which, if infection didn't set in, would heal. The two wounded and one uninjured rustler dug the grave for their two buddies who were killed. The settlers and boatman sent the two wounded men home on one horse and confiscated the rustler's other four horses. The one rustler who was not wounded was conscripted to work on the flatboat with no pay for the consequences of his poor choice.

The boats left to deliver the settlers close to the Perry Point area. On this was the last day of the journey, the flat boaters were anxious to get to the Gulf Coast to pick up badly needed freight for the people in Central East Texas. At 7 p.m. the group arrived at the Bay where the Trinity empties. The landing was about a mile from the small village of Perry Point. The settlers talked it over and decided to camp there by the Bay that night and to go to the only store in the area the next morning. Maggie Logging and Mary Stroud were, of course, worried about their loved ones driving the livestock to Perry Point. The two women spent a lot of time talking and praying over their concerns for their loved ones driving the stock.

5

CHAPTER

The next morning the group moved to the twelve acres A.D. had negotiated for in the village. He had told Maggie to build a fence that would cover another twenty acres. He doubted if anyone would ever challenge their ownership. Perry Point had a general store and a leather-gunsmith shop. The McCoy General Store sold about everything you would ever need. You could also get a meal there.

After the corral was finished each of the families turned their thoughts toward building their own homes. Maggie and the others had made arrangements to get flat boards for use in their cabin. They also talked to Mr. McCoy about where they could get logs to build their cabins.

Gene McCoy said to Maggie, "There is a pretty nice cabin seventy feet from your property. The man that owned it died last year; you could move in there."

"Fix it up the way you want," he added.

The settlers went to look it over. The cabin had flat boards for the floors and a kitchen which was detached by a hallway. It also had a loft and a front porch with an overhanging roof.

Maggie asked McCoy, "If this man has been dead over a year and there is no one to pay for renting the house, can we just move in? Did anyone live with this man who appears to have been a fisherman? And how did he die?"

Mr. McCoy replied, "No one lived with him, and, yes, he was a fisherman. One day we found his boat afloat in the bay, but he was not in it. Everyone presumed he had fallen overboard and drowned."

The women began helping Maggie clean up the place. That night, the group slept in the cabin. The next day they moved some of their kitchen material and clothes out of the wagons into the cabin.

Maggie said, "Everyone can stay here in this cabin until you can build your own."

Mr. McCoy told the settlers, "There is a place about a mile north of here with a lot of trees. I'm sure you could cut down at least two hundred hardwood trees off that place."

After that Frank Sr. and Mr. Smith located their land grants and decided on locations for their cabins. They began to cut logs and haul them to their home sites.

Mr. McCoy said, "All the Indians around here are friendly and there are plenty of deer, ducks, geese, rabbits, squirrels, and fish so no one should starve."

The fourth day they ran out of feed for the mules and the horses so Maggie bought six dollars' worth of corn and oats. She feared that would not last even ten days.

The cabin was cramped with everyone sleeping there. After about two weeks everyone began to get testy. It rained the third week the settlers were there. The men had started playing dominoes at McCoy's store. Of course they enjoyed that, and it got them out of the house, and they met a few other homesteaders.

Meanwhile on the trail, A.D., Frank Jr. and Art had come across what they thought were wild cattle and had added those to the existing herd. All they had to do was to feed them, and the wild cattle followed along with the herd.

One morning Art came running and said, "Dad, our bull is missing."

A.D. immediately told Frank Jr., "You stay here with your guns ready, and I'll try to locate our bull."

It took A.D. about forty minutes to locate the bull by a cabin in a small pasture with four other cows.

He went through the yard to the cabin and hollered, "Is anyone home?"

A man and his son came out and very curtly asked, "What do you want?"

A.D. replied, "You have my bull."

The man said, "Can you prove it?" "As a matter fact, I can," he said. "It has my brand, the diamond double A, on his rump."

A.D. had his rifle and pistol with him and had his pistol drawn by this time. He didn't know if there was anyone in the cabin who would shoot him, but he knew he had his hands full dealing with this man.

The man said, "We got no bull and our cows are no good without a bull."

A.D. asked, "Would you sell me your cows and calves?"

"Yes, if we could get twelve dollars in gold or silver," the man replied.

A.D. said, "It's a deal and gave him two five dollar gold pieces and two silver dollars. Right away they opened the gate and drove the bull, four cows and two calves back to the other livestock.

A.D. told the settlers, "We have been able to catch some of the wild cows."

The man said, "If we should be able to get some more, would you buy them?"

"Yes," replied A.D., "but we will only be in this area for a day."

Before he had proceeded to move the small herd towards his own stock, the boy, Bob, asked "Can you help us with a lame horse?"

A.D. got off his horse and went with them to their barn. Looking at the horse he asked, "Who shoed this horse?"

Bob said, "My dad did."

"The horse will have to be reshod," A.D. replied, "And if you'll bring him to our wagon I'll do it for you." A.D. was worried about being ambushed by these people and didn't like turning his back on them.

The boy got on his horse and rode slowly behind A.D. the two miles to the wagon.

A.D. told Art, "Feed these cows and take them over with the other livestock and have Duke help you." A.D. took all the shoes off the lame horse, trimmed each hoof and put shoes that fit better on the horse. This took about an hour and a half.

Bob was fourteen years old.

He asked A.D., "If I get some cows to you today or tomorrow would you pay me and let me go with you?"

A.D. said, "Yes, I would pay you but what about your family?"

"Mr.," replied the boy, "can't you see there's no future living out here?"

A.D. said, "You could catch wild cows. I know you can successfully do that."

"No, I want to leave and get my own land. I'd be beholding to you if you let me ride along with you," replied Bob as he rode away.

He returned to their camp the next morning. They had already gone seven miles that day. His dad rode with him because he was taking the horse back to his home. That meant Bob didn't even have a horse, but he did bring three cows he had caught and A.D. paid him seven and a half dollars.

A.D. said, "Go saddle up a horse so you can help with driving the cows. That way I can sleep during the day in the wagon, and I can stand guard during the night. I also would like for you to learn how to work the cow dog."

A.D. showed Bob how to work Duke. Bob tried hard and was anxious to learn. That counted for a lot with A.D.

The next three days they covered 36 miles. A.D. figured they still had about forty-five miles to their new home in Perry Point. The next two days it rained off and on and they only covered fourteen miles. Small streams turned into large streams. The boys also found four more wild cows.

Pa said, "We are going to stop and brand all the new cows." It took them all day to brand those cattle. It was a good thing Bob was along because they could not have done the branding in one day without his help.

During the trip they had been able to shoot four deer and on the nineteenth day they shot another one. Everyone hoped it would be the last time they would have to shoot a deer for food on this trip. The next three days the group barely made thirty miles. Everyone now was in a great mood knowing they should get to Perry Point soon. They pushed the cows hard and arrived at their new home after twenty-five days driving the herd.

They came home to quite a celebration. The guys quickly moved the cows, horses and mules into the fenced area. Then a great welcome home celebration took place.

Bob felt out of place until Art asked his dad, "What are you going to do about him?"

A.D. said, "Bob, I'll give you a job working six days a week twelve hours a day. I will pay you fifteen dollars a month. You can sleep in the wagon until we get my blacksmith shop completed. When it is done you can sleep there. You can eat breakfast and supper with my family. Here's the ten dollars I promised for helping us on the trip."

Bob asked, "Would you just keep the money you owe me until I have earned a hundred dollars?"

"Okay, I'll be happy to do that for you," A.D. answered.

After supper the group agreed to rest that night and get together in the morning to talk about plans for their future. The sleeping accommodations were not the best for the returning group but better than sleeping on the ground or in the wagon.

After breakfast everyone met in the small cabin. The Stroud's and Smiths wanted to get started on their cabins. A.D. asked, "Do you have your wells dug or at least located? The first thing we have to do is get some crops in the ground."

All of them asked, "What do we plant in November? Will it even grow?" The women went to the McCoy's for advice. They suggested cabbage and turnips.

It was a brisk, fall day. The general store had the seed they needed to plant eight acres so they could have enough food to help with expenses in the coming winter. Mr. McCoy thought they might be able to have a large garden in January if it was planted now. The rest of the day was spent plowing, and the following day harrowing and planting the eight-acre garden.

There had been little rain in the area so feeding the livestock was a problem.

Mr. McCoy said, "There is a lot of dried dead grass that livestock can feed on. All you have to do is take the livestock to it." That day A.D. and Frank looked for four hours before they found a sixty-acre meadow where there was a lot of dried grass.

The next morning, they drove all the stock to that area to graze. "That sixty acres might be enough food for two weeks," A.D. said, "I'll go out next week and look for more feed for the stock."

Mr. McCoy thought the new settlers could make a crop of wheat and oats if they planted within the next week. For the next five days six people were plowing, harrowing a total of fifty acres each of wheat and oats. The next five days the settlers were cutting and hauling logs to the Stroud's and Smith's homesteads. The next three days Art and Bob were cutting and hauling logs for the blacksmith shop.

A.D. located a two-hundred-acre spot that might keep the livestock fed for two months. It took a half a day to drive the stock over there. A.D. had Bob drive the feed wagon over because he was going to be watching the stock and sleeping in the wagon at night along with Duke.

They thought they had hauled enough logs to the Stroud's and Smith's cabins and it only took four days to put up all the sidewalls with the doors and windows cut in. Now all they needed were the roofs put on. Mr. Stroud and his two boys begin putting the roof on their cabin, and A.D. and Mr. Smith began putting the roof on his cabin. This took a whole two days for each cabin which consisted of two rooms and a separate kitchen. It took another day to put planked boards down for the floors. They then put in temporary covers on the doors and the windows.

The Stroud's and the Smiths hitched their mules to their wagons to haul their belongings to their cabins. It felt so good for them to be in their own place.

The next day they went to McCoy store bought enough food to last for a month. A.D. talked to the leather and gun store owner. He told A.D., "I can make some very good box windows and doors if everyone will cut the holes for them a certain dimension." Fortunately, everyone had already cut the holes to his dimensions. He said, "I will make a box window that you can just set in the cut-out place in the sidewalls of the cabins and then seal it." Everyone thought that was a good idea but not everyone had enough money to do it. A.D. and Frank placed an order.

A.D., Art and young Weldon began building the side walls for his blacksmith shop. In two weeks they had the side walls up and roof frame assembled. He told his boys, "We'll wait until Bob can help us in a couple of weeks. A.D. and the boys rode out to help Bob herd the livestock back to the small fenced pasture behind the blacksmith shop. A.D. went out scouting for forage for all the settlers' cattle, mules and horses. He located his own league of land about four miles North of Perry Point right next to Frank Stroud's land-grant. Frank had finished his cabin and barn. He was now building the corral and working pens. He was trying to fence several pastures. Frank only had four mules, four horses and several head of cattle, but was planning on planting at least one hundred acres of crops with the help of his boys. He thought he would start running hogs and cattle when they had enough money.

When A.D. returned to his blacksmith shop he found two wagons to be fixed and nine horses that need to be shod. He always felt good doing this job because he really knew what he was doing.

Maggie said, "You don't even have a roof on your blacksmith shop and stable. You need to get that done."

A.D. replied, "People need help and I think that's what you do to build your business."

A.D. asked Bob, "Can you get a heavy tarp for the roof? Mr. McCoy hasn't been able to get any more building material we need. He suggested we go to Atascosita where he was sure we would find some. Mr. McCoy also said if you go would please bring back a load of material for him?"

A.D. made up his mind he and Bob would both go to Atascosita in a couple days, and then he got busy on the horse shoeing and wagon fixing. A.D. later changed his mind and told Bob, "We'll go on up to Atascosita in a week or so. Right now, I would like for you to start the fence building at my new homestead."

Frank Jr. went over and helped Bob for two days and during that time they had fenced twenty acres.

Everyone then began cutting roof supports for the two new cabins, two barns and A.D.'s blacksmith and stable shop. Frank was in charge of making the shingles. A.D. and Bob cut and hauled thirty trees while the rest of the settlers helped Frank Stroud with the shingle job. After A.D. and his boys had finished the walls and put up the roof frame on his cabin and two barns, all the help began putting the new shingles on these structures. After that was finished, A.D., Bob, Art and Weldon took two days putting shingles on the blacksmith shop and horse stable.

It was now Christmas and the weather was turning cooler averaging forty degrees during the day and raining at least once a week. Everyone was in their individual homes and celebrated Christmas with their own family in their own home. Frankly, they had had enough of one another for a while! The four days away from each other and just enjoying being with their own family for a change was an enjoyable break.

A.D. had told Mr. McCoy, "We need to make a trip to Atascosita for supplies. I need blacksmith supplies and horseshoes."

Mr. McCoy replied, "I need just about everything for the general store." It would take three wagons to haul all the supplies needed, but

A.D. wasn't sure he had enough money to pay for his supplies. He also hated to go because his blacksmith business was beginning to thrive. Earnings from working on the blacksmith business only one day a week were better than a full week in Fulton, Arkansas.

During the whole time the group had been there they needed wood for burning and could never get enough to last over a month at a time. The pioneers decided they would all go out together to try to collect enough downed trees to last through March. That would take care of the problem and be one less worry. It took three days to deliver that much wood to each of the cabins.

In one of A.D.'s many conversations with Gene McCoy, Mr. McCoy told him, "I am not going to go to Atascosita, to pick up my supplies because they are going be shipped to me by boat. They should be here next week and I would like your help transporting the goods from the Pilot Point dock."

A.D. said, "Sure, I would be glad to help but," he said, "that doesn't solve my problem. I need blacksmith supplies badly and I don't know who I can order them from in New Orleans."

McCoy said, "Make a list of what you want, and we will give it to the first boat leaving from here to New Orleans, which will probably be tomorrow. We'll do it under my name so you won't have to pay in advance. How does that sound?"

A.D. replied, "That would be great!" He immediately went over to his blacksmith shop and began compiling a list of his needs.

In about an hour he took the list to Gene who said, "I will get the order sent tomorrow."

A.D. said, "Thanks, I really appreciate it."

6
CHAPTER

A.D., Bob and his boys spent ten straight days building fence, and in that time, completed fencing fifty acres on their homestead. A.D. knew he had to get three new bulls for his herd, but he didn't really know where to get them.

Mr. McCoy told him, "I know a rancher, Dick Allen, who has a real good herd." "He lives about twenty miles northwest of Perry Point. He comes to my store twice a year, usually just after the new year and again in July."

A.D. said, "I would sure like to talk to him and try to buy some of his upgraded herd of Longhorns."

Sure enough, Mr. Allen showed up January 20. After giving McCoy the list of supplies he needed, he went over to the blacksmith shop to meet Mr. Logging.

A.D. was in the middle of shoeing a horse, but he was sure glad to meet Dick. After he finished with the horse, A.D. and Dick sat down and began a long two-hour talk about farming, gardens and cattle. A.D. invited him home for lunch. Afterward they rode over the homestead to look at A.D.'s cattle.

Dick said, "I am sure my Longhorn bulls are bred much better and could really improve your herd over the next three to five years."

Mr. Logging asked the rancher, "Would you want to buy my three Longhorn Bulls?" Mr. Allen quickly answered, "No, I don't want to buy them, but I have an idea." "I think you should set up a small corral out by the loading dock and keep two or three steers in there at all times. I am sure you could sell them to these boats coming in here."

This seemed like a good time for Dick to mention, "I need some blacksmith work at my ranch."

"Would you come up to work a couple days? I have fifteen horses and mules that need shoeing and a couple wagons that need fixing."

A.D. thought for a moment. "I could do it in February," he replied.

Dick said, "That would be great!" as he handed A.D. directions to his ranch.

By then it was 3:30 in the afternoon. Dick asked, "Hey, do you play dominoes?"

"Of course," answered A.D., "Why don't we go to McCoy's and see if someone else wants to play?"

McCoy himself said, "I'm not busy, and I can play the rest of the afternoon."

They stopped playing at 7:00 and A.D. again invited Dick home for supper.

"I'm sorry I can't," he replied. "I've already accepted an invitation to have supper with the McCoy's, but I wanted to ask you if I could park my wagon in your blacksmith shop. I plan to leave early in the morning to get home in time to spend more time with my family." His new friend readily agreed.

"By the way," Dick added, "you won't win when y'all come to my place."

A.D. laughed and said, "I'm going to look forward to it."

A.D. had a small fishing boat tied up in Trinity Bay that they used for fishing, but there were also two others tied up at the dock. The children enjoyed rowing in these small boats near the marshy water's edge for a couple of hours. That afternoon the families returned to their own homes with tired, sleepy children.

In January 1829, Gene McCoy said, "I need your help. A.D., because the boats have arrived with my supplies and I would like to get them unloaded as soon as possible."

A.D. told him, "It will take me an hour to hook the mules to four wagons; then we'll be out in front of your store."

Luckily, the Logging boys happened to be at the blacksmith shop when Mr. McCoy asked for help. A.D. sent Weldon home to tell their mom what they were going to do. A.D. insisted, "Gene, I want you to check everything that is loaded on the wagons."

"I trust you." McCoy replied,

"I know you do, but this prevents a lot of trouble."

"You're right," he replied, and proceeded to check all the goods that were loaded onto the wagons.

They pulled the four wagons up in front of his store. A.D. said, "My boys and I will unload the larger items, and you can unload the smaller items."

At one o'clock the wagons were parked and the mules unhooked and turned out to the back pasture.

An hour later, A.D. left the blacksmith shop and went to see the local doctor, Dr. Lily. He hadn't mentioned it while they worked, but he had a throbbing toothache.

Dr. Lily said, "You have two bad teeth. All I can do is pull them."

A.D. said, "If that's what has to be done, let's go ahead and get it over with." The doctor pulled the first tooth quickly but the second one took over an hour and a half. Both Doctor Lily and patient were completely worn out when he finally got the two teeth out. The second tooth had broken off during the first thirty minutes so that the gum had to be cut away. The doctor had a terrible time chipping out the rest of the tooth. A.D. paid Dr. Lily two dollars for his services.

"Your mouth will be sore for about a week," Dr. Lily advised. "You should gargle with warm salt water at least twice a day, more if at all possible and eat soft food."

A.D. went on home and told Art, "Go down and lock up the blacksmith shop. I am going to bed." He had a fitful night trying to sleep. His jaw was swollen, he was having trouble talking, plus he had a fever. A.D. stayed in bed two days until his fever finally broke. His jaw stayed sore and swollen for two weeks. He tried to work a little more each day of the two weeks he was recovering.

The day of his full recovery, Mr. McCoy came to the blacksmith shop and said, "All the supplies you ordered are on a boat at the dock."

A.D. said, "We'll be down there shortly to unload." He then sent Art to find Bob to come help. A.D. hitched the mules to the wagons and proceeded to drive them on down to the dock. He had the wagon half loaded when Bob showed up. He checked over everything to make sure he had all the materials that were ordered, and then he thanked the ship's captain for bringing the blacksmithing material to him.

The captain said, "I would buy a steer from you if you can bring it to me within the next hour." Bob took his horse and Duke out to get a steer. He brought it near the dock, then he killed and gutted it and took it to the captain. The captain gave Bob five dollars, and Bob returned to the blacksmith shop, giving the money to his boss. He unloaded most of the blacksmithing material the boat had brought.

It was now about 5:00 and A.D. told Bob, "Stay here tonight. I want to build a small corral for three steers close to the docks tomorrow. I guess you'll come down to the house about 6:00 for supper."

Bob replied, "Yes I'll see you then."

It took Bob and A.D. about three hours to build a 20' x 10' corral for the steers. Then Bob and Duke went out and got three steers, putting them in the dock corral. They had chunked out a tree to hold about three buckets of water for the steers and the boys had spread a small amount of feed on the ground.

The next two weeks A.D. did two days of blacksmithing, and he and Bob also fenced about fifty acres on the homestead.

The boys' education had always included two hours a day of reading, writing, arithmetic and the Bible. Bob did not know how to read or write and was anxious to learn. Therefore, when he was in Perry Point, he always tried to spend one hour each day learning from Maggie Logging. She usually gave him homework for later to practice what he had learned. He was making a lot of progress, and so were the boys.

On March first, A.D., Art and Duke were going to Dick Allen's ranch for blacksmithing work and to try to buy three different longhorn bulls which he had promised. They started off at seven o'clock to the Allen ranch. It took two days to get there.

Dick met them, smiling, "We're so glad you're here". "I have plenty of work for you: a total of thirty horses and mules to be shod and three wagons that need to be worked on. When the neighbors hear that you are blacksmithing at my ranch," he added, "you will probably have a lot more work. A.D., you'll probably have to stay two weeks." Dick gave A.D. and Art a nice big bedroom in his large ranch home.

A.D. was really impressed with this home and told Dick, "We've never stayed in a place this nice, ever!"

A.D. played three games of checkers that night and went to bed at 9:00. They were up at daybreak to start shoeing.

The first morning A.D. had seven horses done. Art was beginning to love helping his dad and was glad he had come along. Pa bragged on him telling him what a great helper he was.

They enjoyed a big lunch and ate too much. That afternoon A.D. shoed eight more horses and mules, finishing all of Dick's stock.

The next day, A.D. planned to fix two wagons, thinking that if he got some help, he could have them fixed by noon. One needed the axle reset and the other repair was a wagon tongue. A.D. told Dick, "All the wheels on those two wagons need greasing."

Dick's daughter, Helen, who was twelve years old came home after visiting a friend who lived about fifteen miles away. She and Art got along really well. A.D. asked her to teach Art for a few days to keep up with his schooling? She agreed. Art worried his dad would need his help while he was studying but Dick intervened, "I can get a cowboy to help your dad." A.D. thought it would do Art good to be around some other kids.

Helen told Art, "It is really lonely out here so most of the time I keep myself busy cooking, sewing, reading and trying to see friends at least once a month." Helen was a good teacher and taught Art for three days. He seemed to learn a lot.

A.D. was well pleased, both with Art's progress and his own. He had shod over thirty horses and mules and repaired four wagons. He had made $60! A.D. had twelve more horses to shoe and one wagon left to fix.

One of the farmers had a beautiful gray stallion. A.D. told the farmer, "I sure would like to have that gray stallion. Are you interested in selling him?"

"No, I really don't want to sell him," replied the farmer. "How much do I owe you?"

A.D. said, "Twenty dollars."

Dick asked, "Would you take thirty bushels of corn and thirty bushels of oats?"

"I sure would," he replied, "And I would buy more corn or oats if you have it to sell."

A.D. was interested in learning as much as he could about how the successful Dick Allen farmed. He told A.D., "The best corn crops I have seen for many years is when I planted a fish with every corn hill, but it wasn't easy."

A.D. ended up buying ten bushels of seed corn and also five bushels of seed oats from the farmer. He paid him twenty-five dollars for those items. For two days, A.D. had been busy shoeing eighteen head of horses and mules and fixing two wagon wheels.

He really wanted to buy the gray stallion from that farmer, but he would not sell him. Mr. Allen had several other blacksmith jobs which were finally finished.

A.D. was about ready to leave the Allen ranch. Dick had picked out three good bulls and six bred gilt pigs to send with him. At 6 a.m. when A.D. went out to the wagon, the farmer that had the gray stallion was waiting for him.

He asked, "Do you still want to buy the gray? I'll sell him to you for seventy-five dollars".

"I've only got forty-five dollars," A.D. replied. "Will you take a note for the rest?"

Dick Allen said, "I'll take your note for the thirty dollars."

A.D. wrote out the note and signed it.

"Thank you, Dick," A.D. said earnestly. "I really appreciate it."

He paid the farmer seventy-five dollars, happy to have been able to buy the gray. He was now ready to leave.

Dick said, "I have a man to help you until you make camp tonight. My daughter is going to ride with Art until noon, then she will ride back home."

A.D. had decided to ride the gray stud so they could get used to one another. The wagon made fifteen miles that day. Mr. Allen's hand helped A.D. build small pens for the gilts for the night. Duke, of course, had been great help driving the bulls and the pigs.

The next morning, it was rough going herding those hogs. A.D. finally told Art, "Untie your horse from the back of the wagon, get on it and help Duke drive those gilts." On the trip home they encountered six snakes. Art was amazed at how the hogs ate those snakes without getting sick from their bites.

When they returned home there was a great reunion with the family. Maggie and Weldon had prepared a wonderful supper. Both A.D. and Art ate a large meal but were so tired that by 8:30 they were asleep, promising to talk about the trip tomorrow.

Everyone slept late the next morning. During breakfast, and for about an hour afterwards, A.D. and Art talked about their trip telling their stories.

A.D. told Maggie, "We got hogs so don't throw away any food because they will eat all our scraps. Just put it all in a bucket and Bob will take it to them every day. If he doesn't take it out every day it will stink and attract flies and mosquitoes."

He continued, "We've got some feed for horses, cattle and mules but we can only feed them a half pound every other day. That way our stock will be in shape when the grass comes in the spring. Lastly, I bought a special horse to breed to our mares. I may race him. Right now, I am the only one that will ride him."

"That's the best horse we have ever seen!" Art and Bob chimed in.

At that point everyone went to their work for the day: Maggie to teaching the boys, cooking and cleaning and also taking an hour to teach Bob. Bob was also preparing housing and a pasture for the hogs so they couldn't escape. A.D. and Art finally fed all the stock and checked the livestock. Later, A.D. went to see Gene McCoy to be filled in on what had happened in Perry Point while he was gone.

Gene said, "There are five horses and two mules in the corral of your blacksmith shop. The lady is in a hurry, so will it be possible for you to get them done today?" He continued, "There is also a boat out there and the captain said he needs you to help repair something. I'll send someone to tell him you are home."

A.D. went out to his blacksmith shop and collected the horses and mules. By one o'clock he had finished shoeing them. He then went to eat his lunch.

After lunch he went back, and his sons went with him. A man came to the blacksmith shop to have his horse shod. At 5:00, the sky looked dark and rainy. Bob came by and said, "The pigs are secure, happy and still tired from the trip."

Everyone went to the Logging's house for supper. After supper, Bob discussed some troublesome math problems with Maggie. She explained them to him and then she gave him more problems to work on that night. He left about 7:00 to go to bed.

When Bob got back to the blacksmith shop to bed down, the first mate from the boat docked at Perry Point was there and wanted to see A.D. about some repairs to the ship. Part of the ship's rudder had broken off and they were having trouble steering.

Bob told the young fellow, "A.D. will come out to the ship in the morning."

The mate said, "No, the captain wants him to start on the repairs tonight."

Therefore, Bob went back to Logging's house to relay this information to his boss. A.D. agreed to go out to the ship that evening to see what could be done to fix it. When A.D. got to the ship, the rudder was still in the water and had not been taken off the rudder shaft.

A.D. told the captain, "The only thing I could do is take the rudder off and take it to the shop to attach a four inch by two-foot piece of metal to it. Then when you get to a larger port you need to replace the whole rudder." A.D. and Bob worked in the water to get the rudder detached so they could take it back to the shop. It took A.D. and Bob five hours to repair the rudder and another hour and a half to reattach it. They finished the job at 4:00 a.m.

The captain said, "I got one of your steers the first day we arrived, and I paid Mr. McCoy five dollars for it. How much do we owe you for repairing the rudder?"

A.D. said, "Twenty-five dollars."

The captain complained, "That is too much." But A.D. stuck to his guns and said, "That is my price and that is what I want." The captain finally paid him the twenty-five dollars.

A.D. and Bob left in the row boat back to Perry Point.

A.D. said, "Bob, let's take today off. Just check the cows and hogs." He then went home, crawled into bed and didn't get up until one o'clock.

After a big lunch, A.D. took the boys down to Gene McCoy's General Store where they visited and played several games of dominoes. They left for supper at five o'clock.

The next morning the whole family went out to check the eight-acre garden. They worked in it all morning. The garden looked great, ready to harvest produce in about one week. The settlers would certainly welcome the cabbage and turnips out of their new garden. If it wasn't for hunting and fishing, they all would have starved by now.

The three settler families that had arrived together at Perry Point met about once a month, ate, played games and visited.

A.D. told Frank and Mr. Smith, "You know you still have six and three cows, respectively, with my cows. In April I would like for you to take them to your own farms. Also, I'll give each of you two gilt pigs if you will give me two three-month-old females from the first litter. I'll get two three-month-old females from each of you in or around June. Is it a deal?" They both agree hoping to get the gilts sometime that week. A.D. said, "We all need to be looking for a good boar we can all use for breeding, and I don't even know where to start looking."

The rest of the day was spent playing games and visiting.

7

CHAPTER

Bob was interested in getting some land for himself and his parents. He wanted to start his own farm in the Perry Point area. A.D. had advised him, "You can spend two hundred dollars and go to a good lawyer. Or you could choose to go to Mr. Austin to give you a league of land grant, but it is not easy making a dangerous trip back up to Nacogdoches." Bob said, "I would like to see if my parents would move down here with me. I will go see a lawyer sometime. You have about sixty-five dollars saved of your money; that's a start."

"You'll need more than that if you pay a lawyer," A.D. said.

The Stroud and Smith families left for the evening taking their two gilts apiece with them. Everyone had certainly enjoyed a good social day. A.D. and Bob went out to the pig pen with them to select the gilts. They also needed to put three steers in the corral down by the dock. A.D. had sold ten head to the boats coming into the port for five dollars each. When he had enough hogs and vegetables he intended to sell them to the ships also. Art and Weldon went to the docks each morning to check for ships at Perry Point. Usually there were two ships a week that were at Perry Point coming out or going up the Trinity River.

During March it turned cold in Perry Point and got down to freezing several nights. During that time, A.D. and the boys fished in the bay three times, and twice they had gigged for flounder. They smoked their catch in the smokehouse to preserve it for a few weeks, adding variety to their meals.

They only went out hunting for ducks and geese twice during the winter and each time they shot nine birds. In the meantime, Maggie had purchased twenty-five chicks from a ship at Perry Point. Most of the chicks survived. By March, the pullets had developed enough to start laying. Maggie was getting twenty eggs a day and selling the excess, about six dozen each week, to Gene McCoy. Some of the hens started setting on eggs as well, and in a few weeks, fifty baby chicks had hatched. She gave one third of them to the Stroud's and another one third to the Smiths.

By March 25, they already had five straight days of 70° temperatures. The folks that arrived in Perry Point with A.D. decided they would plant a total of two hundred acres of corn, with A.D. planting one hundred of those acres. At the same time A.D. planted a new large two-acre garden of peas, onions, potatoes, cabbage and turnips. A.D., Bob and the boys took two weeks to plant the one hundred acres of corn.

In the meantime, a fishing ship that had a large number of dead, rotting fish came to Pilot Point. A.D. paid twenty dollars for about one hundred twenty pounds of dead fish. He and the boys loaded the decomposing fish in the wagons and took them out to where they had planted the corn. They buried a fish beside each plant. There was enough fish to fertilize ten acres of corn. The stench was abominable. They reckoned it was a good thing they didn't have neighbors close by!

Duke was beginning to be a pretty good watchdog for the corn crop. He was good at keeping all the wild animals, mainly the deer and coons, out of the garden.

After harrowing weeds out of the young corn crop, A.D. and Bob finally went to see a lawyer at Perry Point to see if Bob could get a land grant so he could have his own farm.

The lawyer listened, took notes and told them, "I will have the papers needed for you to sign today. I will take them myself to Stephen Austin next week. I have other business with Mr. Austin at that time."

He also alarmed A.D. and Bob by saying, "The Mexicans are going to come in two weeks to start making all of the homesteaders pay tax on their stock and the value of their property. They're going to charge you ten dollars for your blacksmith business and two dollars for your home. Hide most of your stock and tell others to do the same thing."

"All of us together don't have that much money." A.D. said. "How much do you think they'll take from me?"

"I don't know," replied the lawyer. "Gene McCoy may know more."

A.D. stopped by McCoy's General Store before going home.

"How much taxes do you reckon the Mexicans will have you pay for your business, Gene?" He asked.

Gene said, "Probably over $100."

"How much do you think they'll take from me?" A.D. asked.

"Not over fifty dollars." Gene estimated. A.D. was really upset!

He and Bob walked out, got their horses and Duke and they prepared to go warn their neighbors to find a place to hide their livestock. Bob started the search for a place to put their livestock, and A.D. went to talk to the other families about the pending Mexican tax. The news upset them too, and they wanted to know what they could do about this new development.

A.D. said, "You can't do anything about your house, barn and property. They can see your family so if you could hide your hogs, cows and horses, not the mules, then I figure you won't be taxed as much."

Bob returned and said, "I found a good place to hide the cattle and horses. There's a lot of live oaks protecting a pasture in the northeast forty acres." He worked hard to fence a new pasture where they were hiding the livestock. Duke was great at helping them keep the cows in the pasture. A.D. was still feeding the livestock as he had three hundred pounds of corn and one hundred pounds of oats left over. That helped them keep the animals close to the workers until they got the pasture fenced.

They then began to weed the corn crop and get ready to harvest the wheat crop.

The next month went by and no Mexican tax collectors showed up. Everyone was pretty mad at A.D. because he had spread the hearsay about the tax collectors coming. Gene McCoy quickly stood up and took responsibility in the matter.

"I am the one that confirmed the Mexican tax collectors were coming to Perry Point," he reminded the locals. "However, I am glad they have not come."

The same rumor started again in September and again no Mexican tax collectors. A.D. could leave his stock out in the new pasture for about three months to save his own grass.

Progress in Perry Point had A.D. working about one and a half days a week in his blacksmith business. This small village was averaging one new family every other month. A.D. was selling one steer a week out of his corral by the dock. He had forty-three new calves born in the last three months. The Loggings spent two days branding and castrating the new calf crop plus nine other wild cows that they had caught. His hard work was paying off.

In June, the settlers started harvesting their wheat and oat crops, and they were better than expected, right at twenty-five bushels to the acre. Frank, Mr. Smith and A.D. each took the same amount of each of the shared crops. They made sure the storage area in the barn was dry and as protected as possible from insects, mice and other varmints that could cause them to lose the grain.

After that they weeded the corn field for the second time that summer. During the summer, A.D. had his boys mucking out the horse manure in the stable that he owned and putting it on a new two-acre site where he planned to plant their next vegetable garden.

The hogs had multiplied. A.D. now had two sows, eight gilts and four young boars. The other settlers each had two sows and six gilts. A.D. said, "We need a hog pen next to my cattle corral down by the dock."

8

CHAPTER

Atascosa was going to have a big July 4th celebration. They would have horse races, dominoes and checkers tournaments, a greased pig contest, horseshoe pitching and a shooting contest. Most of the people in the area were planning to attend.

A.D. had been having Art ride the gray stud one half mile and running a half mile every day because he planned to enter the stallion, now called Gray, in the horse races July 4th.

They arrived in Atascosa the evening of the 2nd. Luck was with them as they got a barn about half a mile away from where all the activities with guns would take place. They didn't want the horses to be spooked by the gunfire.

The next day, A.D. had Art run Gray on the race track three times and then cooled him off during noontime. He also told Art to find the best place to run on that half-mile track, and Art thought he had found that place. A.D. and a lot of other men had gone out and practiced shooting with their rifles. They had learned they would have two minutes to shoot as many shots as they could at a hundred-yard target. The next morning the rifle shooting contest started. Over two hundred men had entered this contest. A.D. got to shoot within thirty minutes of the contest starting. He put four shots in the bull's-eye. Frank had done the same thing, and his two boys had put two shots out of four in the bull's-eye. Mr. Smith had shot four times in the two minutes, with all shots close to the bull's-eye.

At ten o'clock A.D. had Art start preparing Gray for the first race at eleven o'clock. There were forty-one horses entered and they were going to run ten horses in four different heats, with the winner of each heat would be running for the championship at one o'clock. Art had fed Gray a mixture of oats and corn that morning.

Gray won the first race pretty easily. Art got twenty-five dollars for winning that race, but his dad had bet fifty dollars on that horse and won two hundred dollars.

A.D. told Art to cool the horse off by putting his feet in the stream close by for about twenty minutes, unsaddle and rub him down. Then Art was to have him ready to go at 12:30.

A.D. then returned to the rifle shooting contest where he and twenty others were now shooting at a target one hundred fifty yards away. A.D. was lucky and got to shoot first. He put one shot in the bull's-eye and three just outside of it. Frank got about the same thing. A.D. had seen two men put four shots in two minutes in the bull's-eye and knew for certain he and Frank were out of this shooting contest.

A.D. then returned to watch Art bring Gray out for the championship race. Not to be outdone, this time Maggie had fifty dollars from her egg money that she bet on Gray. A.D. put another fifty dollar bet on Gray. Sure enough, Gray won the race! Art's prize for that race was two hundred fifty dollars, but his parents' fifty dollar bets got them one hundred dollars each!

That evening they had the greased pig contest, and it was hilarious. Spectators couldn't keep from chuckling at the children racing around the arena, diving to get a hold on a greased pig.

The next day several of the group entered the dominoes, checkers and horseshoe pitching contests. Frank won the fifty-dollar prize for the horseshoe pitching contest. The evening of July 4th, a big dance was held with local musicians providing the music. A.D. only saw four fights mostly because those men were drinking. But all of the couples and the children enjoyed the dance.

Very early the next day they headed back to Perry Point and arrived home the evening of July 6th. Bob had stayed home to look after everything. He reported no problems.

9

CHAPTER

August 1, Bob came riding very fast into A.D.'s blacksmith shop. He had finally been able to stake his own homestead. While fencing his own farm, he had found a young part-Indian girl who had been beaten and whipped. It appeared that she was almost dead!

A.D. hooked up the wagon, picked up Maggie and the boys and, on his way, out stopped at Doc Lily's. The doctor couldn't come right away, but A.D. left Art to show him how to get to Bob's farm. Maggie brought water, sheets, ointment, alcohol and some soup. In about fifteen minutes the group arrived at Bob's barn.

It was a very hot day. Maggie could not believe how badly this girl had been beaten and abused. It looked like someone had beaten her with a whip. Maggie immediately began to clean the girl's wounds and try to make her comfortable while waiting for the doctor. Dr. Lily arrived about half an hour later.

"She has several broken ribs and she could have severe internal damage but I won't know that for a couple of days," he said after his examination. "I don't want to move her until I find out how badly she is hurt."

A.D. quickly got everyone together and said, "You can't discuss this with anyone until we talk to her and find out what happened. Whoever did this probably thinks she is dead, and they sure don't want her telling us what happened. Can I count on everyone here to not talk to anybody about this girl?"

Bob said, "I can take care of her, and I have good water from the spring on my place."

"I didn't know you had a spring on your place," A.D. perked up.

"Yes, all I need is some pipe to go twenty-five feet to my big pasture and five thousand, two hundred fifty feet to my cabin, and then I'll have good water for the place."

"You need to get a couple of wooden tanks," A.D. said.

"How much would all that cost?" Bob inquired.

"About fifty dollars, but are you sure you need all this? You only need water for yourself, two dogs, five cows, a horse and a mule."

Since they had settled at Perry Point each man of the group had put out cattle traps. They had each trapped about five wild longhorns, adding them to their cattle herds. Wild cow trapping was done mostly in the winter.

It was decided Maggie Logging would stay with the Indian girl during the day and Bob at night that way no one would notice anything out of the ordinary. The girl woke up and drank some water and then passed out. She did that twice more in the next twelve hours. Then about midnight she woke up for an hour and ate, drank some soup and water then went back to sleep again. Maggie and the doctor came in at 8:00 a.m.

Dr. Lily said, "I think the only serious thing is several fractured ribs." She fell asleep again but had seemed to be disorientated. The doctor returned at 6:00 p.m. and re-examine her, verifying the ribs were the only thing broken. He then wrapped her ribs tightly and told Bob, "I'll see her around noon tomorrow. Keep feeding her all the liquids she will take."

The Indian girl woke up about midnight and stayed awake for two hours.

"Two white men close to Atascocita took me while I was out riding close to my father's farm," she told Bob. "They took me south to a cabin. And after I was there for a week they finally left and went hunting, leaving me tied up. I got loose and wandered two days before I found your farm."

Bob said, "I'll take you home when the doctor says it's okay". He found out her name was Watha.

"I want to go home tomorrow", Watha implored, "if you would take me in a wagon. My family is probably very worried."

"If the doctor says it's okay, I'll take you home." Bob replied.

When she went to sleep Bob rode to A.D.'s to ask to borrow a wagon. "It will probably take me two days."

"Take your pistol and shotgun," A.D. said, worriedly. "That area has a lot of bad people. Be careful and trust nobody."

Early the next morning after seeing Dr. Lily, getting his okay and paying him, Bob and Watha took off. After the long, hot trip, they finally arrived at her parents' home that evening.

What a glorious meeting; crying, hugging and laughing. Watha had two brothers and one sister. Watha and Bob were hungry, so they ate first, she told her story. By then it was 10:00 p.m., and everyone was very tired.

Bob bedded down in the barn and was up at 6:00 a.m. along with her dad, Mr. Adams. He helped with the morning chores. Watha's family mainly ran hogs, cattle and also grew corn and cotton.

"Could I buy a couple of boars from you?" Bob asked.

"No, but I'll give you three, and I won't have it any other way," the grateful father stated. "Just pick out any three of these, and they are yours. I'll build you a crate to carry them in your wagon."

"I'll need to get back home tomorrow." Bob said.

Mr. Adams said, "I want to thank you for helping Watha."

"I like your daughter. Would you mind if I called on her sometimes?" Bob asked.

"Yes, you are welcome here any time," he replied.

"Now you need to find out who these men are that took Watha," suggested Bob.

Mr. Adams said, "I think I know, and I, along with several other neighbors, are going to pay them a visit. Would you like to come along?"

"I sure would!" Bob replied.

Mr. Adams said, "Let's go have breakfast and afterward I'll build a crate to hold the hogs. Then we'll ride off after those kidnappers."

Watha was in the buggy with Bob driving. In a half-hour they got to one of the suspect's farm where they saw the suspected kidnappers working in the field.

"Those are not the ones," Watha said when she saw them.

Bob turned the buggy around and drove to another farm he had seen twenty minutes before. The rest of the posse followed, but she didn't recognize anyone. At the next farm she again said no. They visited two more farms close by and didn't find the suspects. That was the end of the day.

Bob left for his home at 6:00 a.m. after a long conversation with Watha.

"Your dad told me I could call on you," Bob said sheepishly.

"I like you a lot," she said. "I would like for you to call on me. Thank you for all your help and be sure and tell all of the people down at Perry Point how grateful I am. I will never forget them!"

He hoped he could get home without any trouble but he put his pistol and long rifle on the seat beside him and checked to make sure they were loaded.

At about one o'clock two riders rode up ten yards from him demanding Bob give them his mule and wagon. Bob shot the closest man and grabbed his long rifle, jumping behind the seat, he fired at the other man as he was riding away, but he missed.

Bob reloaded both guns put the pistol in his holster and the long rifle on the wagon seat. He went over to see about the man he had shot. Seeing the man was dead he put him in the back of the wagon.

After capturing the dead man's horse and tying him to the back of the wagon, he continued on his trip back home. Bob thought to himself and then he told his mule, "We gotta get out of this area before I get lynched."

Bob moved on for two hours before he gave his team a much-needed rest at a shaded creek where they could all get a drink of water.

They arrived at Perry Point at 7:00 that evening just before dark. Bob went to A.D. and told him about the attempted robbery and the dead man. A.D. and Bob took the problem to Gene McCoy.

Bob told him what had happened.

McCoy said, "Let's bury him and take all his belongings, horse and tack and if anyone comes asking, we'll say we found him dead. We didn't know who he was or where he was from."

That was all accomplished the next day. Bob gave A.D. and Frank each one of the boar hogs he had gotten from Watha's father, keeping the third for himself. Everyone seemed happy with that.

A.D. and Bob had been training Gray to race and thought the stallion might be the fastest horse in South Texas since he had already won the race at Atascosita.

Maggie gave a birthday party for Art and Weldon who turned ten and eight respectively. Most of the pioneer children learned to have fun playing with the dog or even a stick whenever they had free time, after doing their chores. The Logging boys explored all the area around Perry Point.

A.D. had cooked a whole hog and all the children and the parents had a great time and a good meal. A.D. gave the boys each a heifer and told them they could build a herd by the time they were 16 so they would have a good start in their life. Both the boys were well pleased to start their own cattle herd.

"Watha's dad and friends found the kidnappers and hung them," Bob shared the news he had learned from a letter a traveler delivered to McCoy's General Store. Bob thought he should also tell the men about the problem he had coming home because they might know the man that he shot.

They told A.D. and Bob, "We will make sure everyone in the area is alerted and try to find out who the man was."

A.D. wanted to know because he knew they would have to go after the man that got away or he might come after Bob.

Maggie helped Bob write the letter to Watha asking her to come to Perry Point for a visit because he would sure like to see her. He assured her she could stay with the Logging family.

Watha wrote a letter back to Bob saying she couldn't come until the last part of September because everyone around her place would be busy with the harvest. A.D. discovered one of his bulls was missing, and it took him and Duke several hours to track and return him to the herd. Nothing else was wrong that he could see. Both livestock and garden on the homestead looked pretty good. They should start harvesting corn in about a week.

Before they started the harvest, Watha and her dad showed up for a few days' visit. Bob told A.D., "I would like to have four days off so I can show Watha around."

The next day Bob took her and her dad fishing and they caught enough fish to have a big fish fry which was planned in three days. The next day Bob took them gigging for flounder and they had ten flounder for the smokehouse.

Watha's dad brought four horses and four mules that he wanted A.D. to shoe. He tried to pay A.D. ten dollars for doing that job but A.D. wouldn't accept the money, because of the three boars he had given Bob. Watha and her dad stayed with Bob at his farm the entire time.

Weather turned out to be a perfect Indian summer day for a big fish fry. There were about 60 people in attendance and everyone had a great time! All the ladies in Perry Point brought a dish to share. Bob and A.D. told Watha's dad about Bob's trip coming home from returning Watha to her family. He had no idea who the man was or how to even find the partner that had escaped but promised he would check around. The following day early in the morning Watha and her dad left for their home.

September 15th, they began the harvest of the two hundred acres of corn. This took the group three weeks of hard work. The corn averaged forty bushels to the acre. A.D. took four thousand bushels and gave Bob eight hundred bushels. Mr. Smith got a thousand bushels and Frank and his boys took three thousand two hundred bushels. It was decided by the group that everyone would plant their own crops from now on, helping each other out if and when they could. They finished the corn harvest October 1.

That was good because right after the harvest was finished it rained two inches every day for four days. A.D. took a week to get caught up on his blacksmith chores. Bob and the boys went out to the forest area to find fallen trees and began to cut them up for wood for their fireplaces. In eight days, they had delivered one load to the town cabin, one load to the blacksmith shop, one load to A.D.'s barn and cabin and one load to Bob's cabin and barn. That would not be enough for all winter. They would have to go out and get at least the same amount again to carry them through until March.

It was now October 15. A.D. and Bob began preparing 60 acres for the planting of oats and wheat. By the time they had finished it was November 1. A.D., Bob and the boys spent the next two weeks getting eight more wagonloads of firewood.

Snakes were a problem at this time of the year. Every time they collected fire wood they saw a lot of snakes. A.D. and the boys decided before they picked up any more dead trees to use for firewood they would have a snake hunt. They had come close to being bitten by copperheads and rattlesnakes each time.

10

CHAPTER

Most of the pioneers that had entered Texas didn't have much interest in the politics with the Spanish and or Mexican governments. Like all other Americans they believed all people had the rights of life, liberty and the pursuit of happiness, and that the government couldn't arrest them without probable cause or take a citizen's property. The pioneers mistakenly thought they were living under the same laws as the United States.

It was a shock to them when they found out the Mexican government could do anything they wanted, and the pioneers had very limited rights. The only reason they hadn't bothered them was because it took time for the Mexican authorities to realize how these pioneers thought. At first Texas just wanted to be separated and made an independent state of Mexico. They were presently combined with another state named Coahuila. As the Mexican authorities started showing the true way they were going to run Texas, the more unrest it caused with the pioneers. These people were self-reliant and used to being left alone while they tried to build their dreams. The Texans wanted limited government intervention and very little taxes.

Art and Weldon were again cleaning the stable and spreading the manure on the Logging's winter garden area. By November 20, the garden had been planted. A.D. had been selling three steers a month at the Perry Point docks to the ships that were unloading their cargoes or taking on supplies.

A.D. told Bob he also wanted to build hog pens next to the steer corral close to the wharf. It took them about four days to complete the hog pens and put the hogs in them. A.D. was now averaging two days a week working in the blacksmith shop.

The Logging boys had continued to keep a log about the number of ships, dates of arrival and departure, names and cargo. This gave the boys the opportunity to talk to the sailors arriving at Perry Point. They would tell them about the steers and hogs their dad had to sell.

One day in November a captain listened to Art and Weldon about the steers and hogs their dad had to sell and asked, "Would your dad have twelve steers to sell me?"

The boys answered, "He's working at his blacksmith shop in town. You want to see him?"

"Yes, would you show me where his blacksmith shop is?" he replied.

Art anxiously ran ahead telling his dad about the conversation. A.D. came out of the shop and met the captain. They shook hands and introduced themselves.

The captain said, "I need twelve steers in about two hours. I would like to catch the tide at four o'clock."

A.D. said, "It will cost you $120."

The captain countered, I'll give you $100."

A.D. agreed and asked, "How are we going to load them on your ship?"

"I'll show you," the captain offered. They walked down to the edge of the water of the bay. The Captain then walked out in the water for twenty five yards, followed by the others. He said, "You bring them here and I'll bring my ship ten yards out from here, put down the loading plank and you drive them right onto the ship."

A.D. couldn't believe that six of them could load cattle like that. He thought for sure something would go wrong. A.D. thought, "If I could sell cattle like this I wouldn't have to drive my cattle to Opelusus, Louisiana. That would be good for my family if we are able to load the twelve steers on the ship without any problem".

A.D. still worried that other ranchers around might want to put their cattle and hogs in his pens.

There was a big horse race and celebration coming to Perry Point and only nineteen horses had entered. Thanksgiving came to the mouth of the Trinity River, and many families got together at Perry Point for the big celebration. Entrance free for the horse race was twenty dollars.

The racetrack was a straight eight hundred yards. A.D. was running his gray with Art being the jockey. A.D. and Maggie had decided they would both bet fifty dollars on the race since Gray had won the July 4th race at Atascosita. The best odds they could get were two to one. There were two new horses entered that they had never seen run before. Art had practiced riding on the track six times and knew the exact location for Gray to make the best run.

There was also horseshoe pitching, foot races, dominoes and checkers and a rifle contest. There were about three hundred people at the Perry Point first Thanksgiving celebration. A lot of those folks were camping, and McCoy's general store almost sold out of everything. A.D. was also really busy shoeing horses and mules and repairing wagons. Doctor Lily told A.D. that he had made fifty-four dollars during the celebration. That was the most money the doctor had made since coming to the small community.

Bob wasn't available to help because his girlfriend came with her family planning to stay three days. They were staying at Bob's barn that he had recently built. Bob told Watha that he wanted his parents to move to Perry Point and get a farm next to his. Bob now had ten cows, four sows, one horse, two mules and a wagon.

A.D. and Maggie discussed this situation, and they were sure Bob and Watha wanted to get married but were smart enough to want to accumulate some money before this happened.

The day of the race came and the big winner was to be the winning horse in two out of three races. A.D. and Art discussed strategy for the horse race and A.D. said, "Let Gray win the first race, and if he does just walk him in the second race and then try to win the last race."

Art said, "I think we can win all the races."

"Let's do it this way, and it will be easier for Gray." A.D. explained, "You see, son, for a horse to run 800 yard three times with only a thirty minute wait in between each race is too hard on them."

At noon the first race started and Gray won by one length. Art walked Gray in the next race, and rumors flew through the menfolk about Gray getting hurt and that he wouldn't be able to run the last race. The gamblers raised the odds-on Gray up to five to one. Art's mom bet another $50 on Gray after A.D. had told her about the talk that Gray was injured.

At one o'clock the last race took place and Gray won by four lengths. Loggings had won three hundred fifty dollars on the bets and two hundred fifty dollars for winning the race. For the next day and a half, Art, as Gray's jockey, seemed to be pretty popular with all the local folks. Young Art relished in the praise.

At three o'clock the shooting contest started and everyone had to pay a dollar to enter. Each entrant shot a target a hundred yard away. They had one minute to shoot three times. A.D., Bob, Mr. Smith, Watha's dad and brother, Mr. Stroud and his two sons, Mr. McCoy and his son were all contending. The winner, a local man, received two hundred dollars.

The next day and a half there were domino and checker games, sack races, storytelling, and the most popular event, a greased pig scramble with the winners getting a pig. Art and Weldon tried the pig scramble but didn't win. A.D. figured about a hundred children took part in the pig scramble and ten of them won pigs!

For the two-day celebration, they had cooked three steers and twenty geese. The women in the area had prepared fifty pecans pies. At six o'clock the first day, they had finished eating. The dance started at seven o'clock and went on until ten o'clock.

Everyone was tired except the ten men who were drunk and causing problems all day and night. They ended up in a fight with each other during the dance. One woman, whose husband was drunk, asked A.D. and Mr. Stroud to carry her husband over to their wagon. The next morning, he hitched up his team and left. While he was hitching up his team, A.D. told Frank, "I hope he doesn't come over here and want to start a fight."

A.D. and Frank had each given a steer for the celebration, and their wives had prepared two pecan pies each. A.D. sure was not complaining because he had won six hundred dollars off Gray, and he figured his entry and donations were worth about forty dollars. It was a pretty good investment! The second day at noon they finished off all the meat that had been prepared. After eating lunch, most of them began their trip home. No one had complained and the people of Perry Point figured they had had a successful celebration.

A.D. had been busy horse shoeing and repairing wagons, earning about fifty dollars during the week of the celebration. That was certainly a lot more money than he usually made. McCoy's General Store was almost barren. He had sold $1,100 worth of goods. Everyone seemed to have had a good time, and for a few in the area it was profitable. Watha's folks went on home, but she was staying with A.D.'s family for a week. Then Bob would take her home.

A.D. said to Maggie "When Watha is around Bob does less work than he usually does." She said, "Let things run their course. Even doing the smaller amount of work he does better than most."

A.D. nodded agreement.

During the week Watha was very helpful with the Logging boys for the two hours of studying. They showed her things around Perry Point. Maggie sent her out to Smith's house for the remaining time as Mrs. Smith was having a rough time keeping herself together with all of her responsibility of her home and children. Maggie figured Mrs. Smith could probably rest and restore herself with Watha there. The last two days Watha was in Perry Point she spent helping Bob work on his cabin and barn. After that Bob took off three days to take her home and visit with her folks.

11

CHAPTER

Bob's parents, the Tims, had not made much progress and Bob had finally talked them into moving closer to him at Perry Point. Bob started out with eight mules and two wagons to move them next to his farm. In a week, he had moved them to his partially finished cabin and barn. They then decided where to build their own cabin and barn so that they could easily have a good supply of water.

The Logging family rode out in January, 1830 to check on the progress of the Tims' farm. A.D. thought they were making good progress on the cabin, barn and building some fences.

Bob told A.D., "During the move of my parents here we had some confrontation with some Indians but no one was shot. There were ten Indians and they wanted our wagons and mules, but my dad and I fired our guns four times trying to scare them off, and it worked. I have never had any problems with any Indians since I have been living in Texas."

Maggie told A.D., "I have an idea. Let's have a cabin raising. The quicker they have their own cabin the more time they will have to work on your fences and preparing a garden." Three days later in late January neighbors met at the Tims' cabin, and in twelve hours had not only finished the cabin, but had the barn almost finished, plus the corral. Mr. and Mrs. Tims were grateful to everyone.

They told their son, "We will be moving out of your barn tomorrow." Bob said, "I will be coming over to sleep and eat breakfast." Bob worked for three more days helping his dad finish the barn and the small corral.

The Logging boys had been watching other people hunt ducks and geese around the Point and they begged their dad to take them duck and goose hunting. Finally one evening in January, A.D. told the boys, "Get all of the guns ready because we're leaving here to go duck and goose hunting at five o'clock in the morning."

He told Art and Weldon, "Make a list of gear you need to take to go hunting."

The hunters went over the shooting rules while they devoured a breakfast of pancakes and sausage with Maggie.

She warned them, "Dress warm because the day will be cold and windy."

The next morning the threesome walked about a mile to a place their dad thought would be good for shooting ducks and geese.

He told the boys, "I have seen ducks and geese take off and land in this area of water." They set about building a blind out of the reeds and other natural bushes around the area. The blind was about five feet long, three feet wide and three-and-one-half feet tall.

A.D. warned the boys, "If you show your faces the ducks and geese will probably spot you, and they will not land close enough to be shot." By 6:30 a.m. the group was ready have ducks or geese come in close to their blind. Fifteen minutes later a flock of geese flew over, but they were too high and were not interested in landing close enough to the shooting blind.

Each hunter was outfitted with a double barrel shotgun. They would be lucky to get off two good shots at a flock coming close to the blind.

At about 7:15, another flock of ducks was circling their position to land. When they were within thirty yards A.D. and the boys raised up from the blind. Six shots were fired, and six ducks were killed.

A.D. said, "Quick boys run out and pick up the dead ducks." No sooner had they gathered the ducks and reloaded than another group of ten ducks was coming in to land. Again, when they got within thirty yards shots rang out. This time they only got four ducks.

When they gathered those ducks back to the blind and reloaded, A.D. reiterated, "We missed the lead ducks we were shooting at by about a foot."

There was a small marsh behind the duck blind that was within thirty feet of their blind. There were probably one hundred geese feeding in that marsh and the hunters just turned around in their blind and got out six shots, killing four more geese.

They stayed out for another two hours without another shot. The Logging hunters returned home with ten ducks and four geese. Their hunt had been successful. A.D. showed the boys how to dress out the birds and left them out behind the corral dressing all fourteen birds.

A.D. went to the blacksmith shop to repair a wagon a farmer needed that day.

When the boys finished dressing the birds they took them to their mother. She instructed them how to do to better job dressing each bird and then had them redo the chore. Maggie started to prepare two ducks for supper.

"Put the other birds in the smokehouse so they will last longer," she told the boys.

At supper the whole conversation was about the duck and goose hunt that day.

"When can we go again, Pa?" the boys asked.

A.D. promised the boys, "Next week we will go again." That satisfied them.

The boys admitted, "Hunting ducks and geese is harder than hunting squirrels and rabbits like we used to hunt back in Arkansas.

That afternoon the boys went down to see and record any ships that came to Perry Point. While they were around the dock corral, a ship's captain came up to the boys and asked, "Can I buy a steer and some chickens?"

Weldon told him, "Yes on buying the steer but we don't have any chickens. We have eight ducks and four geese." he said.

"Okay, I want one steer and eight ducks."

Weldon said, "That will be $14."

"That is okay if your dad will help me load the steer," the captain agreed. A.D. quickly killed the steer, gutted it, took the hide off, and then they loaded it on the boat. The ducks were already on board.

A.D. told the boys, "You two boys really did a good job today. I really appreciate your help." The boys felt good about their day. They were learning more about business every day.

During the next six weeks, A.D. and his boys went duck and goose hunting five more times. The least number of birds they came back with was ten. As it turned out they sold half the birds that they shot, and the boys now had a savings account of forty dollars plus the five hundred fifty dollars they earned from Gray winning the two horse races.

The previous Christmas the boys had received their 12-gauge double barrel shotguns, and they were beginning to get pretty good at hunting ducks and geese.

Maggie had some big news of her own. "I am pregnant, and will probably have the baby this summer," she told A.D.

"Wow! That is terrific!" A.D. whooped! "How about that, boys? A new baby in the family."

"We think that is great, Pa!" the boys responded, grinning and hugging their mother.

By now, about one new family a month moved into the Perry point area. Most of them had kids, and the boys played with the ones that were close to their age.

It was now 1830, and for the settlers who came to Perry Point in the winter of 1828, things had gone well.

However, into every life, some rain must fall. In early January, Bob came riding in fast and said, "Some kind of animal killed one of your cows and one of mine!"

A.D. and the boys saddled up and followed Bob out see the dead cows.

"I think it was wolves," A.D. said, after examining the dead animals. "Let's get Frank to look at it, but you go to the others close by to see if they've lost any stock the same way. If they haven't, warn them. If they have, come get us so we can see the dead animals."

During the next hours, the group discovered wolves had killed four cows, and they located the place where the wolf pack was drinking water on the Trinity River. By six o'clock, the group had increased to eight men who had herds they were worried about for the coming night.

A.D. told Bob, "Put your dad's few cows in with your herd so you can watch them altogether."

After a lot of other discussion, the group decided they would stay and camp on the river. They would stake out a few calves as bait and try to shoot the wolves when they came after the distressed calves. Frank, Art and one of his boys were going to be close to the calves all night trying to kill the wolves that came around. The first three nights the calves that were staked out did not get any attention from the wolves. The men had placed themselves about twenty-five yards from the decoy calves. The fourth morning Frank said, "I'm getting tired of this all-night stuff, and we haven't lost any more stock in this area. Let's go home, boys."

A.D. added, "That's okay with me, but we need to search along the Trinity every day for at least ten miles up the river from the Bay for at least four more days. I'll do it the first day, Bob the second day, and your sons can do it the third and fourth. If we find anything, we'll let the other folks know."

They all agreed this was a good plan. A.D. was very tired and went home, ate and went to bed. But before he went to bed, he told the boys, "We're going to track wolves tomorrow. I need help so you're going to learn how!"

"We want to learn to track, and we promise to get a long rest tonight!" they said.

After supper the boys went down to the shop and stalled three horses they were going to use the next day. Art and Weldon were really excited were discussing wolf tracking and asked their Mom questions for about an hour before they were sent to bed.

Maggie woke A.D. up and asked, "Are you sure you want to take those boys with you in the morning?" A.D. assured her they'd be okay. "Don't worry," he yawned. "I'm really tired, and I'm going back to sleep."

Maggie said, "I'll come to bed in about an hour."

A.D. asked, "Maggie could you go down to the shop and see what I need for supplies?"

"Sure," Maggie replied. She had done this job before for A.D. She knew she would go to the shop, figure out what he needed and then clean and reorganize everything. She finally got to bed about 11 o'clock that night and was up at 6:00 getting her family fed.

A.D. and the boys left at 7:00 that morning. A.D. led the way to the river and the boys were ten yards behind him. With one boy looking on the left, one looking on the right, and A.D. looking straight ahead, it took the trackers about two and a half hours to check for tracks on Trinity. They found no sign of wolves.

Then they rode over to the place where the wolves had killed a cow, and A.D. showed the boys the paw prints of the wolf. He also talked about ten minutes to Bob asking him to check along the Trinity the next day.

Then they all rode over to check on Bob's dad and see how much fence he had completed. Bob's mother wanted everyone to have lunch. She really was a good cook. After about an hour, they left. As they were leaving A.D. said, "Why don't y'all come have dinner with my family next Sunday?"

They replied, "We would be happy to."

A.D. and the boys returned home at 1:30 in the afternoon. Art and Weldon told Maggie about the Sunday invitation for the Tims family to have dinner with them. She informed A.D. and the boys, "I am not feeling well and would appreciate it if you do not obligate me for anything unless you check with me first."

A.D. examined her tired eyes and hugged her to him. "I'm sorry, honey. I'll tell them not to come."

Maggie said, "No, that's okay."

Two days later A.D. and the boys again were out hunting ducks and geese. They were up at 5:30 and ready to shoot at 6:30. The weather was clear with a beautiful sunrise. The first flocks of ducks and geese were flying very high from the mainland to the bay so there was no way they could hit them. A little later they did get three geese and four ducks. The group was still back home by 7:30. A.D. told the boys, "The birds were flying too high for us to continue to waste our time." Art and Weldon were getting better at the chore of dressing the ducks and geese. When they had finished, they hung them in the smokehouse.

Ed, Mary and Bob came over for Sunday dinner and everyone talked and played dominoes and checkers. Bob's parents said, "We are so happy Bob had come to East Texas and moved us down here. "We have a good cabin, a little money and prospects for making more money by really farming." Bob and his dad planned to plant thirty acres of corn and thirty acres of cotton, plus a big vegetable garden in March.

Maggie thought they were happy to be at Perry Point. The Loggings agreed with her when she said, "It's always nice to be around people that are happy with their lives and not complaining about everything".

It was calm around Perry Point in February. Everyone was hunting and getting ready for the planting season. No one had seen any sign of the wolves in over a month.

Everyone was hoping they had left the area. A.D. was going to plant seventy acres of corn in March and at the same time harvest their turnips and cabbage. Art, Weldon and Bob were busy mucking out as much of the horse manure as they could and spreading it on the acreage where they were going to plant the corn. Even though Art and Weldon complained about the smell, they collected twelve wagonloads of manure. The boys even got some wagonloads of manure from two other farmers.

A.D. knew when he put fertilizer on the plants they grew better. However, he only covered ten acres where the corn was going to be planted, plus the garden. Many farmers would not take the time to do this, and when the land was depleted, they just moved to another plot of land. This took the boys about fourteen days and every day when they finished A.D. had them to go to the shallow part of the bay, wash their hands, feet, shoes, socks and clothes. He instructed them to change clothes in the blacksmith shop.

When finished with the manure hauling job, they also washed the wagon at the Trinity Bay beach. Nobody was happier that job was finished than Art, Weldon and Bob.

The winter garden was just about gone and they began planting their spring and summer garden of squash, potatoes, cabbage, onions, beets, peas and pumpkins. They plowed up the old garden and would leave it until fall.

At the end of February, all the farmers were getting their equipment and mules ready for planting.

A.D. said, "We will plow the first week in March, harrow the next week and by the third week we should be finished planting."

Bob asked A.D., "When you're finished, may I use your plow, harrow and planter so my dad and I can plant thirty acres of corn and cotton?"

"Of course," A.D. replied.

After completing the planting of the 70 acres of corn, the remainder of March was spent blacksmithing. The first week of April all of the farmers worked their cattle. They were branding and castrating the calves and moving all the cattle to an open pasture where they would stay until the fall. The rest of April, A.D. spent harrowing the weeds out of his corn crop. Early May, they took a week and harvested their oat crop. They had 1,450 bushels of oats, and A.D. gave Bob 250 bushels.

Bob thanked A.D. and said, "We're going to have to plant more oats next year." A.D. agreed. By the end of April, Bob and his dad had finished planting their thirty acres of corn and thirty acres of cotton.

At the April Sunday dinner with the pioneer group, the men discussed how easy it would be for rustlers to take their cattle now that most of them were further away from the farms. They had a lot more cattle and horses now and everyone knew it. The only way they could protect their stock was to have someone on guard duty all the time. They decided that Frank and his boys would guard the first week, A.D. and Bob would guard the second week and they would ask the Smiths to be on guard duty the third week. The Smiths had not come to the dinner which concerned everyone.

The next day A.D. and the boys were out checking on a calf that was not nursing properly. A.D. was telling and teaching the boys all the things they could do to help the calf.

"The very best thing we can do is to take it back to its mother and try to get the calf to nurse," he said.

A.D. and the boys decided to go check on the Smith family. Immediately upon arrival, A.D. knew something was wrong because no one was outside. The stock looked like it had not been taken care of recently. A.D. knocked on the cabin door, and Cindy Smith came to the door. She looked terrible and said, "We are all sick don't come in."

"I'm sending for the doctor!" A.D. said, handing her a packet of food he always kept in his saddle bag. "I'm sure he'll be here in a couple of hours. Give me your water bucket and I'll fill it. Is there anything else I can do to help?"

Cindy said, "Yes, please check on the stock."

A.D. sent Weldon to get the doctor and Art to get his Mother to come with the wagon and food and also, two bushels of corn and one bushel of oats.

Dr. Lily had only been at Perry Point for about a year but he had talked to him a couple times and he seemed like a good man. Weldon finally arrived with Dr. Lily. After he checked out all the family, he determined the Smith family had scurvy. They needed fruit, cabbage or maybe even cider for them to get well. A.D. sent Art over to get a few heads of cabbage. After washing a cabbage, Doc gave two leaves to each family member for them to eat.

"Each of you need to eat two leaves of raw cabbage three times a day and eat three good meals each day," he instructed Cindy. "Tomorrow I'll call on you again."

Maggie had brought a lot of groceries and a ham. She proceeded to fix a big meal. All of the children had to be coaxed into eating the cabbage. Boy, that was a chore! Maggie had prepared a great ham and cabbage stew which would last for a couple of days. She stayed for a while, cleaning and helping with household chores.

Meanwhile A.D. and the boys rounded up their two mules and one horse. Their hogs were missing. A.D. had the boys feed each animal a half pound of feed.

"Before you go home with your Mother feed them one more time," A.D. told the boys. They showed the oldest Smith boy how much to feed each animal each day.

Their animals looked so poorly that Art even snuck some meat from the kitchen and fed the dog twice a day. He vowed to feed him the next day also and thought maybe the dog would get strong enough to catch a rabbit or a bird and therefore feed himself.

A.D. had returned home to work at his blacksmith shop.

At five o'clock when Maggie returned home, she told A.D., "I am going to take twenty pullets to the Smiths and also I will be at their cabin all day tomorrow and the next day."

A.D. had already moved the Smith's cattle in with his herd. He also talked to Ralph Smith about planting thirty acres of corn, ten acres of cotton and a garden.

"I don't have a plow, harrow or planter, Ralph said. A.D. volunteered, "I have all that and enough seed left after my planting so you wouldn't have to buy anything."

After a week everyone in the Smith household was feeling a lot better. Maggie told Cindy, "You should come into town every week and visit. There are several new shops you might enjoy." Maggie had also been teaching the Smith kids how to play checkers.

A.D. asked Bob, "Would you go over and work with Ralph for a week and bring back my equipment and leftover seed?"

Bob replied, "Sure thing." A.D. added as an afterthought, "Make sure he gets all thirty acres and a garden planted so they can support themselves. We don't want to have to support them. If they will start working, we won't have to."

Bob said, "You know I'll take my Mom over with me one day. She can visit and help her."

"That's a great idea," A.D. replied.

A.D. and Maggie went over to solve this mess at the Smith farm. They sat down and had a long talk with the Smiths stating, "You can't let things get out of hand like this anymore. The whole family could've died and all you had to do was let somebody know! The other thing is where are your hogs? How long has your family been without food? For at least a month? Plus, your animals haven't been fed and cared for. Why? You owe it to your children to have a chance to have this big farm, but it means you have to get off your ass and work every day, even if you don't feel like it!"

"You need to start schooling these children," Maggie told Cindy.

Cindy explained, "I barely know how to read, write or do numbers, and my husband doesn't know how any better."

"Maybe we could send Art and Weldon each week to school the children," replied Maggie. "I think the boys could teach the two older ones and then they could teach the younger ones, but we need to start next week."

The Smiths agreed with the Loggings and promised to do better. Maggie talked to Art and Weldon about teaching the young Smith children reading, writing and arithmetic. They were more than willing to help. Maggie said, "Now let's talk about what you're going to start teaching. Think about what we started teaching you four years ago." After a month of the Logging boys teaching, the Smith children were really learning and bragged on the boys to everyone.

12

A.D. had struck a deal with most of the fishing boat captains to leave spoiled fish they may have next to the small corral by the docks at Perry Point and he would pay for them later. Every week he was getting about one half of a wagon load of fish with a terrible smell. They would take it out to the planted corn bury a fish beside each corn plant.

"I am trying something another farmer told me would increase corn production," A.D. told everyone. "I want to see if it is true."

At the May settlers Sunday meeting A.D. told the bunch, "I want to talk to you all about an idea I have that you might like." He started by saying, "A fifty-pound sack of flour or cornmeal cost twelve dollars at any store around here. We are now the farmers that provide the wheat and corn that is ground into the flour or cornmeal. I think we can grind our own grain in small grinders. If we find a suitable large flat rock and a big round rock which could move around and across the grain, we could set it up so the mules can pull the heavy round rock around in circles crushing over a hundred pounds of grain at a time. Then we can sift it with a big screen and bag the flour or cornmeal in fifty-pound sacks".

"We could then sell it for ten dollars a sack which is cheaper than everyone is buying it for now. Now ten bags would be a hundred dollars, and that is more than we would get for ten acres of corn. How does that sound everyone?"

Everyone was enthusiastic about the idea. A.D continued, "Of course, whoever uses the rocks would have to wash them off really good after each day of use. When we look for a place we need to find one close to water."

As the group left they all were discussing the possibility of having their own grinding mill for their corn and wheat and the money they could make from this venture.

Two weeks later Frank Jr. stopped by A.D.'s blacksmith shop to tell him, "My brother and I have found two rocks close to the Trinity River that my family thinks would make a good grain mill. We would like for you to come look at it."

A.D. said, "Gimme twenty minutes and I'll be ready."

"Okay I've got to pick up some things at McCoy's store," Frank Jr. said.

"I'll see you there," said A.D, "Just don't discuss the mill with him."

The ride to the location was a quick twenty minutes. A.D. and Frank Jr. looked at both locations, and A.D. voted for the location closest to home because it was high and only twenty yards from the Trinity River.

They parted company and headed for home. The sky threatened rain, and Frank Jr. preferred not to get soaked.

The Loggings were anxiously awaiting the arrival of their new addition to the family. On May 30, Maggie told A.D., "Well I think the time has finally come. I believe you need to get Dr. Lily."

Fortunately, the doctor was in and followed A.D. back to his house. About three hours later a beautiful baby girl made her appearance, letting everyone know she had a great set of lungs. The boys were pleased they now had a sister and agreed she should be named Patricia. Mother and daughter were fine.

Dr. Lily said, "That's a fine healthy baby, and I will come by tomorrow to check on everyone." It was always a happy time for Dr. Lily when he was part of bringing a new life into the world.

In June, the pioneers finally built their grain mill. A.D. and Frank both immediately took one hundred pounds of corn and one hundred pounds of wheat to the mill. After crushing their grain thoroughly, they sifted the grain and each one had 80 pounds of cornmeal and 80 pounds of flour. They were well pleased with the quality.

"This flour and meal looks as good as anything we have ever bought," their wives told them. "We want to try it for cooking before we give our final decision."

Afterwards they had to clean the rock table and the roller rock.

Maggie told A.D., "You men have neglected our garden and the crops. You could knock out the weeds in a couple of weeks."

"We will do it in two weeks," A.D. answered, "because the July Liberty celebration is about two and a half weeks away".

He instructed Art to run Gray every day and cool his feet in the bay. Art began the next day to do just that. He had tried cooling Gray's feet in fresh and seawater and thought the salt water was better.

The men worked hard to get the weeds out of the crops, keep up with blacksmithing and train Gray.

The settlers always looked forward to going to Liberty's July Fourth celebration. Frank Jr. and Gene McCoy's daughter were going to stay home and watch all the farms and businesses. It was a two-day trip to Liberty. A.D. took his blacksmith and regular wagon, plus there were several other wagons in the convoy. They stopped for the night, and A.D. insisted, "We need to post a hidden guard." The guard was to be Pat Stroud. The rest of the group was busy preparing camp for the night. The mules and horses were hobbled, but Gray was not.

While eating supper Pat gave a warning that a group of men were coming in. Art stepped away and got Gray. Pat was back in hiding, and the women and children were in the wagons.

The settler men had their guns drawn when the toughs came into camp threatening, "We are taking the gray racehorse."

"This is my problem, so the rest of you get to safety," A.D. said in a low voice to the settlers. None of the other settlers moved.

"The Gray is not here, and we have two double barrel shotguns on you," A.D. warned. "I can guarantee four of you will be dead if you start anything. Is that what you want?"

The talker said, "You don't scare us. We'll kill the whole lot of you!"

"No mouth," A.D said, "I know the first one I'm going to kill, and that is you! The next one is the person closest to you."

The tough lifted one of his two guns, and A.D. shot him with one barrel. As he fell off his horse, A.D. shouted, "Who's next?"

Another man went for his gun, and A.D. shot him.

The rest of the toughs put their hands up and said, "We've had enough."

Frank, shotgun in hand, tied up the four uninjured men. The settlers gave them water before tying them up.

The women looked after the two gravely injured men. All they could do was try and stop the bleeding and try to make the men comfortable. They wrapped the wounds and tried to put pressure on them to stop some of the bleeding.

To say July was hot and the skeeters were terrible would be an understatement. Without a good mosquito net, the little bloodsuckers would eat you up. The tough guys faced an unpleasant night ahead and made it well-known.

"None of us will get much sleep because the toughs are so mouthy," Maggie told Frank, who gagged the men.

The next morning the two wounded were dead. They put the dead prisoners and the other men in the same wagon.

Loud objections ensued from the prisoners, but as it turned out, everyone got breakfast which quieted them for a while.

Frank rode right behind the prison wagon with a loaded double barrel shotgun. They moved as quickly as possible to Atascosita where McCoy and Stroud turned the men over to the authorities.

"We are taking their horses and tack and if we see these men again, we're just going to kill them." Stroud informed the sheriff.

"You'll have to take care of the two bodies," the sheriff said, but Frank refused.

"We are not!" he responded. "We would have already done that out on the trail but figured their relatives might want to bury them." He boldly dumped the bodies right in front of the Atascosita sheriff's office.

Gene and Frank rode away to find a farmer on the outside of Atascosita with space for them to set up base for the two days of the celebration.

Art immediately took Gray out to walk on the race track and find the best place to run. He also let Gray run for about two hundred yards then brought him back to the river to cool off for about thirty minutes. He then returned him to the barn into his large comfortable stall. Art fed him one-third pound of oats. Gray would run his first race in three hours. Art knew Gray was feeling good and they could win the race. Everyone was busy setting up camp so they could go to the race and enjoy the festivities that afternoon. Art would stay with Gray along with his brother outside the barn ready to run for help if Art said someone was trying to hurt Gray.

The group from Perry Point was going to bet $120 total on Gray. The best odds they could get was two to one since Gray had won last year.

A.D. was already shoeing two horses and fixing one wagon; it looked like he would be busier with his smithy work than last year. But at 11:30 he and everyone else would stop and go to the race.

A.D. went to talk to Art about the race. Art told his dad, "I feel good, and I think Gray is ready to run. I have located the best place for him to run on the track." Art got on Gray and A.D. walked them out to the track leaving him at the starting line soothing Gray to settle him down. A.D. walked away praying neither of them would get hurt.

He then joined his family and friends as they cheered Gray on to another victory. Gray would not have to race again until three o'clock. Art took him to the water and cooled his legs for about 20 minutes then back to his stall and gave him a fine curry. A.D. was staying in the barn so that no one could harm Gray or his jockey.

In the meantime, Watha and her parents arrived, and, of course, that made Bob very happy. Art and Weldon were busy playing with some boys they had met. It was 2:30 when A.D., Art and Gray were getting ready for the championship horse race. Everything looked good and Gray was feeling good.

Three other horses were in this race. Gray started with a good lead and barely beat them across the finish line after being hit by the second-place horse finisher about ten yards from the finish line. Gray had actually staggered and fell across the finish line. With this fall, Art was lucky he was not injured. A.D. thought Gray had broken his leg. He seemed to be able to walk but his left front leg was stiff and he had trouble putting pressure on it. A.D. and Art took him to the river cooled his legs for thirty minutes, and then he seemed to walk better back to the barn.

A.D. decided to splint the leg and build a sling to go under the horse to prevent him from laying down but support some body weight. The sling could barely hold him. A.D. had to reinforce it several times. He left Art and Pat in the barn with Gray, and told them, "Don't let anyone come near Gray or our wagons."

He and the others in the group went over to see the people in charge of the celebration and the mayor.

"What are you going to do about the man that ran into our horse on purpose and tried to hurt my son and Gray?" he demanded angrily.

"Are they okay?" the mayor asked.

"My son is, but not my horse," A.D. exclaimed. "Now, what are you going to do about it? This was no accident don't even try to say it was!"

"Well, the fellow responsible left right after the race was over," said the mayor.

"What's his name, and where does he live?" demanded A.D. "His name is Pete Harbour, and he lives twelve miles southeast of Atascosita," replied the mayor.

Maggie had already picked up the $440 championship money, but she couldn't collect their winnings on their bets.

"Where is that damn man that took the bets?" A.D. grumbled, frustrated with the way events of the day were turning.

When A.D. and the group got to the bet taker's wagon, the man was hurriedly preparing to leave.

"I don't have the money to cover your bets," he told A.D. and the group. "I'll have it soon and make sure you get your money."

"Then what did you do with the money?" asked A.D. "Guess we'll just have to kill you." He put a gun to the welcher's heart.

His wife screamed, "No! I have $200 you can have; just don't kill him."

A.D. took the money, and said, "You still owe us, and you better not come to Perry Point, or I'll do what I should've done to you today."

The group walked off and he gave the money to Maggie and said, "You divide everything among everyone who placed a bet with that scoundrel, and we'll share the loss together."

A.D. turned his thoughts to the problem was how to get Gray home. He immediately measured Gray and then measured his wagon. He went the general store and asked, "Where can I get some plank lumber twelve inches wide?"

"I've got planking eight feet long you can have for $20," A.D. accepted.

He thought it was strong enough to hold the sling to hold Gray up so he didn't have to put pressure on his foreleg. He also put a splint on Gray's leg so he wouldn't have to put any pressure on that leg. A.D. thought to himself, "If I can just get Gray home, I think we can heal him. His racing days might be over, but he is still a great stud".

A.D. was still completing blacksmithing work when the others in the group took off for home. Two days later, the Loggings left Atascosita with $40 earnings from his blacksmithing work.

To load Gray, A.D. pulled his wagon over to a small hill that was level with the wagon floor and guided Gray onto the wagon. He set the sling, and A.D. felt relieved when he was sure his improvisation would work.

Reflecting on this year's celebration, A.D. concluded that none of the group had won anything in the shooting or knife throwing contests. The only one that won anything was the Smith's oldest boy who won a pig in the greased pig contest. Everyone had made a small amount of money betting on Gray. A.D. was still upset about Gray being hurt.

The trip home was a slow two days. A.D. said to his family, "We have to go slow with Gray and watch for the bumps".

"Also," he said, "I am worried about robbers." He had one double barrel shotgun loaded for Maggie and one for the other wagon. Bob was driving the blacksmith wagon, and he had his own double barrel shotgun loaded as well as one of A.D.'s pistols. A.D., of course, had his double barrel shotgun and his double barrel pistol loaded.

Thankfully, the two-day trip to Perry Point was uneventful. Gray took the trip fine. A.D. unloaded him out beside the bay and soaked all the traveling animals' legs as well as Gray's. He then re-splinted Gray's leg and made him walk up to the barn with the others. A.D. took Gray to his own, very nice stall in the blacksmith and stable building.

A.D. sent Weldon over to get Dr. Lily and ask him to come to help treat Gray. About 11:00 a.m. he came by to look at the horse.

A.D. worried that the doctor would be insulted about being asked to help with the horse. To his surprise Dr. Lily carefully examined Gray's foreleg and said, "I'm not sure the leg is fractured, but I'm going to put a different splint on his leg. In two weeks, if it's dry, I want him put in your small pasture out back. Then we are going to take the splint off and begin daily salt water treatments of thirty minutes a day in the bay for another week, putting the splint back on after each treatment. After that, we'll test him to see if the leg was actually fractured."

A number of men who came by the shop told A.D. he should put the horse down, but he ignored their unsolicited advice, telling them he still wanted Gray for stud.

Dr. Lily came by after taking off the splint. A.D. and the boys took Gray to Trinity Bay. They repeated that scenario several times until it was time to take off the splint permanently. Dr. Lily arrived, thoroughly examining Gray, and they watched the horse stagger for the first few steps. He then began to put more pressure on his injured foreleg. He began to walk normally, Dr. Lily got a lead rope on him and told the boys, "Walk him around this pasture for thirty minutes daily, let him stay in the pasture for two more hours then put him back in his stall. Keep doing this for two weeks and we'll see if Art can ride him at a walk for one hour. If everything goes okay we'll put him back in the pasture with the mares. In about a month, we'll see if he can race."

"I'm so glad I did not follow the advice to put the horse down." A.D. said to his boys. "Sometimes you have to make decisions that are different from what other people think you should do."

In about two months everyone thought Gray was completely healed. Art had practiced racing him three times.

In the meantime, all the settlers in the Trinity Bay area were beginning to harvest their corn. A.D. and his boys could definitely see the plants with fish and horse manure had produced more corn. The total 20 acres that had been fertilized yielded 40 bushels per acre, and the unfertilized corn yielded only thirty bushels per acre. All the local farmers told A.D. they didn't believe it, but there were three men who came to A.D. to ask a lot of questions. A.D. thought a few of them were going to try the fertilizer on their crops. Another one of the local farmers told A.D., "I've got an outhouse and I could line you up some more and you could have all that fertilizer you want." The group laughed, but A.D. just ignored them. Fishermen in the area knew A.D. would take their spoiled fish to use as fertilizer.

13

CHAPTER

Perry Point was growing. There were eight stores including the Logging's blacksmith shop and McCoy's General Store. In October, a small detachment of 32 regular federal Mexican troops came to Perry Point to set up a permanent fort, help tax collectors collect taxes from foreign ships coming into Mexico, Texas and also to control U.S. settlers coming into Mexico.

The Mexican Government was alarmed at the number of Americans that were emigrating from the United States. Many of these emigrants didn't officially acquire land in Mexico, Texas. These squatters just came into Texas, built a cabin and started farming and ranching. The legal emigrants got land from appointed impresarios, like Stephen F. Austin. The Mexican Government had promised not to tax the legal emigrants for six years after coming to Texas.

But a new Mexican administration was elected in 1830. They wanted to stop white immigration from the U.S. coming to Texas, Mexico, and reduce the state powers. The new administration wanted all the power centralized in Mexico City. The government's new policy was to station a number of troops at different locations in Texas, Mexico, to run all the illegal immigrants out and to help collect taxes. Policies had changed about taxing the new settlers on goods that were imported into the state of Coahuila-Texas.

At Perry Point, the locals were upset to hear that eight of the soldiers were actually convicts who had volunteered to come on this expedition for Mexico to get out of prison.

Eventually, merchants were disappointed in the amount of business they got from the fort and the slow collection of the money owed by the Fort. Commander Juan Bradburn came to see A.D. with some smithy work. Bradburn was cordial to A.D. and was very appreciative of his taking care of the horses. A.D. told him, "It will just take a few minutes to finish correcting the horseshoes for you." When A.D. finished he told the Colonel, "No charge."

A large crowd of local people had gathered outside the shop to ask Colonel Bradburn some questions.

"Would you be willing to talk to the local folks and answer some questions for them?" A.D. asked the Colonel.

He answered, "Of course, I would."

The number one question that was asked was by one of the wives, "Is it true that you have eight convicts with your company?"

"Yes," he answered, standing up in front of the crowd, "but I can assure you at no time will they be allowed to come to town without being escorted by some of my regular troops, and I do not anticipate any problem from them. Originally, we intended to build a fort at Galveston but we changed our plans. Then we decided on a point south of town overlooking Trinity Bay, but we picked this place because it has plenty of wood and good water. There will be a tax collector sent here. We are to help him collect the import and export taxes now required by the new government of Mexico. At some time, he will begin issuing titles to those of you who have legally immigrated to this country. I am sure that there will be some problems, but certainly we can sit down and work them out together."

The Colonel then left and slowly rode up and down the main street of commerce and made a few notes and returned to the temporary fort. Merchants were happy at this time because they could see a lot of business coming their way. A.D. wasn't so sure!

Within a month, the Mexicans had built temporary barracks and started to build two kilns for cooking bricks for the permanent fort. Bradburn pushed his men relentlessly.

A.D. discussed this with the locals and said, "You don't get people to work by treating them that way. That will eventually cause problems."

From the beginning Bradburn started just taking what he wanted from the locals. One day he took Gray up to the fort for a while. Then he rode him out in the country for a couple of miles.

One of A.D.'s friends who passed them on his way to town asked, "Why did you let the Colonel take your racehorse?"

"I never gave him permission to take any of my horses," replied A.D. indignantly.

He walked down to the blacksmith shop, saddled up a horse and headed out in the direction Bradburn was seen riding Gray.

When A.D. approached him, the Colonel said, "I am just trying him out."

"Like hell you are!" A.D. said. "I'm not like the rest of these people. Don't ever try to do that again, Bradburn."

A.D. took Gray and the horse he was riding and rode back to his blacksmith stables. Blackburn just turned away and walked back to the fort. He didn't speak to A.D. for about ten days.

In November, A.D. and the boys planted thirty acres of oats and 25 acres of wheat. After that was finished A.D. told the group of mill owners, "I need to make ten ten-pound bags each of both corn meal and flour." No one had any objections to that. A.D. said, "I am going to build a place in my blacksmith shop to keep this cornmeal and flour dry. That way I can sell it in any quantity when people come into my place."

Gene McCoy had not liked the fact that the settlers had their own grinding mill and were competing with the general store in selling cornmeal and flour to anyone. They also had to grind more wheat and corn meal for personal use.

Bob said, "I am going to clean off the rocks at the mill, and then I need to work on my place the next two weeks, unless you need me for something, A.D."

"That will be fine," A.D. said. The Logging family had already planted their winter garden with the usual turnips, potatoes, peas and cabbage.

In an earlier conversation with Blackburn, A.D. had warned him, "You should make your men plant a big winter garden." He proceeded to do just that.

Blackburn had also asked A.D., "Will you make 25 iron castings for cooking bricks?"

A.D. replied, "That would take all of the iron I have, and I would have no more available. If you want me to do this I'll need $50 up front." The colonel replied, "If you don't trust me for $50 I guess we just won't do business with you."

A.D. said, "Okay." He walked away and began working.

Blackburn left for the fort, cussing under his breath.

A.D. went over to see Dr. Lily and Gene McCoy who were at the general store. He described in detail his recent talk with the colonel and reported that he had taken his stallion without permission.

"I think this is what we can expect from the colonel from now on," A.D. stated. "I won't be doing any business with the fort because he is going to try to take whatever he wants and do whatever he wants."

Gene and Dr. Lily said, "There will be plenty of others here who will do business with him on that basis."

"Gene, you'll probably lose more money than anyone else here, but if you decide to do business with him, so be it, I ain't!" A.D. was pretty upset and walked out mad.

Dr. Lily followed him out saying, "You can't blame Gene, he has been scraping by for several years and he now has a chance to make some real money."

"I hope he does, but I don't think the Mexican soldiers coming here and building a fort will make him rich," A.D. said. "Remember the soldiers came here to collect taxes and that means from all of us. You know I'm the only blacksmith and when he comes to me, he will have to pay if he wants me to do the work." As Dr. Lily left he said, "We'll just have to see what happens." A.D. then went home and told Maggie and Bob everything that had happened and asked, "What do you two think about that?"

The Mexican Army was busy trying to build temporary and permanent housing for an estimated three hundred troops that would be arriving later. It took the Army until March to finish the two kilns to begin their brick production.

Thanksgiving came and the big celebration for Perry Point had all of the local people as well as the Mexican soldiers were excited. Colonel Bradburn told Art he was going to enter his own horse in the horse race and show these people what a great horse he had. The celebration day came and there was about 350 people in attendance. The first contest was rifle shooting which included ten of the Mexican soldiers and three officers.

A.D. talked to Frank, Bob and Gene McCoy and told them, "We just have to beat them or we'll never hear the end of it." The first target was 125 yards. A.D. and Frank shot first putting six shots in the center along with three others who did the same thing. None of the winners were Mexican soldiers. You had two minutes to shoot and unload six shots. Each of the 250 contestants had paid $1.50 to enter. All five winners received a $70 prize each.

Art had already settled Gray and walked the 800 yards track to see where to guide Gray. Art had been training Gray almost daily, making sure his foreleg was prepared to run again. He thought the horse was almost as fast as he used to be. This, of course, was the first race for Gray since he hurt his foreleg. But the Logging family nursed him back healthy and thought he was in good form. Colonel Bradburn told Art, "Two of the fort's horses will beat Gray." Art replied, "They are talking about that down at McCoy's General Store."

There were thirty horses entered and there would be three races with ten horses in each one. The winner of each of the three races would race for the championship. Gray won the first race, and the Mexican horses were beaten right off. The winner of each race received $100. A.D. had paid the $20 entry fee for Gray and bet $50 on Gray in the first race. Gene McCoy paid A.D. $100 for winning the race and $100 for the bet.

Art was really happy for Gray to be able to race again and win the race! A.D. told Art, "Good job! You beat those two Army horses! Maybe that will shut them up now."

Art replied, "Now they will try to steal him again." At 2:00 o'clock the last race for the championship was going to be run. Gray won second making it the first time he had lost a race.

Just about everyone migrated over to the pistol shooting contest. It was another time-consuming contest. Each participant had two minutes to shoot as many shots at the fifty-yard target as he could. A.D. and Frank, along with two others, put four shots in the bulls-eye. The four of them split $360. None of the Mexican soldiers won.

Art asked his dad in front of several friends, "Are you glad the Army men did not win anything, Pa?"

A.D. replied, "Yes, you know that I am, son."

"A.D., be quiet or you will get more of your neighbors mad at you!" Maggie admonished him quietly.

A.D. said, "I don't care I'm tired of the Mexican soldiers strutting around all high and mighty! They rub me the wrong way!"

The Loggings, Stroud's, Smiths, and Tims contributed a steer, hogs, cabbage, beets and pecan pies to the meal at the town's celebration. That evening the town's folk enjoyed another dance.

The next morning, they had the greased pig contest for the kids and tournaments in dominoes and checkers. Watha and her parents came down to the celebration and, of course, met Bob and his parents. Watha's family, the Adams's, spent four days in Perry Point.

A.D. was extremely busy with his blacksmithing, and Bob only helped one day, but Art and Weldon had become pretty good help at the shop. A.D. made $69 which was a week's record of earnings since he had been a blacksmith.

Most families went out to cut Christmas trees just before December. Maggie and the boys spent two or three days decorating their tree before Christmas.

A.D.'s horse herd had expanded quite a bit since he had arrived at Perry Point as he was always trading horses. He now had fifteen mares, five fillies, six geldings and Gray, his only stud at this time. He spent a lot of time breaking and training the fillies and geldings. A.D. knew it was time to get a new stud for his fillies so he would not be inbreeding. He would, as usual, take his time trying to get a good deal.

A.D. and Maggie presented two quality mares to Art and Weldon for Christmas. The boys knew that they would have to take care of them on their own. A.D. and Maggie also got Patricia a rocking horse and a rag doll.

The boys were excited that they could start their own herd and hoped to have their own horse stock of five or six horses each by the time they were 16. It was a nice Christmas for the pioneers around Perry Point.

14

CHAPTER

Father Muldoon arrived in Anahuac, formerly called Perry Point, in January 1831. Colonel Bradburn had surveyed Perry Point and renamed the town Anahuac. This was part of the new centralized Mexican government trying to make Texas more Mexican, alarmed that Texas was beginning to look like another state of the United States and not Mexico. Even though the Mexican's tried to stop any immigrants coming from the United States, most other countries were still allowed to have immigrants in Texas. The Mexican government had revoked the no tax on goods exported or imported that had been previously given to immigrants. The Mexican government also sent troops and tax collectors to six different locations in Texas to check all shipping going in or out of Texas. In a show of the Texan's displeasure, the Mexican tax collector sent to Nacogdoches to begin issuing land titles to those who could prove they qualified was promptly arrested on trumped up political charges and sent back to Mexico City where the charges were dropped within a few months.

In March, the Mexican Army at Anahuac finally finished the brick kiln to make bricks for their new fort. There were several new businesses also in Anahuac because shopkeepers figured they could sell to the Army and soldiers for a good profit. That didn't work out well because Mexican payroll and money needed for the fort was slow in coming. Bradburn and the soldiers did most business on credit.

In the meantime, the Mexican state of Coahuila-Texas had sent a tax collector to Atascosita and had begun issuing land grants to people that had come to the area before 1828. The tax collector's name was Madera. He insulted Col. Bradburn right away by failing to report to Bradburn letting him know he was in the area. Bradburn felt he should have first come to him and shown him his papers so he could set the rules on how Madera was to go about doing his business. However, this was not in Madero's mind.

A.D. was concerned about the conflict between the two Mexican representatives. He had seen Madera and talked to him. He seemed to think there was no problem since all the land grants had been surveyed. Madera told A.D., "I'll come to see you all at your blacksmith shop next week and look at your homestead and Catholic Church papers and your recommendations from the mayor or whoever's in charge."

A.D. said, "We don't have a mayor and won't have an election until next March. What can I do?"

"Do you have someone that has been there a long time?" He asked.

"Yes, and I know some ranchers that have been here for nine years. Any of them would speak for me." A.D. answered. "Then I'll see you next week."

Before Madera could come to Anahuac he was arrested and put in jail by Bradburn. A.D. went to the Fort and asked permission to see Madera. Colonel Bradburn asked A.D., "Why do you want to see him?"

"He is going to try to help me and several others get titles to our land," A.D. replied.

Bradburn replied, "If you got the title from him it wouldn't be any good because he can't issue legitimate titles."

"Okay, but can I see him?" A.D. asked.

"Yes, it's okay, I guess, but I'd don't see why. We'll have to search you to make sure you don't have a weapon you could give him." Bradburn replied.

A.D. submitted to the search, but inwardly he was angered because there was no reason for this arrogant bastard to threaten him like that.

When Madera saw A.D, he was astonished and explained to him, "Colonel Bradburn and I are from different political parties. My party believes in state control over the country and his party believes in central or federal control of the country from Mexico City. We have had previous encounters, and I know it will be hard to believe but we were both Masons. I need to get a couple of letters to my boss and family."

"I thought as much and brought paper and a pen, A.D. said. "I'll make sure they are sent out this afternoon. They will probably take ten days or so for delivery." A.D. returned with hot biscuits and bacon twice for Madera. He was very appreciative of that. A.D. did it to anger Colonel Bradburn.

In a week, Madera was released and came to see A.D. and his family. He looked over the land-grant property and the Catholic Church verification. He then issued the title for the family's league of land and also his ten acres for the blacksmith shop.

A.D. told Art, "Hook up the buggy and show Mr. Madera where the other land claims are. Tie your horse on the back and come home after you show him where the Stroud's live." He asked Madera, "Will you be agreeable to see the Tims and Smiths also?"

Madera said, "Yes, I will and I appreciate all your help. I'll bring your horse and buggy back before I leave this area which will be in about a week."

A.D. asked, "Are you still going to issue titles?" "Yes," He said, "I'm going to the Atascosita area and change the name to Liberty. I will set up an election for Mayor, Prosecutor, Judge and Sheriff for that area. Liberty would be the county seat for the area, which would also include the town of Anahuac."

The Logging family was surprised that Madera had told them so much information. He said, "I will be staying at the Ted Orr farm but don't tell anyone, especially Colonel Bradburn. I hope I can spend about four weeks there without getting arrested again. I really appreciate all your help and support in the Anahuac area."

They had been harvesting their spring gardens and Bradburn attempted to buy the produce from several of the farmers on credit.

"The Colonel would not dare ask me because he knows I wouldn't sell anything on credit," A.D. told Maggie. "In fact, I think some of the soldiers have stolen some produce."

Many of the people were trying to entertain Bradburn and his officers. A.D. on the other hand had tried to make friends with the Sergeants of the Mexican soldiers. In fact, Bradburn had told Master Sergeant Gonzales to handle any business between A.D. and the Fort.

In March, A.D. and his group planted 70 acres of corn. Other farmers were also preparing for planting. It took them fifteen days of hard work before the job was completed.

A.D. bought a load of fish and he told Art and Weldon, "You have to bury a fish with ten thousand corn plants. That is all the fish I can afford or find." Bob and his dad also added fish to ten thousand more plants in the next two weeks. They had still only used fish on twenty percent of the crop. The boys had Duke out protecting the young corn plants from wild critters.

Meanwhile Madera had secretly returned A.D.'s horse and buggy.

Madera advised A.D. and his friends, "Go register your titles on your allotted land at the courthouse in Liberty." They all did so immediately.

In May, at one of the Sunday dinners at the Loggings' house, the owners of the grinder mill had a meeting. Mr. Stroud said, "We need to grow more wheat because we can sell more. This would give us quick money."

"We also need to have someone selling in Liberty and maybe other villages," A.D. said. "Well, out of a total of 60 acres," he continued, "I have about fifteen bushels left over from last year. We can make a few barrels of flour and cornmeal". They planned to send someone to peddle the flour and meal in Liberty, Harrisburg and other small towns for $5 for a ten-pound bag."

Frank Jr. and Pat Stroud volunteered for that job. They were thinking how they could go see other parts of the country without their parents hanging around. They would be on their own! On May 30, Frank, Jr. and Pat left with eight barrels of flour and cornmeal, to go to Liberty and Harrisburg.

Frank Jr. told Pat, "We can stop each night and sleep in a farmer's barn. Maybe they will even give us supper".

They stopped at nine farms on the way up to Liberty and sold about a barrel, total, to all those farms. Then when they got to the general store in Liberty and they got them to take one barrel of flour and one of cornmeal. When asked, they sold two pounds for a dollar, increasing their profit margin. After a week the Stroud boys returned.

"All of the flour and cornmeal was sold," they stated proudly. "We brought home $280 and got six barrel deposits which is $30."

In May, A.D.'s family and Bob had harvested their fifty acres of wheat. A.D. got 1,200 bushels and Bob got 600 bushels. They had tried a new way of harvesting the wheat which they all thought had helped the yield quite a bit. Everybody took the wheat they wished to have ground to the grinding mill. A.D. wanted six barrels, Frank wanted five barrels and Bob wanted two barrels. Smith, who had not raised any wheat, bought one barrel from Bob for $8.

A.D. told Bob, "You need to stick with the agreed prices we set or you can't use the grinding mill."

"It is my wheat and I will do what I want to do with it." Bob retorted.

A.D. told Frank who told Bob, "You cannot use the grinding mill anymore since you will not stick with the prices we agree upon." This, of course, made young Bob mad at both A.D. and Frank. Bob loaded all his flour and the wheat that he had and left for home. After giving his parents one barrel and taking a small amount for himself to use at home, he put the rest in his barn. A.D. put one barrel at home and the other five down at the blacksmith shop. He was now selling an average of thirty pounds each week. All the pioneers in the area had planted their gardens back in March for the summer crop. These were usually two-acre plots. Weather had cooperated, so the gardens would produce quite a bit for late summer and fall. That meant the women would have their hands full trying to preserve enough vegetables to last through the winter.

Bradburn announced a cornerstone laying program, inviting all the residents in the area. For this celebration he roasted one steer and one hog to serve his guests. It was a nice dedication and everyone enjoyed themselves. Maggie had told A.D., "The family is all going because I am not cooking supper that day!" A.D. had thought about not going but then he discarded the thought of objecting and went to the dedication. Actually A.D. and his family had a good time. He told Maggie, "I enjoyed talking to a lot of farmers and ranchers that I only see once or twice a year."

During this time A.D. had worked in his blacksmith shop repairing two wagons and shoeing nine horses. The boys were extremely helpful because A.D. had not seen Bob since the problem over the cost of flour back in June. They began harvesting their garden for their own use. In July the garden produce was usually used for canning because the sweltering August sun burned up the plants.

Art spent a lot of time with Gray, trying to get him ready for the horse race July fourth in Liberty. A.D. explained to him, "Gray is almost seven years old. He just might not be as fast as he used to be."

Art said, "I think he can still win. Please let me ride him and try."

A.D. agreed. "You know I'm looking for a new stud for the farm though. Gray will probably be going to some other farm."

Art replied, "All I know is he's one of our family." To that A.D. mentioned an idea he'd been considering. "I've been thinking about maybe keeping him at the blacksmith shop's pasture and charging people a stud fee of $6 when they bring their mares in for breeding.

Art said, "I'll do anything to help out so our old friend Gray can stay around"

A.D. said, "Then we will have to partition off part of the pasture behind the shop."

"Okay, Weldon will help me," Art exclaimed. The boys did a fine job fencing off the part of the pasture and still getting Gray ready for the race.

The Smith family had told the group at the regular Sunday get together in June they were not going to the Liberty celebration July second through the fifth. The group was worried about all their crops, livestock, and homes while they were gone, especially A.D. He said, "I'm going to pay Sergeant Gonzales $10 to check my home, shop and ranch. He says he can get two other trustworthy soldiers that would also be available to check the other farms for the same amount of money." Frank said, "A.D., you don't trust the Colonel and most of the soldiers!"

"That's what is so good about this! A.D. said. "I wouldn't put it past Bradburn to steal our stock, burn our homes or even kill us. He is probably afraid we would retaliate. Many of the soldiers and the prisoners take delight in confronting our women unless we are with them. They are using six convicts and three slaves from the merchant Morgan. I intend to make as many of the soldiers as I can our friends, and you all should be doing the same thing!"

After that speech all the settlers agreed to have Sergeant Gonzales hire the other two men to watch over their livestock and homes. "Mr. Smith, you and your family might just as well go to Liberty with us and have a good time," Frank recommended.

Frank Jr. and Pat were going to drive a wagonload of flour and cornmeal to the celebration to sell. That sounded like a good idea to everyone. A.D., Frank, Mr. Smith, Bob and his parents talked to Sergeant Gonzales.

He said, "I have two more men already selected. They thought they could do the job for $30."

The settlers decided they would leave at 4:00 in the morning of the July second. If they left that early they could travel until they got to Liberty without having to camp out. It was 9:00 p.m. when they arrived in Liberty. They went out to their friend's barn where they had stayed every time since first going to the celebration.

Sergeant Gonzales used two Army friends to help him guard all the property. They also wanted to try and find some land they could homestead on their own. Sergeant Gonzales was at the blacksmith shop when he saw three men he had never seen before. During the night, they broke into A.D.'s house and trashed the place looking for money. Then they came to the blacksmith shop and busted down the door before the Sergeant stopped them.

The next two days he made these men repair everything that had been damaged in the house and in the blacksmith shop. When Sergeant Gonzales let them go, they met up with three more tramps and rode to A.D.'s farm. Gonzales and his two soldier friends followed them. The six rustlers now had all 90 head of A.D.'s herd. There was a big shootout in which Gonzales and his buddies killed three of the men and wounded two more men. Only one man was not wounded. They buried the three dead men. One of the soldiers was shot in the leg but it did not hit the bone so they thought he would heal. Gonzales took his buddy, the soldier that was wounded and the two wounded rustlers to Dr. Lily. Gonzales told the man that was not wounded, "I will kill you if I ever see you in Anahuac again." The two wounded rustlers stayed at Dr. Lily's for over a week recovering from their wounds.

Gonzales took his wounded friend out to A.D.'s cabin so they could also watch over the surrounding area to stop anyone from stealing anything. About the third day while patrolling the farms, Gonzales' friend rode in and told him there were two men stealing a lot of horses and they were driving them up the Atascosita trail. Sergeant Gonzales and his friend got in front of the rustlers and ambushed them. In the gunfight that ensued, the two rustlers were killed. The Mexicans took the rustlers' horses, money and guns. Then they buried them.

Gonzales didn't know what to do with the wounded men. Eventually he took them out to A.D.'s cabin and made sure they were tied up and fed and watered twice a day. He was saving them for the settlers to punish.

The night before the settlers returned, the two rustlers got loose. They rode away on their own horses and were never heard of or seen again.

When the settlers returned from the celebration they realized how dangerous it had become with the additional people coming into the Anahuac and Liberty areas because of the fort, shipping, fishing and agriculture in the area.

The settlers had had a real good time at the annual Liberty celebration. Frank Jr. and his brother Pat J. had sold all the flour and cornmeal they had taken to the celebration for $205. Art and the whole Logging family were happy because Gray won his two races and was the champion racehorse again! Gray won them $300 for his winning and $300 for their bets. Mr. Stroud and his boys, Mr. Smith, Bob, A.D and his boys all entered the shooting contest. All put four shots in the target at one hundred yards except Art and Weldon. They each put four shots close to the target. All the other friends of the Loggings were in the final shooting which Smith actually won. The six hundred people in attendance all knew with that kind of shooting no one should dare come around Anahuac. The group also had a great time with checkers, dominos, horseshoes and sack races. The greased pig capture was truly enjoyed, plus ten children took new pigs home. The Smith's son was one of those. Maggie had a sign made for Gray's stud service.

Three people told the Loggings they were bringing their mares to Anahuac to leave them for six weeks for breeding purposes. When the settlers were leaving a rancher north of Liberty brought two good mares for the Loggings to take home and have Gray breed them. He also paid A.D. $20 and said. I'll come get them in 45 days." Art told the rancher, "We'll take real good care of them don't worry."

After an uneventful trip to Anahuac the group was confronted with all that had happened while they were gone and what people were trying to do to their property. A.D. and the other ranchers paid the soldiers $30 with many thanks. They also paid the wounded man's bill to Dr. Lily.

These pioneers were realizing they had to be always on alert. Sergeant Gonzales who regularly went on patrol once a week told A.D. "Every time you find a group of men that are hungry and despondent, they will do whatever is necessary to survive."

After three weeks, another rancher brought three good mares to breed with Gray. A.D. told him, "Better let the mares stay for eight weeks." Mr. Logging was afraid Gray was getting overworked. The rancher also bought a barrel of flour and cornmeal and paid A.D. $68, thanking him when he left. Art and Weldon were well pleased with being able to keep their pet, the gray stud while they could still ride him every day.

September came and all the local farmers were busy harvesting a decent corn crop. A.D., Bob, Frank and his boys had harvested a lot of hay in May and June so they had plenty of fodder for winter. The first of October the grinder mill owners ground fifteen barrels each of flour and cornmeal. This took about two weeks. Frank Jr. and Pat set off with six barrels each of corn meal and flour on another selling trip. The boys thought this was a great opportunity for them to see and meet other people, especially girls. They could also make money and get to know some other neighbors. The boys tried to get to stay in some barns. Several of the farmers let them stay in their homes and have supper with them. Frank Jr. told Pat, "I enjoy all the calm occasions, I don't want to play dominoes, checkers or cards because it takes time away from when we could be visiting."

Pat told his group of friends and family about their trip when they returned with $195. All the pioneers were informed of the boy's success. Art and Weldon hoped they could travel like Frank Jr. and Pat in a few years. They like listening to them tell about their trips. A.D. and the boys planted fifty acres of oats in late October and they would plant fifty acres of wheat in November.

15

CHAPTER

The big news was Mexican General Mier Teran, committee member for the colonization of the territory, came to inspect Fort Anahuac. He was the commander over Texas, Mexico and brought a new tax collector, named Fisher, with him. The new tax collector tried to collect taxes for imported and exported goods. Fort Anahuac now had over 200 soldiers.

A ship that arrived at the same time as General Teran had goods for a local man named Reid. Fisher, trying to impress his supervisor, the General, demanded that Reid pay taxes on the goods.

"I don't know anything about any taxes," Reid objected. "I will not pay you, Mr. Fisher; Mexico can just impound the goods."

General Teran tried to intervene by telling Reid the truth, "Your taxes are only twenty percent of what Fisher told you".

Reid was determined not to pay anything for taxes. Fisher confiscated all of both merchants', Reid and Morgan, imports, storing them in a local warehouse.

Fisher had set the tone for himself as a tax collector for this area! When Reid threatened Fisher, Colonel Bradburn got involved. He had Reid arrested and put in jail at the fort. Morgan tried to see him, but Bradburn refused. Reid and Morgan were defiant. They were not going to pay the $600 Fisher wanted for taxes. Morgan appealed to General Teran who gave Morgan a note for the release of his merchandise. He promptly went up to Harrisburg and sold the merchandise to a general store there. The owner came to Anahuac with four wagons and a $300 offer for the taxes. Bradburn was ready to let this situation expire. Fisher was furious when he found out.

"You've got to be flexible sometimes and negotiate these things," Bradburn said. Fisher was so despised he was always fearful that the locals were going to kill or hurt him. As soon as they built the temporary tax collector's house in Galveston, he set up his headquarters there, ignoring the protection of Fort Anahuac. At the same time, he requested a transfer to Matamoros.

At first Fisher incurred the wrath of the boat captains by unreasonably insisting they come to Anahuac, even those going up the Brazos. Anahuac was only convenient for boats going up the Trinity and San Jacinto. It was out of the way for any boats going up the Brazos.

Meanwhile, Teran had stayed in the Liberty, Anahuac area for six weeks, interacting with settlers and observing. His discussion with A.D. was precipitated by previous discussions with others who suggested Teran talk to Mr. Logging.

The General rode to A.D.'s blacksmith shop to ask him, "Can you look at my horse? I think he has lost a shoe.

"This horse has lost two shoes, and the other two shoes are loose," A.D. informed him upon inspecting the horse. "It will take me about an hour and a half to shoe this horse. Can you wait? Your stableman should not have sent you out with this horse."

Teran replied, "Yes, please fix the horses' shoes and make sure they are put on correctly." A.D. offered to go to the fort to bring a replacement for this horse, but Teran insisted he could wait.

"I'd like to hear your thoughts about the fort and the soldiers," Teran suggested. "Will you talk to me?"

A.D. replied, "Yes, and I will tell you the truth! If you don't like that you can go somewhere else."

A.D. said, "Well, here goes. I guess you really want to hear about the first three days Bradburn was here. Without asking my permission, he took my prize racehorse, named Gray, and rode him about a mile when someone came to my home and asked why the Colonel was riding Gray. I saddled one of my other horses and rode out to confront him. He told me he would take whatever he wanted and there was nothing I could do about it. I pulled my pistol and told him to get his butt off my horse or I would kill him. He got off my horse and I rode away with Gray and the horse I was riding. I also told him not to come to my home or my business ever. If anything happens to any of my family or possessions, I'd come after him. I left him two miles from the fort. Now I only do business with Sergeant Gonzales from the Fort."

A.D. continued, "Second thing is he allows his soldiers to harass our women. This has happened many times and he ignores it. He also expects people to give him everything. He buys or takes material from others in Anahuac and never pays them. He does not have the support of one half the people because he does not know how to treat people".

"Is that what you want to know, General?" A.D. asked.

Teran said, "No, I told him to stay out of local politics and help the people! I will discuss this with him and see if he can change."

A.D. said, "Thanks for listening. Your horse will be finished in about 20 minutes."

Bradburn had carefully kept General Teran away from the half of the population, mainly the people who didn't like him or how he was doing his job.

After talking to A.D., Teran next went to talk to Bradburn. He asked him, "Why aren't the fort's horses blacksmith by Logging?"

"Because he doesn't like us." Bradburn said.

Teran said, "You mean he doesn't like you stealing his stud horse, and the soldiers harassing the civilian women! I had to have Logging re-shoe my horse when I rode out today. Since I've been here the only people I meet are the ones that are your friends. You were told to foster good relationships with all the civilians here. From now on use A.D. Logging to take care of all your horses. Your Calvary would not be able to ride out if you sent them on a horse that was shoed like the one I rode today. I know you send out patrols daily. What I don't know is how you're going to change and show these people you're here to help?"

General Teran left after six weeks. He instructed Colonel Bradburn, "Shut down the County seat in Liberty and move it to Anahuac but stay out of local affairs. Don't make these local people worry about titles to their land. Make sure these soldiers don't harass their women. Inspect all the titles that are issued by Madera. Order lawyers who practice in these courts to show you their Mexican license. Only one attorney in Texas ever secured a Mexican attorney's license, and that is Thomas Jefferson Chambers. Local Anglo lawyers, such as David Burnett, William Travis, Patrick Jack and Robert Williamson, all rode circuit from the Brazos to the Trinity, or practiced in American-style English common law. That is not the same as Mexican law. Do what I told you to do in the first place." Bradburn promised he would obey.

Early the next morning, he watched as a schooner carrying Teran sailed out into Trinity Bay, getting stuck on a reef. A merchant on another ship pulled over to help the schooner off the reef.

When the tax collector, Fisher, saw the schooner had imported goods that were taxable he told the local merchant, "Your tax will be twenty percent."

The merchant said, "I haven't heard anything about a new tax."

Teran, suspecting there was trouble on shore, had his boat return to the Anahuac dock. Upon hearing the issue, Teran offered, "How about a compromise of $150 total for the load?"

The merchant replied, "That seems fair me."

Fisher said, "Well, that is not okay with me."

Teran quickly made Fisher change his mind and accept the $150 from the merchant.

The merchant also demanded a signed letter signed by you two men stating he had paid his tax.

Fisher was furious with Teran and threatened, "I am contacting my superiors in Mexico City." The General told him, "Please go ahead and do it but I'll see you lose your job." Fisher immediately left Anahuac, never to return.

Bradburn had also come down to see if he could help. Teran told Bradburn, "Get two wagons and take this merchant's merchandise up to his store in Anahuac." Bradburn knew Teran was trying to embarrass him and put him in his place. All of this had made Bradburn furious with the local resistance. They were not the Tories who liked Mexico and Bradburn.

A small crowd from Anahuac had gathered to observe what was happening at the wharf. Most of them got a kick out of it. However, the settlers at Liberty were upset with the order from Teran to move the courthouse to Anahuac. They thought Bradburn was being capricious only to annoy them.

When two soldiers who were from Mestizo Indian background assaulted a woman in early 1832, irate citizens demanded that they be turned over to them for tarring and feathering. Bradburn refused; the angry men organized a vigilance committee. They elected a lawyer, Patrick Jack, captain of a regular militia whose purpose was to guard against attacks by the Indians, as their leader. The only Indians in the vicinity were the peaceful Coushatta who lived north of Liberty. They also traded with the settlements. Under Mexican law, only Bradburn or the mayor could call up a militia. Bradburn immediately arrested Jack, imprisoning him on board an armed schooner in the harbor, out of fear the man's friends would attempt to rescue him.

Another lawyer, Robert Williamson, visited Bradburn three times trying to secure Jack's release. On the final visit Williamson shouted he would kill Bradburn. Either to save face or prevent an incident, Bradburn announced that Jack's release was set for three o'clock that afternoon. Jack's associates hurried down the bluff to the landing and formed two lines to greet their captain. They cheered Jack when he was released. Bradburn believed the incident was meant to embarrass him and retaliated by dismissing Jack from his position as surveyor for Mexico.

Another unpopular instance developed when members of the U.S. Schooner, *Topaz*, crew did mutiny on Galveston Island in February of 1832. Their plan was to seize a Mexican payroll of $3,000. Lieutenant Colonel Ugartechea and one hundred Mexican soldiers were escorting the payroll to Fort Anahuac. Rough seas forced the soldiers below deck and the sailors quickly sealed all the hatches trapping the personnel below deck. The United States sailors tossed the Captain and the steersman overboard. The troops below deck realized what was happening and broke out of the hole and quickly overpowered the crew except for one man who climbed into the rigging and was shot. When the vessel, Topaz, reached Anahuac, Bradburn arrested nine American sailors and put them in prison at the Fort. The sailors began telling a different story to their countrymen who visited them in prison. In a letter that appeared in a New Orleans newspaper, an American citizen claimed that Bradburn's charges were false. The writer contended Bradburn wanted to confiscate the ship and money for his own use. The writer also contended the U.S. seamen would not receive a fair trial and that Bradburn was holding runaway slaves from Louisiana and using them to work at the fort. An Eastern newspaper also published another letter which confirmed that the sailors did mutiny and deserved their fate.

In late February, most of these local farmers and ranchers were branding, castrating and checking on all their livestock. The middle of

March they would move their stock out to the larger pastures for the spring, summer and fall. In addition, the pioneers were putting in their big gardens and plowing, harrowing and finally planting their corn crops. A.D. and the boys had been very busy at the blacksmith shop in addition to planting fifty acres of corn.

Bradburn, by now, was pretty well known but detested. His troubles were about to increase! William Travis had been retained by a Louisiana slave owner to recover runaway slaves to whom the colonel offered sanctuary. Mexico did not approve of slavery and the only place it was legal was in Stephen F. Austin's colony. This was done under an indentured servant agreement. The master and the illiterate slave signed a paper before a notary which stated the black would work for a number of years, usually some ridiculous number, in exchange for his passage to Texas and the cost of his keep until the end of the contract. This agreement did not exist outside of Austin's colony. Mexico, through Bradburn, offered freedom to fugitive slaves, a fact that disturbed slaveholders who feared their servants might learn of the Mexican law and try to go to Texas. Bradburn had of course refused to release the slaves to Travis and the owners. Travis appealed to Teran, but he also would not turn over the slaves. The General advised Travis that the only recourse he had was through diplomatic channels between Washington D.C. and Mexico City.

Travis and Warren Hall, a former associate of Bradburn in Louisiana, decided to try tricking Bradburn. Late one night during the second week of May, 1832, a tall man dressed in a cloak delivered a message to the sentry at the fort. The note was signed by Ballou, the ferry keeper on the Sabine River, who knew John Bradburn. The letter warned that one hundred armed men were poised in Louisiana across the Sabine River and were forcibly recovering slaves.

Accepting the letter as authentic, Bradburn dispatched two local ranchers who regularly drove cattle to Louisiana, Taylor White and Silas Smith, to check it out. They returned several days later to report there were no men between Anahuac and Louisiana. Nobody in that area had ever heard of such an invasion.

Deciding that he had been tricked, Bradburn sent a patrol to arrest Travis at his law office and bring him in for questioning. If Travis was guilty of passing the bogus note to the sentry, he was guilty of sedition against a military post and he would be tried in a military court. On May 18, Anahuac was in turmoil. Settlers wanted to know under what authority the military could arrest a civilian and hold him without bail, not allowing him any communication? Why would he be tried by General Teran? The Americans were accustomed to the protection of the United States Bill of Rights and saw Bradburn's actions as lawless.

Travis' law partner, Patrick Jack, went to Bradburn's office, demanding the release of Travis. Jack made threats and used abusive language. He was promptly arrested too and joined Travis in the jail. One of Morgan slave named Hannah tried to slip a note in to the pair along with food and clean laundry. An alert sentry confiscated the note which detailed a plan to free the men two nights later. Bradburn immediately transferred Travis and Jack to a recently emptied brick kiln where he placed two guards at the entrance and increased the other guards throughout the fort.

Discovering that a clerk in Morgan's store had sent the note, Bradburn had him arrested and placed him in jail with Travis and Jack. Anyone remotely involved in the plot quietly left Anahuac because tension was so high. The Tories supported the cause of law and order and Bradburn. The rebels were favoring arming to free the prisoners.

The next week A.D. and all the other local wheat farmers were busy harvesting a half good crop of wheat.

William Jack, a resident of the Brazos, had come to Anahuac to try to free Travis and his brother. They were not going to let him even speak to his jailed brother until he became belligerent. William Jack set out for his home on the Brazos determined to raise an army. That force then marched to Liberty where more men joined the force, making it a total of one hundred fifty men.

John Austin paid a diplomatic call on Bradburn to discuss his prisoners, and the Mexicans had convinced him that Travis and Jack had committed sedition and should be tried under a military court. Austin returned to the Brazos where he heard of the escalating tension at Fort Anahuac and raised a volunteer force of thirty to go back and help free Travis and Jack. Before leaving the Brazos, Austin called on Lieutenant Colonel Ugartechea who advised Austin to try to get the men turned over to the local mayor. He also sent forty men under the command of Lieutenant Dominguez to accompany Austin's party. In the meantime, tensions were escalating. Several more men had been arrested trying to overthrow the Bradburn forces or trying to steal the fort's horses.

Owners of three Anglo ships blockaded the approach to Anahuac with three small five-ton vessels. Not only did this stop Government supplies from reaching Bradburn, but they carried messages from the insurgent volunteers to the Brazos. When John Austin reached Anahuac, Bradburn called for a formal review of the case. Lieutenant Paco presented the facts and convinced him under military law Travis and Jack had committed sedition by formatting rebellion against military authority. The Mexican Republic had adopted old Spanish military law without any revision.

More Anglos were arrested for trying to steal the Mexican Calvary's horses. The rebel volunteers were now camped about six miles south of Liberty. After finding this out, Bradburn sent nineteen of his Calvary to spy on the rebels.

Sergeant Gonzales told A.D. this when he brought three horses to him to be reshod. After Sergeant Gonzales left, A.D. rode to tell Frank Stroud to go up to warn the rebels. Frank Senior and Frank Junior were already with the rebels so A.D. asked Pat Stroud if he would go warn them that the Mexican Calvary would be there shortly spying on them. The rebels set a trap to capture the Mexican Calvary. The leader of the rebels did so without firing a shot. The rebels then moved their camp closer to Anahuac on Turtle Bay, approximately six miles north of the fort. Frank Johnson and Warren Hall were elected to command them in the field.

When the rebellion began Bradburn had sent for help from Nacogdoches, Velasco, and San Antonio to help him put this uprising down. On June ten[th], the rebel forces entered Anahuac and secured buildings on the north end of town that had formerly served as barracks for the Mexican army. At midday a committee of rebels asked for a meeting with Bradburn. They asked him to turn over the prisoners to Johnson, the mayor of Liberty. The rebels left the unsatisfactory meeting because Bradburn refused their request.

They spent the next morning skirmishing with Bradburn's patrol. About noon an offer was sent out from Bradburn to parlay. A schooner had brought Lieutenant Colonel Felix Subaran to Anahuac along with his Sergeant. Both were political prisoners banished by Mexico City to the frontier of Texas and bound for Fort Teran near Nacogdoches. The two paroled officers were supporters of the Federalist coup led by Santa Anna that began in January 1832. This was intended to overthrow the ruling Mexican centralist administration. Bradburn asked the paroled Subaran to temporarily serve as his second in command. The rebels, as requested, came to the meeting.

A prisoner exchange was set up. The rebels would release their nineteen Mexican Calvary men, and the next day Bradburn would release his Anglo prisoners, specifically Travis and Jack, along with a total of fourteen of Anglo prisoners. Johnson accepted the offer for the rebels, but most of the rebels did not trust Bradburn to keep his word.

Sure, enough Bradburn said, "Several of the rebels stayed in Anahuac last night and that violates the treaty. I do not have to release my prisoners." He also warned, "I am going to begin shelling the village within two hours." At that time all the women and children left Anahuac for safer places. A.D. had sent his family and several of his friend's families to his ranch outside of town. The rebel Texans felt Bradburn called a cease fire so that he could recover stored ammunition in the temporary barracks which the rebels had not discovered. The rebels remaining in Anahuac skirmished with the troops. One settler and five soldiers died during the skirmishes. The commander Johnson and others had learned that Subaran intended to overthrow Fort Anahuac and claim it for the Sandinistas'. Once that was accomplished, the new commander would view the Anglos as allies working to overthrow Bradburn, the representative of the Centralist Government.

The Texans decided to capitalize on the information about the Sandinista movement. A committee drew up a series of resolutions explaining they were not disloyal to Mexico, but rather had attacked Bradburn because he was an oppressive Centralist officer. This made the rebels squarely on the theoretical side of Santa Anna and the Federalist. The Turtle Bayou resolutions, adopted on June 13, 1832, charged Bradburn with violating the Constitution of 1824 by substituting military order for civil authority. As free men devoted to the Constitution, they pledged their support to aid Santa Anna. They also called upon all Texans to join in this movement. They sent one copy of their resolutions to the Brazos with John Austin who was returning there for cannons stored at San Felipe and Brazoria. The rebels realized they needed artillery in order to capture Anahuac.

While waiting for the cannons, the local rebels returned home to continue their farming, ranching and other chores. Other Texans that had come some distance camped on farms close by. A.D. and many of the other townspeople were alarmed that Bradburn would threaten to fire cannons into the town. It made A.D. so mad he just wanted to grab him by the throat and kill him, but of course he couldn't get close to him.

Stopping those cannons was just about all that was on A.D.'s mind that day. In the meantime, A.D. had continued his work. That evening, he rode out to see Johnson and Hall, the rebel commanders.

"I have a plan," he told them. "If we could put clay down the barrels of the Bradburn's cannons and then add water to the clay to harden it, the cannons would be worthless until they removed the clay."

Both leaders thought it was a good idea. They asked, "How could we possibly get enough time to accomplish this?"

A.D. said, "Sergeant Gonzales told me all the guards leave for twenty minutes and sometimes longer to have supper." Everyone agreed if they could spike the cannons so nobody would notice would be the way to do it.

Twelve men were assigned the task. They immediately filled four sacks full of clay and headed for the blacksmith shop where they would stay until the guards left for the evening meal. A.D. had made a metal funnel with a wide mouth and four of the men were carrying five-gallon buckets of water to pour on top of the clay once it was in the cannons.

Everyone knew they had to keep the area policed so that nobody would notice the cannons had been sabotaged. They had several wet rags to help accomplish this. A.D. would serve as a lookout, and if caught would tell the soldiers he needed to see Bradburn.

The guards finally left to eat supper, and the sabotage crew swung into action. Swiftly they poured the clay into all the cannons, adding water and plunging it down. They wiped the cannons down, finishing the job in twenty minutes and quietly making their way back to town.

Johnson was waiting for the crew at A.D.'s blacksmith shop to make sure all of the group was safe. The men were anxious to explain to him what they had done.

"If we get a couple of hot days it will probably take them a week to get those cannons in shape to fire," they predicted.

Johnson said, "A.D., you are doing more to help us here than many that are actually out ready to fight.

"Bradburn has many spies in your group," A.D. warned. "Be careful and try to eliminate those people because if they report me, Bradburn would have another prisoner. Call all the men together and tell them that you're going to attack the fort at six o'clock in the morning. Watch carefully who has to leave the camp. Have five or six riders ready and concealed to follow. The ones who go to the fort are your spies."

Johnson said, "I'll try it if you will watch the road close to the fort and identify people going in and out."

Johnson and his men returned to their camp and he immediately told the men they would attack at six o'clock in the morning. Four of the rebels left within an hour of the order.

One of the men went to his home and took care of some chores; the other three went to the fort as quickly as they could, telling the guards they must talk to Bradburn. After telling him the attack time they each received some silver and left to return to camp.

A.D. left for the rebel camp at ten o'clock and identified the three informants who Johnson promptly had arrested. When the rest of the rebels found out what had happened they wanted to hang the rebel traitors.

Johnson warned them, "We might be able to use them for bargaining at a later time. We need to protect them until it's time."

That seemed to satisfy his men. This had made everyone in the Texans' rebel camp more aware and more observant of everyone else's activity around the camp. They still knew there were other spies in their ranks and they intended to discover who they were.

16

CHAPTER

Colonel Jose Piedras, in response to Bradburn's plea for help, had started from Nacogdoches to Anahuac with fewer than one hundred men plus some Indian scouts. He was worried that the rebels would outnumber his relief force, and that settlers on Ayish Bayou might attack him from the rear. He had had trouble with this group of settlers from the time he arrived. Piedras approached Liberty and sent a delegation to talk with Johnson, asking the settlers what they wanted. The delegation returned with a list of grievances against Bradburn and asked for an interview with Piedras, which he refused because he was afraid that his forces were badly outnumbered. Piedras agreed to most of the Texans' demands. He said, "The mayor of Liberty will be re-established immediately, so that the civilian prisoners at Anahuac can be released to his supervision."

Piedras also agreed that Bradburn surrender his command. He instructed the settlers to petition Teran to rectify the injustices committed by the commander at Anahuac.

These terms were favorable to the Anglo rebels. Colonel Piedras conceded to the demands of the Anglo settlers without even talking to Bradburn. The agreement was immediately signed June 28th.

Piedras arrived at Fort Anahuac July 1st, discovering that Bradburn was willing to resign. Therefore, he assumed temporary command of the garrison on July 1st. He released Travis, Jack and the others to Liberty's Mayor Hugh Johnson. The prisoners were supposedly under arrest in the company of Johnson and went back to Liberty with him. Liberty didn't even have a jail, so all the prisoners were soon released.

Travis and the other prisoners planned to seek revenge against

Bradburn as soon as Piedras left Anahuac. Piedras stayed at the Fort until July 8th and then left for Nacogdoches. He named Lieutenant Juan Cortina as Fort Commander. Three days after Piedras left, Travis opened up a barrel of whiskey for the fort's garrison, and they staged a drunken atmosphere everywhere. The soldiers were asked to join the Sandinista movement. Unable to control his soldiers, Lt. Cortina turned over the command to the Sandinista-backed officer Subaran.

A party of men, with John Austin, had arrived at the Brazos where there were three cannons stored. Austin organized a meeting in Brazoria on June 20th to endorse the Turtle Bayou Resolutions. The following day he put three cannons on board the schooner *Brazoria,* which was in port loading cotton. The *Brazoria* set sail downriver where the insurgents expected Commander Ugartechea to challenge them. In addition to forty men on board the vessel, one hundred volunteers marched overland to Velasco.

Ugartechea would not join the Sandinista uprising and prepared to defend his small fort with sixty-four infantrymen and nine artillerymen. Austin parlayed with the Mexican colonel, trying persuade him to surrender so there would be no loss of life. Of course, Ugartechea refused.

Austin's force attacked the Mexican fort on the night of June 26th. The next morning the Mexican commander surrendered. Not only was he almost out of ammunition, but many of his troops had been wounded and needed medical attention.

One half of Austin's troops attacked the fort by land and his other troops from the *Brazoria.* Austin had lined the ship with cotton bales and had three cannons on board. The Mexican losses were heavy, and the Anglos losses were few. The *Brazoria* had been so heavily damaged during the short six hour battle, she could not sail the Mexican troops to the Rio Grande. Austin had agreed to send the Mexican troops back on that ship but he could not keep his word. The captured troops marched cross country back to Mexico.

As Austin was preparing to bring his volunteers and cannons to the Texans at Turtle Bayou he learned that Bradburn had resigned, so his goal was accomplished.

When Colonel Piedras got to Nacogdoches in late July, many Sandinista victories against the Centralist government had increased

Santa Anna's power. Piedras believed the Centralist Government would soon be victorious. He further thought that his agreeing to the Texas Rebels demands at Fort Anahuac would stop the rebellion and they would soon be made to obey Mexican laws and be obedient to them! When he reached Nacogdoches Piedras found all the local residents were supporters of Santa Anna's coup. He then left his command August second trying to reach safety.

Travis had already made an assassination attempt on Bradburn and he knew he had to leave Anahuac quickly but he could not get passage on any ships. Three small ships had actually blocked the entrance to the Bay not letting any supplies get to the Mexican Army while the Anahuac revolt was taking place. Also, this made it impossible for Bradburn to escape via boat. Bradburn eventually got some friends to guide him to Louisiana. He got to New Orleans and safety on August 6th. The centralist officers in Nacogdoches, San Antonio and Anahuac could not control their troops and had to resign their posts and travel overland back to Mexico City. The Mexican civil war ended in December 1832. Santa Anna was elected president of Mexico in April of 1833. He entered the office as a Federalist Reformer, a guise he continued for approximately one year.

Federalist Victories on the Rio Grande made Colonel José Mexia fear the Mexican Texans were staging a separatist rebellion and sailed for the Brazos River. Stephen F. Austin was returning from a session of the state legislature and happened to be in Matamoros.

General Mexia defeated the centralist army there. Mexia had asked both Austin and the Centralist General to accompany him to Texas in an attempt to settle their differences. The fleet of five vessels reached Velasco July 16th. John Austin and others quickly convinced Mexia that their activities had been for Santa Anna's cause. Even before Mexia could travel to Anahuac, Subaran had commandeered sufficient vessels to rejoin Mexia's Army. Subaran's fleet met Mexia in Galveston Bay on July 23rd. The entire Federalist Army then returned to the Rio Grande.

When the Garrison departed, Anahuac went back to having four businesses in place of the twelve they had before the Army was there. Many of the merchants now used their buildings for storage. Most of the wooden buildings were set on fire in August of 1832. A lot of the practical folks got bricks from the Fort to use for themselves. The backers of the

Mexican troops, who were called Tories, had greatly benefited by the occupied Fort so they were either tarred and feathered or taken to the Bay and scrubbed with corncobs. Even A.D. had been approached by these rebels accusing him of being a Tory and demanding that he answer to them. A.D. was at his blacksmith shop when he was approached. He picked up both of his double barrel pistols and slung the shot gun on his back and ask the man making the accusation, "Who appointed you judge and jury over this matter?" They answered by saying, "You better tell us or you're going be tarred and feathered." A.D. replied, "Not before four or five of your people are shot. I will not answer to you or any man that comes to me about such a matter." "Well," the Rebel said, "You weren't with the group that was fighting against the Mexican Army." "Yes, that's right," A.D. answered, "But what I did was more useful than you out camping and shooting a rifle once in a while! I know most of you thirty people that are here and do not bother to come back to my blacksmith shop anymore for any work or anything else because I won't do it. Now, you people get the hell off my property and you better hope I don't catch you alone sometime." He pointed his two pistols at the three leaders as they said, "We'll get you sometimes." "Thanks for the warning but you just remember what I have already said." A.D. was furious and rode over to see Frank Johnson persuading him to come back to Anahuac and address the mob. This took a whole day and after Johnson had set the mob straight about what A.D. Logging had done for the rebel cause, several of those people came to him to apologize, but not the leaders. A.D. was now calm and felt he had been cleared of any accusations from the mob. Frank Stroud found out about it and told A.D., "You should have just come to me. I would have set them straight." A.D. replied, "I just didn't think they would believe you since they already know we are friends." A.D. quietly thought I hope those leaders come to my shop sometimes so I have the pleasure of running them off.

17

Most of the loyalist were grateful to the Mexican Republic for their large land grants and took the oath of allegiance very seriously. They were treated better than the other settlers and also benefited monetarily while the Mexican soldiers were present. The rebels tended to be young unmarried newcomers without land grants and were very pushy. Most of their leaders were lawyers or former supporters of the Mexican Independence movement. The Anglo-Americans seem to believe that the United States and Mexico were republics and their laws must be the same. However, they were very different. Mexico had adopted Roman law which had been inherited from Spain. Mexico wasn't even thinking of adopting the English Common Law protection of the United States Bill of Rights into their judicial system. This was hard for the American settler to understand and were continuously involved in many problems. Most of the early emigrants were grateful for their generous land grants and of course they had discovered and settled on the best land they could find. The newcomers after 1830 favored separation from Mexico in the hope that they could get some of the land previously claimed.

Of course, there were many politicians in the United States that wanted Texas to become part of their country. There were other politicians who did not want Texas to become part of the United States. It was at this time that Sam Houston made his way to Texas. There were many people who had come to Texas because they were debtors and in the United States you could be sent to jail for not paying your debts. There were also a certain number of settlers that come to Mexico because they had committed crimes in the United States. There were also a number of settlers who really had no interest in politics as long as they were left alone. These were mostly big ranchers that were in the Liberty area of Texas.

After the Mexican Army left the blacksmith business had been pretty scant for A.D. He decided he would take his blacksmith wagon out to the various farmers and ranchers within a 20-mile radius of Anahuac to see if that would be more profitable. But before he started on this venture he and the boys had harvested the fifty acres of corn with a yield of 40 bushels to the acre. A.D.'s cowherd was now around one hundred and he was probably going to have to go with one of the other large ranchers on a cattle drive to sell some of his cattle. The Loggings then planted their two acres fall garden. It was now September 24th. A.D. rode out to see ten of the larger ranchers to tell them about his availability to come out to their ranch to shoe horses or mules and repair wagons. There were three of the ranchers that thought it was a good idea. He set up times beginning the next week to go out and work.

The next week he was at the Taylor White ranch where he worked for two weeks shoeing 35 horses and mules and repairing three wagons. He had also shoed ten horses and mules for some of Mr. White's neighbors who had come over asking for A.D.'s help. During the two weeks, A.D. stayed at White's ranch for four nights and went home the other evenings. Mr. White always treated A.D. respectfully. The four nights A.D. had stayed they played dominoes with Mr. White and two other hands for two hours each night. They discussed the cattle drive which would begin in a couple weeks. A.D. said, "I would be interested in going on the cattle drive." Mr. White said, "That would be okay. You can go on the drive to Opelousas, Louisiana. We will probably get between $12 and $15 a head for the cattle."

After finishing the work for Mr. White A.D. began compiling the number of steers he and his close neighbors would want to send. Between him, the Stroud's, the Smiths Tims and A.D. they would have 150 head. He would need help. He rode over to see if ex-Sergeant Gonzales would like to make $25 helping him drive the herd and protect the money when returning to Anahuac. Sergeant Pedro Gonzales and his two cohorts, Corporals Juan Hernandez and Ernesto Diaz had stayed in Anahuac and together were homesteading over 18,000 acres. When the Mexican Army had left Anahuac these friends of A.D. and others had decided to try ranching in the area. The Mexican government had given them six thousand acres each to homestead. They only had ten cows and had been running those with A.D.'s herd because they did not have a bull. They also had five horses and two Mules, three bred gilts and had planted 20 acres of wheat and 20 acres of oats. Their plan was to plant one hundred acres of corn in the spring. They had planted a ten acre fall garden and had been selling and eating much of the produce. They were hard pressed for cash. Ernesto and Pedro asked A.D., "Do you think we could also get a job helping with the herd going to Louisiana?" A.D. told them, "Go see Mr. White, you could probably get a job." The two ex-army men went over to see rancher White and he said, "I know I can use you on the drive." Meanwhile A.D. was getting his ranch, home and shop ready for protection while he was gone. Bob Tims was going to stay at his ranch and watch the remaining livestock. A.D. had decided not to take his cow dog, Duke, on this cattle drive for fear of losing him to snakebite, theft or being run over by the cattle. He felt the dog would be more valuable protecting the herd at home. His wife and boys would take care of the shop and home in Anahuac. Rancher White estimated they would be gone for 25 days. Before leaving A.D. made sure all of his stock was branded.

It was the largest herd anyone had ever seen going to Louisiana. There were approximately 1,650 steers. There were a lot of families watching including A.D.'s and the pioneers who came to Anahuac with him. The largest owners of the herd were James White, Sol Barrow, Williams and of course A.D. The three largest owners had about five hundred steers each in this drive. The first day they got about three miles past Liberty. James had sent the Mexicans riders out ahead of the herd to see if there were any rustlers out there who were going to try to attack the herd. In 8 days, they came to the Sabine River. It took all of the 9th day to cross the cattle, horses and mules. The tenth day everyone rested.

That evening some rustlers tried to take part of the herd but the Mexican cowboys had warned them and after a brief gun battle the rustlers surrendered. They tied them up and took them with the drive to Opelousas. The 20th day of the drive they arrived in Opelousas and had the rustlers placed under arrest by the local authorities. Mr. White was quite pleased because there were three buyers wanting their steers.

They got $15 a head. A.D. had insisted that he be paid in silver dollars and knowing this he had brought a draft horse along on the drive to carry the three hundred pounds of silver on his back. The draft horse never slowed them down and had no trouble carrying the money. There was a total of 32 people involved in this trail drive. They all went out and celebrated that night. The next morning A.D. and several others were ready to go on the return trip. The big ranchers warned A.D., "Do not trust anybody going home because robbers will be waiting to steal the money on the Atascosita trail." Mr. White said, "There is a group of people all along the trail home named Yoakam and are well known for stealing cattlemen's money when they are returning from Louisiana. I put my money in the bank and it is transferred to my bank in New Orleans. If I ever need that money I can always get it in a few days." All of the drovers had been paid and were cautioned, "Do not even stop at the Yoakam home." There were 14 including A.D. that were ready to leave the next morning. This also included the three Mexican ex-soldiers.

They left 7 a.m. and made thirty miles the first day. The next two days, they made thirty-five miles each day which put them across the ferry at Sabine River. The 4th day they made another thirty-five miles and picked out a very defendable place to camp. They decided to double the guards for the night. Early in the evening Mr. Yoakam himself came out and told the group, "You should be staying in a nice home, sleeping on good beds with good company and plenty of liquor." Mr. White respectfully declined his invitation telling him, "We have already pitched camp and intend to stay here." Yoakam was quite insistent about his invitation until A.D. and two others stepped up and told the thief, "Too many people had lost their money and some even their lives by accepting your invitation. Our invitation to you is for you to leave. If anyone comes around tonight or tomorrow or anytime we will be glad to meet them." A.D. was sure the man understood what he was saying. He turned and went off in a huff hollering some threats to the group. In their position there were 3, three foot tall mounds, one on the North, one on the South and one on the West. Their hobbled horses were in the middle of the earthen walls with the protection of several large trees. They had three men on each wall, two were sleeping and one was on guard duty at all times. Two men were taking care of the horses. Those two men could also go to any wall that was having trouble with an attack. Most of them only got about three hours of sleep that night because they knew they were being watched for an opportunity to attack. A.D. sent a lone rider back to the Billew ferry to warn the other cattle herders about the Yoakam's threat and to tell them what had happened. He cautioned them to be careful and let them know that Yoakam intended them great harm and intended to steal their money.

No attack came so they rode out of their camp the next Morning, riding two men side by side and the next two men ten yards behind. Gonzales was already scouting ahead for them. They didn't see him for the rest of the day because he didn't encounter any problems. The herders made another 35 miles finding an abandoned cabin at the end of the day. They were certainly lucky because it had begun to rain and they could stay dry. They had also found an abandoned barn about thirty yards from the cabin. It was so rickety they didn't know if it would hold up thru the night. The horses appreciated it though because they were also out of the rain. They put one guard at the barn, one at the cabin and rotated guard duty all night. Most of the group got six hours of sleep because they were not bothered by intruders that night. The horses were plum given out and they had no feed for them the last two days. Many of them wanted to rest the horses plus themselves. But they knew if they made good time that day they could be home late the next night.

The group stopped in Liberty to rest and feed their horses and ran into Mayor Williams. They told him about the Yoakam threats and what they had to do to prevent him from trying to take their money. He asked the group, "Is anyone willing to join a posse to go in there and clear him out?" A.D. said, "We don't have enough evidence on him but someone needs to go out and help the other half of our cattle herders who will probably see him tomorrow." Williams said, "Well, will one of you lead us back to this place if we send a number of men to help the other returning herders?" Pedro Gonzales volunteered saying "I am the only single one here and I am sure the others want to get to their families." He also asked, "Could I have a fresh horse and place to sleep tonight?" Williams took care of his request and then went to get the sheriff to see if he could build a posse. The next morning the 11-man posse rode out to meet the other herders and possibly to arrest Yoakam. As it turned out the posse and the herders returned to Liberty without incident. Williams had told the group, "There are a lot of stories about Yoakam but there really hasn't been any proof that he has done anything wrong." They would, of course, warn people coming through Liberty about the danger when taking the Atascosita Trail to Louisiana.

They arrived home late that night. Everyone got someone else to take care of their horses and the exhausted herders went to bed. The trip had been quite profitable to everyone who took it. A.D. slept until noon the next day when his wife finally woke him up for breakfast. She told him, "You have about fifteen horses and mules to shoe down at the shop along with three wagons to repair. I think the people are pretty anxious to get their animals and wagons back." A.D., Bob and the boys worked until 8:00 o'clock that night and had shoed over one half of the horses and mules and went home to a late supper. During the afternoon, rancher White brought three horses in that had the colic, he had unsuccessfully tried to treat. A.D. had treated cows and horses since he had the blacksmith shop. He made a mixture of coffee, whiskey and coal oil and administered it with a three-foot tube. After two hours the three horses seemed to be ok. Mr. White also bought five gallon of hoof dressing, paid A.D. $25 and left.

The next morning while A.D. and the boys were working at the blacksmith shop Frank Stroud and his boys rode in wanting to get their money from the cattle drive. They had sent fifty steers and A.D. paid him $750 dollars. At the same time A.D. paid Bob Tims $225 for his fifteen steers. He still owed Ralph Smith $225 for his fifteen steers and would probably ride out and pay him the next day. He would go over to his own ranch and hide his money in his special tree which was not far from his barn. There were no banks anywhere close to Anahuac so everyone had to hide their money in a safe at home or somewhere else. That was all right with A.D. because he didn't trust banks or even safes. He put the proceeds from the cattle drive plus $375 he had saved from his blacksmith business in a special small box that was supposed to be fireproof. He finished the shoeing of the remaining horses and mules at 6:00 o'clock and went home for supper. After supper they went to bed because everyone was really tired.

The next morning early, after breakfast, the Logging family rode out to see the Smith's and give them $225 for their fifteen steers that A.D. had sold for them on the cattle drive. They were so glad to receive the money because, now they could pay off their bill at McCoy's general store and buy enough seed for planting the corn crop. Plus, they would still have $40 left to live on until the corn crop comes in next fall. The Logging family then rode on to their money hiding tree and added $900 in a special metal box where they kept their money. They then continued on to the cabin and Maggie fixed lunch while A.D. and the boys went out and fed the hogs and cattle. After eating and checking his livestock the family rode home to the cabin in Anahuac. They dropped Maggie off at the cabin and drove back down to the blacksmith shop. The boys put up the wagon and the mules, fed all the stock in the pastures behind the shop and also went down to feed the steers and hogs near the boat dock on the Trinity Bay. A.D. in the meantime began trying to repair one of the three wagons that needed fixing. He greased the four wheels after repairing one of them that was missing two spokes. At that time, it was 7:30 and all the crew went home for supper and rest. The next day A.D. fixed two wagons and shoed two horses. Most of the other customers who had left horses, mules and wagons at the blacksmith shop came in that day, got their animals and paid A.D. so he had $39 at the end of the day. That was pretty good money!

It was the end of February and the next day the Logging family spent the day planting their two-acre spring garden consisting of onions, potatoes, cabbage, pumpkins, carrots and peas. A fisherman had come to the dock in Anahuac and wanted to sell about ten thousand pounds of fish that had spoiled. A.D. gave him fifty dollars for the fish and he was going to use them as fertilizer on his corn crop. The following day, A.D. and Bob spent most of the day getting the plow and harrow ready for planting. The next three days it rained and they waited two more days for the land to dry so it could be more easily plowed and harrowed.

The front of most cabins and shops in Anahuac were on stilts raising the buildings about thirty inches above the ground. This was done because when there was a storm or hurricane, water could flood the village up to two feet. A.D. had never liked the stilts supporting his home and business. He asked Dick, the local carpenter, "Is there a way to build something more substantial to ensure the stilts will hold even in flooding?" Dick suggested to A.D., "We could get some bricks from the now non-occupied Fort and build more substantial stilts." The back part of the building was setting on a small hill that ran behind all these buildings on Front Street. In this planting lull A.D., Bob and Dick drove the wagon up to the Fort and loaded it with brick. Dick, with Bob's help, began to build brick supports for the front of the Logging business and home. This cost A.D. $15 for Dick's work but they thought the brick stilts would last much longer than the wooden supports.

A.D., Bob and the boys began plowing and harrowing the one hundred acres they were going to plant in corn. That took ten days to complete. They then began to plant corn and that took five more days. It took the boys five more days to spread stinky, rotting fish on ten acres of corn. They were finished planting by April second and were done with de-weeding the corn by April 25th. The next week they spent working mainly with the new calves, branding, de-worming and castrating the males. They also had to brand 5 new wild cows captured during the winter in the traps. In a week they would start the harvest of 25 acres of oats and it looked like a good crop this year.

All the fall and winter Art and Weldon had been training a young two-year-old stud named Gray Boy for racing. He, of course, was the son of the famous racing horse stud, Gray. They had a lot of advice from their dad on what and how they should be training the horse. In May they tried racing the young stud so they could enter him in the summer and fall races. A.D. thought Gray Boy would be ready to race by that time. The horse was still sometimes skittish but that was becoming less and less. June 15th, they had two mock races with Gray Boy and Gray. Gray Boy barely beat him both times. A.D. was still getting about one mare a month for the old great stud to breed. On May 25, they finished the harvest of the oat crop which made twenty-five bushels to the acre. A.D. gave Bob two hundred twenty-five bushels and kept the rest for himself. After the cattle drive A.D.'s blacksmith shop business had kept him busy about one day out of each week.

The two large ranchers, Williams and Barrows, said they wanted A.D. to come out and spend a couple of weeks at their ranches, shoeing their horses and mules and repairing wagons. A.D. needed to get more bulls for his herd and was going to try to trade his present bulls with one of the ranchers. Art and Duke accompanied him helping him to do the blacksmith work.

When they arrived at Williams ranch A.D. immediately asked Mr. Williams, "Would you trade me three bulls and I will buy one more?"

The rancher told A.D. "Sorry I can't work a deal." This rancher was not as friendly and helpful to A.D. as some of the others. He and Art shoed fourteen horses, nine mules and repaired two wagons in a week's time. They were then ready to go home, where they received a grand reception! A.D., Art and Duke were really glad to be home.

Weldon and Art spent the next few days getting Gray Boy ready for racing. They raced him against Gray and he won this time by a couple of lengths. Gray was getting older and A.D. doubted if he would ever race him again, A.D. had already made arrangements with Pedro and his two ex-Mexican soldiers to protect the Logging's ranch, home and blacksmith shop while they spent six days at the Liberty July celebration. A.D. took his blacksmith wagon and another wagon for his family. There were six other families and one racehorse going to the Liberty celebration.

Of course, the Stroud boys were driving a wagon used to sell flour and cornmeal. They had talked each of the other families into carrying one barrel of either flour or cornmeal for them to sell at the Liberty celebration. It was decided by all that they would start early in the morning, like 4:00 a.m. so they could arrive in Liberty by 7:00 p.m. However, it was 8:00 a.m. before they arrived at Liberty.

Watha and her parents met the group at one o'clock. When they arrived A.D. immediately went to the farmer who rented his barn to him and the Anahuac family, the Stroud family and the Smiths. They prepared their camp and because they were all so tired, including the mules and horses, they slept late the next morning and didn't finish breakfast until 9:00 a.m.

A.D., Art and Weldon took Gray Boy down to the race track and had him race a couple of times. They could tell the horse felt good and thought they would have a chance to win the big horse race. The boys then took Gray Boy to the river to wash him down and cooled his feet. They brought him back and since it was a nice day put him in a small pasture close by.

The boys asked their parents, "Is it ok to go play with some of the other kids that are camped close by?"

Their parents answered, "Sure, have a good time." They enjoyed the afternoon and didn't return to camp until 5:00. Their mother was preparing supper and the boys jumped in and started helping her.

A.D. and Maggie had paid the twenty-dollar entry fee for the race. Gray Boy had ten to one odds on winning the race. So, they decide to bet a hundred dollars on him but not that day because they didn't trust the man taking the money. They figured he could take the money and just run off that night if he wanted to. The bet was placed the next morning.

The first contest was the rifle shooting contest which started at 8:00 a.m. Over three hundred men had entered this event. A.D. had his usual luck and was the tenth shooter at the hundred-yard target with a two-minute time limit.

He put four shots in the bull's-eye and left. The next two contests were the knife and hatchet throwing contest, which none of their group entered, but the winners won two hundred dollars each.

As A.D. was coming back to the camp the boys met him and said, "Gray Boy is not in the pasture."

He told the boys, "I think I know where you should go and look."

Then he told Maggie, "Go tell the Sheriff that someone has taken Gray Boy."

A. D in the meantime got his horse saddled and began trying to find the tracks where Gray Boy had left the pasture. He was really upset when he determined two people had led him out of the pasture to where they had two horses waiting and had taken off with him.

A.D. told Smith, "Show the Sheriff the tracks I have found and the direction I am tracking the horse and the rustlers."

A.D. caught up with the rustlers in about forty-five minutes, because both of their horses were sick from eating some harmful weeds. They offered no resistance when A.D. approached them with his gun drawn. The rustlers and their horses were a pitiful sight. He didn't think any of them had a meal for several days. A.D. did what he could for the horses hoping they didn't founder and die.

He asked the boys, "Why did you take my horse?"

"We don't have a stud," They answered, "and our three mares are over ten years old. If we had a stud we could probably get some new colts."

A.D. asked, "What do you feed your horses?"

They replied, "We don't have any feed so they eat grass in spring, summer and fall and a little bit of hay in the winter. Mister, we don't even have enough food for ourselves much less for the horses." On the way back, the Sheriff and Maggie caught up with A.D. and the rustlers.

Sheriff said, "Do you boys know that stealing horses is a hanging offense?" After a period of silence, he continued, "Well, I'll have to take you over and lock you up."

A.D. said, "Please don't do that let's try another approach. Maybe if we care for their horses and cure the sickness we can feed them. Then feed the boys, because I am sure they haven't eaten in sometime."

The Sheriff said "Okay, A.D., if that's what you want but don't come crying to me if they steal from you again because, I won't help you out."

A.D. said, "Actually, I think I'm the one who caught these guys, not you." The Sheriff just shook his head and rode away.

When the group got back to the campground Maggie fixed a large lunch and the rustlers ate as if they were starved. A.D. and Weldon had not eaten because they were getting Gray Boy ready for the first race at one o'clock.

In the meantime, Frank came back to camp and told A.D., "You tied with another man named Pete in the shooting contest and split the three hundred-dollar winnings handing him one-hundred fifty dollars." A.D. told him what had been happening over the last five hours, then everyone was off to see the horse races. Gray Boy was running in the second race with ten others as there were a total of forty-four horses entered. Gray Boy won his first race by three lengths. A.D. was worried that he was probably too tired but Gray Boy had the championship race yet to run which would be at 3:30. The boys went to cool the hooves and legs of Gray Boy and then brought him back to the stall in the barn. The two rustlers had stayed close by A.D. and had sincerely apologized for what they had done. When everyone got back to the barn, A.D. tried to treat the rustler's two horses. They were improving. Frank then put the two horses in the pasture. Maggie in the meantime had picked up her winnings and bet one hundred dollars on Gray Boy in the championship race. At three o'clock they all started to the horse track for the championship race. In the meantime, Art had become sick with a fever and he, of course, could not ride. Weldon was going to have to ride Gray Boy. Art told him what part of the track he should run on and gave him other pointers which would help.

A.D. told Weldon, "Just let him go and stay on him and I think you'll win the race."

Sure, enough Gray Boy won the race by a half a length winning seven hundred dollars. Also, Maggie won five hundred dollars from the bet she had placed on Gray Boy. Weldon was the happiest they had ever seen him, because he had ridden Gray Boy to a victory in the greatest race for the area. Even the two boy rustlers, Matthew and Mark May, were happy.

Later that afternoon they had a greased pig contest and the only ones eligible to try from their group were the Smith's two sons and one daughter. As it ended up, one of the sons won a pig. Some of the group entered the big checker tournament which was also going on that afternoon. Mary Stroud had entered a canning contest for peas and won seven dollars for first place. She was really happy about that!

At 7:00 that evening they all went over to the big dance complete with a band. A lot of people there were selling food, beer and liquor. The dance started off pretty good and there was no trouble the first two hours. Suddenly a single boy who was dancing with a married woman was attacked by her husband and a great fight commenced. A.D. and Maggie finding their kids and Matthew and Mark, made their way a short distance away from the dance. On the way off the dance floor A.D. had been slugged twice.

"I'm going back to get the two guys that slugged me."

Maggie begging said, "Please don't go. Just come on and let's get all our group together and leave."

A.D. was determined to go back. Finally, he returned and you could tell he had been fighting. The Stroud's, Smith's, McCoy's and Tim's families had gotten together outside the dance and decided to call it a night. They went back to their wagons in the rented barn, checked all the horses and mules to make sure they were okay.

The group then decided they would start for home at 4:00 a.m. in the morning and try to make it to Anahuac by nightfall. Watha's family would ride with them for about five hours and then veer off west to their home. From that point they only had to drive about an hour to get to their farm. Watha's parents were going to allow her to go to Anahuac with the group and spend a couple weeks visiting with Bob and his parents. That was fine with everybody.

The evening before they left, A.D. had decided that he would give Mark and Matthew ten dollars each and send them back home to their mother. He had told them, "If you want to come to Anahuac and work for me, I will give you room and board plus twenty dollars a month each."

Frank gave them five pounds each of flour and cornmeal to take home with them. A. D. also sent them home with some horse and mule feed.

He told them, "If you come bring only your horses with you and we will try to nurse them back to health."

A.D.'s entire group was surprised when before they left, Mark, Matthew and their mom, Bea, returned to Liberty with a loaded wagon and most of their possessions.

She introduced herself and asked, "Can I come and stay with the boys while they are working for you?" She further stated, "I understand they'll be staying in the cabin by themselves, and I would not be a burden to anyone. I could cook for the boys and make improvements to your cabin, which you told them you wanted."

A.D. quietly talked it over with the group and no one objected. The only problem now was, would their rickety old wagon make it to Anahuac?

The rest of the trip was uneventful. Bea had told Maggie, "I left a note for my husband in the cabin in case he came back home. I'm not certain he will come back or if he even wants to."

Before getting to Anahuac, A.D. and his family took Matthew, Mark and their mother to the Logging cabin on their ranch and unloaded their wagon.

A.D. said, "Make a list of what you need. I'm taking your wagon into my blacksmith shop because it needs a lot of work done and I want you to be able to use your wagon. I can pick up what you need while I am there." After that the Loggings went to their cabin in the village of Anahuac.

The Loggings family slept until ten o'clock the next day. The rest of the day was spent unloading the wagon and putting things where they should be. Then they went down to the blacksmith shop where there were ten notes stuck under the door. Also, there was a total of ten horses and mules to be reshod plus two wagons to be repaired. A.D. did none of the work that day, he just took time to restock his blacksmith wagon. The following day Maggie and the children drove out to see Matthew, Mark and Bea May. Maggie was going to show them where all their neighbors lived and introduce them to the other neighbors they had not yet met. Also, she was going to bring them to town show them the cabin, shop and the General Store in Anahuac.

When they got to the general store Maggie insisted, "Bea, you get whatever supplies you think you need and we will charge them to A.D." They were very grateful.

The May family asked A.D., "What do you want to do with your cabin and land?"

He told them, "I will be out tomorrow morning and we will go over all the things that I want to see done out on my ranch." He did get their wagon repaired and wheels greased so they would be okay for a least another couple years.

The next morning when he rode out he took the wagon pulled by their mules and the horse tied onto the back of the wagon. He was carrying three bushels of corn and three bushels of oats to feed their stock. Also, he took Duke, the cow dog, with him so they could get acquainted with him.

He showed the boys a pasture of one hundred fifty acres and told them, "I want the pasture fenced." He also showed them the spring that was located on Bob Tim's place and told them, "I want to divert some of that water all the way to my house. I also want water just outside this corral and a place to water the stock between the spring and my cabin." "You," he continued, "will have to build the water troughs for those two areas. I have already made sure the slope from Bob's spring will easily flow freely through a pipe system. Over here is a place you can plant a fall garden so you will have enough to eat through the winter."

He then took the boys to where his cows were and told them, "I will expect you to go out each day and check on the condition of all my stock." Next, he showed them how to take care of the eight sows and one boar. A.D. was also running ten mares in a fifty-acre pasture about one hundred yards from the house.

He said, "I want you to check the horses daily."

A.D. asked them, "Have you ever built wood fence for pasture before?"

They replied, "Only for small areas."

A.D said, "Well if you have any questions about how to do it, please talk to me now." They asked him a few questions, and A.D. thought he could come out in a few days and check out what they had done. They had two axes, a crosscut saw, a hand saw, and a hammer & nails. A.D. had also told them where to cut the wood for the pasture fence. He showed them a two hundred acre fenced pasture about five hundred yards from the cabin so they could see how it was fenced. The boys spent a week cutting wood for the fence then asked A.D. to come out and show them how to get it started. A.D. spent about a half a day with them showing them the easiest way he knew to build the cedar-wood fence for the pasture. He then went over to his money tree and put another nine hundred dollars in his metal box.

From there he went straight to McCoy's store and told him, "I want to pipe water from Bob's spring to my house. Could I order the pipe, a couple cutoff valves and drops? How much would this cost?"

Mr. McCoy said, "It will cost you seventy-five dollars for all of that."

"Okay, Gene," he said. "Go ahead and place the order." Then he paid him. A.D. also spent the rest of the afternoon playing dominoes with Gene and several different farmers and ranchers that had come into the store. The next two days he spent in his blacksmith shop shoeing horses and mules and fixing two wagons.

The third day, Matthew, Mark and their mother came into town.

They told A.D., "We have several ideas on how we could improve the cabin but it will probably cost some money."

A.D. approved all their suggestions then told the boys, "After you get the fence built, I want you to build three three-sided sheds to protect the stock." He continued, "Also, I want you to help with the corn harvest the next few weeks."

The next day A.D., Art and Duke left for the Barrow ranch for at least a week of blacksmithing. They left at 6:00 o'clock in the morning and got there in the evening about 8:00 o'clock. A.D. parked the wagon outside the barn where they would be working. Mr. Barrow had a cowboy put away their team of mules and A.D.'s horse. He took them into the house and introduced them to his wife, two sons, one about Art's age, and his daughter. They ate a meal of steak, greens and buttermilk. A.D. and Art both ate heartily. They were very tired and went right to sleep in a small bedroom that had assigned to them. Mr. Barrows had told A.D., "Just call me Sol and I'll see you at breakfast at 7:00 in the morning." They slept well, ate a big breakfast and were ready to work by 8:00 a.m. There were twenty horses and ten mules that needed shoeing. Sol showed him two wagons that were in terrible shape and A.D. told him, "It will take a day each to repair those wagons." He said "That's fine just fix them up for me." A.D. observed that the horses and mules had not been well taken care of, as far as their feet were concerned. He had to do more cutting on the hooves than he had ever done before. Therefore, the work went very slow even though he had appointed a man to help. They had only shoed seven horses by 5:00 when Sol came to the barn. A.D. told him, "Your horses' hooves are in terrible shape, you will need to put this hoof dressing on every horse and mule once a week for six weeks."

"Okay," he said. "I agree with you that is what needs to be done. Now," he continued, "I want to show you my place."

They rode over twenty thousand acres and saw a lot of longhorns.

Sol said, "I have about two thousand head of cattle."

A.D. told him "I need about four good bulls."

Sol said "Great, do you want to pick them or do you want me to?"

A.D. said "I would appreciate you picking me four really great bulls."

"They will be ready when you finish with the horses and mules," Sol said.

A.D. asked, "How much will it cost me?"

Sol replied "Sixty dollars for the lot."

"Agreed," A.D. said, "I want to thank you."

The last three days Art and Sol's son Emmett were beginning to get acquainted. They were enjoying playing together and Art didn't want to go home. A.D. had two other farmers come with a horse, a mule and a wagon to be repaired after he finished Barrow's work. A.D. charged them ten dollars each. So not only was A.D. returning home with four bulls, he now had an extra twenty dollars.

"Art tells me you have a great race horse stud named Gray," said Sol, "I would like to buy two of his stud sons. If you'll deliver them to me sometime this winter I'll pay you one hundred fifty dollars," A.D. replied

"That's a deal and, Sol, don't let your horse's and mule's feet ever get as bad as they were again," he said.

"I won't because I now know a good blacksmith." With that they said their goodbyes and the Loggings left. Emmett went along to help A.D. with the Bulls and visited with Art for half the day then returned to his father's ranch. The Loggings got home at 9:00 that night, put the bulls in the pasture behind the blacksmith shop and then took care of the mules and horses. They had a late supper and went to bed sleeping until ten o'clock the next morning.

The next day A.D. and the May boys rounded up the four bulls that had been with his herd for the past two years and returned them to the pasture behind his shop. They then took the new bulls out to the rest of the herd. The boys asked, "Are you going to sell the bulls we just took out of your herd?" A.D. replied, "Yes, I am going to sell them for fifteen dollars each. He could see the boys really wanted to buy one of the bulls.

The May's brothers told A.D., "We have caught some wild cows that are unbranded, fed them some ear corn and put them with the rest of the herd. It looks like the wild cows are staying."

A.D. told them. "The next two wild cows you catch are yours. I will make you a brand at my blacksmith shop." A.D. checked all the cows, hogs, horses and mules and was satisfied they were okay. He then checked the fencing the boys had been doing and felt it was pretty good. Then they rode over to the cabin and A.D. paid each one sixty dollars, and told them, "Okay, you are now paid through October."

The May boys and their mother seemed to be pretty happy. He had eight horses that needed to be shod and one wagon to fix at his shop. Then he went over to McCoy's general store, played dominoes for three hours and then returned home for supper.

He informed the family, "Art and I are leaving day after tomorrow to go to the Williams ranch to do some blacksmith work. Everything around the village and home seemed to be okay." The next morning A.D., Art, Weldon, Bob and the Mays brothers were looking over the corn crop and decided they would start picking the corn in ten days. A.D. said, "Yawl will have to wait until I get back from the Williams ranch which could be a week or two.

Bob said to Matthew and Mark, "We need to make more corn crib storage in the barns.

A.D. said "You will need to get flat boards from the carpenter in Anahuac." He also stated, "You need to have that job finished before I return from the Williams' ranch." Then A.D. and his boys returned to the blacksmith shop proceeding to shoe the remaining eight horses and by eight o'clock had the wagon fixed. He told Weldon how much to charge for each horse and the wagon. Weldon was pleased to have the confidence that his father had placed in him to collect the money.

A.D. and Art left for the Williams' ranch at 4:00 a.m. and arrived there at 6:00 p.m. Mr. Williams and his wife sat at the table while A.D. and Art ate supper. The Williams family had six boys who came in and talked after they had finished eating. A.D. learned that they had thirty-one horses and nine mules to be shoed. Mr. Williams wanted all his boys to watch while A.D. did his job. At 8:00 they got out the dominoes and had two different games going.

At 9:30 A.D. announced, "I am really tired and need to get to bed. If you would show us where we are to sleep I would appreciate it."

Mrs. Williams led them to a small cabin beside the barn. She gave them sheets and blankets and said, "Breakfast will be at 7:00 in the morning."

Before they went to bed they cleaned up the cabin as best they could but didn't get in bed until about 10:30. They were up by 7:00 a.m. had breakfast and got to work by 8:00. The Williams boys held the horses while A.D. was busy moving the horses in and out quickly. Art was getting nails and whatever size horseshoes were needed for A.D. He had to trim the hooves on one half of the horses. They worked until 7:00 p.m. quitting when they were called to supper.

This went on for three days with the last day mainly shoeing mules. The oldest Williams boy got to shoe two horses and one mule. He did a good job on the horses but not as good on the mule. A.D. thought he might be a little bit afraid. The 4th day several nearby farmers came in with a total of eight horses and eight mules to be shod. They finished all of those the following day. During that day the Williams boys had shown Art around their ranch. He thought they had a pretty good operation with two thousand head of cattle, eighty head of horses and thirty mules. The next morning, they had a 6:00 o'clock breakfast and left at 7:00. Mrs. Williams had packed them a picnic lunch and she sent some blackberry jam home for the family. A.D. and Art were returning with over $110 which was a great week's work. They arrived home at 7:00 p.m. had supper and went to bed exhausted. The next day they prepared to start the corn harvest plus A.D. shoed five horses and two mules before starting the harvest.

The corn harvesting crew consisted of Art, Weldon, Matthew, Mark, Bea May and A.D. Bea May had asked, "May I work with the boys picking corn? I need to get outside and do some real work because I am going crazy in the cabin." It took them ten days to harvest and store the one hundred acres of corn. This was the first year Bob Tims had not helped A.D. with the corn harvest. The corn crop averaged 35 bushels to the acre and A.D., of course, stored most in the barn at his ranch. He gave Mrs. May, Mark and Matthew the job of shelling one hundred bushels of corn which would be used for cornmeal after it was ground and sifted. A.D. had all that crew help him with the production of cornmeal. A.D. told Mrs. May, "I'll pay you $15 for helping with the cornmeal and harvest of the corn crop." "Oh no," She objected. "I insist so take the money." He insisted because he now had ten barrels and one hundred ten pound sacks of cornmeal ready to sell. He put a barrel at his ranch cabin and a barrel at his home in Anahuac. The rest was put in his blacksmith shop where he could more easily sell it. During the whole process he had made sure the May family fully understood how to make the cornmeal and cleanup after the process. A.D. had in mind letting them handle that chore from now on. After all that was finished everyone spent three or four days planting their fall garden.

Frank, Ralph and Bob had come to A.D. and said, "We want to all get together and make cornmeal so we can sell it and make some cash money." A.D. told them, "I have already made 11 barrels of cornmeal and won't need to make any more until December, I think." They said, "We thought we were going to do this together." A.D. said, "Well I've already made my cornmeal so I think ya'll should go on and make your own cornmeal whenever you get ready." Frank got mad and told A.D. "My boys and I will not sell your cornmeal anymore." A.D. replied, "You go on and sell your meal and flour where and when you want to. Just make sure you clean up after you have finished with our grinding mill." Frank said, "Well my boys found the grinding stones so they are ours." A.D. replied, "Don't even go there, because I will use that grinding mill whenever I wish to whether anybody around here likes it or not. You know you can't stop me so don't ever try." Frank and Ralph told A.D. "Don't expect us at anymore of your Sunday dinners." "Okay," replied A.D. and went back to work in his blacksmith shop. Art and Weldon had witnessed all of this arguing and, of course, told their mother. Maggie asked A.D. "Is what the boys said about the argument true?" He confirmed they had an argument and further stated, "I am tired of trying to get things together for our entire group. It's time that they start doing things on their own." Maggie said "Maybe so but ya'll don't have to get mad about it." She said, "I'll go out and talk to them." A.D said "No you won't I forbid it. Give them a month to cool off and then if you want to go talk to them you can." "Okay," She replied, "That's the way I will handle it."

18

CHAPTER

Following the defeat of the centralist Mexican Government in Texas in 1832 the insurgents called for a convention of delegates from each district to come to San Felipe. The convention participants, under the leadership of Stephen F. Austin, adopted a list of changes they wanted and sent it to the National Government of Mexico. These changes were:

1. Reaffirmed their loyalty to the Mexican government and constitution.
2. Tariff exemptions for necessities be extended to Texans for three years.
3. Change the law of 1830 which prohibited Anglo- American immigration.
4. Separation from the Mexican State of Coahuila. Admission of Texas as a separate State in Mexico.
5. Land commissioners be appointed to issue title to East Texas lands.
6. Custom officers be appointed by the mayors of their Jurisdiction.
7. Additional towns be established for areas east of Austin's colony.
8. Government lands to be donated for primary Schools.

The Mexican government disapproved of the convention in January 1833. The convention met again April first with William Wharton presiding as president of the convention of 1833. At both conventions the Atascosita district sent delegates to San Felipe along with 16 other communities in Texas. Representative Warren Hall, Patrick Jack, James Morgan and Claiborne West went to the first convention. For the second convention they sent Patrick Jack, David Burnett, William Harden, Samuel Whiting and Jesse Woodbury. The convention of 1833 adopted the same grievances of the 1832 convention but also framed and adopted a state constitution for Texas. They requested that the Mexican Congress approve all of this. The convention sent Stephen F. Austin to Mexico City seeking approval of the Texans action in the 1833 convention. When the house of deputies delayed taking action on the request, Austin warned the Mexicans that the Texans might organize a State Government without approval of the Mexican authorities. Austin even argued with Vice President Farias about the matter. Austin realized the Mexican government was not going to address the Texans grievances so he wrote the mayor at San Antonio advising them to proceed with plans for a state government.

This letter was intercepted by the Mexican authorities and Austin was arrested in Saltillo. He was jailed without trial and not allowed to talk to anyone. The Texans were upset about Austin's treatment and sent two lawyers, Grayson and Jack, to Mexico City with a petition demanding Austin's release. They were unsuccessful in obtaining Austin's release. Late in 1835 Stephen F. Austin was at last released by Mexico and returned to Texas. Austin had really tried to be a loyal Mexican citizen but in January 1836 he publicly repudiated his loyalty to Mexico. Father Muldoon, Austin's friend was the only one allowed to visit him during his imprisonment. Father Muldoon got in trouble himself in 1834 when he published a paper in favor of the Texas Settlers.

In the meantime, A.D. and his boys, with the help of Matthew and Mark, had planted thirty acres each of oats and wheat the last 2 weeks in October. This crew had gone out to the grinding mill with the wheat leftover from last year's crop and ground six barrels of flour plus one hundred ten-pound sacks of flour. A.D. put a barrel at his ranch cabin and a barrel at his home in Anahuac. In November A.D. had taken his wagon loaded with flour and cornmeal plus two, two-year-old colts from Gray to rancher Solomon. A.D. also sold him one barrel of flour and barrel of cornmeal. He went by another rancher named, Williams, and sold him a barrel of cornmeal and a barrel of flour. A.D. had shod a few horses and mules at both places. He had stopped at some of the smaller farmers in the area and ended up selling fifty sacks each of cornmeal and flour. When he returned home he had two hundred thirty dollars. This venture had taken him a week.

It was now the middle of November and A.D. had a week's worth of work shoeing horses and mules that had been left over from the past two weeks. He planned to spend this week making sure his boys were training Gray Boy for the race that would be held in Anahuac the week of November 24th and 25th. Gene McCoy said, "You know I am concerned about the number of people entering this year since the soldiers have left. We only had 25 horses entered so far." A.D. replied, "We might have a little less but I'll bet it's not much. I know a lot of the people from Harrisburg, San Felipe and Velasco had expressed an interest in coming to the horse races in July and November which took place in Liberty and Anahuac respectfully." Sure, enough a total of 20 more horses from those towns entered the race which gave them a total of 45. Of the original pioneers that came to Perry Point with A.D., only the women were talking because Frank, Ralph and Bob were still mad and not talking to him.

The day came for the big horse race and other competitions. Art thought that Gray Boy was feeling good and ready to run. The best odds given on Gray Boy were two to one so Maggie bet fifty dollars on him just before the first race. There were actually twelve horses in the first race and just eleven in each of the other three races. The entry fee was twenty dollars a horse. Gray Boy won the first race by one length and therefore Maggie claimed her winnings. Art also got one hundred dollars for winning that heat. Gray Boy would have to race in the championship race which would be twelve hundred yards in place of the customary eight hundred yards.

In the meantime, the rifle contests had started and there were three hundred men shooting. A.D. was lucky, he was the tenth shooter and put four shots in the bull's eye at one hundred yards. Frank and another man from Harrisburg did the same thing as A.D. so they split six hundred dollars three ways. The final championship horse race would be at three o'clock for the four horses that had won their heat. Maggie bet one hundred dollars on Gray Boy with four to one odds on him winning. The longer race was harder on Gray Boy but he still won by one length paying Maggie four hundred dollars. Gray Boy received three hundred dollars for winning the final race.

After that race was the greased pig scramble. Ten younger children got a pig to take home with them. Weldon had been cooking two steers and Gene McCoy was cooking a hog and a steer all day to feed the 400 plus people at the Anahuac celebration. The next day they had horseshoe pitching, a checker and domino tournament in the morning. It began to rain around noon so most of the people left. They had certainly had a good time. A.D., of course, was shoeing horses and mules two days before through days after that celebration. He made about $60 for his blacksmith work. The Loggings had made over $900 during the celebration and as usual Gene McCoy had very little supplies left. Even the Carpenter had sold over 20 of his homemade box windows and doors. It would take him three months or more to build and install them. Ralph who made homemade whiskey sold 25 gallons. Even though saw milling was at an early crude stage, a man had established a saw mill in Anahuac. He also got a lot of orders during the celebration. The May family made some money during the celebration by betting on Gray Boy. They were now $100 richer. They had never seen that much money before and were very happy!

They continued working for A.D. building fence and now building his famous water line from the spring on Bob's place. A.D. had spent a day going out and brazing the pipe pieces together. It was working fine and would save a lot of time. He told the May family, "You should think about finding a good place to raise cattle and hogs." He also told them where this should be and his plans for them for the next two years so there was no hurry. They had built several traps near the Trinity where they didn't think anyone would mind them trapping cows.

Christmas was coming and A.D.'s boys, who are now twelve and ten respectively, were more interested in what they could do to increase their cow or horse herds. They each had four cows and two horses. A.D. showed the boys a place about fifteen miles from home where he thought there were some wild cattle. He told the boys, "I think if you build a couple of cow traps at this location, you might get 5 or six cows this winter." It had taken them two hours to ride to the place and A.D. watched while they began to build the two traps. When he saw they were constructing them correctly he gave them a 1/3 of a sack of corn he had brought along and told them, "When you finished ride on home." They would have to check the traps weekly to see if they'd captured any cows. It was about 6:00 p.m. when they finally arrived home and their mother was worried to death. A.D. also gave them $10 each to put in their savings.

Maggie had expressed to A.D. that she wanted a new stove which would make preparing the meals easier. Mr. McCoy had ordered the stove for A.D. and it arrived two days before Christmas. The Logging family also got Patricia some clothes and a few small baby toys for her to play with. Maggie had negotiated peace between the pioneer families and they had decided they were coming to the Christmas party. Everyone seemed to have a good time. A.D. found out Frank and his boys had sold out of all of their cornmeal and flour with their sales trips into the rural areas. Pat had brought a young filly with him and he wanted the gray to breed her. Art told him, "Just put her in the pasture and come get her in about six weeks." Since the Stroud's and Smiths were out of flour and cornmeal and, of course, also out of corn and wheat they asked, "A.D. will you sell us all your corn and wheat so we can make some more cornmeal and flour?" A.D. was not really happy about what they wanted but he said, "I guess I can spare five hundred bushels of corn and 250 bushels of wheat." A.D.'s answer was not what they wanted to hear and said, "We figured we need at least twice that much to be able to continue selling cornmeal and flour." A.D. replied, "That's all I can spare if you want it that's fine if you don't that's fine too. I want $750 for the grain" That was a fair price in the area. Frank and Ralph quickly said, "That will be okay, when can we pick it up?" A.D. replied, "Any time this next week, how about Tuesday at 9:00 a.m. at my ranch?" "Okay," They said, "That's a deal." A.D. would still have 1,000 bushels of corn and five hundred bushels of wheat left and that was enough to feed his cows and horses and still be able to make some cornmeal and flour for himself.

They proceeded to eat and play checkers and dominoes while the kids went out in the Bay in the rowboats making themselves completely exhausted. When the company left, everyone was ready for bed. A.D. talked to Maggie that night and told her, "I really didn't like the way I was forced to sell some of my corn and wheat. It was like they expected me to give them the corn and wheat. I'm kind of tired of that attitude from them. I wanted to keep peace but I will not be run over." They picked up their corn and wheat Tuesday.

A.D. went to have a long talk with the May family about what they should be doing this winter. The boys told A.D., "We have been building fence on the good days and just looking after the livestock on the bad days, making sure they are fed and as comfortable as they can be." They had plenty of food, in a warm cabin and told A.D., "We have captured three wild cows already from the traps we built. We hope we can catch a lot more." A.D. said, "When spring roundup comes we'll have to put your brand on them." They had shot three deer and gave A.D. one to take home. He was upset because Frank and Ralph had told him they could not pay him until the first of March. So, A.D. made them sign a paper to that effect. They did not like that at all and A.D. said "If you don't want to sign a note then give me my corn and wheat back I really didn't want to sell it to you in the first place." Frank and Ralph thought to themselves, A.D. has become really bad about money, and A.D. thought, those so called friends believe I should just give them anything and everything they want. They signed the note.

1833 was beginning and A.D. spent a month at home taking care of his blacksmith shop. The boys were still checking on the ships coming to Anahuac or going up or down the Trinity River. The Logging's were still selling about three steers and three hogs every two months from their small corral near the dock.

A pretty large rancher, named Henderson, had brought in two mares to put in with Gray. Henderson asked, "In about six weeks will you bring those mares back to my place? I will have at least a week's worth of blacksmith work ready for you?" He continued, "I have two friends that have a number of horses and when you come to work on my ranch they would also like you to come to their ranches, which are nearby." A.D. said, "That would be great."

He proceeded to work until it was the middle of February then went to Mr. Henderson's ranch. He spent two and 1/2 weeks in that area shoeing over 70 horses and 40 mules plus he repaired four wagons and came home with over $200. In his absence 20 horses and ten mules had been left at his blacksmith shop.

The May family had come into the village to buy some supplies. They asked, "Would it be possible for Maggie to start teaching us how to read, write and do arithmetic?" "Of course," responded Maggie, "I would be happy to teach yawl." The boys would ride in Monday and Thursday morning for three hours of school. Mrs. May also told Maggie, "The Stroud's and Smiths have been coming by and picking up a bushel or two of corn about every week. They said you told him it was ok." A.D. assured, "It is not okay and I will ride out and let them know tomorrow. But, I want the boys to come with me." They were okay with that and the next morning A.D. went to the Stroud's and Smith's place telling them, "Do not come by my ranch and pick up corn or wheat because I will not have enough to feed or for planting seed this coming spring." He also told them, "I expect to be paid $1 a bushel for all the grain you have picked up on the six trips to my ranch." They agreed and said, "We will not pick up any more grain from you and we will pay for the extra grain we have already picked up." That took a half a day of A.D.'s time and he thought it was uncalled for. He thought that these people have a lot of gall and if you don't stop them they will just keep on borrowing what they want.

A.D. rode over to his ranch cabin with the Mays' boys and paid them $60 each telling them, "You are paid through March." He also gave their mother $15 for her help. While he was there Bob Tims rode up and asked A.D. "When am I going to paid?" A.D. replied "Bob you have not worked with me on anything in the last six months, why should I pay you for not working?" A.D. paid him $20 anyway. He told A.D. "Start including me when you have the spring roundup, planting, de-weeding and harvesting." A.D. assured him, "I will do that." He then asked, "How are you doing on your home place?" Bob told A.D., "I have finished the cabin, barn and corral. Also, I have fenced 2, 150-acre pastures so that I can run cattle on them if I need to. My dad and I now have twelve cows but we still need a bull." A.D. said "I've got a bull you can have for $15. Do you want to pick him up today?" He said "By golly, I'll just ride back to your shop with you and drive him back to my place."

A.D. had told his kids, the May's brothers and Bob "I want to start working the ground for the corn crop next Monday. I plan to plant 150 acres. I want all of you to be ready to work two solid weeks straight at that time." Monday came and most farmers were busy in the fields planting corn. In one week, they had plowed all 150 acres and the next three days they finished harrowing. Four days later they had finished the planting. Art and Weldon were mucking out the barns while the rest of them were spreading horse manure and covering fifteen acres. A.D. was well behind in his blacksmith chores and spent three days shoeing horses, mules and repairing wagons.

A.D. and Art went to the two large ranchers, White and Solomon shoeing about 35 horses and mules and repairing four wagons.

While working for Mr. White, he asked A.D., "Are you going to take any steers to Louisiana this year?"

A.D. told him, "No, but I would sure like to go on the drive next year."

"That's fine," he said, "but I wondered if you would ask those three Mexican friends of yours if they wanted to help us with the drive this year?"

"I sure will and I am certain they want to help you."

When they returned home, it was time to work the cattle by castrating the male calves and branding all the new calves and other stock that needed branding. The Loggings were now building up quite a herd of horses and none of them had the Double Diamond A brand on them. A.D. had asked the three Mexican friends to come over and help him brand the horses. It turned out to be quite a chore and they were great help with the project. After that the Mexicans rode over and verified that they would help with the cattle drive to Louisiana this year with rancher White.

It was time to harvest the fifty-acre oat crop which yielded one thousand two hundred fifty bushels. They then began weeding the corn crop. A.D. had all his young help handle that chore. He worked in his blacksmith shop, all week and was finally caught up. The following week they ground five hundred pounds of cornmeal and five hundred pounds of flour at the grinding mill located close to the Trinity River. He took some to his ranch home and some to his town home. The rest of it he took to his blacksmith shop where he was able to sell most of the cornmeal and flour. A.D. always fed the hulls from the wheat and corn grindings to his hogs. They loved it!

Art and Weldon had been preparing not only Gray Boy for racing, but another horse named Checker. They took Gray, Gray Boy and Checker out to the race track in Anahuac and raced them twice. Gray Boy barely won both races and the boys decided that they would race them twice a week until the Liberty celebration in July. They again began to weed the corn crop after that week. A.D. had to spend four days working in the blacksmith shop. It was early June and they began to harvest the wheat crop, which yielded thirty bushels to the acre. A.D. stored all of it in the barn at his ranch. His Mexican friends had gone on the thirty day cattle drive and returned at the end of May. A.D. and the boys spent the rest of June training their racehorses and building fence for a two hundred fifty acre pasture. He was trying to use the abundant cedar as posts that had been cut in the winter. There was plenty of cedar, and if this wooden fence lasted over five years that would be great.

A.D. had made arrangements for his Mexican friends to guard the Logging livestock, ranch, cabin, blacksmith shop and village cabin for five days, while they were gone to the Liberty celebration. They agreed on a payment of forty dollars total. The Logging's were going to take two horses to enter in the races this year. Gray Boy who had won before and Art was going to ride him. The second horse, Checker, was going to be ridden by Art's brother Weldon. They began their trip at 4:00 a.m., July 1st, and arrived in Liberty at 8:00 p.m. They immediately went to the local farmer who had rented them his barn the previous years, paying him the usual twenty-five dollars for the use. Things were so bad between the pioneers, who went to Texas together and settled in Anahuac, that they didn't even discuss traveling with the Logging's this year. The McCoy's, Tims and Mays were the only families that went with them this time. A.D. had brought his blacksmith wagon and another wagon so that they would have room for his family to sleep in the wagons. Gene had only brought one wagon because he, his wife and daughter could sleep in one wagon. They ate and went right to bed, not rising until eight o'clock the next morning.

After breakfast the boys took their racehorses over to the track trying to find the best location for the horses to run on this track. They practiced racing two times and it seemed like both the horses were feeling good. Finding the best spots to run in these rough small-town tracks could be the difference between winning and losing. A.D. and his boys and Gene McCoy went out to shoot their long guns practicing for the shooting contest July 4th. A.D. spent the rest of the afternoon shoeing 11 horses and mules. He finally stopped working at 8:00 that night. The boys found a couple of friends they had met the two previous years and had a lot of fun playing with them. July 3rd the Shrouds and the Smiths arrived. They were all upset that their friends had already arrived.

The Mays had come along to see if anyone was living in their old house. They specifically wanted to see if Mr. May had returned to their house. They found out no one was living in their old cabin and that Mr. May had not returned. When they found that out they insisted on returning to the cabin in Anahuac. A.D. told them, "It will not be safe for you to return without the other wagons. Just relax and enjoy the celebration." They finally decided that was the best thing to do. The next day A.D. paid for himself, his two boys and the Mays brothers to enter the long gun shooting contest. As usual A.D. shot tenth out of three hundred twenty-six shooters and put four in bull's-eye within the two- minute limit. Art and Weldon each put two in the target but missed the other shot within the two-minute limit. Mark and Matthew did the same thing Art and Weldon did. Even though the boys knew they had not won, it was a lot of fun just to compete in the contest. A.D. and Frank tied for first place and split four hundred dollars. Everyone hurried back to get the horses ready for the afternoon runs. Weldon and Checker had won the first race. Art and Gray Boy won the third race which meant they would run against each other and three other horses for the championship. At 3:30, the five horses that had won previous races competed for the championship. Gray Boy won and received a total of six hundred dollars for winning two races. Checker received one hundred dollars for winning the first race. He finished a close second almost beating Gray Boy for the championship. Of course, Maggie won three hundred dollars betting on her two sons riding Gray Boy and Checker. The boys were in great spirits after the races. Everyone wanted to talk to them when they saw 'em.

That night they had the usual big dance and everyone got along pretty good until nine o'clock. Three separate fights broke out within five minutes and within ten minutes there were at least twenty men fighting. The entire group went about ten yards from the dance floor and watched the fight. Ralph Smith who had been drinking was also fighting and not doing very well so A.D. and Frank went out on the dance floor to try and rescue Ralph. They had to fight just to get to him and then again to get themselves off the dance floor. Ralph was mad because he wanted to go back and fight.

A.D. told him, "We're not going out there anymore to save your ass."

"I don't care," he said, and proceeded to go back out on the dance floor and start fighting again. That meant that the entire group had to stay there and make sure he wasn't too badly hurt. Otherwise, his wife and kids would've just been waiting there helplessly until the fight was finished. Fighting finally stopped after about twenty minutes but most people were not in the mood to dance anymore and returned to their campground for the rest of the night.

While returning to the Logging camp area, Ralph Smith was bragging, "I sold over fifty-one-gallon jugs of liquor, which I made at my ranch."

He told A.D., "I made more money-making liquor than anything else I have ever done."

A.D. said, "Yes, I know the next thing you'll be doing is opening a tavern."

"I sure wish I could," Smith replied. That night the skeeters and the heat made sleeping pretty hard.

The next day A.D. was busy shoeing horses and mules while the greased pig contest was going on along with the checker and domino championships. That night there was another dance scheduled. A lot of people had already left and there were only three small fights that night. The band stopped playing music playing at eleven o'clock. The group had decided to leave at five o'clock in the morning trying to get home to Anahuac at a decent time. On the trip home they had a couple of wagon problems and didn't get home until eleven o'clock that evening. The men that had been protecting their stock and homes reported there had been no problems. Everyone was exhausted and slept late the next morning. A.D. spent the rest of the week working at his blacksmith shop.

The following week, A.D. and Art went to the Solomon ranch and the following week they were going to the Williams ranch to do blacksmith work for those large ranchers. The first week they shoed forty horses and mules and repaired two wagons. The second week they shoed 35 horses and mules and repaired four wagons. Art had one boy at each of the ranchers about his age and they had a good time playing together.

When they returned to Anahuac, the Mays brothers told A.D., "We think there are four or five cows that are sick. You really need to come and inspect them." A.D., Art and Weldon rode out immediately to check the sick cattle. No one seemed to know what was wrong with these cattle, but A.D. immediately separated them from the rest of the herd putting them in a small pasture close by. They then rode to see the big cattleman, James White, to ask him to come check on the sick cows.

He told A.D., "I will be there in the morning. I can't come right now."

The boys and A.D. returned to Anahuac preparing to meet Mr. White the next morning. Mr. White arrived at ten o'clock and spent an hour checking the sick cattle.

He stated, "A.D. I really don't know what's wrong with these cattle. It could be something they ate." He proceeded to go to the other pasture to see if he could discover any harmful plants.

At noon Mr. White told A.D., "I am sorry I don't know what's wrong with your cows, but I'm glad you separated them like you did. I would keep close watch on your stock and separate them just as you've been doing." His final words to A.D. were, "Keep me posted so that I know what is happening to your herd."

A.D. assured him, "I will definitely do that." A.D. paid everyone working for him through September, mainly because he had enough money at this time to do it.

He told the Mays brothers, "Keep a close watch on the herd and if even one cow gets sick, come get me."

A.D. spent the next two weeks shoeing horses and mules. During this time, he also asked the human Doctor, Dr. Lily, to go out and look at the sick cattle.

He reported, "I don't know what is wrong with your cattle".

Mr. White had told a neighboring cattleman about the Logging cattle problem and he had come over and looked at the cows.

Mr. Crawford said, "I really don't know what is wrong with the cattle either. But there is a man just south of Liberty that is a pretty good cow Doctor and maybe you should try him." The next two weeks there had been no more sick cattle and the five sick ones were well. So, A.D. put it out of his mind for the time being.

It was time to prepare for the big corn harvest which they would start in about a week. A.D. tried to get all his blacksmith work caught up so he could spend all his time on the corn harvest. It took two weeks to harvest the one hundred fifty acres of corn, which only yielded twenty-five bushels to the acre. Next everyone planted their fall garden.

Politics and fighting had taken a lull, except for West Texas where the Indians had made several raids capturing women, children, horses and killing most of the men that opposed them on those raids. In West Texas the folks had tried to organize militias to oppose the Indians when they attacked. In Southeast Texas they did not organize a militia but thought someday they might need them.

Sunday, while the Loggings were having dinner with their friends, Gene McCoy came over and told the group, "I think we are going to have a hurricane. Most of us should go to our cabins outside of Anahuac. The last storm they had the water was almost knee deep everywhere."

It rained heavily for two days and then the winds picked up to hurricane force. As soon as these settlers had been warned they began to move all their livestock away from the water. They picked up everything on the ground in their cabins or shops and moved it up higher.

Bob Tims told A.D. "Your family can stay at my cabin and I'll go stay with my parents." The Loggings loaded up their essentials in one wagon and drove that wagon along with the blacksmithing wagon to the Tims' ranch. After three days they returned to the cabin and shop in the village. On their return, A.D. and the boys killed four poisonous snakes, which alerted them to be careful entering the buildings. The Logging's cabin and shop seemed undamaged from the storm. But many of the other buildings had the support beams outside washed away. This meant they would have to put up more supports or their cabins would collapse. The local Carpenter was urging them to get bricks from the Fort and build their supports out of them. He used the example of what A.D. had done to support the front of his building. A.D. and the boys, helped by collecting three wagon loads of brick and bringing it to three different merchants along Front Street. A.D. and the boys then went snake hunting along Front Street. That day they killed nine more snakes and warned every one of the danger. They then began to put their house and blacksmith shop back in order. A.D. and the boys then rode out looking over their livestock. They drove the horses, three steers and three hogs that were in the dock coral back to the back of the blacksmith shop.

The Smiths had come to town and informed everyone on Front Street they were setting up a tavern in one of the abandoned buildings. They had again asked Maggie, "Will you start teaching our kids the basics of reading, writing, arithmetic and Bible study three days a week from 12:00 until 4:00 p.m.?"

Maggie replied, "Of course, I will be glad to do it." She was never paid for teaching children and never asked to be paid. A.D. thought it was just their way to have her babysit the kids while they ran the tavern. It took them a week to get the tavern set up the way they wanted. Ralph had Gene McCoy ordered him some other liquor from New Orleans and that arrived in Anahuac the week they were setting up. They put a sign up at the tavern and on A.D.'s corral down by the docks. Ralph planned on selling mostly his own homemade whiskey. A.D. and Maggie were not happy about them setting up a tavern but were glad it was at the other end of town.

Ralph told A.D., "The Mexican soldiers are going to look after our cattle and hogs."

A.D. asked "How are you going to pay for this?"

He said, "The ex-soldiers said they would do it for a gallon of whiskey each, every month."

A.D. asked, "What are you going to do about planting your corn, oats and garden?"

Ralph replied "I'll get the ex-soldiers to help me."

A.D. said "Good, I won't have to sell or give you grain to get by anymore."

Ralph just said "Oh no, I'll have plenty of money to get by without your help."

All of the locals at that time were planting wheat and oats. This took A.D. and his boys two weeks to get fifty acres of wheat and fifty acres of oats in the ground. A.D. had bought two loads of spoiled fish which the boys had to spread on twenty acres of those crops. The May brothers and Bob each planted twenty acres of wheat and twenty acres of oats. They needed the grain for their own families and livestock. They borrowed A.D.'s equipment and mules to plant their crops. Actually A.D. was glad to loan them his equipment, they were showing their independence.

The Anahuac celebration was about a month away and the hurricane had torn up the racetrack. Everyone spent three days rebuilding the track as best they could, but it really wasn't the way they wanted. Art and Weldon had begun the last part of training of Gray Boy and Checker for the upcoming races. Their two horses were closely matched and A.D.'s two boys were really competitive. Finally, it was the week of the Anahuac celebration and it appeared there were going to be about fifty horses competing in the horse races. The entry fee was twenty dollars. That was a lot of money for most of the people that had entered their horses in the race. Frank and Ralph each donated a steer and a hog for the celebration. This was the first year A.D. had not been forced to donate the meat for the celebration. November 24th was the first day of the celebration and the first competition was long rifle shooting. There were over four hundred men competing by hitting a target one hundred twenty-five yards away as many times as you could, within two minutes. A.D. and his son, Art, where in the first bunch of fifty shooters. A.D. put four shots in the bull's-eye and Art put three shots in the target.

Ralph smartly said to A.D. "I guess you think you'll win."

A.D. replied, "Yes I do. If I lose it certainly won't be to you, Ralph." A.D. hurried on over to the blacksmith shop because he had a large number of horses and mules the people had left to be shoed while they were attending the celebration.

He told Art and Weldon, "Go over and run your horses on the track at least twice, and then cool them down. When you've finished come back and help me blacksmith." All the businesses in Anahuac were busy including Ralph Smith and his tavern.

At one o'clock, Frank came over to the shop and gave A.D. two hundred fifty dollars which was his half for tying for first place in the rifle shooting contest. A.D. thought Frank had tied him again, but that wasn't the case, a man from Harrisburg had tied him this year.

That afternoon they had one hundred kids trying to catch ten greased pigs and if they caught one they got to take it home. It was good entertainment for about thirty minutes. The dance started at 7:00 p.m. About seventy-five men were already drunk and they caused nothing but problems all evening long. Ralph was not at the dance because he and his wife were serving as much booze as they could to the people that came in the tavern.

The dance finally ended at eleven o'clock and A.D. had made the boys stay with the horses to make sure no one fooled with them before the races tomorrow. After the dance, A.D. sent the boys home to make sure they got a good night's sleep, and he guarded the horses the rest of the evening.

About 2:00 a.m. A.D. was awakened by someone trying to open the doors to his shop. He grabbed his double barrel pistol and opened the door. There were two men standing there. They didn't say anything, they just walked off.

A.D. told them, "I'll see y'all in the morning."

Race day was here. Gray Boy won by one length in his race and in the third race Checkers won by two lengths. The championship race was scheduled to start at three o'clock, and the best odds they would give on the Logging's horses were two to one. Maggie had already bet a hundred dollars on both the boys' race and now had four hundred dollars. She again bet a hundred dollars on each of her boys. A.D. would be happy if either one of them won. Weldon thought he would not run checkers on the most favorable ground because he was afraid of being boxed in by the other horses. The race was on and it was Art who got boxed in. Checkers won the race by two lengths winning a five-hundred-dollar purse. After the race A.D. made sure the boys took care of their horses and brought them back to the blacksmith shop where he could protect them. A.D. still figured someone was going to try to hurt those horses because his horses had won every race in that area for over two years.

The man that handled the bets had gone to Ralph's Tavern and A.D. had to go in there to pick up the winnings. While he was in the tavern he spotted the two men that had tried to break into his shop the previous night and he confronted them about it. They gave A.D. some lame lying excuse. A.D. said, "If you come around any of my places tonight, I'll kill you." One of the men then pulled a knife and tried to cut A.D. He knocked the knife away and left telling everyone in a very loud voice, "I'll be back and if you are still here I'm going to kill you right here. So you better not be here when I get back." Ralph tried to calm him down. A.D. thought things had gone too far, so he couldn't stop. He got his two double barrel pistols and slung the long rifle on his back, loaded all of them and returned to the tavern. Ralph told A.D., "The two men took off right after you left. I think they have left the area." A.D. then began to ask around who were these men and where do they live? He was told their names and that they lived in Harrisburg. A.D. left the tavern and looked all over the Anahuac area but could not find them. When they went to the dance that night, A.D. wore his two pistols. This made many people nervous but he didn't care. A.D. and Maggie left the dance at ten o'clock, and everyone breathed a sigh of relief. The boys had been watching the shop, horses and house while their parents were at the dance and had no trouble. A.D. had decided he would again stay in his blacksmith shop to make sure the horses or any other material was not harmed. There was no trouble that night.

A.D. and the boys worked for twelve hours the next day to get all the horses and mules shoed so the attendees could finally go home. Mark, Matthew their mother, Mr. and Mrs. Tims and their son Bob had all attended the big celebration and had a good time. A.D. had talked to the boys and Bob about protecting all the livestock each and every day because some of these people that came could have been looking to steal stock or anything they could find of value. They had taken the hint from A.D. to closely check the stock during the Anahuac celebration. The area had one day of rain since they planted the wheat and oats. It did seem like most of the seeds were sprouting but several good rains were needed to make a crop by May or June.

Christmas time came and the Loggings had ordered new store-bought mattresses from New Orleans to make their sleeping more comfortable. That was all anybody got with the exception of Patricia and she got some toys from Santa.

January of 1834, A.D. took off to blacksmith at the Henderson ranch and spent two weeks shoeing fifty horses, 25 mules and repairing six wagons. He made $250 for that two weeks work. During his time there he had seen a small farmer who had some outstanding bulls. A.D. needed some new breeding stock for his cows, so he bought 6, one-year old bulls to put in his herd in about six months. This cost him of $120 plus free blacksmithing for a year. Duke and A.D. drove the bull's home and put them in the small lot behind the blacksmith shop. Later they were moved to a small fifteen-acre pasture close to the fort.

A.D. got home late and Maggie said, "Weldon is running a high temperature and you should to get Dr. Lilly." He went right over to get the Doctor who came right over saying, "It looks like Weldon has yellow fever. Everybody will have to stay in the house until this is over." A.D. said, "I just got home and I really haven't been here." Dr. Lilly said, "Just don't sleep here or come down for any meals until we get this thing stopped. The only thing you can do is try to keep the fever down by bathing the patient with cool water." He admitted, "There are several cases of yellow fever in the area. I am going to try to get some medicine that will reduce the fever and pain." Dr. Lilly asked A.D., "Will you find a willow tree and get a big quantity of bark from that tree, then grind it up as fine as you can and bring it to me?" After A.D. brought the ground willow bark to Dr. Lilly, he then further ground the bark to a very fine powder and put some of it in one hundred capsules, which he planned to use later. He then made up a liquid of honey and ground willow bark. He told Maggie, "You can give one ounce of the willow bark every twelve hours for pain and to help keep the temperature down." He also gave them some black cumin seeds that were ground up into oil that should be taken twice a day. Patricia, Art and their mother eventually got a milder case of yellow fever. It took four weeks for everyone to be cleared. At that time, Dr. Lilly gave them one gallon of alcohol and said, "Rub down all the cooking utensils, pots, pans, silverware, plates, beds, sidewalls and floors before A.D. can come back and resume a normal life with this family."

In February they got two inches of rain two different times and that made the oats and wheat look a lot better.

March started off as a warm, no rain month, but A.D. and the others knew they needed to plant corn in order to feed their stock. A.D. had his corn planted by March 15th and the day after he finished planting they got a one-inch rain each month right up until the corn harvest. The harvest was the first part of September because it'd turned out to be an extremely hot summer for this area. In April they de-weeded the corn crop and A.D. spent two weeks doing Mr. White's blacksmithing work. When he returned it was time to get his herd ready, along with the other ranchers to drive them to Opelousas, Louisiana. A.D. was going to sell more of his herd this year than he usually did, because he thought he would be short on feed next year. A.D. had 150 head, Frank had 70 head, Bob had 20 head and Matthew and Mark Mays had 20 head and Ralph Smith had ten head. The three large ranchers had 1,500 head together. A.D. and Frank were going on the drive and asked Sergeant Martinez, "Would you go to help on the drive? "I will be glad to," He replied, "I will do it for $30 if I can take twenty head of my cattle with me." So that was settled.

19

At four a.m. on May 1, the cattle drive started. As usual, a slow start encumbered progress. The men camped just one-mile past Liberty on the first night even though they didn't stop until 8:00 p.m.

The next morning, they didn't get started until 7:00 and only made eleven miles that day. The pace was set for the next nine days until they arrived at the Sabine River. One day was eaten up getting all the cattle and horses across the river.

That evening some cattle rustlers made off with fifty head from the herd. Mr. White informed the local sheriff about the theft.

"We are going to track down the cattle rustlers and get our cattle back," White informed the sheriff. "You can count on that."

The sheriff wanted nothing to do with their posse and told them, "Don't take the law into your own hands." He got an earful from their group.

"He's probably in cahoots with them," A.D. surmised. The drovers agreed they should continue on with the drive while A.D., Sergeant Martinez, Mr. White and his foreman formed the posse to go after the rustlers. They figured the rustlers had about a six-hour lead on the posse.

They rode hard until eight o'clock, just about dusk, when they finally caught up with the stolen herd. The posse saw there were only four unsuspecting rustlers who were just beginning to have their supper, leaving no one to guard the herd.

A.D. quietly got their horses as the other three rode in, shooting and threatening the rustlers. The rustlers never got off a shot. They had butchered a steer for supper. The four men looked starved and claimed they didn't have any money for food and that their families were starving.

Mr. White took their guns, gave them four steers and let them keep their horses.

"I will leave your guns with the ferry man on the Sabine River," he told them. "You can pick them up in two weeks."

The rustlers and the posse spent the night at the same camp and had supper together from the steer they had butchered. Everyone left at 6:00 a.m. with the posse driving the cattle back to the rest of the herd. It took two days to catch up with the main herd, and it looked like they would get to Opelousas in about three more days.

Mr. White had warned the ranchers that he thought the best we would be able to get was about $12 a head. Everyone was happy that he was wrong because they sold for $14 a head. Even Mr. White was pleased. They went out had a big meal and celebrated that night.

"I am leaving early in the morning" A.D. informed the other settlers. "How many are coming with me?"

A.D., Frank, Sergeant Gonzales and his other two Mexican friends were the only ones that left that morning.

Mr. White cautioned them, as usual. A.D. took all precautions he'd learned from experience on his previous trail ride. He had all of his group's money on the extra horse he had bought.

The group averaged forty miles a day. They got to the ferry and crossed the river on the fourth day. On the fifth day of the return trip, they traveled another forty-five miles, reaching the abandoned farmhouse with the dilapidated barn where they could stable the horses.

Lo and behold, in the middle of the night, eight men rode in shooting. The real advantage the ranchers had was that the riders didn't know about the guard in the barn or that the man guarding the cabin was hidden out of sight. A.D.'s group shot and wounded three men plus they captured one more, but the others rode off.

The group turned the captured man over to the sheriff in Liberty and told him about the incident. Frank was the only one of the group that was shot, both in the arm and leg. Both of the bullets had gone clean through, so they cleaned up the wounds, stopped the bleeding and bandaged him tightly.

The group was still a two-day ride from Liberty and the nearest doctor. Frank was in a great deal of pain by the time they reached Liberty.

The local doctor tended his wounds, advising that he shouldn't travel for a couple of days. However, the next morning Frank wanted to get home and they all accomplished that together.

He asked A.D., "Will you have Dr. Lily come out and see me tomorrow?"

"Sure, I will," he said.

Frank took his $980 and the $140 that went to Ralph Smith.

"Why don't you just drop it off at the Tavern?" Frank asked.

A.D. said, "No because I don't want to put up with him!"

The next day, A.D. distributed the proceeds to Bob and the Mays brothers for their cattle.

A.D. had a grand homecoming. He hid $2,000 more in his money tree. It now contained over $10,000. By all standards in the area which they lived, they were considered rich!

The middle of June was fast approaching when the farmers had to start harvesting their wheat and oats. The crops didn't look very good this year. They only yielded ten bushels to the acre for both wheat and the oats.

Since Bob and the Mays brothers had planted twenty acres of wheat and oats, they had the same poor yields as A.D. Realizing the area would be short of all grain, A.D. bought half of Bob's and the May brothers' wheat and oats for $500 each.

Those boys thought they were rich and they still had enough grain to feed their family and livestock for the coming year.

Art and Weldon had been working hard the last three months to get Gray Boy and Checkers ready for the big race in Liberty this coming July. They thought they were unbeatable and would win just like they always did.

Bob and his new wife, Watha, planned to make the trip to the Liberty celebration and to meet her parents there. The Stroud's were going and the boys would take four hundred pounds of flour and cornmeal in a separate wagon to sell at the celebration. Ralph Smith and his family were going, and A.D. thought he had about fifty gallons of homemade whiskey he was going to try to sell.

A.D. was taking one wagon for the family and his blacksmith wagon. Mr. McCoy and his family were also going in this nine-wagon train. Mrs. May and her sons were taking their wagon to check on their old cabin on the farm outside of Liberty, always hopeful that the boys' father had returned.

The wagon train arrived at their destination on the evening of July 1, after a full day of travel. Everything was arranged for the group to stay around the same barn and pasture where they had previously stayed. They all ate and went straight to bed because it was late and besides they were tired. The next morning the boys were taking their horses out to run on the new racetrack.

Amazingly, the May family found their father had returned after a three-year absence. The old codger hadn't changed a bit. He lit into Bea with a vengeance for taking it on herself to leave their cabin.

Late that afternoon, the May brothers and their mother returned to the encampment.

"Well, the old man returned to our old cabin," they told A.D. "He tried to beat our mother so we left him." Bruises on Bea's face testified to the incident.

"I don't know what I would've done if the boys had not been there," Bea explained. "The two of them actually fought their father. I had to pull them off of him, or I think they would've killed him."

A.D. and Maggie were sympathetic to Bea, encouraging her to resume her life in Anahuac.

All the men in their group entered the shooting contest including the teenagers. They shot early with A.D. only putting three in the bull's-eye and one slightly outside this year. Art and Weldon each put two shots in the target. The rest of the group shot well, but even Frank was a little bit off.

That evening Frank found A.D. blacksmithing.

"We tied with three others for first place. There will be shoot off at 8:00 o'clock in the morning."

A.D. couldn't believe he was still in the running for this contest! After supper, he went out and shot about twenty practice rounds. His competitors were doing the same thing.

The next morning A.D. had to shoot last out of the five that were shooting. He put two in the bull's eye and two just outside the bull's-eye at one hundred twenty-five yards. All his competitors did the same thing so they declared a tie with all five splitting the $500.

When A.D. returned to the camp area, the boys told him, "Checkers and Gray Boy both won their heats! Now we have to race in the final!"

A.D. looked over the winning field and thought the boys would be lucky to win this race because there were a lot of fast horses racing this time. The championship race started at three o'clock and, sure enough, another horse won by a length over Gray Boy and Checkers who were tied for second place.

Art and Weldon were devastated but their parents tried to console them, telling them they were not going to win every time. The money they had won betting on the boys winning the first heats was lost on the bets they made on the championship race. Maggie said, "At least we came out even and didn't lose any money."

Out of all the excitement, Mr. May provided the biggest flurry of this year's celebration. He came to town with a gun, determined to harm his wife.

Matthew and Mark saw him first and came running up to Frank and A.D. screaming, "We need to kill him!"

A.D. quietly told their mother and the boys a plan.

"Y'all go twenty yards past our location and stay there. He will see you and that means he will have to come very close to us in order to get to you."

The plan worked because in just a short time later that old man May came running past shouting, "Everyone get out of my way,"

A.D. and Frank simply walked up behind the old badger and clubbed him over the head.

"Who hit me?" he demanded when he came back to consciousness. "I'll kill him, whoever he is!"

There was a long pause. A whispering crowd had gathered.

"You have a gun," A.D said. "Do you know how to use it?"

"Oh no! If I kill you," May said, "they'll hang me, so I'm just going to beat you to death with my fists."

He dropped the gun to the ground as he started toward him. A.D. also dropped his guns and knocked the man on the ground as he came charging. May got up, and A.D. kicked him in both knees. He went down again. As he was getting up slowly, A.D. hit him with a right and a left, and he went down again. The crowd oohed and ahhed, some of them egging the old man on.

A.D. became so riled up, he picked May up and took him to the corral where he tied him up with rope in a spread-eagled fashion.

"Mr. May," he said, "if you ever hit anybody around here again, specifically a woman, I'm going to hang you myself!"

A.D. turned to the crowd.

"Anybody takes the ropes off this man will answer to me."

He left him tied up at the corral all night. About sundown, May, began to holler, so A.D. went over and gagged him.

In the meantime, he took Mrs. May to see the sheriff, and they explained everything that had happened.

The sheriff thought they had handled it well. He asked, "Will you let him go in the morning?"

A.D. promised, "Yes, I will."

Frank said walking towards his camp, "I think I'll take his horse and give it to his family."

"That's a good idea, Frank," A.D. replied.

The May family was in fear that the old man would try hurt them or someone else when he was let go.

"I think he's too embarrassed to try to come back here and do something," the Sheriff said.

That day, A.D. shod horses and mules until dark-thirty while Frank and Pat peddled the rest of their flour and cornmeal. Ralph Smith had already sold out of all of his homemade whiskey. The others played dominoes, checkers and watched the greased pig contest, enjoying the leisure of the holiday.

A.D. was really tired but he knew the rest of his group wanted to start for home early in the morning. So, he got up before sunrise to finish up his blacksmith work and pack the wagon to be ready to leave by six o'clock. The wagons got back to Anahuac safely at ten o'clock that night. Everyone was tired and slept late the next morning.

Sergeant Gonzales told A.D., "We had no trouble protecting your stock and buildings." He also told him, "The second day you and your family were gone, three men rode past the cow herd so a friend and I followed them into Anahuac. They stopped in the store and finally the tavern." "We made sure these men knew we were following them," he continued. "They left the Tavern about 10:00 o'clock, and we followed them until they were ten miles out of town."

"Thanks," A.D. replied. "That was a good job, and I appreciate it." He then paid him $40.

A.D. and the boys spent two weeks catching up with his blacksmith business, shoeing several horses and mules. The corn crop looked bad as they had not had much rain in June or July.

A.D. had plans to go to Sol Barrows' and Mr. Williams' ranches in August to do his yearly blacksmithing for them. This usually took two weeks, and A.D. planned to take Art with him so he would have help. They left with the blacksmith wagon August 1st and spent one week at Sol's place. While they were there they shoed thirty-five horses, fifteen mules and repaired four wagons. The income for that week was $120, which was the largest amount A.D. had ever been paid for one week's work.

A.D. really got along with this rancher. They played dominoes every night he was there. Sol's son and Art had also become good friends. They were about the same age. When A.D. got ready to go to the Williams ranch, Sol said, "Why don't you let the boy stay with my son while you're working over there? They seem to get along pretty good."

A.D. replied, "Are you sure it will be okay?"

"Sure," Sol said, "If anything goes wrong we know where to get in touch with you."

A.D. said, "Okay that's fine and, Art, you better be on your best behavior."

A.D. went on the Williams ranch and shoed twenty horses, five mules, repaired three wagons. Williams' charge for the work was $60. Every time A.D. went to the Williams' ranch, he had the same Williams boy work with him to try to learn the blacksmith business. That way he could begin doing the blacksmith business for their ranch.

On his way home to Anahuac, he picked up Art who was excited because that was the first time he had been away from his family all on his own.

A.D., Art and Weldon spent the next week blacksmithing and by September 1st they were again caught up with that work.

Everyone began harvesting their poor crop of corn. Since the 200-acre field of corn that A.D. had planted was fenced, he decided to harvest just the ear corn and leave the stalks for the cows to graze in October and November. He only harvested two thousand bushels of ear corn. That would not be enough for his herd and his cornmeal business. He immediately began to try to find people that would sell what little corn they had for $1 a bushel. He was able to eventually buy another two thousand bushels. He had all his help shelling one hundred bushels of ear corn so that he could grind eighty pounds of corn meal.

Gene McCoy had raised the price of cornmeal in the general store. A.D. noticed immediately that it was going for $8 for a ten-pound sack. A.D. followed suit, matching the price.

The cattlemen were all working their herds in October by branding new calves or captured cows and castrating the bull calves that had been born since May. A.D. now had one hundred twenty-five cows; Frank and his boys had the same number. Bob and his family, the May family, Ralph Smith's family and the ex-Mexican soldiers all had herds of fewer than fifty head. None of them had near as many as the five large cattle owners in the area. That was one of the reasons the smaller cattle herd owners had to make sure their cattle and horses were branded, so the large cattle herd owners could not accuse them of stealing their stock. Most of the time the cattle in this area could graze on the grass left after summer but this was going to be a problem this year because of the drought. Most of the smaller cattle outfits probably would have enough feed to last through January or February, but that would be it.

A.D. had built one of the better horse herds in Southeast Texas, and he sold his horses for a higher price than most others. However, the people who had bought them thought they were well worth the price.

The area had finally gotten two three-inch rains in the last week so A.D. and the others in the area had decided to plant wheat and oats right away. In two weeks they had planted fifty acres of oats and fifty acres of wheat, hoping they would have enough rain to make good crops this year.

Maggie had decided she wanted a schoolhouse on Front Street in Anahuac before the big celebration in November. There were seven vacant buildings on Front Street, and one of the owners just happened to be coming through Anahuac at that time.

"How much do you want for your building?" A.D. asked him.

He replied, "I will sell it for $150."

A.D. countered that offer saying, "I would be willing to pay $125."

The owner quickly accepted. While he signed over the deed and bill of sale, A.D. went to get the money from his cabin.

"You now have a schoolhouse," he told Maggie. They were all excited. The whole Logging household went to check out the building.

Maggie began making plans to change the building into a classroom. She had Dave, the local carpenter, come over and make some tables for the classroom. Since she wouldn't be using the whole building, A.D. planned to use the rest of the building for storage. Maggie then went down to Gene McCoy's and ordered two big slate boards, books, chalk, ink and a few sheets of paper. The whole family worked at the new school building for an entire week. Dave worked off and on for three weeks getting the school room in order.

Within six weeks, Maggie had received all of the materials for school. The carpenter had mounted the slate board in front of the class and cut up the other slate boards so that each student could have one. During that time, Maggie had located a desk and chair which she put in the front of the room. Dave had made benches for the tables the students would use. A.D. and the boys had set up four swings at the side of the school. Maggie continued to teach her own children, the May brothers, Bob, and the Smith children at the new schoolhouse twice a week.

Maggie made some flyers telling about the school opening in January. It would cost $3 a month per student to attend. If anyone paid until the end of the school year, they would get a ten percent discount. Also, she would have school four days a week, eight hours a day. Subject matter would be reading, writing, arithmetic, geography and the Bible.

The boys, in the meantime, had been getting Gray Boy and Checker in good shape for the 1,200-yard horse race track. The race track in Liberty was only 800 yards long.

A.D. and Frank each donated two steers and two hogs for the celebration. The May brothers and their mother were in charge of cooking the meat this year. The other local women had promised to cook fifty pecan pies for the celebration.

A.D. was really busy two days before the celebration began because one settler brought twelve horses and two mules to be shod. Another man brought in three bad wagons that he wanted repaired so he could use them. A.D. spent one day working on each one of those problems.

When he charged the wagon man $60 for repairs, the man had a complete fit and told him, "I will only pay you $20."

A.D. explained, "I had to repair the tongue on all three wagons, put one new wagon wheel on each, re-greased all of the axles, plus repair the seats on all three. The charge amounts to $60.00."

"I will not pay it," he shouted, "and there is nothing you can do about it. I'll just take my wagons."

A.D. pulled out his double barrel pistol and said, "You're not taking anything anywhere until you pay me! If you're not going to pay then get out of my shop and stay away from here."

That evening A.D. had the three wagons in the back of the new schoolhouse so the man could not come up and take them while he wasn't there. That man was extremely unhappy, and A.D. knew he had not seen the end of him.

The next morning was the long rifle shooting contest and there were four hundred entrants. A.D. shot thirtieth and his boys shot right after him. At one hundred yards within 2 minutes, A.D. put two shots in the bull's-eye and two just outside.

The boys got off three shots during the two minutes and put one in the bull's-eye and the other two only hit the target.

As he and the boys were walking back to the blacksmith shop, they saw the man he had trouble with the day before. He said, "That was pretty good shooting."

A.D. replied, "Just remember that," and kept on walking. As it turned out he and Frank were declared first place winners and split $400.

The boys went on to give their horses a workout and A.D. went back to blacksmithing. He had both pistols loaded and convenient for him to grab at the shop. While A.D. was talking to a customer, the troublemaker and three buddies came into the blacksmith shop and paid A.D. the $60 he owed.

A.D. walked them down to where the wagons were stored, opened the doors and they pushed the wagons out. Then they went to get their mules while A.D. returned to his work at the blacksmith shop.

Maggie had been talking to people about the school and now had twelve students enrolled for January through May. She was sure she would get more.

The next day at noon, Checker was running in the first race of four, and then the four winners would run for the championship. Checker won by three lengths and got $100 for winning the heat. Gray Boy won the third race by four lengths and also got $100 for winning that heat.

Maggie had placed $100 on each of the boys in the horse races. A.D. had his eye on the troublemaker and his buddies making sure they didn't try to hurt his horses or his sons. At three o'clock the championship race was run and Checker and Gray Boy tied so they split the $400 winner's prize. All in all, the Logging family carried away $1,200 in winnings from the celebration.

That evening they had the big dance. It seemed to A.D. they had more drunks than usual. He noticed that the troublemaker and his friends were among those looking for trouble. Several guys stepped in when they had tried to cut in on various couples while they were dancing.

When they came to A.D. and tried to cut in, he politely told them, "No." The troublemaker spat out a long list of names for him, Maggie and his boys.

Before he could finish, A.D. hit him three times. His buddies rushed in and grabbed him and at that time Frank, Frank Jr., Bob, and the May brothers joined in the brouhaha against the troublemaker and his friends until they surrendered.

The men were marched up to the old Fort Klein and locked up with a guard put on them for the rest of the night. The next morning, the guard said they complained the whole night. The troublemakers were released and escorted ten miles out of Anahuac.

"We'll get even," they promised.

But the local men responded, "Don't even think about it, and don't ever come back!"

The next three weekends, A.D. and his boys went duck and goose hunting, killing seventeen ducks and ten geese. The boys were well pleased with the bird hunting.

"I'll take you guys hunting at least twice in January," their pa promised.

December 20th the families went out together to cut a Christmas trees for each home. The kids spent two days making decorations to hang on their tree. All of the children under ten were excited and looking forward to Santa Claus coming.

Santa brought the younger children several presents and the older children's present would be a horse, cow, saddle, buggy, or some of the girls got dresses or jewelry. The Loggings had a big Christmas party at the new schoolhouse. A.D. gave his help each $10 which was a tradition he had started when he first moved to Anahuac.

The younger ones wanted to take the rowboat out about two o'clock in the afternoon. At three o'clock a storm began to blow up in Trinity Bay. The kids' parents all worked quickly together getting them back safely on land. Immediately after they got the children on dry land, the area received a gully washer of three inches of rain in an hour. The guests, of course, had to stay until the rain stopped before they could venture on home.

20
CHAPTER

Through the summer and fall, the main discussion among the settlers in Texas Mexico was the imprisonment of Stephen F. Austin. Austin had stuck to his policy of remaining neutral in Mexican politics, not taking sides in the revolutions in Mexico City or Texas. In fact, he was the leader of the Peace Party which had no intentions of breaking away from Mexico. He had been arrested only on suspicion of planning to start a revolution because of the intercepted letter.

His arrest had the opposite effect than what the Mexican government intended. Tension against Mexico had actually grown among the settlers because of Austin's imprisonment!

In January, 1835, the Mexican government sent Captain Antonio Tenorio and troops to occupy the fort built in Anahuac. This was the principal port of Galveston Bay and would again be responsible to force the Texans to pay taxes on goods going in or out of Texas. Anyone that didn't pay taxes on imports or exports was considered a smuggler and would be punished for that crime. Capt. Tenorio knew what had happened to the last tax collector and Mexican soldiers in 1832 and was determined to establish a good relationship with the locals. He had no cannon, horses, mules, wagons and no lumber or brick to repair the ransacked fort.

A.D. offered the use of a wagon and two mules down to help the Mexican troops take their material to the fort.

When the Captain and another soldier returned the wagon and mules, they asked A.D., "How much will you take for this wagon and two mules?"

A.D. replied, "$100"

"Sold," said the captain.

Tonorio further asked, "How much for six horses with saddles and enough oats to feed them for three months?"

"$650," A.D. replied.

"I'll have to think about that," Tonorio said, "but is it possible to buy two steers?"

A.D. said, "Yes, for $10.00."

The two Mexicans immediately went down to A.D.'s dock corral, separated two steers and drove them up to the fort to feed the soldiers.

The next day Capt. Tonorio came back to see A.D.

"I would like to ask for your advice," he began. "This is my first assignment like this and I have no one else to talk to. What would you do if you were me and running this new fort?"

A.D. answered, "I would appoint my best three hunters and three fishermen to go out each day looking for food. Then I would appoint ten men to immediately plant a twenty-acre garden and let those men be responsible for taking care of it. Also, I would put my four best cooks in charge of the kitchen. Of course, I would begin making brick to repair the fort. I would appoint sentries and have a six-man patrol ride out daily if to do nothing else but talk to the locals and get the lay of the land." "Now," he continued, "for the lumber I would have four men go out and cut trees then bring them to the fort for other necessary wood repairs and firewood."

The Captain thanked A.D. for his candor. "That is almost exactly what I was thinking I should do." He also paid A.D. $650 for six horses, saddles and enough oats to last the horses and mules for three months. He asked for a bill of sale for all his purchases. Within a week, the Mexican Army was building and repairing the fort.

Maggie's school for the local children had begun January 4th. After talking to the parents of the children attending school and the fort's captain, Maggie decided to add Spanish three hours a week to the curriculum. Her Tuesday morning Spanish lessons enabled her students to have simple conversations in Spanish.

The captain was trying to win the locals over to his side. However, the locals were not friendly to the soldiers at the fort, and there were several desertions. Two of the soldiers deserted and went to work for a ranch about thirty miles away. When Captain Tenorio sought help from the local law, they would do nothing.

In January, A.D. allowed his boys to go duck and goose hunting twice by themselves. They killed seven ducks and seven geese, a good haul for the youngsters.

By March, Captain Tonorio had run out of money and was trying to charge most of his purchases. Also, in March, the farmers and ranchers in the area were busy planting corn. It took A.D. and the boys, with the help of Bob, Matthew and Mark, three weeks to prepare and plant two hundred acres of corn. Bob and his father planted thirty acres of their own, and Matthew and Mark also planted a total of thirty acres for their stock. The crops looked a lot better than last year because they had received so much more rain.

Finally at the beginning of May, a ship carrying supplies and money for the fort arrived. The Mexican captain paid every debt. The ship had also brought six more soldiers and sixteen muskets. Ten of the Mexican soldiers hadn't even had a rifle when the first troops arrived in January.

Meanwhile, Captain Tenorio had stopped eighteen ships so far and collected taxes from them. There were also two Mexican tax collectors actually doing the assessing and collecting, relying on the Army for enforcement.

People in Southeast Texas did not object to paying those taxes; the problem was at other collection points; tax collectors could be bribed or would take a lesser amount of tax. This did not happen in Anahuac which meant people in that area thought it was unfair. Also, the settlers in Southeast Texas were convinced they were the poorest of all the settlers.

The first part of June, most of the farmers including A.D. were harvested their oats, and two weeks later harvested the wheat crop. A.D. had twenty five acres of each oats and wheat planted. Each crop made twenty-five bushels to the acre. A.D. immediately started grinding one hundred bushels of wheat, producing four hundred ten-pound bags of flour.

Things went along pretty well until June 1835 when the captain had two prominent merchants who were well liked in the area arrested. Briscoe, from Anahuac, and Harris, from Harrisburg, were charged with selling goods without paying the import duties. Harris was released shortly, but Briscoe was detained. When Harris returned to Harrisburg he told the story about what had happened, and the residents were enraged!

This information was taken to San Felipe where William Barret Travis was practicing law. About sixteen settlers formed a company and elected the young lawyer, Travis, as their captain. They obtained the sloop, *Ohio*, sailing from Harrisburg to Anahuac and put a six-pound cannon on it. They added a few more men through Harrisburg and Morgan's Point.

When they arrived at Anahuac, Travis with his company of twenty-seven men, fired two cannon shots at the fort. Tenorio had no cannon. Travis had caught the Mexicans completely by surprise. On June 29th shortly before nightfall Travis fired one more well-aimed cannon shot which scattered the soldiers into the nearby woods. That night the Texans were busy. They captured seven Mexican soldiers, including the tax collector, Hernandez. Tenorio surrendered his troops, with no loss of life, on the morning of June 30th.

The settlers had captured sixty-four stands of muskets and bayonets along with all the powder and lead needed to fight with those weapons. Briscoe, of course, was released immediately. The Mexicans agreed to leave Texas and never to fight against them again.

After the surrender, the Mexican soldiers sailed to the town of Harrisburg where a barbecue was held for the departing soldiers, the Texas settlers who had opposed them and the locals. Afterward, the Mexican soldiers marched from Harrisburg overland to Labia with a few of their weapons for protection and hunting.

This was the second time Travis had overthrown the Mexican fort at Anahuac. He thought the people of Texas would be happy, but the Peace Party had meetings all over Texas, condemning Travis's action. The War Party really gained more of the settlers into their group when they intercepted a courier with a message, intended for Captain Tenorio, from General Martin Perfecto de Cos, the brother-in-law of Santa Anna, the dictator of Mexico. The message read that more troops would be sent to Anahuac and other tax collection centers in Texas. A strong division of troops which were now in Zacatecas, Mexico, could easily defeat the Texans if they came right away.

The two cannon shots had surprised the townsfolk of Anahuac and most, including the Loggings, loaded their wagons and left the town. They did not want to be involved in a big fight or have their families injured. A.D. and his family invited several of the other families that lived in the village to come to his farm. There were a total of twenty-one people sleeping in the cabin or in the barn!

At noon the next day Mr. McCoy rode back into the village and found out that the Mexican Fort had surrendered, and the defeated soldiers returned to Mexico. Everyone at A.D.'s cabin was relieved that they could sleep in their own beds that night! A.D. took the boys and went to the Fort retrieved the six horses two mules he had sold them earlier.

Life was back to business as usual in Anahuac. On July 2, an eight wagon caravan headed to Liberty for a big July 4th celebration and horse race. The wagon train arrived to their usual barn campground at eight o'clock p.m.

The long rifle shooting contest was held the very next morning, and every man and boy in the Anahuac group entered. A.D. only put three shots in the bull's-eye and one just out of the bull's-eye. Art and Weldon put one in the bull's-eye and another one in the target. None of the men or boys won anything in the long rifle contest. This was the 1st time in 3 years A.D. or Frank had not won. A.D. had to explain to his daughter, Patricia, why she couldn't shoot in the contest.

The boys got busy getting their racehorses ready for the next day, and A.D. began shoeing the horses and mules' people had brought to the celebration.

The big talk was about Travis and his men making the Mexican soldiers leave the fort. Many people condemned this action, including the mayor of Liberty who was a known Tory. He promptly put out a flyer warning everyone not to disturb the peace and asked Ralph Smith to post it in Anahuac.

The next day, Gray Boy and Checkers each won their heat races, but lost in the championship race. This was also the second time, A.D. or his boys had not had the winning horse, and the boys were disappointed.

Two nights of dancing were pretty rough. Ralph Smith had sold over one hundred jugs of homemade liquor so there were a bunch of drunks fighting which messed up the dance for everybody. The dance only lasted two hours each night because of all the disturbances!

A.D. earned $80 blacksmithing during the celebration. The Stroud brothers had sold eight hundred pounds of flour and cornmeal. On July 6th, the group started for home at before sun up and arrived at eight o'clock p.m. The May brothers, who had looked after things, had had no trouble on the home front.

21

CHAPTER

Lorenzo de Zavala, the former ambassador to France for Mexico, had resigned and returned to Velasco because of his opposition to Santa Anna's growing dictatorship. He hoped to align the Texans with the Mexicans that opposed the dictator and together overthrow him. He quickly realized that the best thing to do was for Texas to become independent. Zavala would become one of the signers of the Texas Declaration of Independence. He was also vice president of the provisional government at the Convention of March, 1836.

At the end of July, Tom Thompson, an Englishman in command of the Mexican schooner, *Correo*, entered Galveston Bay and seized a ship bound for the Brazos. After discovering it was not carrying clearance papers, Thomas agreed to issue a permit to the seized ship the next day at Galveston Island. The Englishman continued to Anahuac where he saw the notices, published by John Williams and William Harden, warning against the San Felipe's political chief's order to organize a militia. Thompson added his own order to forbid citizens' meetings on the grounds, stating this was illegal under Mexican law. Congress had disbanded all state militias.

As Thompson returned to Galveston Bay, he seized a sloop from Mr. Allen for his own use. Instead of providing the ship that had been seized in Galveston Bay with the promised permit, Thompson put Allen's cargo on Galveston Island and announced that the entrance to the Brazos River was blockaded. On the Brazos, he seized a U.S. schooner unloading cargo. Thompson warned that he would seize all of the vessels he found without permits, especially the two steamers. He also declared that if he found

Travis, he would hang him. His last boastful threat was that Santa Anna intended to free all of the slaves in Texas. This information spread like wildfire through the region and helped more fence sitters join the War Party. Thompson was one of those men that people instinctively disliked.

In September, he started out for Matamoros. However, while still anchored in the bay, the armed schooner, *San Felipe*, returning with Stephen F. Austin from his long captivity in Mexico City. The *San Felipe* was owned by Thomas McKinney who was still disgruntled over the loss of his schooner, *Brazoria*, in May due to the lack of proper papers. That night McKinney had a nearby ship, the *Lara,* towed the *San Felipe* out to Thompson's ship, the *Correo,* and by dawn had overtaken the ship. McKinney captured Thompson and his crew and sent him to New Orleans to be tried as a pirate.

Austin, who had been a moderate man joined the War Party and called for a consultation to discuss meetings about opposing Santa Anna. Austin wrote to the various communities throughout Texas to explain why he had changed his mind, warning that war with Santa Anna was inevitable.

In the state capital of Monclova, Coahuila, Santa Anna had delayed the opening legislative session from January to April. The Texas deputies to that legislature, Sam Williams, John Durst, and Jose' Carbajal all went along with a plan to raise money for the Coahuila-Texas state by selling land. They sold three four-hundred-acre leagues of land just south of the Red River. The six men that received this land did not pay any money but were supposed to raise armies to oppose Santa Anna. When the news reached San Felipe, the Texans were upset. Especially upset were all the land speculators who were jealous because they didn't get the land. The men that got the land didn't lift a finger to help in the Texas Revolution.

General Cos and his troops arrived in Monclova, the new capital of Coahuila-Texas, and he dissolved the state legislature. It would never open again. Cos then took his five-hundred-man army to San Antonio Landing at the port of Copano, Texas. At the same time Santa Anna was leading his army north into the Mexican state of Zacatecas, which was also in revolt. Several large battles took place there. Santa Anna won and captured two thousand of his enemies, and he ended up executing most of those captives. For three days, he also allowed his army to loot, rape and pillage the defeated state. When this news reached the Texas settlers, most of them were extremely upset.

As early as April, 1835, Mexican military commanders in Texas had requested more troops to handle the Texas citizens in case they revolted. Mexico was not prepared for a large civil war because the country had limited funds to conduct a war. Unrest in Texas posed a real danger to the power of Santa Anna and the Centralist Mexicans. Mexico faced losing a large portion of its territory if the Texas Revolution became successful.

Mexico feared without Texas, United States influence would spread and the other Mexican territories of New Mexico and California would also be at risk. When General Cos arrived at San Antonio he was to investigate the troubles in Anahuac, arrest Travis and other Texas patriots, and expel all colonists who had entered Texas after 1830. Austin called on all municipalities to raise militias to defend themselves.

The Mexican Army had loaned a small cannon to the citizens of Gonzales for protection against Indian raids. After a Mexican soldier killed a Gonzales resident, in September, 1835, tensions rose even higher. On October 2, 1935, Mexican troops tried to disarm the people in Gonzales and retrieve the cannon. The residents refused to surrender their cannon and weapons. Instead the Texans with a force of one hundred forty volunteers attacked the Mexican troops causing them to retreat back to San Antonio. Two Mexican soldiers were killed, and one Texan was injured when he fell off his horse.

News of the skirmish went all over the United States, encouraging many adventurers to come to Texas and volunteer to fight. Volunteers continued to arrive in Gonzales. On October 11th the troops elected Stephen F. Austin, who had no official military experience, the leader of the group that he called the Army of the People. These men lacked discipline which made fighting with them difficult. The Texans were determined to drive the Mexican Army out of Texas and started preparing to march to Bexar.

On October 6, Texans marched on the Presidio la Baha'i, a fortified base set up by the Mexicans in Goliad, trying to kidnap General Cos and steal the $50,000 that was rumored to be with him. Unbeknownst to them, General Cos had left Goliad a day earlier to take his troops to San Antonio.

On October 10, Texan troops, including thirty Tejanos, stormed the Presidio. The Mexican garrison surrendered after a thirty-minute battle. Two Texans were wounded, and three Mexican soldiers were killed with seven more wounded during the battle.

The Texans set up their defenses in the Presidio, under the command of Captain Philip Dimmitt. He immediately sent the local Tejano volunteers to join Austin on the march to San Antonio (Bexar).

At the end of the month, Dimmitt sent some men under Ira Westover, a Refugio settler, to capture the Mexican garrison at Fort Lipantitlan near San Patricio. The Texans took the undermanned Mexican fort without firing a shot.

After dismantling the fort, they prepared to return to Goliad. The remainder of the Mexican garrison, who had been out on patrol, approached the Texans, and a fight ensued. The Mexican troops were accompanied by fifteen to twenty loyal Centralists from San Patricio. This included all members of the Ayuntamiento, or town council. After thirty minutes of fighting, the Mexican soldiers retreated to Matamoros.

That meant that the Texan army controlled the Gulf coast, so all communications with the Mexican interior would have to be transferred overland. Therefore, it would be more difficult for General Cos to quickly ask for reinforcements or supplies.

On December 5, Colonel Domingo Ugartechea returned to Texas with five hundred more troops. On December 8, Ben Milam, a Kentucky native now colonizing Texas, led a five-day attack on the Mexicans at San Antonio. He and others were killed.

Colonel Ned Burleson, a former soldier in the War of 1812 and experienced military man, took charge of the small Texas army. He negotiated General Cos' surrender of over one thousand Mexican troops and the Alamo to the Texans. After this battle, most of the men returned to their homes. Burleson had already earned the reputation of a great Indian fighter. He was also a great commander under Sam Houston and very helpful in holding the unruly Texas army together.

In January, General Cos finally left San Antonio with his defeated army. They were destined to meet Santa Anna's army coming to San Antonio.

The first session of Consultation of 1835, which served as the provisional government of Mexican Texas throughout the revolution, was held in Columbia on October 16 and 17. The second session met at San Felipe, November 1 through 14. At that time, the Consultation was not in favor of leaving Mexico, but was against the dictator, Santa Anna, and the restoring of the Mexican Constitution of 1824.

Members of the Consultation set a date for a convention on March 1, 1836, which was to establish a permanent government. Archer, Wharton and Stephen F. Austin were sent to the United States to seek aid, but found it difficult because of the friendship treaty the U.S. had with Mexico.

The provisional government of Texas set a plan in motion in November, 1835, to establish a Texas Navy. The rebels knew the four-hundred-mile coast line would be a weakness if not addressed and set about to beg, borrow or whatever necessary to secure the coast. A financial negotiator was sent to New Orleans. Four schooners were obtained in January and retrofitted for fighting.

In February, the schooners were ready for action. They were to allow ships bringing helpful goods to Texas and stop any cargo coming to help the Mexican Army. They were also to stop Mexican ships from going up the Texas Rivers, Colorado, Brazos and Trinity, stopping shipments to Santa Anna. The Texas rebels also signed a letter of marque to privateers who were allowed to keep a percentage of the booty they captured from the Mexican ships.

The Texas ships were and *Independence*, *Liberty*, the smallest, *Invincible*, the largest, and *Brutus*, that had a ten-foot cannon capable of firing an eighteen pound ball over two miles in any direction. The Texas Navy and the privateers did a great job of capturing Mexican ships and their content, including Mexican soldiers. The Texas Navy continued the defense of Texas from Mexico until the fall of 1837.

The *Liberty* was confiscated by New Orleans creditors, the *Invincible* and the *Brutus* were in badly damaged in a fierce battle off the coast of Galveston with two Mexican war ships. They were scrapped.

Sam Houston was named commander in chief of the Texas Army in November, 1835, but he had no authority over each town's militia. Houston was to proceed to Goliad where he would meet up with several small volunteer armies which were prepared to march on Matamoros.

The Consultation organized a general counsel and elected a

Provisional Governor, named Henry Smith. All the towns had established a central committee charged with maintaining regular correspondence with each other on all subjects relating to peace and safety of the frontier.

Houston was not part of the Navy and never admitted how successful they had been. He never reinstated the Navy the rest of his term as President of Texas. However, the second president, Lamar, did!

When Houston got to his army, he found his troops were mostly fresh recruits from the U.S., unprepared and in a state of confusion. He discovered the Texas forces at Refugio and Goliad were also disorganized and untrained. He then concluded that the Matamoros expeditions would be a failure and even made a number of speeches at Refugio opposing the venture. Then he returned to San Felipe where Governor Smith and the general council agreed with him on his decision. More guns, more men and more training were needed before Texas could go on the offense.

Houston also informed the Council that the Alamo could not be defended and should be destroyed. The Council sent Jim Bowie to the Alamo to destroy it and bring back the much-needed equipment that was there. The Alamo Commander, Colonel McNeil, persuaded Bowie to help him defend the Alamo. So, they disobeyed orders and decided they would defend the Alamo.

Meanwhile the Council sent Sam Houston to talk to the Cherokees to get them to refuse to participate against the Texas settlers during the coming conflict. Houston got this agreement covered.

Gov. Smith had angered many of the rebel leaders, and his authority rapidly went to nothing. Gov. Smith was impeached as the Provisional Governor. However, he maintained the General Council didn't have the authority to impeach him and tried to continue on as Governor.

Houston, for one, remained loyal to Gov. Smith. When Houston's business with the Cherokees was settled, he returned to Washington-on-the-Brazos.

Refugio citizens had elected him a delegate to the March 1 convention because of his opposition to the Matamoros expedition. On March 2, the convention approved a Declaration of Independence from Mexico. George Childress, a lawyer, politician and illegal immigrant to Mexico from Nashville, Tennessee, actually wrote the Texas Declaration of Independence. He had arrived in Texas just six weeks earlier.

At Washington-on-the-Brazos, a new interim government was set up to take the place of the Provisional Government and finally elected David Burnett as President. Burnett was not an elected representative sent to this convention. He actually had come to Washington-on-the-Brazos to get a pardon for two convicted murderers sentenced to hang. He was their defense attorney at the trial. Eventually his clients were pardoned, after he became Provisional President.

Burnett was a stocky built man, forty-seven years old and a native of New Jersey. He carried a double barrel pistol in one pocket of his black frock coat and a Bible in the other. He was a teetotaler and would reprimand anybody who was cursing in his presence. He had participated in a rebellion where Venezuelan rebels had tried to free themselves from Spain. After the rebels' defeat Burnett escaped from Venezuela and came to Texas. He had developed tuberculosis and rode out to live alone. The Comanche Indians took him in, and he lived among them for two years while he was cured of TB. The Comanche's had treated him well, yet Burnett was intolerant and suspicious in all his dealings with the Indians.

Lorenzo De Zavala, a medical doctor who was a native of Yucatan, was elected vice president. During the struggle for the Mexican Republic's fight for independence from Spain he had been held in chains in the Spanish dungeon for three years. As long as Santa Anna had appeared to support the Constitution of 1824, De Zavala had supported him. When Santa Anna turned into a dictator of Mexico, De Zavala would no longer support him. He had become a wanted man by the dictator, and was an instigator of the Texas rebellion against Mexico.

Sam Houston had come to Texas because the U.S. President Jackson had been trying to buy Texas and he needed someone there that he trusted to tell him what was happening in this frontier state. Jackson had paid Houston $500 to check out what was going on in Texas. Houston was raised in Tennessee and had Cherokee Indians as his neighbors and friends. When he was fifteen, he ran away to live for three years with the Cherokee Indians. When he was eighteen and on his first job, he took a calico cloth as part of his wages which he gave to his Cherokee girlfriend.

In the War of 1812, Houston had participated in Battle of Horseshoe Bend. Jackson was the commander of the American forces in this battle which was part of a campaign against the Creek Indians who were English allies. Early in the battle an arrow struck Houston in the thigh, but Houston kept on fighting with saber and pistol until the Indians were driven back. After that, Houston had a lieutenant in his company pull the arrow out. This made a large wound. When General Jackson rode past, he paused to order him to the rear for medical attention and then continued on his way. After a short time of being treated by the doctors, Houston returned to the fighting front.

When Jackson called for volunteers to storm a ravine where the Creek Indians had a very strong position, Houston enthusiastically moved forward calling for his platoon to follow. In the ravine, the young officer fell after being shot twice in one shoulder and once in the upper part of his right arm. His bravery inspired the American forces, and they went on to route the Creeks at Horseshoe Bend. This earned Houston the attention and admiration of Andrew Jackson. He was greatly influenced by the future president for the rest of his life.

While he was still a United States Army officer, Houston once appeared in Washington in his buckskins and feathers of a Cherokee warrior. John C. Calhoun, who for many years was a very powerful politician in Washington and at that time Secretary of War, gave him a severe reprimand. Houston and Calhoun became bitter enemies. In later years it might have been Congressman Houston who kept Calhoun from running for president. Houston was Jackson's protégé. From 1823 through 1827, Sam was a congressman, and from 1827 through 1829 he was Governor of Tennessee. His name at that time was sometimes mentioned as a candidate for the Presidency of the U.S.

In 1829, Houston was married to a young Tennessee beauty, Eliza Allen. After a few months of marriage, she left Houston and returned to live with her parents. No one really knew what happened, but there was a lot of speculation. Houston announced publicly before he left Tennessee that the problem between himself and his wife was his fault, and if he heard anyone had spoken ill of Eliza, he would return and kill the person. Coming from Houston that was not an empty threat.

Several years before Houston had fought a duel with a General William White from Kentucky, and General White had been severely wounded. General White was known to be a skilled duelist; therefore, most people did not want to duel Houston.

In April 1829, Houston resigned as governor of Tennessee. He went to live with the Cherokee friends who were at this time living in Indian Territory near Fort Gibson, Oklahoma. He settled down as a trader and planter and soon he was married under Cherokee law to an Indian girl named Tiana. She must have loved him very much or she would not have put up with him. He had brought with him a wagonload of whiskey, most of it for his own use, as he drank almost continuously. The Cherokees gave him the nickname which was to haunt him the rest of his life. They called him Big Drunk.

Houston and his wife had accumulated a big plantation house with a lot of land and slaves. Houston wanted his wife to come with him when he went to Texas, but she refused. Houston took nothing but the expense money Jackson had given him when he left Oklahoma on his way to Texas to try to make treaties with the hostile tribes there.

Houston was a big good-looking man. He was six foot two inches tall and weighed two hundred thirty-five pounds. Houston was able to talk to the Indians because they knew he kept his word. This was helpful to Houston all of his life. Houston's first message to President Jackson was that the Mexican province of Texas was ripe for revolution.

Houston rode over much of settled Texas. He settled down in the bachelor's quarters in Nacogdoches, a town in a pine forest near the Louisiana border. Houston was a self-educated man and had passed the bar to practice law in Tennessee earlier. He was very popular in East Texas, especially with the ladies. He, like other settlers that came to Texas, joined the Roman Catholic Church so he could own land in Texas. He even took some Spanish lessons because he thought it would actually help him get along better in this country. For two and a half years he had practiced law in Central and East Texas. This was a very calm part of his life.

22

CHAPTER

Santa Anna had massed an army amounting to over six thousand troops. Over half were inexperienced conscriptions into the Army. He also gathered money and pledges from the rich in Mexico. Sana Anna began his march from Mexico to Texas in December and arrived at the Alamo, February 23, 1936. During the march to San Antonio his officers trained the raw troops. While on the march, the Mexican Army was plagued by hypothermia, dysentery and raids by Comanche's.

Weather was unseasonably cold and rainy during the winter and spring in Texas which caused problems for both sides. Most people thought that Santa Anna would not come to Texas until the spring so he would have plenty of grass for his animals, but here he was!

When the Mexican Army crossed the Rio Grande, Santa Anna sent General Urrea and his army of one thousand men to Matamoros first to secure that city from Texas attacks, then on to sweep along the Gulf Coast of Texas, destroying what resistance they encountered. Santa Anna had intelligence that there was a large force of Texans at Goliad. If that was true he wanted General Urrea to defeat that army.

The first action of the March Convention was to select Sam Houston the commander in chief of the Texas Army with the rank of Major General. This meant he was also over all the militia and volunteer forces, rather than just the regular army. At this convention, Burnett and Houston developed a dislike for each other. Burnett was a shy man and probably envied the big profane hard drinking General. No doubt Houston had the greatest personality of anyone at the convention. Burnet actually had a great hatred for Houston from then on.

De Zavala told fellow Latin delegate Navarro of San Antonio that never before had such an incompetent person as Burnet been named to such a high office. De Zavala was elected vice president. The Secretary of War was Thomas Rusk. He was Houston's drinking buddy. Rusk seemed to be the only one in the cabinet that could keep peace and harmony among the esteemed group. Sometimes he used physical force to accomplish this task. Rusk was a large muscular sandy haired man. He was thirty-two years old and came from South Carolina. His father was a stone cutter on the plantation of John C. Calhoun. When Tom was old enough the great statesman sponsored his law studies because he had great faith in the young man. This was ironic because there was animosity between Houston and Calhoun when they were in the U.S. Congress together.

Burnet's closet associate in the new cabinet was secretary of the Navy, Robert Potter. This thirty-six-year old North Carolina man had been a junior officer in the U.S. Navy for a short time. That was the only qualification he had for that job. He was sentenced to jail because he castrated two men he thought were having relations with his wife. There was no evidence to back up his claim. After he served his jail sentence, his wife divorced him and his father-in-law tried to shoot him.

Potter was elected to the state legislature and was considered a great speaker. The state legislature of North Carolina in 1835, invited him to leave because he cheated at cards. He went to Texas and was elected a Nacogdoches delegate to the Washington-on-the-Brazos Convention. Potter hated Rusk and disliked Sam Houston. So, two different factions existed between the president and his cabinet. This would factor in many criticisms of the way Texas handled this war.

Houston and Rusk were well aware that two days of forced marches by Santa Anna dragoons could have brought the enemy troops to Washington-on-the-Brazos. They frequently reminded the long-winded delegates to hasten the business.

The delegates received Colonel Travis' report that if he did not receive help quickly, they would be overrun at the Alamo. This caused a great stir from the delegates. They all wanted to go help him but both Burnet and Houston told them they must first form the government and take care of the government business. They both believed the colonies like Anahuac,

Goliad and the Alamo having small battles against the Mexicans did not effectively help their cause.

Burnet was elected president on the third ballot. March 2, this Provisional Government passed the Texas Declaration of Independence. Orders went quickly to Colonel Fannin, then at Goliad, to make ready to help Travis and his men at the Alamo.

Finally, two days later Fannin started his one hundred mile poorly planned trip to San Antonio. Before he arrived, he decided to return to Goliad because of troubles on the trip. He also had heard that General Urrea was going to attack Goliad. His officers disagreed with Fannin about turning around and were beginning to lose confidence in his leadership.

As it turned out, Fannin's four hundred men might have made a great difference in the defense of the Alamo. The Alamo had a large area to protect and one hundred eighty men were simply not enough to effectively defend it.

There was a lot of apprehension about Burnet. Many people felt he did not fully support the revolution. They thought he was going to get a high post appointment from the Centralist Mexican Government. Burnet's stance on this hurt him all the time he was Provincial President. Santa Anna, quickly put a price on the heads of the President, Houston and the rest of the cabinet hoping someone would kill them.

When Houston finished his business at the convention he and three aides rode to Gonzales to build a force. Then he was to rendezvous with Fannin at Cibolo Creek near San Antonio. Houston started toward Gonzales to begin planning the fighting operations against the Mexicans surrounding the Alamo.

Houston arrived on March 11, and rumors were rampant about the fall of the Alamo. He believed the rumors, but was afraid to tell his men because it could cause general panic. Travis had probably been defeated before Houston's own force was even organized so he faked his disbelief in the news. Houston had the two riders that brought the news arrested for treason, held in a secluded place and guarded. Within an hour they were released with Houston's apology. He did send a messenger to Fannin telling him that he should disregard the earlier plans to rendezvous near San Antonio and instead quickly retreat past Victoria Guadalupe.

When the Alamo fell March 6, all the combatants that had surrendered were executed and the Mexican Generals allowed their troops to defile the bodies of the dead Texas soldiers by bayoneting them, throwing the bodies up in the air and eventually burning them. All the non-combatants that were captured were personally interviewed by Santa Anna before they were released. Mrs. Susanna Dickinson, who had seen all the fighting and the defiling of the dead men, had the entire Mexican army parade before her to show the might of Santa Anna's force before she, along with her child and a slave, were sent on the road to Gonzales. Santa Anna's objective was, of course, to put fear in his enemy.

When she arrived at Gonzales and began telling her story, the civilians and many soldiers were afraid for themselves and their families. Some soldiers deserted and others just got a leave to go home and see to the safety of their families. The last thirty volunteers to enter the Alamo had been from Gonzales and these families were devastated. Houston only had $300, and he gave all of it to the thirty widows from Gonzales.

Houston immediately sent out riders to warn people in the surrounding areas and also check on the location of Santa Anna's troops. He ordered Gonzales burned and allowed all his civilians to cross the Guadalupe River, before crossing his Army.

His retreat began the night of March 13. After crossing the river, the settlers burned all boats and rafts within five miles of Gonzales. General Houston had the only two small cannons that he had thrown into the river.

The spring rains were heavy this year causing all rivers to be flooded. The prairies were extremely muddy which caused a lot of problems for wagons, horses, mules and even humans.

The civilians were ill-prepared to make this trip. In their rush, they were poorly prepared for travel, not having enough clothes, food, or proper transportation. This was the beginning of the runaway scrape where thousands of Texas settlers were running away from Santa Anna's army toward the safety of Louisiana.

Fannin waited days before he began his poorly planned retreat. Fannin had the best equipped and trained men in Texas, but General Urrea's force of one thousand men overtook the Texas force crossing a huge open space on a hot Texas day, with no cover or water. Fannin had neglected to plan for water and food for his retreat. He had no horses or mules and was forced to use oxen which were already tired and hungry. Fannin had wasted time trying to repair an oxcart and allowing the oxen to graze while his force was within five hundred yards of trees they could have used for cover and desperately needed water. Also, the oxen could have more easily grazed there. The other officers with Fannin warned him not to stop and unload the oxcart to repair it or allow the oxen to graze in the open area, but he paid them no heed.

The Texans formed a box formation three deep and repelled the Mexican force three times that day, with few casualties. Urrea sent two hundred men back to Goliad to retrieve cannons, more ammunition and fresh troops. His troops returned with all that the next morning. Fighting went on the first day all day and the Mexican Army lost between one hundred and two hundred men. Fannin's men had no water and very little cover to hide behind so they dug trenches. The lack of water meant they could not take care of their wounded and cool or clean their cannon.

The next day when Urrea got reinforcements and made the first attack, Fannin surrendered with terms that his men would be treated fairly as prisoners of war. This all happened March 20 and 21. Urrea's army left two days later to continue to obey Santa Anna's orders to sweep the Texas coast.

Urrea left a force of two hundred fifty men to guard the Texas prisoners with orders not to harm them.

The Mexican Army had very few doctors and medical people, whereas Fannin had over twenty doctors so they became doctors for both armies. Fannin himself was wounded along with a number of Texas and Mexican soldiers. The Mexican Army used a number of Texas men who were skilled blacksmiths, gunsmiths and carpenters. In fact, Urrea, with his one thousand five-hundred-man army took most of these doctors and skilled men with him.

When Santa Anna found out that Fannin's men that were captured had not been killed, he sent a high-ranking officer to Goliad with orders to execute all prisoners. When the commander of the prisoners' detail received the order from Santa Anna, which contradicted the order he had from Urrea, he was in a quandary about what to do. The officer messenger Santa Anna had sent cautioned him to do what the dictator had ordered. On March 27, Palm Sunday, the Mexicans marched the prisoners two miles from the camp and began shooting them. Over thirty of the Texans escaped and most of them returned to their families, but some went to warn Sam Houston. The wounded Texans were taken out of the hospital and shot.

Santa Anna had sent a letter to U.S. President Jackson stating that he would treat all prisoners as pirates and, therefore, would be able to execute them immediately. This letter was not widely known about, especially among the Texas rebels.

On March 26, Urrea captured the important port of Copano. This meant that the Mexican Army could now receive supplies from Mexico in the fastest and easiest way. Urrea set up defenses and gave orders for the two hundred fifty men that were at Goliad to come to this port and hold it, ensuring that Mexican supplies could safely come to Copano.

General Urrea listened to some local residents of the Gulf Coast area and adopted a policy that was non-threatening to the local population. This enabled him to get more information so he could safely move through the area without fear. Santa Anna figured the rest of the fighting was routine and planned to return to Mexico City. His officers talked him out of returning to Mexico City, and they also got him to return some of the heavy cannons and other equipment that would make travel difficult in these spring rains.

Santa Anna also returned Melchora Barrera, his seventeen-year-old fake marriage wife, to have her comfortably set up in Mexico City. He sent a high- ranking colonel with several thousand dollars' worth of silver to be deposited in his personal bank account in Mexico City.

He immediately sent General Joaquin Ramirez y Sesma with seven hundred fifty men after Houston. He also had sent General Antonio Gaona toward Bastrop with a brigade of seven hundred fifty men. Santa Anna followed with the remainder of his Army behind Sesma's force.

The next morning fifteen miles east of Gonzales, the Texas Army met reinforcements of one hundred twenty-five men. Of these volunteers, twenty-five left when they heard what the Mexicans had done at the Alamo. Many of the recruits wanted to stop and fight while others wanted to desert.

There was very little sleep for anyone during the first three days of retreat. At nighttime, Houston would post one third of his Army as sentries for the night. Houston was hard to live with because he was riding up and down the column urging everyone to hurry because the Mexican Army was right behind them.

On the fourth day of the retreat, the Army was joined by fifty mounted Texans who turned their horses loose to graze within the lines of the sentries. Houston cursed the newcomers for this and told them if they stayed with the Army they would be foot soldiers and their horses would be used for draft animals. Some of these new Calvary recruits mounted their horses and left. Others allowed themselves to be converted into the infantry. These people all relied on their horses and mules for needed transportation. Houston knew he could not allow animals to graze and had no grain to feed them while they were retreating because the Mexican Army was too close.

By this time Houston was getting accurate reports about where all the Mexican troops were located and a more accurate number of their forces. In fact, the most outstanding job that was done by the Texas army at this time was the ability to get accurate information on what the Mexican Army was going to do.

In Gonzales, Houston had set up Captain Henry Wax Karnes as head of his spy scouting organization and he had recruited eighteen other outstanding individuals like Deaf Smith.

Houston's Army was fed by the cattle and game that were in the area. When the troops halted most of them were doing guard duty finding wood or boiling, roasting or smoking dry beef. Each mess had at least one portable corn grinder and each man was rationed one ear of corn a day. Some of the soldiers had bread called pinole which was a mixture of ground corn meals, dried wild berries and sugar. His men seldom had coffee and the only commodity the commissary had in a large enough supply was chewing tobacco. Houston chewed tobacco constantly. Houston was no better provisioned than his men. His saddle bags contained several ears of corn along with this lucky double barrel pistols. Mary Bowles had made Houston Indian moccasins which he wore when he wanted to spare his boots or his feet and she had also given him a vial of ammonia spirits made by distilling liquid from the shavings of deer horns. Houston believed this ammonia prevented colds and he carried this vile in his breast pocket. He applied the spirits to his nose regularly. During this rainy cold season Houston never had a cold. This led to the accusation that Houston was taking opium and in fact, he intercepted a letter to Secretary Potter from one of his subordinates stating just that. Houston used his saddle for a pillow and his horse blanket to lie on because he didn't have another blanket.

The Texas soldiers, who were supposedly reluctant to travel on foot, made pretty good time and, by March 17, they were on the Colorado River. The civilians crossed the river on March 20. The next day, General Sesma's division arrived at the west bank of the Colorado and camped about two miles upstream from the Texans. The Armies maintained their positions for six days.

Houston had in mind attacking Sesma. Thinking about Fannin's surrender made the idea of attacking the Mexicans vanish. He worried that Gaona would come the sixty miles north of the Texas position and Urrea could come from forty miles south and the three divisions would have the Texans trapped. Houston estimated they had about eight hundred fighting men at the time and four hundred refugees looking for his protection.

The Texans were, indeed, in a poor defensive position so, on the evening of March 26, despite most of his officers wanting to attack the Mexicans, Houston had his Army fall back to the Brazos. Between two hundred and three hundred men left the Army at that time, disgusted with the retreat. Some of them got furloughs to take care of their families and some just plain deserted. For the first time, but certainly not the last, there was talk of naming a new general. If there had been, in this army, a man with a strong personality with more military experience, Houston would have been relieved of his command for not fighting at the Colorado River. There were not any really qualified people in the army that could have handled this rough assignment.

The Texans got to San Felipe on March 28 and stayed overnight.

The next day there was really a lot of dissatisfaction in the ranks when Houston led his smaller Army northward twenty miles up the Brazos to Groce's plantation, the home of the region's richest man. There was an abundance of food supplies and Houston knew the one hundred sixty-foot-long steamer, *Yellowstone*, was there taking on cotton cargo.

Houston also knew he could more easily defend that position and planned to try to organize his Army which he had really not had time to do so far. Houston, at this time, gave a speech to his men as to why he was going to Groce's plantation. This was unusual for him because he usually kept his plans to himself, not even telling his officers.

Wiley Martin and Mosley Baker, two company commanders, refused to follow Houston to the plantation. Baker wanted to guard the San Felipe crossing of the Brazos. Martin wanted to move downstream about twenty-five miles from San Felipe and protect the crossing near old Fort (now Richmond). Realizing they were not going to follow him anyway, Houston gave them the defense orders they wanted. He warned them to pick up all the boats on either side of the river and make sure to guard the ferry at old Fort.

Burnet and some cabinet members had fled from Washington-on-the-Brazos a few miles upstream from Groce's to Harrisburg which was southeast of Washington-on-the-Brazos. The Provisional President wrote Houston a scathing note telling him he was to stand and fight. Burnet said Houston was a laughing stock of Texas because he had not already whipped the Mexicans. He also said that his retreats had caused panic with the Texas civilians causing the runaway scrape, or settlers' evacuation. Houston replied he thought the Provincial Government moving had caused the runaway scrapes.

Burnet and Houston had exchanged some terse letters throughout this campaign. The mad scramble of the civilians was to get out of the way of Santa Anna's army. Most Santa Anna sympathizers among the colonists joined in the runaway scrape, because after the Goliad and Alamo massacres, they were afraid of the Mexican dictator. This was causing the breakup of many families in Texas. The older people, women and children were headed toward the Sabine River and the younger men were headed to join Houston. The runaway scrape was hard on the civilians; some died, and many got sick because it was so wet and cold. Walking was very hard for the women and children and also for the soldiers, in both armies. It took twice as much effort when it was wet and muddy like it was to walk and by the end of the day people were completely worn out.

Many acts of kindness were extended to the people in the runaway scrape along the way; this included the Indians, who had stayed out of the fight as they had promised Houston. When these pioneers finally crossed the Trinity River into Liberty County, they were welcomed by the people in Liberty and Anahuac with food, shelter and dryness, which they desperately needed. The Logging and Stroud families had gone to Liberty in April with one thousand pounds of flour and cornmeal along with one thousand pounds of oats.

The runaway scrape people were also plagued with measles and yellow fever. Some of the people died because of this further devastation. The Logging and Stroud families gave away all of the food in one day and told the refugees if they needed covered shelter to come to the Fort in Anahuac where they could house over three hundred people. When the two families returned home the next day over a hundred people followed them to the fort. The community quickly made them as comfortable as they could by taking bedding, quilts, sheets, blankets, food, wood and water to the fort. Most of them rested there for eight days before resuming their trip to Louisiana.

23

CHAPTER

A.D. and other farmers in the area had spent the first part of April weeding their corn crops. The men in the area had been talking about going to help Houston.

By mid-April, A.D. told Maggie, "I have been thinking of going to help Houston and taking Art with me. We could shoe their horses and mules which would help them greatly."

He was astonished when she said, "That would be a good idea."

A.D. and Frank contacted Sergeant Gonzales and his friends to take care of the livestock. He wanted all their cattle and horses pastured on his land so it would be easier to watch over them. Driving the cattle and pastured horses over to Gonzales's ranch took all day for the Logging family, along with Duke.

The next day, A.D., Art, Frank, Frank Junior, Pat, Bob, Matthew and Mark, along with eleven other men decided they would be ready to leave on April 18. A.D., obtained a schooner to take this group to Harrisburg where they would meet Houston, his last known position.

At three o'clock, the schooner docked at Lynch's ferry on the San Jacinto River below its confluence with Buffalo Bayou in Harris County, and the Anahuac group found out Houston had left Harrisburg but was close by. The group disembarked on the South side of the San Jacinto River hiding in the trees a mile from the landing. They thought it best to wait for the Texas Army at that position because they didn't know where the Mexican Army was at that time.

There were at least one thousand Texas civilians waiting to board Lynch's ferry. Nathaniel Lynch was charging two dollars a head for people or animal to cross on his flatboat service with a hand-pulled rope for power. Many people did not have any money and therefore weren't going to be able to cross. The schooner's captain that brought the Anahuac group to San Jacinto found out that Lynch had been charging to convey refugees, and he offered to take four boatloads to Anahuac for free. Within two days he transported three hundred civilians, saving them from having to cross the San Jacinto and Trinity Rivers. The rivers of Texas were swollen way beyond their banks and many of the people in the runaway scrape had drowned trying to cross.

On April 7 Santa Anna rode into the burned-out town of San Felipe de Austin, which is on the west bank of the Brazos River. He was at the head of about one thousand four hundred troops.

Baker's company, one of the two that had refused to retreat to Groce's with Houston, had burned the town and crossed to the east bank of the river gathering all the boats within ten miles in each direction on the Brazos. His company dug trenches there and fortified their position. Some hours before the Mexicans arrived Baker had sent three men to warn him of the Sandinistas approach. The three men were sleeping when the Mexican column surprised them. Two of the Texans escaped in a canoe. But the third man, named Bill Simpson, told Santa Anna everything he knew.

Houston, with around five hundred followers was only twenty miles upstream. Simpson told the Mexicans that the Texas Army was still on the west side of the Brazos. The Mexican dictator sent new orders to Urrea and Gaona to rush their armies to San Felipe. His plan was to crush Houston close to this location.

Meanwhile Santa Anna brought up two cannons and started shelling Baker's trenches on the other shore. Baker's company's firing made sure that Sandinistas could not launch any boats. On April 9, Santa Anna left Sesma with eight hundred fifty troops to deal with Baker and to wait for columns under Urrea, Gaona, and Filisola, an Italian-born empresario.

It was near freezing when Santa Anna with five hundred grenadiers and fifty dragoons rode down the west bank of the Brazos and stopped at Powell's Tavern for the night. The next day the dictator started down the Brazos toward Thompson's ferry, arriving there early on April 12. Martin's company was supposed to be guarding the crossing from the west bank of the river. The Mexican advance guard, who had been warned not to let the army cross at this point, could see a black ferryman on the opposite shore. Colonel Juan Almonte called out in good English in an attempt to lure the black man over to the west bank. His plan was accomplished. Almonte wrote and spoke perfect English and Spanish. He had traveled over the Texas area before and was continually writing Sam Houston offensive notes saying the Texans were giving up because they had no chance against such a large force. At Fort Bend, Santa Anna learned, from the captured civilians, that the unguarded and uneasy rebel government was at Harrisburg, which was less than thirty miles east of Fort Bend. General Sesma arrived as ordered the next day and told Santa Anna, the other generals had not made it to San Felipe.

On April 14, the Mexican Army crossed the Brazos with one thousand men, including fifty of his best grenadiers, Santa Anna's staff, Calvary escort, mule-skinners and others, including women camp followers.

Santa Anna was trying to catch the Texas government at Harrisburg and hang the rebels. Santa Anna only knew Houston, De Zavala and Austin. He was vague on the names of the other Texas revolutionaries. He also thought that the reason the rivers were flooding was because of all the snowmelt on the mountains during his campaign in Texas. It was evident that he couldn't swim and had a fear of water. Santa Anna was so eager to get to Harrisburg that he didn't take time to protect his supplies on the backs of two hundred pack animals against water damage. He ordered his men to swim the animals across the deep creek. Of course, all the supplies got wet. Many of Santa Anna's Generals and aides considered him a maniac.

Santa Anna was in one of his daring moods on the night of April 15. He and one officer took fifteen dragoons and rode up within a mile of Harrisburg at about eleven p.m. They dismounted and sneaked into the town hoping to catch the so-called Texas government, but Burnet and others had already fled. The only Texans Santa Anna found were three printers busy putting out Texas' only newspapers, the *Telegraph and Texas Register*. The printers didn't withhold any information and said the Provisional Government had left the morning before on the steamboat, *Cayuga*, to New Washington which is now Morgan's point. According to them, Houston and his Army of about eight hundred had left Groce's plantation after camping there two weeks. The printers figured that night they were about fifty miles northwest of Harrisburg. They believed the Texas Army was headed for San Jacinto.

Santa Anna was disappointed at this failure to catch the government leaders in Harrisburg and burned the town. He threw the printing equipment into the bayou. The Mexican dictator now had two major objectives: to catch the fleeing Texas government at New Washington and to intercept Houston's army at Lynch's ferry.

On the morning of April 16, Santa Anna sent fifty dragoons, under Colonel Almonte, in pursuit of the Texas government leaders in New Washington. Ms. McCormick had sent her son with a message for Burnet via Mike McCormick, whose mother owned a ranch close by. The Mexicans followed Mike to New Washington and were only one thousand yards behind him. Mr. and Mrs. Burnet and the rest of his cabinet were waiting on a rowboat to take them to the schooner, *Flash*, and had just shoved off from the shore when Almonte's men reached the shore's edge. They could've easily blasted the boat out of the water, captured, or killed the Texas president but Almonte ordered them not to shoot because there was lady in the row boat. Santa Anna found out that Almonte let the Texans get to safety where they got to the *Flash* and sailed off to Galveston.

However, Almonte's trip to New Washington was very profitable because they captured Morgan's warehouses which were loaded with large food stocks meant for the rebels. The Mexicans were glad to get the food because they were short of many supplies. Almonte sent a message to Santa Anna, suggesting that they hurry up with the rest of the forces since his small detachment was exposed to danger from enemy ships, or men who might land to recapture the food supplies or the Mexican soldiers. The reinforcements finally arrived at noon.

Morgan's servants had been helping the Texans load the food stock out of his warehouses onto flat boats for transport to Houston's army. Emily, one of those servants, had caught the dictator's eyes and she was assigned to be a servant to him. Santa Anna spent the rest of the day trying to arrange passage back to Mexico aboard a German schooner which was lying off of Morgan's plantation. The plan was for him to board the vessel the night of April 19. He seemed to be bored with the Texas expedition and they were worried that he was losing his power politically in Mexico City.

Santa Anna did not even know there was a Texas Navy until April 19. On that afternoon an armed schooner appeared off of New Washington, attacked and burned the German ship before the dictator's eyes. This Texas warship was one of four pressed into service at Galveston by Robert Potter, the Secretary of the Navy. The dictator was not in favor of the long horseback ride to get home for a hero's welcome in Mexico City.

That evening, the Mexican Army burned the town of New Washington and was preparing to leave the next morning when the new leader of the dragoons, Captain Miguel Barragan, excitedly came galloping into the burned-out town, shouting, "Houston is close on our rear and his troops have captured some of our stragglers and killed them."

The Army was then in a dense wood on the narrow land about four thousand yards in length which only allowed for passage of pack mules single file and mounted men. The lane was filled with hundreds of men and hundreds of pack mules. When Santa Anna heard Barragan's report, he got on his horse and galloped through the crowded lane of men and mules. He knocked over several men, running into several mules and shouting, "The enemy is coming! The enemy is coming!"

Santa Anna regained partial control of himself and formed a confused column of attack, giving incoherent and contradictory orders. The frightening excitement of Santa Anna had a terrible effect so that order could no longer be preserved. Every man thought of finding a hiding place or running. Santa Anna ordered the men to drop their knapsacks to the ground without breaking formation. He was determined to intercept the Texans before they could gain control of the crossing over the San Jacinto. The dictator and all of the horsemen dismounted and went forward on foot, leading their horses. The day was overcast, and dark clouds moved overhead. The Sandinistas left the woods and marched out over a very grassy plain. On the horizon were dense forests of live oaks draped in Spanish moss with a few tall pines among them.

General Manuel Fernandez Castrillon was still mad at Santa Anna over the fake marriage to Melchora Barrera, who was the daughter of his friend in San Antonio. Santa Anna, invited himself to share the services of Castrillon's personal chef he had brought along. Santa Anna had chronic stomach trouble, and the chef could prepare food so that it was both bland and appetizing. Castrillon rejected Santa Anna's proposal which made him mad.

Everyone crossed the bridge at Vince's Bayou. The mules would not pull the cannon, named *Golden Standard*, over the bridge. General Castrillon was told to take a company of men the long way around, which was nine miles through boggy high wet grass. The men were all afraid of snakes that they could not see.

At 2:00 p.m. a position on the plain of San Jacinto had been established for the Mexican Army. It was also part of Peggy McCormick's ranch. Santa Anna was again the confident general and ready to fight Sam Houston because most of his officers had seen him eat some opium during the hike. The Army then began to dig in and fortify their position until late that night.

At Groce's plantation, Houston was aware of the men's displeasure with him because of his failure to meet in battle so far. He was a very busy man during those two weeks. At no time prior to his arrival did Houston have adequate time for organizational work. He began the task of forming his command into some semblance of an Army. Discipline was the first problem because the raw troops in this Army had little experience with military regulations. Some of the men believed that Houston was deliberately trying to shake out unruly elements when he led them to this plantation. The men had been marched from Gonzales in a zigzag fashion through swamps and bogs and had been subjected to all military discipline and practice. They stood guard twenty-four out of each forty-eight hours and were not allowed to go to sleep even at the guard fires.

The delay at Groce's had good effect on the men, giving them military training and discipline. They were supposed to be on watch but he also showed the Army that he could be firm when four men were caught robbing and raping women refugees. The four men were hanged.

Houston had already developed a great scout and spy service but during this time he added ten more men to the original ones. The spies would hang around the edges of Santa Anna camps and then come back with information for Houston. Deaf Smith and his black friend, Hendricks Arnold, obtained critical information for Houston.

Houston also formed a medical staff which was necessary because the revolution had drawn together frontiersman who had previously led isolated lives and not been exposed to many of the contagious diseases. The

Texas Army was plagued by many childhood diseases such as whooping cough, mumps, measles and pinkeye. Bad food and worse water caused dysentery. Houston selected Dr. Alexander Ewing, a twenty-seven-year-old who had studied medicine in Scotland, to be the chief of staff over the other eight physicians whose duty it was to cope with these problems.

Men in the army used whatever arms they had available. The large plantation had well-equipped shops and much of time during the rebels' stay was given to weapons repair. Although Houston was aloof with his officers, he was quite sympathetic and helpful with the men in the ranks. When the regular gunsmiths were too busy he would pitch in and help with the repair of rifles.

Houston said that sedition was rampant among his own officers. He used his loyal spies, Deaf Smith and Karnes, to find out what was going on among his staff members. As a result of Karnes' investigation, Houston placed one of his aides, Colonel James H. Perry, under arrest. He was in correspondence with Secretary Potter in Galveston, and it was he who reported that Houston was using opium to excess. Perry also put in that letter that the big drunk wasn't drinking. Apparently, the Texas General who had previously used a lot of liquor for so many years drank only water from a gourd canteen.

When Tom Rusk arrived, Houston called all of his officers together and held a trial for Colonel Perry. Houston told Perry, "You have accused me of taking opium during this campaign, now I want you to prove it." Perry said, "That won't be necessary." Houston said, "No, I want you in front of all these men to show me where the opium is and when I am doing it." Perry then went over to Houston obtaining the vile he had been sniffing and asked two of the doctors that were there, "Would you please sniff the contents of this vile and tell us if this is opium in it?"

They both replied, "No, it is an ammonium substance which I am sure he sniffs to try to protect himself from colds and pneumonia."

Houston told Colonel Perry, "You and the others that have been sending messages to Burnet, or Potter, find the opium you say I've been taking! You and whoever is helping you have two hours to find the opium you claimed I've been taking. The rest of us will wait right here until you have had your time to find it."

None of the other officers made a move to help Colonel Perry and after he made a halfhearted search of all of Sam Houston's possessions he came back to the meeting. He told General Houston, "I cannot find any opium, and I don't think you were ever taking any. I hope you will forgive me."

"No sir, I will not forgive you and if we were in a civilian situation I would demand satisfaction. In place of that you are under arrest, and I will court martial you later. If I find any other person of this Army sending messages to anyone, without my knowledge, they will also be court martialed. Some of these messages that you have sent have been intercepted and we cannot have that. This will be a hard fight without our officers, telling everyone what we plan to do. I say to every man here, if you have something to say to me, say it to my face now."

No one had really said much of anything in the last hour and a half during this meeting, outside of Houston and Perry. Houston told Perry, "Confine himself to your tent for the night and consider yourself under house arrest."

Rusk showed the letter to Houston from President Burnet, and Houston confided in Rusk his plan for Texas was to win their independence.

"We are a force of one thousand men going against an enemy that has six thousand men so we must be careful where we fight. When we fight we must not only win, but we must capture Santa Anna and make him send his troops back to Mexico. I have tried to stretch out his supply line and weakened his troops with nature's rain and mud more than we have been weakened by these events."

He continued, "We have no cannon, but I believe our Army with the long rifles is better than the Mexican Army with muskets. At no previous time have I felt that we could defeat the Mexican Army. Most of these men wanted to fight at the Colorado River, however, we had a total of five thousand Mexican troops within sixty miles of us that would've entered into any fight. The odds were just too great at that time. I have tried to keep up the location of Santa Anna. Knowing that is a critical part of my plan. I have not discussed these plans with anyone here because several of them are sending the messages right back to other cabinet members."

Rusk told Houston, "I believe in your plan and will support it."

After the officers' meeting and his talk with Houston, Rusk was then besieged by the unhappy officers wanting to tell him how fed up they were with the general's failure to act. It was soon evident that Rusk believed that Houston was doing the right thing, but the officers felt he had fallen under the spell of their leader. Rusk's backing of Houston strengthened his position.

In mid-April the Army was joined by a private named Mirabeau Bonaparte Lamar, who saw himself as a candidate for Houston's job. Lamar was a thirty-eight-year-old Georgia poet and newspaper editor who had joined the Army under the influence of Burnet. Lamar began undermining Houston's leadership as soon as he got into the Army. He started by explaining a plan he had where he wanted three hundred volunteers under his leadership to take the *Yellowstone* steamship and make raids on Mexicans along the stream.

He also said he planned to attack Gaona, however, at that time the Mexican general was leading his division many miles inland from Brazos. That night, Houston posted notices throughout the camp that anyone who tried to get volunteers to raise a personal force within the Army would be considered a traitor and would be shot immediately. Private Lamar lost interest in his plan and he quietly acquired a horse and rode with the Calvary.

Two other candidates for Houston's job were the only two high-ranking officers with full tailored uniforms. Colonel Sidney Sherman, the commander of the new second Regiment and Adjutant General Colonel John Austin Wharton, the same who had written to Houston urging him to come to Texas and lead the rebel forces back in 1832. Wharton had originally helped quiet the negative attitudes toward Houston and gradually under the influence of Burnet's friends in the Army had cooled toward the general. If Houston had shared his plans, Wharton would probably have backed him. He wore a well-tailored blue woolen uniform with brass buttons and a pair of good boots. But he also wore a Mexican sombrero and carried a gourd canteen. He was a tall, wiry man of thirty years. Colonel Sidney Sherman, the commander of the new second Regiment was a tall, brown bearded thirty- year-old native of Massachusetts. He was new to Texas and war. Before the revolution he lived in Newport, Kentucky, where he was a prominent industrialist and innovator in his field. When the Texas revolution broke out he sold his factory and used the funds to outfit and finance a company of fifty-two volunteers for the Texas Army. His volunteers were the real problem children of this Army. The company was composed of the most reckless, drunken and lawless men in the Army. Many times, fights would start between two men in the Kentucky company ranks and would soon bring about a big fight among many of the other men, which included officers. Only a few of this outfit were native Kentuckians; the others came from Maine, Massachusetts, Illinois, Maryland, Mississippi, Ohio and Tennessee.

Colonel Burleson was a sharp contrast to Sherman or Wharton as he wore faded blue homespun and had no arms except for a pair of pistols. Burleson had a lot of military service, both in Texas and in the United States, while Sherman had none.

Actually, Burleson was the one man who might well have succeeded to set himself up as Houston's rival. Burleson was a patient, effective officer, a veteran of both fighting and controlling an Army. He was popular with the men and was already, at the time of the San Jacinto campaign, a famous Indian fighter. He had been commander of the hastily assembled Army that defeated general Cos at San Antonio the previous December. His satisfaction with this post as regimental commander under Houston was understandable because of what happened to him in the siege in San Antonio.

A man named Ben Milam had decided that the commander was too slow about attacking. It was Burleson who had negotiated the surrender of Cos and his men. Throughout the San Jacinto campaign, Burleson had never acted like he wanted to take over the Army. But now, Milam went through Burleson's camp baying, "Who will go to San Antonio with old Ben Milam?" He got four hundred soldiers to follow. They stormed the town, but some of the sting was taken out of Milam's success because he himself was killed in the fighting.

Houston's spies had not been able to find out if Santa Anna was still with the Mexican forces in Texas. On April 12, Houston obtained dependable information on Santa Anna's whereabouts. This report came from Joseph Powell, the son of the innkeeper Ms. Elizabeth Powell, who had been forced to entertain Santa Anna two nights previously.

Powell told Houston and Rusk that Santa Ann was at Fort Bend and reported that the Mexican president planned to make a quick drive to

Harrisburg to capture the Provisional Texas President and cabinet. Powell had heard that Santa Anna with a small force might go on occasional raids out ahead of his main armies. This information gave Houston and Rusk fresh hope and something to build their plans upon. They could look for a chance to isolate Santa Anna and his smaller force and defeat him before the other Mexican columns could come up to his relief. After the report from Powell the General determined cross the Brazos and march the army seventy miles down the road from Groce's to Harrisburg.

The Texas Army got its first two cannons sent by some citizens of Cincinnati, Ohio, on April 11. It was against the law in the United States to ship arms to Texas so the *Twin Sisters*, as the cannons were called, were labeled hardware and smuggled to Texas by ship. The guns were landed at Harrisburg and hauled to Groce's plantation. Houston placed Lieutenant Colonel James C. Neill in command of the brand-new artillery corps.

April 12 and 13, the army crossed the river using the *Yellowstone* and marched in the direction of Harrisburg. As usual, it was raining. A group of civilians fell in behind the army. These fleeing pioneers begged Houston to furnish them an armed escort to the United States border. They had heard wild stories that the Indians along the Trinity were ready to go on the warpath.

The Coushatta had promised Houston sometime before that they would not attack the rebels, but would even help them. Chief Kalita, a good friend of Houston's, also said that he would furnish ninety warriors for the Texas Army but this never materialized. In a short time, the road would split with one road going east to Louisiana but the Army was going to take the other fork, going to the Southeast part of this territory, to find and fight Santa Anna.

Several days after the Army left Groce's, Moseley Baker's and Wiley Martin's companies rejoined Houston and the Army. Baker retreated back from the Brazos crossing at San Felipe, meeting the column on April 15.

The minute he saw Houston, Baker reproached him, "You said you didn't attack the Mexicans on the Colorado because you didn't have any artillery. Now you got two brand spanking new Cannon's and you didn't stand and fight on the Brazos? Are you going to Harrisburg or not?"

Houston refused to answer and Baker threw his company in with Burleson's regiment. Wiley Martin who had come back from the hopeless job of trying to guard the Fort Bend crossing was convinced that Houston was not going to fight. He didn't want to go on serving under the General. Houston, Baker and Martin had once been good friends and the General did not make an issue of Martin's insubordination. He ordered Martin's company to guard the crowd of refugees clinging to the army. The next day the civilians turned left at the fork in the road to take them to the Louisiana border while Houston turned right and headed for Harrisburg.

A civilian woman, who had allowed Houston to use her team of oxen to pull the new cannons, took her oxen back when Houston turned toward Harrisburg causing a lot of consternation. This meant that many of the soldiers would have to pull the cannons out of any mud holes and down the road the rest of the way.

When they got to Buffalo Bayou opposite Harrisburg and camped, Deaf Smith brought word of Santa Anna. The Mexican general was headed down to New Washington on San Jacinto Bay. Houston then gave orders to move out at daylight.

On the same day, Karnes and Deaf Smith crossed the hundred-yard Buffalo Bayou, ambushed and captured a captain and two other Mexican couriers.

"The captain has come all the way from Mexico City," Rusk commented, "judging by the saddlebags he is carrying. It seems he had been in on the assault of the Alamo and picked up some of the spoils. The deerskin saddlebags are inscribed with the name of William Barrett Travis."

An indication of Houston's control over his head- strong followers is the fact that the courier captain was not killed for the sight of Travis's name on the saddlebags which must have been like a red flag to the Texans. Smith made the captain swap trousers and headgear. Smith, the larger man, had trouble getting into the captain's new blue trousers but these wool pants were a lot more comfortable than Smith's mud stiffened buckskins. The captain looked like a clown riding into camp wearing the large mud stiffened buckskins.

The captain was also carrying dispatches from General Filisola at Fort Bend intended for Santa Anna at New Washington. The letters were translated for Houston by one of his new aides, Major Lorenzo de Zavala Jr., the vice president's son who had just recently joined Houston's army. De Zavala was the best dressed of Houston's aides for he was accompanied by a Parisian valet he acquired while his father was Mexican Ambassador to France. One of the letters was congratulating Santa Anna on his Goliad and Alamo victories. But the other correspondence revealed that the Mexican dictator was farther ahead of the three large columns than Houston suspected. It also told them that Santa Anna had a force of a thousand men and General Filisola was sending five hundred reinforcements that had been requested. The capture of these dispatches at Harrisburg was extremely important to the battle that would be fought at San Jacinto. Houston thought it better to attack the dictator because he was on the east side of the Brazos and unconnected with his other forces.

To attack the Mexican forces, Houston sent the steamer, *Yellowstone*, down the Brazos River, running the gauntlet of Mexican troops on the west shore. He didn't lose a man or sustain any serious damage. Those on board were protected from Mexican fire by cotton bales.

Before the Army left Harrisburg, fresh cases of mumps, measles and other children's diseases broke out among the men. A snug camp was made in the woods near Harrisburg to hold the two hundred twenty-five men, either ailing or who were ordered to stay there to guard the Army's baggage, a few prisoners and over one hundred fifty sick Texans.

The others with marching orders set out on April 19 along the Buffalo Bayou to find the nearest possible crossing of the flooded stream.

Before the Army crossed Buffalo Bayou, Houston made his first formal speech of the campaign. The soldiers were in a hollow square formation with Houston and Rusk in the center. Houston sat astride his big white stud, named Sarasin, and delivered his words in a booming voice. While he talked, Houston could see behind him across the plain where smoke was rising from the tall timber around New Washington. Santa Anna was burning another Texas town!

"Victory is certain!" Houston said. "Trust in God and fear not! The victims of the Alamo and the names of those who were murdered at Goliad cry out for cool deliberate vengeance. Remember the Alamo! Remember Goliad!"

The ragged, muddy Texas soldiers took up the cry. Among Houston's men were seven survivors of the Goliad massacre. Most of the others had known men that died in the Alamo or had been murdered at Goliad.

That speech made sure of one thing: no man in this Texas Army would be taken prisoner! These men who had been close to mutiny many times, until they heard the Houston speech, were ready to die if it meant saving Texas from Mexico! Houston ended his speech saying, "There is no use looking for help. There is none at hand. Colonel Rusk is with us and I rejoice in that."

Only ten of the fifty-nine signers of the Declaration of Independence for Texas were with the Army. That day Rusk in his speech referred to the missing delegates, "Many of those at Washington-on-the-Brazos had promised to raise big forces of riflemen and yet for various reasons are not here."

The Secretary of War said, "Santa Anna himself is just below us within the sound of a drum. A few hours more will decide the fate of the Army. One of the alarming facts is that when the fate of our wives, our homes and all that we hold dear are suspended on the issue of one battle, not one quarter of the men of Texas are here. I look around and see that many I thought would be here first on the field are not."

The secretary, growing increasingly moved himself, cried out suddenly, "May I not survive if we don't win this battle!" Rusk, at this point seemed to realize that these angry, lice-ridden men needed no more prodding to stir them against the Mexican Army. Rusk stopped abruptly saying, "I am done."

The cries went up again, "Remember the Alamo! Remember Goliad! Remember La Bahi!"

Houston had three scouts each watching the three remaining Mexican armies checking on their locality and how far they would have to come to be involved in this coming battle. The Texas Army proceeded to cross Buffalo Bayou and rested for a few hours. Then in the early morning crossed via Lynch's Ferry.

At that point, A.D. and the Anahuac group met Houston and his Army. A.D. said "We are here to help you fight the Mexicans. I have a blacksmith wagon with supplies, so that we can shoe any horse or mule you have. We also have five hundred pounds of flour, five hundred pounds of cornmeal, and five hundred pounds of oats. We are good horsemen and want to join your Calvary and believe we can be of help. We are the only men that will use our own horses!" Houston agreed.

Houston said, "You have four mules pulling your wagon, would you unhook two of them so they can pull these two cannons? We don't have far to go, so I'm sure your two mules can easily pull your wagon the next few miles without any trouble."

Of the Texas Army, only one hundred seventy-one men were presently landowners. That meant that eighty percent of the men who participated in this Texas Revolution were newcomers who wanted to get land for their participation in this fight. Only one company in Houston's Army was composed entirely of Native Texans. All these men had Latin names and many of them spoke no English. They were commanded by a strong thirty-one-year-old captain named Juan Seguin. He was a son of one of the wealthiest, most respected patriarchs in Texas, Erasmo Seguin, and he had been the political chief of San Antonio.

While General Cos had occupied San Antonio, the Santanistas had made the mistake of mistreating Erasmo Seguin and, as a result this influential clan, which probably would have remained neutral, became staunch revolutionists. Don Erasmo had turned over to the colonists the resources of his big ranches around San Antonio. He made huge contributions of food, horses and mules to the rebels when San Antonio was stormed and taken from General Cos in December, 1835. Juan had led a company of Latinos. Of his original Seguin company, seven died in the Alamo. Seguin himself escaped the fate of the others only because late in the Alamo siege, Travis had insisted on sending the Latin captain through to Mexican lines as a messenger.

During most of Houston's retreat Seguin's company had been rear guarding and they had several bloody skirmishes with Santa Anna's advance men. The Army left Harrisburg and Houston asked Seguin's men to stay and guard the sick. Houston was afraid some of the rebel Latinos might be shot by mistake in a general fight.

Sequin and his men were insulted by this suggestion and told Houston. "We did not join your army to ride herd on sick folks. We men from San Antonio have more grievances to settle with the Sandinistas than anyone else. For we have suffered the most from them. We want to fight!" Doing the translation was a large six foot two inch Latino named Sergeant Manchaca who became a great fighter during this battle.

There were also two companies of regular infantry from the United

State Army stationed in Louisiana who had been allowed to desert for a short time, taking a fighting vacation with the Texas rebels. The two regular companies were the most disciplined men in Houston's Army of stubborn individuals. These regular companies were commanded by a twenty-nine-year-old lieutenant colonel from Mississippi named Henry Millard. His second in command was Captain John Allen, a tough idealist and great leader.

The Texas Army band consisted of three fifes and a drum. Ned Burleson's first regiment, the real foundation of the Texas Army, included two hundred men who had walked all the retreat from Gonzales.

The quarreling Kentucky Company was still in Burleson's Regiment commanded by a tough officer named Captain William Wood. This company had the only flag in the Texas Army. On the flag was a well painted nearly nude Ms. Liberty carrying a sword in one hand and a streamer in the other inscribed, "Liberty or death."

Another troublesome company "D" was led by Captain Mosley Baker, who knew nothing about military matters and would not give written orders. During the whole campaign Baker denounced Houston and believed he deserved impeachment.

The toughest soldiers in the first Regiment were frontiersmen's that were commanded by Captain Jesse Billingsley. He had fought the Indians since organizing The Texas Rangers consisting of eighty Rangers he commanded and was known for getting the job done. The oldest man in this Army was Private James Curtis who was sixty-four years old.

24

CHAPTER

Wednesday, April 20, all of Houston's men were tired of retreats and safe camps. They were ready and eager to fight the Satanists. After they took their position in the woods near the McCormick Ranch they would have their chance. It was a chilly, partly cloudy day when Colonel Sherman was sent out at the head of forty horsemen to scout around New Washington early in the morning. About two miles from New Washington, they encountered Captain Marcus Barragan and other mounted Sandinistas scouts. The Mexican Captain thought he had stumbled on the whole Texas Army. As Barragan's men fled four stragglers were shot by Sherman's scouts. Near New Washington Sherman's men broke off the pursuit of the Mexican dragoons and hid in the woods so they could observe Santa Anna's force. At about 1:00 p.m., Sherman's scouting patrol came riding into the Texas camp in the San Jacinto live oak grove. Sherman informed General Houston the enemy was close by.

Afterwards the Mexican Calvary was observed in motion passing through the prairie about a mile away. Upon the trail of the Texan Army, they advanced toward them with trumpets sounding. The Mexicans could only see a few rebels, two cannons and about thirty artillerymen. The cannons and men were about ten yards out on the prairie in front of the trees.

Unbeknownst to the Mexicans, right behind the rebels at the edge of the timber were two companies of regular infantry. The Calvary was in the woods behind the regular infantry. Sherman's regiment protected the left side of the camp, and Burleson's riflemen were on the right wing.

When Santa Anna looked at the woods by Buffalo Bayou, he only saw a few men and two small cannons. The site, of such a small force, together with a fresh dose of opium, made the dictator eager for battle. His officers believed that Santa Anna was trying to bring on a regular battle. He ordered a company of skirmishers out to a cluster to trees halfway between the two armies and had them fire on the rebels. While they were doing this, Santa Anna had his buglers play the sinister El Deguello, the signal of no quarter, which he played during the Alamo siege.

Under the protection of the Calvary, Santa Anna advanced his twelve pounder, named the *Golden Standard*, about fifty yards and fired one shot. It cut through the trees over the Texas camp and lobbed into the Bayou.

The *Twin Sisters*, which the rebels had never fired before, answered with a blast of broken horseshoes. The shots landed a little to the right of the Mexican's advanced position.

Colonel Delgado was not happy that Santa Anna had him put the *Golden Standard* out without proper protection. The Mexican skirmishers who had been firing at the Texas positions had hit nothing. They were the only protection the *Golden Standard* had.

Delgado was surprised when Santa Anna rode out in full medal-laden uniform and Napoleon style hat mounted on a big bay stallion. The Dictator certainly made an easy target, but the Texas riflemen failed to pick him off.

General Castrillon quickly came out telling the Dictator, "This is a good way to lose a war that we've already won." Santa Anna ignored the Major General and ordered Delgado to fire on the Texas artillery.

The *Twin Sisters* returned fire with a better affect at the three-hundred-yard range very near Santa Anna. A young Mexican Captain who was about to mount his horse was shot in the rump.

The rebel Colonel Neill was also shot. Santa Anna then ordered Delgado to give up his twenty mules, which were used to haul ammunition for the *Golden Standard*, to the Captain so he could go pick up knapsacks that the Mexican Army had dropped on the road from New Washington.

Luckily, Delgado kept six mules to haul powder and ammunition back to the main Army, three of those mules were killed while doing that. The Mexican army then went about a thousand yards and camped on a hill that gave them an advantageous position with water on the rear and heavy woods to the right as far as the banks of the San Jacinto, open plains to the left and a clearing in front for about two hundred yards. Late in the afternoon Houston sent Sherman to scout with the Calvary, but not to provoke any main encounter.

A.D. and his fellow Cavalrymen from Anahuac had not been used that morning with the skirmish of the cannons and the small number of infantrymen. Colonel Sherman came to A.D. and said, "I am going to use your horse because mine has a problem."

"Like hell you are," A.D. said. "When my son and I signed our enlistments, we put a statement on that paper that we would be the only ones to use our own horses. So, you ain't taking any of the horses that we have here. If you've got a problem with that, I suggest you talk to either Houston or Rusk."

Colonel Sherman said, "I'm taking the damn horse."

A.D. pulled his pistol and said, "Let's go see Rusk!"

There was such a commotion about the confrontation that Rusk met the men, almost in the middle of the camp. He verified A.D.'s story. With that, A.D. turned around and went back to his horseshoeing which had not let up since they arrived in camp.

Sherman was furious and told Rusk, "I will not have any of those people from Anahuac riding in the Calvary that I am in charge of."

"You ain't in charge here," Rusk said. "Houston makes the assignments. I would not forget that. Now let's go on this patrol."

Houston came by later and asked A.D., "Is everything okay now?"

A.D. assured him, "Things are going okay. I only have eight more horses to shoe and will be caught up by midnight."

Houston said, "It might be a good time to spread some of the oats for the horses and cornmeal for the soldiers." The men who had come with A.D. and Frank took ten pounds of corn meal to each of the fifteen mess stations around the camp. The men were grateful.

When the Calvary returned from their scouting expedition, A.D. and the others took two hundred-pound sacks of oats and gave it to Sergeant Black who assured them he would make sure every horse got half a pound each day.

Sherman had taken sixty one Cavalrymen on this patrol and met fifty Dragoons under Captain Marcus Barragan's command. They immediately drove the Mexican Calvary back, throwing them into confusion. Santa Anna ordered two companies of riflemen to attack them and this drove the Texas Calvary back. The Texans had to dismount and load leaving at least half of the Calvary men on the ground having to fight however they could. They reloaded and got back in the saddle and forced the Mexicans back a second time. Rusk, in front of the second Calvary charged, was hemmed in by several Mexican dragoons and might have been killed, or captured, if Private Lamar had not come to his rescue.

Lamar, with his pigsty charged in, knocking down a Mexican horseman backing out in an opening through which both could escape. As the Texas Calvary retreated to the woods, Lamar saved Walter Lane, a nineteen-year-old boy from Ireland who had been brushed off his horse by a Mexican lance.

Lamar rode up in time to shoot the Mexican lancer, and Lane jumped behind another Texas Cavalryman and made it back to the Texas camp. Santa Anna watched this fight and ordered out the buglers sounding the El Delquello.

If Houston had brought out his main force there would have been a pitched battle there on the evening of April 20. That day two Texans were wounded and one died because of improper medical treatment.

When Sherman returned from the Calvary skirmish, Houston had heated words with him, but Sherman, by that night, had become the hero of the camp. Not only had he led his men into brushes with the enemy during the day, but that morning a group under his command captured a flatboat full of supplies that Santa Anna had dispatched the day before from New Washington for use by his Army. When the Texans, who were hidden on the bank, hailed the boat as it neared the shore, the Mexican boatman jumped over the side and made it to the opposite side of the Bayou. A man laid flat in the boat, finally put his head up and exclaimed in English, "Don't shoot! Don't shoot! I'm an American."

They had not only captured a prisoner of the Mexicans, but also had captured flour and coffee. For the first time in three days, the Army had bread and coffee to go with the usual boiled beef that night.

That evening there was a huge uproar because Colonel Sherman had demonstrated that they could stop those Mexicans. Various members of the Army were seen publicly going from company to company soliciting volunteers to fight the enemy without Houston's consent. In the Mexican Army, Santa Anna ordered his men to sleep on their arms in battle formation while keeping good watch.

The elderly Cherokee Chief, Bowl, at his camp in the Piney Woods about a hundred miles north of San Jacinto, put on his military hat that Andrew Jackson had given him and greeted two courteous officers from Filisola's division. Filisola had a contract with the Mexican government to settle thousands of acres of East Texas land. Some of the land was occupied by the Cherokee with the permission of the Mexican Government but without secure land titles.

The previous February, Houston had called on the Cherokee seeking cooperation with the Texas rebels. In addition to the usual gifts he gave his word that the Texas government would confirm the Indians' ownership of their lands. The two Mexican officers firmly suggested to the Cherokee chief that the Mexican Armies would soon be swarming all over East Texas, and he'd better get his warriors on the winning side.

"The Cherokees will remain neutral," Chief Bowl politely but firmly said. The Chief did not say that he had just received a letter from Sam Houston, promising him again that the Cherokees would be able to keep their present land.

Also, on April 21, the Mexican General Urrea, who had defeated Fannin and other Texas rebels, joined the three other columns on the Brazos, about fifty miles from San Jacinto. Not only was there no opposition, but the Sandinistas received a good reception.

Early in the Texas campaign, Urrea had captured Dr. Harrison, who bargained for his release: he would ride ahead of Urrea's division, telling the colonists that Urrea would not harm them if they lay down their arms. Urrea, not ruthless like Santa Anna, was deeply haunted by the execution of Fannin's men, which was ordered by Santa Anna. Urrea drove along the coast where he found goods, food, supplies and liquors in abundance. Compare that with Santa Anna's main column marching through the heart of settled Texas which usually came into burned out settlements with very little food. Many English, American and German colonists awaited Urrea as the result of Dr. Harrison's ability to allay their fears. Many offered to lead the general to Houston because they desired his defeat and knew the greater part of the men under his command were adventurers who were worse enemies of the colonists than many others.

On April 21, Houston's Army began at four o'clock in the morning. When they beat the drum to reveille, Houston himself, lying on his saddle blanket with his head on a coil of rope and getting his first unbroken sleep in over a week, slept through the drum roll. A 38-degree Blue Norther was sweeping off the water all over the flat plain of the San Jacinto. But by sun up, the skies were clearing and the north wind had died down.

In the early morning, reinforcements of nine young recruits from the United States arrived to enlist in the Texas Army. They had sailed from Galveston and were hoping they would meet up with Houston in place of Santa Anna. The scene was twenty campfires and many groups of men: English, Irish, Scots, Mexicans, French, Germans, Italians, Poles and Yankees, all unwashed and unshaved their long hair, beards and mustaches matted, their cloths in tatters and plastered with mud. A more savage looking band had never assembled anywhere. Yet many were gentlemen, owners of large estates and their guns were of every size and shape. The Texas Army numbered fewer than eight hundred.

Beyond the sheltering timber, the new men saw a prairie with islands of big trees in it, and there was a gentle rise in the land about eight hundred yards away. About a mile across, the ground of the prairie and in another location along the San Jacinto was the camp of the Dictator of Mexico, Santa Anna.

In the Mexican camp the day had begun early and the Dictator was watching his enemy position through a spyglass. Smoke rose from the woods by Buffalo Bayou and a few rebels were out on the edge of the timber in the prairie grazing horses. Santa Anna was satisfied with his position. The enemy was shut up in a low, marshy angle of the country where retreat was cut off by Buffalo Bayou and the San Jacinto River. Everything was favorable for the Mexican Army and the cause they were defending.

After making those observations, Santa Anna fussed around his camp supervising the building of breast works and cursing his officers. Santa Anna's officers did not agree with their leader that the camp was a good one, but their caution to the Dictator was ignored.

At nine o'clock, General Cos arrived with five hundred reinforcement troops.

From the direction of Nance's bridge, Deaf Smith had whispered to General Houston that the Mexicans were getting reinforcements.

"This is going to be a damn good day to fight a battle," Houston said when he arose and he tested the wind and the weather. Fair weather was important to Houston for the old muzzle loading rifles with flint locks carried by most of these men were very unreliable weapons in rain and wind. So were the *Twin Sisters* which had to be ignited by flares.

The arrival of Mexican reinforcements was not a complete surprise to Houston since he had seen Filisola's acknowledgement when they captured three Mexican couriers. Houston was out on the prairie about fifty yards from the edge of the timber.

The condition of the ground forced Cos's men to move slowly, as had Santa Anna's own troops. Even after the bulk of his force was established at San Jacinto, Cos's rear Guard lagged far behind.

At 10:00 a.m., Deaf Smith rode out with another member of his spy company to a group of trees about four hundred yards from Santa Anna's camp. Houston had given him orders to get an accurate count of the number of tents and other materials the Mexican Army had. Smith had climbed a tree and took about twenty minutes to count the tents, horses, cannons and number of stacked arms. After he had been up there about ten minutes, Mexican infantry appeared from the timber about three hundred yards away and began firing.

The balls whistles over the spies' heads, but Smith did not appear to notice as he proceeded to count. Next, some Mexican Calvary came from under the trees where their infantry was shooting at them. Smith quickly came down from the tree jumped on his horse and the two men returned to the safety of their camp.

Smith reported to General Houston that he estimated the Mexicans had approximately fifteen hundred men.

"Take the boys from Anahuac that joined us yesterday," Houston then told Smith, "and burn Vince's Bridge."

Smith went over to A.D. and said, "Get a total of eight men mounted and be ready to ride with me in five minutes." He further stated, "Bring some material so we can burn a bridge."

A.D. selected, Art, Mr. Stroud, his sons Frank and Pat, Matthew, Mark and Bob. They gathered a small can of coal oil, matches, five four-foot-long sticks, an axe and five burlap sacks. Art strapped all that on an extra horse. When Smith returned, he looked over the men and material that were going to accompany him approvingly.

The special detail moved rapidly eight miles on the road leading to the Brazos, reaching the mouth of the lane on the north side avoiding a cabin where the enemy could be hiding. They tore down a fence where it joined Vince's Bayou and a hundred fifty yards from the fence came to Vince's bridge where Smith told them, "Fire the bridge." He and two others watched for the enemy. In thirty minutes, the bridge was in flames, and they were on their way home.

When they reached a deep, dry ditch about a mile from their camp, Smith told the volunteers, "Rest while I ride up to high ground and see whether any of the Mexican horsemen are near." When Smith got up on the rise he dropped his head down around the horse's mane and headed back to their hidden location. He shouted to the other men, "The prairie is full of Mexican horses. What will we do now?"

All of the men answered, "We will follow wherever you say."

Smith said, "Get your guns ready and follow me single file to where this hollow joins Buffalo Bayou. Then turn right and run for the level above. If the Mexicans see us, raise a Texas yell and run through their line. General Houston's orders are for us to get back to camp, dead or alive." Smith warned, "Don't tell anyone about the burning of the bridge." Houston had planned to have Smith announce what had happened to the only bridge on the road to Brazos later.

Upon returning they found out that the big news was Houston had made Lamar a colonel because of his heroic actions the day before, and he was made commander of the Calvary. While the burn detail had been gone Houston had his first and only council of war during this whole campaign with Rusk, Bennett, Sherman, Burleson, Wharton, Lamar, Somerville, Lieutenant Colonel Henry Millard and Lysander Wells. Houston asked the Council, "Do y'all think the Texans should attack this afternoon or remain in our position, and let Santa Anna attack?"

Rusk and all but two others were against attacking the veteran Mexican troops behind fortifications. They said that the rebels didn't have bayonets to charge with through an open prairie. They were all confident that their position was strong and in this position, they could whip all of Mexico. Millard and Wells voted to assault Santa Anna's position that afternoon. Houston had received their opinions on this subject silently. He never commented himself.

Bennett was riding out to graze his horse on the prairie and take a look at the enemy. Houston spoke to him and said, "Don't be gone more than thirty minutes, Colonel, as I'll want you." He came back in less than a half-hour and Houston sent him through the camp to see the captains and men and ascertain their feelings about fighting that afternoon.

"The men are ready to fight," Bennett reported back to him.

Houston then ordered the troops to be prepared between 3:00 and 4:00 pm. Houston and several others thought there were seven hundred eighty or so Texans in the battle line. The Texas Army strung out two deep over nine hundred yards. The *Twin Sisters* were in the center of the formation about ten yards ahead of the line. The Calvary was hidden in the woods ahead of and to the right of the attack line.

Houston had left twenty men at the camp ready to repel anyone that got through the line. A.D. and Frank had been told to ride their horses behind the line and once the attack started to go directly to the *Golden standard*, capture it and make sure to hold it during the entire battle.

The observers that were in the trees reported to Houston that they could see no Mexican dragoons and really could not even see a single Mexican sentry. Rusk was to ride with the second Regiment, only until it contacted the enemy and then he was to gallop over to the center of the line and give a report to Houston. The reason for this was the Second Regiment's attack could not be seen by Houston or most of the rest of the Army.

Houston mounted on Sarasin, his white stallion, gave the order, "Trail, arms! Forward!" At around 4:00 p.m., the men began to move toward the silent camp of Santa Anna. At two hundred yards, the Mexican artillery and infantry opened up, but they overshot and the rebels never fired a shot until they got within forty yards.

The command all along the battle line was halt, fire and then charge. When the Texans went over the small hill in view of the enemy, which was about two hundred yards away, Houston gave the order to fire. Most of the Texas riflemen made their own decisions about when to fire because they thought two hundred yards was too far away to be effective.

The Texans' band began to play "Will you come to the Bower." It had been extremely hard for the men to pull the *Twin Sisters* up over the hill, but with that accomplished, they began to effectively fire on the Mexican camp.

Deaf Smith came riding along the battle line, shouting, "Vince's bridge is down! Fight for your lives! Vince's bridge is down!" The battle was now in full swing, and Sherman on the right side had met little resistance but there was tough organized resistance in front of the Texas Army. The smoke from the cannon and small arms made it hard to see anything after about seven minutes of fighting.

When Houston was about forty yards from the Mexican lines and almost directly in front of the *Golden Standard*, a volley of five shots caught the General's horse, Saracen, and the big stallion sank to the ground, slowly without a sound. Houston landed on his feet and was immediately given a rider less horse by one of his men. When Houston got into the saddle, the stirrups were so short he could not use them so he rode away with his long legs dangling.

When Houston was at the breast works of the Mexicans defense, he was hit just above the right ankle by a three-ounce copper ball. At the same time, a second horse in the battle was blasted from under him. An aide dismounted and gave the wounded General his horse. Then Houston rode off inspecting all the tents the Mexicans erected looking for officers or cowering soldiers. The Texas Calvary had been advancing on the right and had tried to block the Mexicans' only exit from the battlefield, but Lamar didn't have enough men in his command to do this. Even so, the Texas Calvary did manage to take a lot of Sandinistas out of their saddles, horses added to the mass confusion in the Mexican camp.

When the Texans made first contact with the enemy, the infantrymen were no longer in their two-man deep formation. They covered the last hundred yards at a run, and, in the process, they had moved into a line at least 1,500 yards across.

Colonel Delgado was watching the artillery men repair the *Golden Standard* when the Texans charged over the rise of the plain. He jumped into an ammunition box so he could see better. What he saw was a line very extended that advanced upon the camp firing their rifles.

The Texans were yelling furiously. All the other Mexican officers were asleep or having a party. The Dictator had retired to his tent taking the slave girl, Emily. When the Texans attacked, the bugler who gave the first warning to the Mexicans did not live to play very long.

Sherman's regiment had sneaked within about sixty yards. They had come up through the timber, just inside from the marshes and the San Jacinto River. They were a complete surprise when they fell upon the relaxed Mexican Army. Sherman's men were ordered to fire. Then all discipline, as far as Sherman's regiment was concerned, was at an end. Each Texan appeared to be fighting and charging the Mexicans on his own. During this time, it was hard to tell friend from foe.

General Castrillon tried to take charge of the *Golden Standard*, which was discharged three times and was loaded for the fourth shot when the Texans cannon hit the Mexican cannon's water bucket. The same shot stunned and put most of the gunners in flight. By that time A.D. and his group shot the General and prepared to control the twelve pounder. A Mexican officer and nine men tried to advance on the *Golden Standard*, but none of them got off more than one shot before they were either killed or wounded. After that Rusk sent several more men over to help keep the huge gun out of the enemy's hands. By now, all of Santa Anna's Army was in complete disorganization, and most were running and begging not to be shot. Most of the Texans were so mad that their officers could not control them for over an hour.

"We must reform the Army," Houston told Rusk, "and be prepared for either a counterattack or being attacked by one of the other Mexican columns. We must have Santa Anna!"

By that time, Houston had rounded up a company of men and they were taking charge of over two hundred prisoners who had already surrendered.

Houston and Rusk contacted all their officers and told the men, "We must prepare for another column of Mexicans to attack us, and we must stop the killing. We need the officers to get intelligence about what the Mexicans have planned, but above all, we need Santa Anna!"

Most sensible people knew that the Texans had been lucky to have actually surprised the Mexican Army. Houston was in a great deal of pain from his wound and he went to his tent, staying outside by the fire laying on a good mattress an aide had dragged over.

The prison had been set up about a hundred yards from the Texas camp and the three-foot-high wall around it was made of large trees and other material taken from the Mexican camp. The *Twin Sisters* and the *Golden Standard* were loaded and pointed at the prisoners from three positions. Later that evening fires glowed inside the prisoner containment area, allowing them to warm themselves up and to dry out wet clothes. Almost every Texas soldier now had more than one pistol, plenty of ammunition, a full powder horn, a saber or Bowie knife, in addition to a rifle or musket or carbine. The one hundred men that were guarding the prisoners had discovered a large number of small candles. The Mexicans had walked around the temporary prison with those burning in their hands. This made it an eerie sight. A small number of the prisoners were women.

At first the Anahuac bunch was assigned to prisoner guard duty until A.D. complained to Colonel Rusk, "I have at least twenty horses that need to be looked after tonight."

Rusk agreed and told A.D. and the others, "Go on over and work on the horses and I will get replacements for you." Frank and the others helped A.D. tend the horses all the following day.

Colonel Ned Burleson had placed two men to guard Santa Anna's tent and told them they could have anything that was edible out of that tent. There was a lot of food and two six-foot-high mountain baskets of champagne. Several of their buddies came by, and the guards gave them each a bottle of champagne. This information spread through the Texas camp quickly and there were a lot of soldiers and officers that visited them during the night. The two soldiers thought the Colonel would agree that champagne could be classified as edibles.

In addition, Houston knew they had captured Colonel Altamonte, so he sent for him. He questioned Altamonte for about an hour and told him he wanted him close by and wanted his tent set up where it would be more convenient to talk to him. Ten Mexican soldiers along with five Texans to guard them moved Altamonte's tent twenty yards from Houston's tent. That night, Houston asked Rusk, "How many men did we lose?"

"Nine dead and fifteen wounded, including you. It is a remarkable victory, Sam. No one can deny it."

"Still we must catch Santa Anna," Houston said.

ART ANTHONY

"Sam," he said, "there are a lot of Mexicans still in the swamp, but we have it surrounded and don't intend to go in there until in the morning. We have approximately four hundred prisoners, and we do not have a final count on the number of dead Mexicans. There will be more prisoners in the morning because they were bottled up in two different marshes. When daylight comes, they will have to surrender."

This battle was won because the Texans had been able to surprise the Mexican Army in daylight. The real fighting lasted only about twenty minutes. After that, most of the soldiers were murdering any of the Mexicans they found alive.

Houston had Colonel Millard's men secure the Mexican camp so that looting would not take place. The final count was six hundred thirty dead and two hundred eight wounded Sandinistas. The prisoners and the wounded numbered seven hundred thirty. Santa Anna's Army had almost been annihilated. Yet Sam Houston knew that the San Jacinto Battle would not be a real victory until they had captured the Dictator of Mexico, sometimes called the Napoleon of the West.

208

25

CHAPTER

Just before dawn, a search party of 30 was formed under Colonel Burleson and Houston told him to look hard at all captured soldiers because he thought Santa Anna would be dressed in a private's uniform. Santa Anna, General Cos, and Caro, Santa Anna's secretary rode the seven miles to the destroyed Vince's bridge. They decided to get off their horses and walk because it was so muddy the horses were bogging down. They also decided to split up to easier avoid detection and they were in tall grass which would easier hide a man.

The dictator feared water, and he certainly couldn't swim the swollen Vince's Bayou. Santa Anna was trapped in a pocket of overflowing rivers, bayous and creeks. He spent the night in the tall grass and early in the morning of the April 22, he worked up enough nerve to ford a waist-deep creek, where he found some slave quarters and put on different clothes owned by the slaves.

The colonel had sent six men in a different direction than some of the other searchers. Sgt. Sylvester, Privates Sion Bostick, Alfred Miles, Charles Thompson, Joe Vermillion, Joel Robison. Joel was the only one that could speak Spanish. These men started back on the road between the Vince's bridge and the Lynchburg ferry, which ran through tall grass as high as five feet, when one of them spotted some buck deer. While the others waited for him, he galloped in to the high grass and stopped about a hundred yards from the road and began to sight a bead on one of the bucks. Something startled the animals, and they ran off.

A moment later, the soldier saw a hat appear in the same location where the deer had been. He hollered to his companion, and at the same time spurred his horse to that location. Santa Anna ran only a few paces and then fell to the ground, covering himself with a muddy blanket. The other Texan rode up, dismounted, kicked Santa Anna to his feet and searched him for weapons. He wanted to shoot the captive, but one of the others interceded.

When Joel Robison rode up and started talking to the captive in Spanish, Santa Anna kissed the Texans hands. Joel saw the fine shirt and the diamond studs under the rough clothes and he asked; "Are you an officer?"

"No, soldier."

The captors let him ride out of the tall grass to the road. When they got to the road, they made him walk, but he complained so much, they discussed killing him or having him walk by himself back to the prison camp.

Most of these six men wanted to go hunt deer and three of the captors, including Robison, decided they would take the prisoner on to the prison camp. Santa Anna rode with Robison because he spoke Spanish. He asked a lot of questions on the way back to the Texas prison camp and could not believe the Texans had fewer than eight hundred men. The prison compound was in a state of excitement because the guards were teasing the prisoners.

At 2:00 p.m. the Dictator, dressed as a private, with his three captors arrived at the prison area. The prisoners began to exclaim "El Presidente! El Presidente!"

The Mexican officers were saying, "Shut your mouth! Shut your mouth!" at this point.

Colonel Hockley and Major Ben Fort Smith took charge of the prisoner and led Santa Anna to where General Houston was lying.

"General Houston, here is Santa Anna!" Colonel Hockley announced.

Santa Anna, speaking in Spanish told General Houston, "I am Antonio Lopez de Santa Anna, Commander in Chief of the Mexican Army, and I put myself at the disposition of the brave General Houston. I wish to be treated as a General should when a prisoner of war."

Tom Rusk and Lorenzo de Zavala Jr., were walking up to see Houston when Santa Anna was led up. Santa Anna recognized young De Zavala and immediately went up and embraced him, saying, "My young friend."

De Zavala's expression was plainly mortified as he stared at the president full in the face. Santa Anna was more than mortified when he stood before Houston with curious Texans not wanting to miss the culmination of their recent battle and most of them in favor of execution on the spot. Houston ordered the men who made threats against Santa Anna to be removed.

Excitement burned through the entire camp. Houston's Spanish was inadequate for this discussion, so Almonte and young De Zavala acted as interpreters.

"General Santa Anna, please have a seat," Houston invited. The General took a seat on an ammunition box nearby while Houston propped himself against the oak tree in a seated position. His wound was forgotten for a while as he cut himself a chew of tobacco. The Mexican Dictator clutched his knees to control them from shaking and asked that his opium box be brought to him. At the same time, Houston ordered Santa Anna's tent and other camp effect be brought up by some prisoners and set up next to Almonte's tent.

Santa Anna took some opium which calmed him for a while. Finally, he had full command of his voice when he stated, "That man may consider himself born to know common destiny which had conquered the Napoleon of the West. Now it remains for him to be generous to the vanquished."

Houston replied, "You should have remembered that at the Alamo and before you gave the order to assassinate Texans at Goliad."

Santa Anna desperately tried to justify his actions, but Houston would have none of it.

"The less you say about your own crimes the better it will be for you, sir," Rusk interjected.

Several times Santa Anna would take another piece of opium to calm himself. Thomas Rusk did a lot of talking during the two-hour conference with Santa Anna.

His Excellency ultimately said "I will stop the war and send Filisola and the other troops out of Texas."

"Then tell Filisola and all the troops with him to surrender," said Rusk.

"I will do nothing to disgrace myself and my nation," answered Santa

Anna with more spirit than he had shown since his capture. "I am but a single Mexican and you can do what you want with me."

Houston agreed, to a solution, of Mexican troops a full-scale retreat. Caro, Santa Anna's secretary, was summoned to prepare his dispatch to General Filisola. Several copies of this document were made. He said that the division under his command was killed or taken prisoner yesterday afternoon. I am a prisoner of war in the hands of the enemy who have treated me kindly. With these circumstances, I recommend you to order General Gaona to march back to San Antonio and await orders. You will do the same thing with the troops under your immediate command. General Urrea is to take his division back to Victoria. I have agreed with General Houston to call for an armistice, pending negotiations, which could put an end to this war. It was dated April 22, San Jacinto, Texas.

When Caro had prepared Santa Anna's dispatches, Houston summoned, Deaf Smith, and two of his trusted friends to deliver the orders to Filisola, and the canny scout took off that night for the Brazos.

Houston and Santa Anna discussed the large number of dead Mexican soldiers on the battlefield and whether Santa Anna would allow the Santanistas to bury them.

"It is a very small item of my concern," Santa Anna replied, "and I will not have my men bury their comrades. We never buried the dead in the battle of Zacatecas, and I will not have my people bury their dead in this battlefield."

Houston replied, "Someone will write your statement down and I want you to sign it, so that everyone knows this was your decision." The stink of dead bodies was beginning to be too much for everyone. These bodies also attracted wolves, coyotes and other wild animals as they ate the carcasses.

Houston explained to his men why he didn't kill Santa Anna.

"If Santa Anna is held a prisoner, his friends will be afraid to invade Texas because they will not know if and when we would kill him. His political enemies couldn't attempt to take over in Mexico or prepare for another Texas invasion, because they don't know that one moment he might be released upon them. So, I guarantee peace to Texas, so long as he is a prisoner."

Word of the battle and its outcome spread quickly to the refugees near the battlefield and actually within two days, most knew the Texas Army had annihilated the Mexican Army at San Jacinto.

Houston and Rusk had begun to reorganize their army on April 22 in preparation for another battle with the other Mexican troops presently in Texas. The Texas Army was certainly eating much better and getting some much-needed sleep and rest.

Deaf Smith and his agents were close to Fort Bend the next morning when they came upon a lone Mexican rider. They knocked him off his horse, then caught and questioned him. He was a courier from San Antonio, bringing Mexico City dispatches intended for Santa Anna. He was riding along so casually because he thought the Mexican Army had control of the Brazos country. Smith confiscated all the dispatches intended for Santa Anna. Then he told the frightened courier about Santa Anna's defeat and capture showing him the dictators' letter to Filisola. He put a copy of the letter in the Mexican's wallet and told him to deliver it to Filisola at Fort Bend.

While Smith's crew was trailing the messenger to Filisola's camp, he encountered another lone Mexican, this time walking. Smith did not realize that he had captured, General Cos. He didn't know that the General had offered $1,000 for Deaf Smith's head, saying he would cut it off and send it to Mexico City. Smith found a horse for the Mexican soldier, and they returned to the San Jacinto battleground. Smith was really surprised when he learned he had captured General Cos. The presence of General Cos at the Mexican prison created a sensation among the Texans, and they crowded and quarreled for a sight of him. All Cos wanted to do was lay down comfortably in a blanket. There were many of the Texans who would have liked to murder him.

Colonel Mariano Garcia, the commander of Cos's straggling rearguard on the morning of the battle, had not arrived at the Vince's bridge until Smith had burned it. Garcia's unit apparently camped near the burned bridge where they heard the noise of the battle and then intercepted fleeing Mexican survivors. There was only one horse in this infantry unit and the commander sent a courier with a note describing the Mexican defeat to Filisola.

The courier arrived in the early morning hours of April 22 and the general who had 1,000 men on the east bank of the Brazos quickly brought them to the west bank, where they were joined by Gaona's division. He did not send a message until 3:00 o'clock that afternoon to General Urrea telling him of the lost battle and asking him to meet him at Powell's Tavern as soon as possible. Urrea, who was not friendly with Filisola, received his message at 9:00 a.m. the next morning. He set out up the west side of the Brazos at once and on the way picked up two survivors of Santa Anna's division who explained the battle to him. When Urrea's commander of the unbeaten brigade arrived Filisola, Gaona, and Sesma were already there.

"With a force of three thousand backed by rearguard of fifteen hundred crossing at Brazos and attacking Houston's army," Urrea began, "how could anyone deny the success of that operation against Houston's reported seven hundred fifty men?"

All of the Mexican Generals felt that Houston's force might grow to over twelve hundred because of his victory against Santa Anna. But, they rightfully pointed out that the new troops arriving would be green and not trained.

Filisola, the new commanding general, said, "If the Mexicans went on the offensive, Houston would merely kill all the prisoners and the mobile rebels could easily continue keeping one or more of the raging rivers between them and our forces." He also reminded the assembled generals, "Realize that the average Mexican soldier has a belly full of this wilderness called Texas." All the generals finally voted for retreat, and the Mexicans headed for San Antonio and Victoria.

Houston's eight hundred ragged rebels settled down in earnest to the labors of the victorious and began to count the spoils. In Houston's official report, there were about six hundred muskets, three hundred sabers, two hundred pistols, six hundred mules and horses, and nearly $12,000 in specie. There were also almost eighty loads of ammunition and powder, forty carts and wagons, all of this under guard. Most of the Texas soldiers had picked up a lot of the ammunition, arms and horses from the dead and captured Mexicans for themselves but, of course, this was not in the report.

Houston had been going over Santa Anna's private papers and had discovered that he had the names of many prominent Texans who were backers of the Mexican Government. Many of those same collaborators had relatives who fought well for the rebels out of wisdom and kindness.

Houston never released the names of the Tories. In place of that, he sent out a company of men under Captain Dan Kokernot to inform these known Tories that they were now working for a lost cause. Kokernot did a good job of convincing the Tory leaders, and he kept their names a secret.

The day after the battle, Houston began to dictate his official report of the battle to Burnet, but he took three days to finish the report because he was in such pain from the infection of his ankle. Two of Houston's Doctors told him he should take some of Santa Annas opium to help reduce his pain. Houston did that and it helped!

A.D. and Frank took an idea to Houston about a place to house some of the prisoners of war.

"We know a place where you could keep a third of these prisoners, the housing is already built and it would be easy to control them," A.D. said, "in the fort in Anahuac."

They continued, "It would require very little repair, and it has held as many as three hundred soldiers, but we think it would more easily hold two hundred fifty." Houston and Colonel Rusk agreed to consider their idea. "We will make a decision by tomorrow," Houston promised. "If we say yes, we will want to move out right away with them."

A.D. replied, "I also think it would be better to take Texas guards that live around our area."

"Yes," they both replied.

Houston asked, "Have you been busy with the horses and mules?"

"Lord, you wouldn't believe in the four days that I've been here, I have worked with over a hundred head."

Rusk followed the settlers back to their wagon and told them, "Make plans so that you know exactly what you will need, the men you need and how you're going to get to the fort with the prisoners."

As luck would have it Captain Briscoe, who was over the Liberty volunteers, had three horses he needed shod, and A.D. promised he would have them done in about three hours. A.D. and Frank discussed their plans for the prisoners for up to six months.

A.D. was pleased with their practical plan.

"It makes more sense for men in our area to guard those prisoners because they are closer to their homes and farms," he told Frank. "We need about sixty-five more men to get the job done."

Captain Briscoe agreed to talk to his company from Liberty while the blacksmithing work was being done.

"I have twenty-five men who volunteered for prison guard duty," he told A.D. when he returned to pick up his horses, "and I'll send them over to you in about an hour."

Vice President De Zavala was the first member of the government to arrive after the battle. He had not come to celebrate because he did not find out about the victory until he docked at New Washington to get supplies from James Morgan. He was accompanied by an armed company of men from Galveston Island led by John Linn. The steamer, *Cayuga*, was carrying flour, coffee, sugar, gunpowder, lead and other items.

Also, on the steamer was Tom McKinney, one of the financiers of the Revolution. All the men on the steamer were appalled to see all the dead Mexicans lying unburied and immediately turned on Houston and Rusk with indignation!

Houston gave them a copy of the statement signed by Santa Anna stating he did not care. He would not order his men to bury these dead comrades.

"I won't have my men do it either," Houston quietly added. The men then calmed down.

De Zavala went out to the battlefield to find his friend Castrillon's mutilated body and had his servants take the body to his family burial ground, less than a mile from the battle. He was buried there.

The owner of the land where the battle was fought came, complaining to General Houston about the dead Mexican bodies. Houston did nothing to remedy that situation to the owner's satisfaction.

Finally, at nine o'clock that night, Houston, Rusk, Zavala, Linn and McKinney had a meeting about the prisoners and were told of the option of taking two hundred fifty of them to the fort in Anahuac. They all agreed that it would be a good thing to begin tomorrow and not wait for President Burnet to give his okay.

Rusk immediately informed A.D. and Frank, "Get everything packed by noon tomorrow and leave. You have been promoted to Captains, and here is paper stating that."

A.D. asked, "Can we enlist some local men from our area, especially ones that speak Spanish?"

"Yes, up to ten men;" Rusk agreed. "Just get me their names. But you cannot tell anyone where you're taking these prisoners."

A.D. asked, "Who picks the prisoners?"

"I'll get Colonel Almonte to do it because I know he will be fair. We will have them picked tomorrow so there's less to worry about."

A.D. said, "Here is a list of what I need and you'll probably have to give me authorization to get it."

"I can do that except for the $1,000." Rusk answered. "That'll have to be Okayed by Houston."

Of course, he did.

Houston also insisted, "An extra company of men need to escort the prisoners to Anahuac and return after a week of helping the guards and prisoners settle in."

On April 24, one hundred soldiers escorted two hundred fifty Mexican prisoners on their march toward Anahuac. They crossed the San Jacinto on Lynch's ferry and crossed the Trinity on a sloop they hailed coming down the river. They arrived at the fort on April 26.

There was a lot of joy with the local men returning home victorious and the possibility that they would be guarding prisoners for at least six months. The forty men that had been sent to help guard the prisoners helped for two days and two nights before returning to the battleground.

During those two days, A.D. and Frank gave various assignments to the prisoners: fourteen men as cooks, four men to fish for food, six men to hunt for food, twenty men to plant a fifty acre garden, ten men make bricks, ten men to make cots, thirty men to clean and repair the fort, twenty men to gather firewood, and twenty men to rebuild the corrals and fences for the livestock. The rest were assigned to help plant two hundred acres of corn for the fort.

A.D. quickly enlisted the three ex-Mexican soldiers that were homesteading in the area as interpreters with orders that one would be at the fort at all times. The prisoners were allowed to take much of their own clothing and boots, but the captors knew they would have to wear some identifying piece of clothing to indicate they were incarcerated. Several of the local women showed twenty of the prisoners how to cut out and sew gray shirts that they must wear at all times.

On the two day trip, they had killed eleven deer which would feed everyone for at least five days, along with the beans which would become a staple for every meal. The men built a building for drying venison, beef and pork. A.D. had also bought three hundred chicks in hopes that in a few months they could start having eggs. They assigned ten men to build a five-acre chicken yard. He also bought twenty sows, and the prisoners had to make a hog lot for them. Every Saturday the prisoners were marched to the Trinity River where they washed the clothes on themselves and bathed. They were served two meals a day, breakfast and supper. On Sunday, they rested.

Back at the battleground, Houston and Santa Anna had further agreed for the Dictator to send a new dispatch to Filisola ordering the Mexican troops to retreat to the Rio Grande. The message was to be handed to the Mexican commander in person. Ned Burleson, with three hundred cavalrymen was to deliver this order.

They started in the early morning of April 25 in search of Filisola's camp. They located it on the Colorado River. After receiving Santa Anna's letter and orders, the Mexican commander told Burleson, he would give an answer the next morning.

By nine o'clock the next morning the Texans had not received Filisola's answer. They went to inspect the Mexican's camp, but found the enemy had left leaving tents, wagons, muskets, lances and everything they couldn't carry conveniently on pack mules. They had retreated burning the carriages of six pieces of artillery and throwing the guns into a pond.

They had also left twenty sick and wounded Santanistas. The Texans fed them and tried to treat their ailments. Colonel Burleson also left eight men to try and help the sick men get well enough to send them back to Mexico.

Six of the prisoners died within six days, but the others were soon well enough to travel back to Mexico on their own. The Texans equipped them with two wagons, eight mules, four muskets, four pistols, powder and lead so they could hunt or defend themselves against Indians or irate settlers.

Burleson ordered ten men to retrieve the cannons from the water, clean and oil them and take them, along with other salvageable materials the Mexican Army left behind, back to General Houston.

Burleson and the rest of his men trailed General Filisola and his four-thousand-man army until they crossed the Rio Grande. The Colonel left thirty of his men at the Rio Grande, making sure the General did not re-cross for another attack on Texas.

Some of the men with wanted furloughs to go home and check on their families. The rest headed to San Jacinto to rejoin Houston's Army.

The Texas Army and the remaining Mexican prisoners had moved seven miles from the San Jacinto battleground because of all the stink. Distrust of the Mexicans prevailed. Houston and Rusk worried that the Mexican Army would try to return an attack. The new location gave them peace of mind about a better defensive position until they got confirmation from Burleson that the army had crossed the Rio Grande.

Before moving the prisoners to Anahuac, A.D., Frank, Houston and Rusk had discussed the possibility of the Mexican Navy attacking Fort Anahuac. As a result, A.D. had requested the captured *Golden Standard* cannon and two smaller cannons to protect the fort from the Bay. Houston had not sent the cannons, but when Burleson returned with the six Mexican cannons, he sent A.D, the big *Golden Standard* and two of the captured cannons with twenty artillery men and Lieutenant Kraft on a steamship to permanently protect the Fort from attack from ships.

Upon arrival, Kraft and his men began to replace the frames from the two six pound cannons. After two weeks of making repairs, the lieutenant began firing the cannons, marking his range. The cannon's firing upset the townsfolk so much that Captain Stroud ordered Kraft to stop. The local population was informed and forewarned of why the cannons were firing. Afterward, Kraft was allowed to fire another forty shots until he thought he had his range marked.

Kraft then gave half of his men thirty day furloughs. Three of them did not return at all. Then he let the other half of his men go on thirty day furlough, and two of those did not return. So, the lieutenant was down to fifteen men in his detachment. He then took a thirty-day furlough himself.

Rusk completed his brief report of the battle for Burnet. He decided to dispatch this message at once instead of waiting until Houston was ready. The four messengers could only get a row boat to take them the forty-five miles to Galveston.

The men left on April 23 with the dispatch and finally reached Burnet five days later with the great news. One of the dispatches Houston had sent telling of the victory had finally reached the United States Army forces under General Gaines on the Neches River. Gaines sent his own messenger to relay the news to President Andrew Jackson in Washington, D.C.

People say Texas has two seasons: summer and the rainy season, and this winter and spring had testified with frequent precipitation. Before and after the San Jacinto battle, rainstorms, followed by near unbearable heat and humidity plagued the soldiers and prisoners and kept them in low spirits most of the time.

Finally, on May 4, the travel-worn Texas Interim Government led by President Burnet arrived on the steamship, *Yellowstone*. The President and Secretary of the Navy Potter suggested that Houston should be court martialed for mismanagement of the San Jacinto campaign. Their complaint was Houston could have just as easily stopped the Mexicans on the Colorado River and saved the country between the Colorado and the Brazos River from being overrun by the enemy. Rusk, De Zavala and many others saw to it that Potter's suggestions were ignored. Houston's new tremendous popularity with the majority of the soldiers would have saved him from a court martial anyway. The regular soldiers had criticized the general during the retreat, but after San Jacinto, they were well reconciled to Houston's management of the campaign.

There is no doubt that Houston had done a great thing in managing this war against the Santanistas. He knew he had limited forces and was badly outnumbered, so he picked the battle where he knew Santa Anna could be confronted. All the delaying tactics were to wear down the Mexican Army and to also train his many untrained troops. Burnet and the many others that opposed him knew his tactics had been the correct ones for the Texas rebels. This fact really galled Houston's critics. The president and his cabinet spent little time at the Army's headquarters.

Houston's wound was so much worse, that Doctor Ewing feared the General would die if he didn't get better medical attention. The doctor suggested that Houston be sent to New Orleans by way of Galveston. On the May 5, Houston resigned his commission and turned his command over to Rusk. He would return to Galveston with Burnet who was leaving in only two days.

Santa Anna and others of the more prominent Mexican prisoners were to be taken back to Galveston with the Texas Government officials. In the evening of May 7, Burnet and the cabinet including the new Secretary of War, Mirabeau Lamar, went aboard the *Yellowstone*.

Thomas Rusk, his brother David and others carried Houston on a cot, down to the dock where Burnet informed them, to their astonishment, "Since Houston is no longer in the employ of the Republic, he cannot have passage on this government ship."

Captain J.E. Ross of the *Yellowstone* came to the rescue, "This ship is not sailing unless General Houston is on board!"

A few minutes later the Rusk brothers put Houston aboard the vessel. A few days after the *Yellowstone* reached Galveston, Houston left for New Orleans to have his badly infected ankle wounds treated. For six weeks he was seriously ill in the hospital. He recuperated for another six weeks.

The Texas cause was popular in most parts of the United States. Even the abolitionists had developed a liking for the rebels after they heard of Santa Anna's cruelty at the Alamo and Goliad massacres.

Santa Anna was imprisoned in Texas for many months during which time his influence in Mexico waned. The Mexican government made announcements that all arrangements Santa Anna made as a captive were illegal. Also, Texas hadn't fulfilled all the provisions of the Velasco treaties because the Mexican President had not been returned to his own country.

Burnet had other problems. There was no money in the treasury. He was unpopular with the people. The Army continued to give trouble, and their soldiers had grown tired of guarding the herd of prisoners. Many of the prisoners were already farmed out to work on farms and ranches. The big plantation owners acquired the most skilled prisoners to replace the hundreds of slaves that ran off during the runaway scrape.

Within a week of the Texas victory the victorious soldiers were given from $3 to $12 each. The commissary officer, Colonel Forbes, fell under a lot of criticism because by the time the money was divided with the soldiers, much of it was already lost! Most of the captured Mexican equipment was auctioned off. Each soldier was given $16 credit to buy auctioned articles. A.D. had picked out ten horses that he wanted.

Frank Jr. stayed to buy stock and other items for all of the Anahuac soldiers with $100 A.D. had given him. He was able to buy three of the horses A.D. wanted for $116. He also bought twelve mules and other items which he drove home. He paid another soldier $5 to help him drive the animals and equipment to Anahuac.

With Sam Houston out of the way, Burnet thought that things would go smoothly for him, but that wasn't the case. From Galveston, the Interim Government moved to Velasco, where the Brazos River meets the Gulf, and settled down to consider the case of the Republic of Texas versus Santa Anna who was charged with murder.

Lamar and Potter argued for Santa Anna to be executed immediately. Burnet believed, as Houston had, that Santa Anna should be spared, at least for a while, as a hostage to keep peace. Rusk, the new commander of the Army, sat in on the case as expressing his views in support of the president.

So instead of killing Santa Anna on May 14 at Velasco, the Texans signed two treaties with Santa Anna. The first treaty, which was made public, provided that all hostilities should cease, all Mexican troops should retreat beyond the Rio Grande and all prisoners should be exchanged. This treaty also stated that Santa Anna would be returned to Mexico as soon as possible, after having promised that he would never again take up arms against Texas.

The second treaty was a secret one. It differed from the first only in that there were more details on the promised conduct of Santa Anna. Once he was back in Mexico he was to use his influence on the Mexican government to acknowledge Texas independence and to make arrangements so that Texas diplomatic and trade missions could visit Mexico City. Because of the second treaty, it was imperative that Santa Anna be returned to Mexico before his Dictator organization had broken up. Most participants of the Texas Army tried to overthrow Burnet's political agenda because soldiers demanded Santa Anna's execution. Burnet defied the Army and held on to his position. On June 1, 1836, in accordance with the treaties, Santa Anna was taken aboard the *Invincible*, off the shore of Velasco. Santa Anna, Almonte and his secretary, Cato, and other aides sent a farewell message to the disgruntled Texas Army units at Velasco which only inflamed them more. Unfortunately, adverse weather prevented the ship from sailing for the next two days.

On June 3, several hundred-armed volunteers from the United States arrived on the steamboat called the *Ocean*, and they were looking for trouble. The leaders of the newly arrived volunteers made speeches against Burnet, and finally the mob gathered around the President's house.

Burnet came out to address the crowd, defending his views and insisting that the treaty should be carried out for the faith of the nation to be preserved. He was followed by the Attorney General and John A. Wharton giving speeches. They vindicated the treaty, repelled most questions and stated the interference of the military in the affair was unfair.

Wharton protested especially against the interference calling it defiance of armed strangers who had just landed on Texas shores. He could not understand the idea that they should become the dictators of the country and said the Texas government would not relent.

The mob finally prevailed and Captain Brown sent word from the *Invincible* that he wouldn't sail, even if ordered to do so by the President. Burnet, then saw the impossibility of carrying out the treaty. Men went on board and took Santa Anna and marched him to McKinney's store.

McKinney, one of the revolution's financiers, commented, "We already have a failing government."

"May I be excused from further connection with the Burnet government," De Zavala asked, "which has lost the support of the Texas people?" Actually, the speeches by Burnet, John Wharton and Grayson disparaging the government may have saved Santa Anna from being lynched.

On June 18, Henry Clay offered a resolution to the United States Congress that the independence of Texas be recognized. The resolution was not adopted until March, 1837. The fact that it was offered did serve to bolster the Texas position in relation to Mexico, and it also must have made everyone in Texas happy.

26

CHAPTER

Meanwhile, back at old Fort Anahuac, the prison routine had become well established. The area's ten largest ranchers asked A.D. for five workers each to work on their ranches. A.D. permitted the work release, but required the ranchers give one steer to the fort for each month they kept the Mexican prisoners. The ranchers signed a paper that they were responsible to give them a place to eat, sleep and not allow them to escape. In lieu of driving the steers back to the fort, the ranchers could opt to pay $20 each to keep the prisoners for four months.

In May and June, A.D., Frank and all other farmers in the area had the prisoners harvest their oat crops. The farmers, except the overseers – A.D. and Frank, provided twenty bushels of oats to the prison fort in barter for the prisoners' work. The prisoners also built a varmint-free storage area large enough to hold a great deal of grain. A.D. and Frank took four mules and ten prisoners out to the grinding stone, crushed and sifted three thousand pounds of flour in a week. Half went to the fort and the other fifteen hundred pounds were split between A.D. and Frank.

The men also discussed moving the grinding mill to the Trinity River where water would power the crushing rock in place of the mules that they currently used. The time was ripe to make this adjustment while they had the prison manpower to complete the arduous task of moving the massive stone.

Liberty cancelled the annual July celebration, which disappointed the locals.

In June the prisoners harvested thirty-five large wagons of hay for A.D. and Frank. They split two dozen wagonloads and sent the rest to the prison. This was the most hay they had ever had. As wardens of the prison, they were keeping all the prisoners busy and self-supporting.

Almost monthly, Burnet or Rusk visited the fort to check on the prisoners' conditions. They approved of the management methods A.D. and Frank employed.

"Prisoners held in other parts of Texas certainly are not this well off," Rusk indicated to Frank on one such visit.

The Anahuac Prison population was down to one hundred seventy; the rest were working on farms and ranches in the area. Five had died during the first four months.

In September, A.D. harvested his two-hundred-acre cornfield with an average of forty bushels to an acre of field corn. One month later, prisoners harvested the two hundred acres they had planted at the fort, averaging thirty bushels to the acre. By the end of September, the ort, A.D.'s and Frank's corn had provided almost four thousand five hundred bushels of corn for cornmeal, split three ways.

President Burnet had grown weary of his office, and on July 3, he issued a proclamation for a general election on the first Monday of September, 1836. Three candidates ran. Sam Houston won an overwhelming victory, receiving 4,373 votes to Henry Smith's 745 and Austin's 587. Houston and the first Congress took office in October. President Houston appointed Austin Secretary of State and Smith Secretary of the Treasury. He also relieved Rusk of the command of the rough Texas Army, consisting of 2,500 men and returned him to his old post as Secretary of War.

When Rusk took the cabinet post a new problem arose. The soldiers chose a wild man named General Felix Huston as their leader. Sam Houston and the Texas Congress nominated Albert Sidney Johnston as Senior General, but when Johnston tried to take over command of the Army, he was challenged to a duel by Huston. He accepted and was wounded badly and spent a long time recovering.

General Huston went to the Texas capital to report on the Matamoros operations. Huston wanted to extend the revolution by leading an expedition against Matamoras, a Mexican town on the Rio Grande. Houston entertained the young general for a week, even sleeping on the floor while allowing his guest have his bed.

While Huston was with the President, Secretary of War Rusk rode to all the Army camps, giving most of the troops furloughs. When Huston returned from the capital, he found that his army had been reduced to only a thousand men. Deprived of his army, he stayed in Texas for a few years, participating in Indian wars from time to time but never again making his ambition felt as he had when he first arrived in 1836. He went home to Mississippi in 1840 and never returned to Texas.

At the end of October, 1836, the fort prison guarding detail counted sixty enlisted men, plus Captain Stroud and Captain Logging. The artillery unit consisted of fifteen enlisted men plus, Lieutenant Kraft. He had also volunteered half of his men daily to help with guard duty while the other half were look outs, day and night.

At 6:00 a.m. on October 24, a lookout spotted a Mexican man-of-war steamer five hundred yards out in the bay, and a rowboat with an officer and two men approaching the fort under a white flag. The men in the row boat were headed toward the base of the fort. A.D. immediately sent Weldon to warn all families close by. He also sent Art to Liberty to get as many volunteers as possible to help defend the fort. He made sure his wife and daughter went to his out-of-town ranch.

A.D. and Frank met the boat with its Colonel at the bank of the Bay. They did not want him to come into the fort to see their defenses and cannons.

"Unless you release all the prisoners the man-of-war will began shelling the town and the fort," the Colonel warned. "We will then invade the area."

Frank asked, "How much time do we have to make our decision because we'll have to talk to the Mayor and others in this village?"

"You can have three hours before we start shelling," As the Colonel left, he said, "Remember, nine o'clock."

A.D. and Frank agreed they would not surrender or turn the prisoners over to the Mexican Colonel. Everyone began preparations to fight. The prisoners were all fed breakfast and marched off to do their various details. Fifteen guards took care of that chore.

The Texans only had forty-three men ready to fight, but most of them had Halls Breech loading rifles. With this rifle each man could shoot four rounds a minute, whereas the muzzle loading muskets the Mexicans had could only shoot two rounds a minute. The Halls rifles were much more accurate which gave the Texans an advantage if the Mexicans landed. A.D. and Frank were confident that the *Golden Standard* would be their secret weapon, and Lieutenant Kraft agreed with them. The artillery officer's first concern was to get the Mexican man-of-war, *Aztec*, in closer. He needed it to be about three hundred yards to be in range of *Golden Standard*. All of them felt if they could hit the *Aztec* three times the ship would start retreating.

A.D. sent Pat and a prisoner to move all the livestock in town to a small pasture three miles out of town. By eight o'clock the Texas soldiers had their orders to move to a defensive position.

The *Aztec* had moved to within a one hundred fifty yards of the fort, and Lieutenant Kraft asked permission to open fire. He was extremely lucky with his first two shots, hitting the Mexican steamer. Then the big cannon missed twice, but the fifth shot hit.

In the meantime, the Mexicans had launched three large rowboats loaded with soldiers. At the same time the rowboats were moving toward the shore, the *Aztec* had begun to shell the town.

The small cannons of the Fort turned their aim toward the rowboats. Lieutenant Kraft had already marked the distances in the Bay from the Fort and when the small rowboats hit the 100-yard mark, the small cannons sunk two of them.

A.D. had twenty men mounted to intercept the rowboats where it looked like they would land. Frank also had twenty-three infantrymen to meet the rowboats at the same location.

The *Aztec* retreated trying to avoid the fire of the *Golden Standard*. The big Cannon hit the ship twice more before it could get out of range. The Mexicans were now more concerned about saving their ship, not the rowboats. All the men from the rowboats, including the ones in the water, were trying desperately to get ashore. At the same time the *Aztec* had struck its colors, raised a white flag and was trying to get back to a small dock close to the Fort. When the ship finally made it to shore everyone worked hard to secure the man-of-war so that it wouldn't sink.

A.D. asked the local carpenter, "Will you supervise building of scaffolding, so that the *Aztec* will not sink and can be repaired?" He agreed to do that.

A.D., Frank and their men had rounded up ninety-five Mexican soldiers and fifteen sailors that were all from the Aztec. Five soldiers and five sailors were missing, assumed to be dead from the brief pounding from the fort's cannons.

The Texans allowed the sailors and officers of the *Aztec* to work with the local carpenter, under his orders, to repair their ship. The newly arrived Army prisoners were taken to the fort and processed into the system. The carpenter and the sailors of *Aztec* had it repaired and ready to sail within two weeks.

Immediately after the capture of the *Aztec*, forty militiamen arrived from Liberty to help defeat the Mexican attack. When they understood the attack was over, they told Frank, they would return home immediately. Frank tried unsuccessfully to reason with them; they were needed the help in guarding the new prisoners.

A.D. rode after the retreating volunteers explaining how much they needed them. Then the leader, James Hardie, offered a compromise.

"My men need to get home and take care of their families, before properly preparing to ride back down in a week and spend two weeks at the fort helping guard the prisoners," Hardie promised.

A.D. and Frank wrote a report to President Houston asking what to do about the new prisoners and the man-of-war. In a month Secretary Rusk visited Anahuac and informed them the *Aztec* was now Texas property and would not be returned to Mexico. In a few weeks he would send a Navy Captain and crew to take charge of the *Aztec*.

A.D. asked, "When are we going to send all the prisoners back to Mexico?"

He answered, "I think it will be in the next two or three months."

The Texans had also confiscated the ship's safe and found 20,000 pesos and 5,000 silver dollars. Rusk signed for $5,000 in silver saying, "I will put this in the Texas treasury. You Captains can do what you want with the Mexican money."

The Captains also discussed with Rusk the land claims and what was going to happen to all of those pioneers who had farms and ranches. Rusk indicated that Sam Houston was going to appoint lawyers and surveyors for different areas of Texas to settle the land claims. A. D. and Frank hoped the appointees would be of the honest variety.

A.D. also asked, "What about the land that was promised to the military men for serving in the Army and guarding these prisoners?"

"Will you make a list of all the men that fought at the battle of San Jacinto and also the ones that were guarding the prisoners including the time they served?" Rusk asked. "If you have a man that you want to fill the position, please tell me, and I will tell Sam Houston. I am sure he will consult y'all first."

"We would like to have attorney and surveyor Jack Jack appointed for this position in this area."

Rusk said, "Fine, I will relay your suggestion immediately, as I am bound for Velasco."

Houston realized that Santa Anna was becoming less viable as a hostage, so he decided to send the "Napoleon of the West" back to Mexico as soon as possible. His plan was for Santa Anna to go to Washington D.C. for a conference with President Jackson. From Washington, he would be shipped to Veracruz. The purpose, of course, was for the Mexican people to see the apparent respect shown to Santa Anna as their dictator and for him to be impressed with the power of the United States. Santa Anna and his aide, Colonel Almonte, traveled under guard to Washington in late 1836. Not long after the dictator reached Washington, he was released and sent back to Mexico on a United States ship. He was received coolly when he got to Mexico, but the old Santa Anna luck held. His participation in Mexico politics lasted for many years.

November 1836, back in Anahuac the Fort was operating with maximum capacity of two hundred seventy-five prisoners. Sure enough, as promised, the Liberty volunteers had returned with seventy-five men to help guard the prisoners for two weeks. The regular Texas guards took two weeks off to go home and take care of their families.

Life rocked on as usual for most of the farmers and cattlemen in the area, planting fall crops and working their herds. The town of Anahuac prepared for the big celebration for the first time since canceling it because of the Revolution. Art and Weldon were busy getting their horses Gray Boy and Checkers ready to run. Nine other Texas soldiers prepared to run their horses. The entrance fee was $15 each, but the winner got $400 and the heat winners got $100 each.

As it turned out, fifty-one horses were entered. A.D. and Frank allowed the prisoners to watch the horse races and other contests. The two commanders were hopeful that some of the celebration attendees would want to take some prisoners home to work as farm or ranch hands. As it turned out forty-five of the prisoners were farmed out to local farmers.

On the last Saturday in November. The long gun shooting contest started at eight o'clock in the morning. A.D., Frank and four others put four shots in the bull's-eye area in the allowed two minutes. The six finalists then shot at 150 yards. This time, A.D. and Frank were the only men to put four more shots in the bull's-eye area. They split the winnings.

The next events were knife throwing and hatchet throwing. Over 150 men paid their two-dollar entry fee for the chance to win. Two men from Harrisburg won the knife throwing contest and split $150. Six men tied for the axe throwing contest, and after six extra tries, it was declared a tie and each man received $40.

The horse race commenced at one o'clock with five different heats of ten horses each. Gray Boy and Checker won the first and third heats, both qualifying for the championship race. They tied for the championship race and split $400. Maggie and A.D. had also won $350 betting on their own horses.

There was no trouble at the dance this year, but A.D. had his boys guard his blacksmith shop and the racehorses. The May brothers guarded all the pasture animals and had no trouble.

The greased pig contest, horseshoe throwing, checkers and Domino tournaments took up most of the next day. The greased pig contest was the most fun to watch. Of all the children six and under who participated ten got to take home a pig. The prisoners enjoyed the two days, were very helpful and asked Frank if they could have checkers and dominoes at the prison. That request was granted. The prisoners had also helped cook the eight steers and six hogs plus four hundred pounds of potatoes. Local women contributed one hundred pecan pies. Of course, the prisoners ate lunch at the festivities since they were cooking and serving it. An estimated six hundred civilians and two hundred prisoners attended the festival.

Each of the Texas soldiers at the fort received one hundred pesos in December. Each member of A.D.'s family except young Patricia, received pesos for working. Maggie was still teaching the prisoners English two days a week.

"We still have 11,140 pesos left," Frank said. "What are you planning to do with it, A.D.?"

A.D. replied, "I want to give all the prisoners who have been here since they were captured at San Jacinto fifty pesos each to get them started when they get to Mexico."

"How about the ones we just captured?" asked Frank.

"They would get twenty pesos each for a total of 9,500, and we will still have about 1,900 left which we will need to help feed them. I would like for them to think we treated them right," A.D. responded.

The locals also celebrated Christmas at their homes since there was still no church within eighty miles. The prisoners were allowed to celebrate Christmas by cutting and decorating trees. Every prisoner received two pesos to shop for themselves at McCoy's store.

A.D. and Maggie gave the boys one more head of cattle and a horse to increase their existing herds. They gave their daughter, Patricia, some dolls and books.

The Loggings had their usual big celebration dinner with their family and friends. Their friends were all in the Texas Army, guarding prisoners at the Anahuac Fort and were getting very tired of this assignment.

December had been mild and the children had enjoyed fishing and hunting ducks and geese. All the area, including the prison, would be harvesting their winter garden soon which was critical for keeping the locals and prisoner fed.

On January 10, everything changed along the Gulf coast as a Blue Norther arrived, causing a sudden drop in temperature, heavy precipitation, and dark blue skies moving rapidly. . Forty days of near freezing temperatures followed. Luckily, the men of Anahuac had been able to kill more wild game and had their fall gardens harvested, keeping everyone fed.

27
CHAPTER

At the end of January, 1837, Navy Captain Walters arrived in Anahuac with fifteen sailors and five soldiers to take charge of the captured Mexican man-of-war *Aztec*. He gave his orders to Frank and said he would now be responsible for the newly renamed ship, the *Austin*. After they physically checked the vessel out, they sailed it in Galveston Bay for two days. This would be the homeport for the ship. They would be guarding Galveston Bay for at least four months. The present crew would be sent to the fort.

Captain Walters asked A.D. and Frank to supply the ship for two months. He said Rusk left enough pesos here to supply the Navy with food. A.D. and Frank got potatoes, onions, cabbage, turnips, twenty pounds each of cornmeal and flour, plus twenty pounds of sugar from McCoy's. Also, they were given one steer, one hog and some lard. "How about eggs?" Walters questioned.

A.D. lied and said, "We don't have any eggs. You might try buying some at Morgan's Point, Lynch's ferry or even Galveston."

Walters said, "Give me some money then so I can buy some."

A.D. said, "I won't give you any money. There are no orders to do that, and I'm writing to Rusk to see about furnishing your supplies."

Walters replied, "Good. You do that!"

A.D. did write a letter that day to Rusk. He answered within two weeks and said Captain Walters had been allocated $500 to buy provisions for his men to last at least four months. Do not give him anything, but you can help him obtain supplies at the best price. When his men are in the homeport let them sleep in the fort barracks used for guards.

When Walters returned in two weeks, A.D. showed him the letter from Rusk and said, "Pay me $25." He paid A.D. without any trouble. The *Austin* stayed in port for two weeks, mainly because Walters wanted his men to eat free at the prison Fort.

The *Austin* sailors started a fight with the regular prison guards after ten of them had been drinking heavily at the Tavern. Walters refused to punish them, but A.D. refused permission for the men who had been fighting to continue sleeping at the fort.

"We will probably be gone for two months," Walters informed the fort captains when the man-o-war prepared to sail.

Frank reminded Walters, "We captured and defeated the Mexicans in the last attack and expect the *Austin* to protect us in Trinity Bay!"

Walters didn't even respond. He paid A.D. $55 for food provisions for the ship, hoping they would last four months. Many watched as the ship sailed away.

It was the end of January and A.D., Frank and all the other soldiers guarding the prisoners were really, really tired of their job! They had been guarding Mexican prisoners of war nine months after Filisola led the rest of the defeated and demoralized Mexican army back across the Rio Grande into Mexico. Even U.S. President Andrew Jackson had recently released Santa Anna and transported him back to Mexico. The local guards began to grumble, wanting to be released from military duty.

February was unusually cold. To make matters worse, the prisoners had an outbreak of smallpox and were isolated in their barracks. Dr. Lily separated the sick prisoners.

"Will you recruit some wives and others in the area as volunteers to nurse these men?" Dr. Lily asked A.D. and Frank.

A.D. told him, "Absolutely not! You train other prisoners because our wives are not going to do it!"

"Then," He said, "I need to find some cows that have cowpox so I can vaccinate at least a thousand people, including all the prisoners and guards. I also need at least twenty pounds of willow tree bark. I'll prepare it because it is the best pain killer I can get now."

Frank told the Doctor, "We should have taken some of the opium from the dictator when we could."

The Doctor said, "They could sure use it."

A.D. wrote a letter to Sam Houston that day and told him about the sickness and that they could sure use two boxes of Santa Anna's opium." Frank put the letter on the steamer going up the Brazos that afternoon.

Houston actually got the letter in three days and sent two boxes of opium on the same steamer that had brought the letter. Houston sent a note to A.D., stating, "Santa Anna really didn't like giving up his dope even if it was going to his own men."

The smallpox ran its course in about six weeks; ten of the captured soldiers died. A few of the local guards got the disease, but survived.

Finally, the Captains received an order at the end of April from Rusk to release all prisoners as soon as possible. After the prisoners were released they were to discharge all the soldiers that were guarding them at the Fort. He also requested a report stating the length of service of each soldier and whether they had fought in the battle of San Jacinto.

A.D. and Frank finally completed the report and sent it to Rusk May 15, along with their resignations. The captains had decided to send a Mexican Sergeant to be in charge of twenty-five enlisted prisoners each and give each man fifty or twenty pesos, depending on the time they had spent as prisoners. They also went to each of the farms and ranches where several prisoners were working giving them the option to return home or to stay at their present jobs. Most of the prisoners chose to return to Mexico.

The prison officers thought it would be best that the prisoners take ships to Matamoros, Mexico, or other Mexican ports. That would probably cost them two or three pesos each, but would get them out of Texas faster to safety. Most of the prisoners agreed but it took two weeks or until May 14 to get all the prisoners on ships to Mexico.

A.D. and his boys would receive one thousand twenty-five acres for their service. Frank and his boys would get one thousand two hundred acres for the same service. Each of the three local Mexican ex-soldiers who had worked for a year, mainly with translation, would be given five hundred acres. Other soldiers would receive an amount of land depending on their service.

28

CHAPTER

During the time the local settlers had been in the Trinity Bay area they had longed for a local church. Within the last three months Liberty and Harrisburg had built churches with pastors from the United States. A committee of local Anahuac women had visited the two pastors. The pastors told the committee they would write letters to people they knew in the United States telling them of the need for a preacher in Anahuac. It had been decided that church could be held in the back part of the school building. The locals even built a steeple with a bell on that building.

The church committee received a letter from an ordained preacher named, Buck Bills, from Tennessee. He also came to visit the area and talk to the church committee and other locals. He accepted their offer of a guaranteed $45 a month and would be moving his family to Anahuac within the month.

While he was visiting, Pastor Bills purchased ten acres right outside of town and planned on running two dairy cows, one sow and two horses. Before he returned to Anahuac, forty locals spent two days building a small home and barn on his property.

When his family returned with him, they were pleasantly surprised to see how hospitable the local people had already treated them.

The following Sunday, August 1, one hundred fifty people showed up for the church service. They had to move the service to the abandoned fort because it was the only shelter available to hold that many people. Pastor Bills preached a two-hour service. Most of the churchgoers had brought picnic lunches and stayed to fellowship until three o'clock. Many of the children went swimming in the bay.

The pastor took the opportunity to meet all the attendees. The collection for the day was $98 which meant they could pay the preacher for the first two months.

Pastor Bills had brought only thirty hymnals to outfit his church, but realized he would have to purchase more if the congregation remained so large.

Most of the locals were worried about their land and titles to those lands, so they sent. A.D. to see Houston. The other congressmen told A.D. they would recognize the Mexican grants by name in Congress on the floor, stating the name, amount of acreage and when issued. Then they would send a copy of the bill that contained the name date and acreage amount issued in the Congress. A.D. thought that would be proof enough for the pioneers in the Anahuac area. The soldiers that were due land would have to wait until the new Texas state legislature worked out how the soldiers could claim their land. Each man received one hundred sixty acres for each three months served. Rusk, was in charge of compiling a list and A.D. gave him the list of the men's records that were at the Anahuac fort.

Most of the farmers and ranchers of Southeast Texas that didn't have Mexican deeds felt their ownership was in jeopardy. So, they hired a local lawyer Jack Jack to represent them. They distrusted the politicians of Texas to do this correctly. The other concern of the locals was the Mexican Army or Navy would return to attack this area. That had happened in several places along the Texas border after San Jacinto. A.D. and Frank had hidden the cannons and ammunition in the fort, just in case.

The young men who had been helping A.D., like Bob, Matthew, Mark, and the three ex- Mexican soldiers, had all built cabins, barns and stock pens on what they considered their own land.

Before the prisoners had left, A.D. had the Fort grain storage facility moved down to the back of his blacksmith business because he had made up his mind to start selling the crops in addition to his blacksmith, flour and cornmeal business. All the local pioneers had split the crops from the fort. A.D. had also taken three wagons, four mules, and three grade mares. Two great Mexican four-year-old stud horses immediately improved the Logging horse herd.

Good news for the local area, lawyer Jack Jack had been appointed legal title claims adjuster and had set up an office in Anahuac. He had begun to issue Republic of Texas land titles. A.D., Frank and several others had received their first titles for the Mexican grants and then the additional land for serving in the Texas Army. Jack worked for four months and thought he had finished issuing all titles within a fifteen-mile radius of Anahuac. He was going back to the Texas legislature for approval of these titles and when he returned to the area, he would give each of the official titles to the landowners. Some of the larger ranchers in the area had not even tried to get Texas title, even though Jack and others had warned them to do so.

July 2nd the Anahuac settlers began the trip to Liberty for their 4th of July celebration. They had rented this site several times before. This had been a 10-caravan wagon train and Frank, for the first time, paid the farmer and found out he had raised his rates to $35. Frank paid it, but was not happy, swearing to himself, "I'm gonna find another place."

But A.D. knew there wasn't another place, not like this one.

Art and Weldon had brought two new two-year-old stallions named Jon and Lon to run in the local horse race. The boys had been training them for only two and a half months but thought they were the fastest. They were still having some trouble with them. Art and Weldon had sold their previous racehorses, Gray Boy and Checker, but still had Gray.

Matthew, Mark, and Bea May who used to live in Liberty came to enjoy the celebration. They found a poor family of three, the Shaw's, which included a father with a thirteen-year-old daughter named Ione and an eleven-year-old son named Onnie, living in their old cabin. Not only did they need food and clothing but their animals needed grain and care. The May family asked the Shaw family to come to Liberty for the celebration where they could feed them and their mules. The Shaw's lost a wheel on the wagon about a mile from Liberty. A.D. was fetched to replace the wagon wheel.

Mr. Shaw told Mr. Smith, one of the Anahuac settlers, "About 3 months ago we each caught a fever and it took two months for the family to recuperate. Then we were headed for the Gulf coast when our wagon broke down near the May's old cabin. We have been living off two wild hogs we shot."

"Don't worry," Mr. Smith told the Shaw family, "Just relax, eat and sleep at the campsite, and we'll try to get your mules back to good strength." The settlers gathered some clothing for the Shaws. Each of the Shaws had a bath in a nearby stream.

Smith generously gave each of them a silver dollar to enjoy the Liberty celebration. After cleaning up and eating, they slept eighteen hours straight until the next morning. When they got up, they ate eggs, bacon, biscuits and gravy and washed it all down with fresh milk. The Shaws enjoyed the Liberty celebration and Mr. Shaw even placed third in the checkers competition, winning three silver dollars. You would have thought he was rich! The Shaw family had been invited by the Smith family to homestead in Anahuac where they could build a place of their own.

A.D. condemned their wagon, but salvaged three wheels, both axles, the bows and canvas off the old wagon telling them, "I'll give you another wagon when we return to Anahuac."

At 8:00 a.m. on July 4, the long gun shooting contest followed by knife throwing and hatchet throwing. The Anahuac settlers represented themselves well as usual.

A.D. went to check on his boys to make sure they had their horses ready to run. The first and second heats were barely won by them. For the championship race, the boys had made their own plans. Weldon's horse tried to box in the other racing horses which allowed Art and his horse Lon to win the championship.

The other horse owners strongly objected. The judges discussed the situation and still declared Lon the winner. A.D. made the boys return $100 to each of the other seven horse owners.

After all that, A.D. finished up his blacksmithing work before the big dance that night. Mr. Shaw and Onnie guarded the campsite. Several strangers came around but left when they saw Mr. Shaw with a shotgun.

The dance took place that night with few problems. After the dance the 6 other horse owners whose horses lost in the championship race gave a challenge to A.D. They wanted another race in the morning with everyone putting up $200.00 each. A.D. readily accepted the challenge and the time was set for 9:00 a.m. in the morning. He said, "My 2 sons will be there," A.D. said, "I will pay you my money in the morning when the race officials can hold all the money," he continued. A.D. really did not trust the people that were racing the other horses. The boys and their dad got shovels and walked out to the track picking the places on the track that looked like needed fixed. This took 2 people with shovel 30 minutes. After this the boys picked out where they would have the best chance for their horse to win the race.

On arrival at the track the next morning, A.D. and the other owners gave their entrance money to track officials. The race officials were at the track to make sure this race was run fairly. Art and Weldon were going to run on the route they had secretly prepared the day before. The other horse owners in the race couldn't believe the Loggings were going to run on the north side of the track.

Actually, Lon and Jon tied for the win that day! The boys pocketed $1,400, and Maggie got $300 more for betting on the boys in this race. The boys cooled and rubbed down their horses and put them in a small pasture next to the campsite. A.D., his boys, Mr. Shaw and his son shoed horses and mules for the rest of the day.

Everyone except the Shaws went to the dance that night. They were watching the stock and possessions. A.D. paid Mr. Shaw $6 and Onnie $2 for helping them.

Art was now sixteen and Weldon fourteen so they really were glad to go to the dances. They had both met girls at the dance the night before and intended to meet the same girls tonight. The dance lasted until 11:00 p.m., and the only problem was when Art got in a fight with another boy who wanted to dance with his girl. A.D. and the other boy's dad broke up the fight and let the girl choose who she wanted to dance with. Art was happy to be chosen by Lara and also find out that she lived in Liberty. She told him they would come to the big Anahuac celebration and that he could write to her. She promised she would write back.

The next morning the group left at 4:00 a.m. and arrived home in Anahuac that evening. The Loggings took the Shaw family by their log cabin on the ranch which would be their home in Anahuac for a while. A.D. told him, "Come to the village day after tomorrow in the morning and I will have a repaired wagon ready for you."

Juan Ernesto told A.D., "There was no trouble while you were gone."

A.D. paid him $40 and said, "Thanks for protecting our livestock, homes and equipment."

When Mr. Shaw showed up, A.D. outfitted him with a used wagon along with his two mules loaded with needed supplies for the cabin. Mr. Shaw bought his kids some candy, checkers and dominoes plus a deck of cards.

"I'll be out to the place day after tomorrow to show you what your job will be," A.D. told him. "Relax and get your cabin in order. This will be your home. Make it comfortable."

The Shaw family set to work making their new cabin more livable and even scouted around the area. A.D. and his boys went out to see the Shaw's, taking a horse and tact for them to make life easier. He told them, "The first of September you will be working to help me harvest over a hundred acres of corn. In October you will be planting your own garden. You will also be planting wheat and oats in October and November. Whenever you have time start cutting cedar posts and building fence for a new hundred fifty acre pasture and replacing some old fence posts. If you want to go to church it is every Sunday at 10:00 a.m. Everyone usually stays for a picnic and visiting in the afternoon."

Sure enough they came to Sunday church and brought two turkeys they had cooked.

A.D. was surprised when twenty locals came to him, asking him to run for mayor in Anahuac. He reluctantly accepted and won the election in September with nine hundred fifty votes. He ran against one other opponent who received fewer than one hundred votes. A.D. figured the ones that voted against him were the people he didn't want to see or do business with anyway.

All the farmers and ranchers began harvesting their corn crops in September and the Loggings averaged thirty-five bushels per acre. They also help harvest one hundred acres of corn at the fort that the prisoners had planted before they were released. The same crew shelled out five hundred bushels of corn at the grinding mill which made five seventy five pound barrels and four hundred ten-pound bags of corn meal. A.D. put most of the cornmeal at his blacksmith shop, one barrel at his log cabin home and one barrel at his home in town.

A.D. planned to plant thirty acres of oats in October and thirty acres of wheat in November. Mr. Shaw was also planning on planting twenty acres of wheat and twenty acres of oats and spend the rest of the time building fence after the corn harvest. A.D. had paid Mr. Shaw $100 and Onnie and Ione $30 each to get them to help the rest of the year. They were so happy! Their fortune in life was improving.

In October the village council, composed of the Mayor, Sheriff and the village attorney, held the first regularly scheduled monthly meeting. The other members of the Council told A.D. there was no business to report.

A.D. told them, "I hope we can plan to run a grader and improve our roads within fifteen miles of town."

The Sheriff said, "You make the grader, and we can easily do it."

A.D. replied, "Let's order the metal, and I think I can make one."

In November, Anahuac began preparations for the big celebration and horse race, November 24 and 25. Folks planned to cook two steers and one hog. The ladies again prepared pecan pies and coleslaw. The Loggings would only have Jon running the horse race because Lon was sick.

Sixty horses entered, paying the entry fee of $20 each. The news had gotten around the area that A.D. had some good racehorses. Of course, many men thought they had horses that could beat anybody else. There would be six different heats.

The week of the celebration A.D. was always busy horse and mule shoeing and repairing broken wagons. All the other businesses were either sold out or really busy. Mr. Shaw was told to stay up all night guarding the horses and cattle. During the day he and the kids came into town to enjoy the celebration.

The day of the 24th would start with the long rifle shooting, next would be the knife throwing and last in the morning would be the hatchet throwing. A.D. and his boys shot 25th, 26th and 27th. A.D. put four shots in the bull's-eye at 125 yards. The boys put one in the bull's-eye and just three apiece in the target. As usual, Frank was the only one that shot as well as A.D. so they split $500.

A.D. and Weldon immediately went over to check on their racehorse, Jon. He was running in the second heat on the twelve-hundred-yard track. He placed first in that heat, winning $100. Also, Maggie had bet $100 on Weldon and Jon and $100 on the championship race. Jon finished second, being beaten by half a length in the championship. Weldon felt he was boxed in at the start of the race but only complained to his parents.

That evening Onnie, came riding into the dance telling A.D. rustlers were stealing his horses. A. D. and Frank quickly rode out to the area of the horse rustling, telling Weldon, "Go get Sheriff Jones and bring him out."

After a brief gun battle, the three rustlers surrendered, and A.D. rounded up the thirty mares they had collected. Anahuac had no jail so these prisoners would have to be guarded night and day. It was decided to put them in a small room with no windows at the fort.

Sheriff Jones got a chain lock at the McCoy store locking them up unguarded for the rest of the night. The Sheriff made sure the prisoners were fed breakfast and supper letting them out of their cell periodically.

After one week of this everyone wanted a change. Sheriff Jones and A.D. decided the prisoners should build a fence on two hundred acres and rebuild an old cabin for A.D. No one paid much attention to the prisoners that were working on the Logging's farm and when A.D. went out looking for them, the day before Christmas, he found they had left without permission. He informed Sheriff Jones but no one really cared, figuring they had served their time. Certainly no one wanted to go after rustlers the day before Christmas!

Christmas was upon them and since they had a church, there were two special services to celebrate Christ's birth. Two hundred people attended and the collection was over $200 in each service. The congregation could pay the pastor for another four and a half months.

Christmas had a little more meaning since they could celebrate it religiously in a church. Art and Weldon got their usual two cows and a horse each for their own herd. Both the boys now had twenty cows and ten horses each. Patricia was given a young colt to take care of and train herself.

The year 1839 arrived, and Maggie's school was up to twenty full time students. Only Matthew and Mark were part time, still coming only on Tuesday and Friday mornings. The Shaw children were in school for the first time in their lives, but they tried hard and wanted to learn.

On January 5, everybody that owned property in this county was given a letter from Thomas Chambers, Mexico's lawyer in the area. He claimed the Mexican government had given him claim to much of the land in the Trinity Bay area. His letter told all the locals that they needed to abandon their property or come see him to pay for the property.

A.D. was still the mayor, and the locals packed in to a town meeting, raising hell and demanding the town do something about the problem. The people finally accepted that it was their individual problem and not the town's.

"All that got the letters get together and fight Chambers for your land," A.D. suggested. "We must fight this together or we will lose."

The locals set a meeting date to get together in two weeks in Anahuac to plan their strategy for fighting Chambers. It was thought they should also get the best attorneys and be prepared to pay their share to the men that would actually do the fighting.

Many people present at that meeting openly stated, "The real solution to this problem is just kill Chambers."

A.D. told them, "It isn't worth it to sacrifice your life for something like this." A.D. went to see lawyer surveyor Jack Jack to get some advice.

Jack advised, "Go see your local Republic Representative. You know Sam Houston; see if he can help. Then I would go to President Lamar, and any other Representatives in the Republic and plead your case."

A.D. and the others contacted forty representatives and they all promised to help with the problem. The legislature failed to protect the land rights of Anahuac citizens. A.D. and Frank had given $200 each to the defense against Chambers but there were no positive results. This legal dispute actually went on for the next twenty years.

The next two years Chambers tried to force people in the local area to leave, threatening to hurt them. He even tried to bribe the Sheriff to go along with him. None of the pioneers would move and most of them threatened Chambers right back. He tried to send out surveyors and when the pioneers found out about that, they ran them off, threatening them if they came back! Chambers had built a nice home in Anahuac. This problem died down somewhat when it was corn planting time in late March.

Frank's two sons had left for central Texas to join the Texas Rangers because they wanted to see some other places. Bob Tim's wife had left him and gone back to live with her parents so he went with Frank Jr. and Pat J. A.D.'s sons also thought they might want to go but they knew their dad needed them to help him with his businesses. Besides, A.D. was smart enough to promise them when they turned eighteen, they could have their own farm or ranch and go where and when they wanted. There always seemed to be turbulence between Texas and Mexico and this continued until the U.S. - Texas war against Mexico. By that time many of the old warriors had died or just settled down to peaceful endeavors.